SHADOWS MADE REAL

BOOK SIX OF THE TALES OF THE TERRITORIES

PETER WACHT

Shadows Made Real
By Peter Wacht

Book 6 of The Tales of the Territories

This book is a work of fiction. Names, characters, places, and incidents are the product of the author's imagination or are used fictitiously. Any resemblance to actual events, locales, or persons, living or dead, is coincidental.

Cover design by Ebooklaunch.com

Published in the United States by Kestrel Media Group LLC.

ISBN: 978-1-950236-46-6

eBook ISBN: 978-1-950236-47-3

Library of Congress Control Number: 2024910652

❀ Created with Vellum

ALSO BY PETER WACHT

THE FALLEN KNIGHT SERIES

(Forthcoming)

The Death of the Dragon (short story)*

The Dragon Awakens

Duel With a Dragon

Beware the Dragon

The Dragon Returns

THE REALMS OF THE TALENT AND THE CURSE

THE TALES OF CALEDONIA

(Complete 7-Book Series)

Blood on the White Sand (short story)*

The Diamond Thief (short story)*

The Protector

The Protector's Quest

The Protector's Vengeance

The Protector's Sacrifice

The Protector's Reckoning

The Protector's Resolve

The Protector's Victory

THE TALES OF THE TERRITORIES

Stalking the Blood Ruby (short story)*

A Fate Worse Than Death (short story)*

Death on the Burnt Ocean

Monsters in the Mist

The Dance of the Daggers

Bloody Hunt for Freedom

A Spark of Rebellion

Shadows Made Real

Shadow's Reach (Forthcoming 2024)

Storm in the Darkness (Forthcoming 2025)

THE SYLVAN CHRONICLES

(Complete 9-Book Series)

The Legend of the Kestrel

The Call of the Sylvana

The Raptor of the Highlands

The Makings of a Warrior

The Lord of the Highlands

The Lost Kestrel Found

The Claiming of the Highlands

The Fight Against the Dark

The Defender of the Light

THE RISE OF THE SYLVAN WARRIORS

*Through the Knife's Edge (short story)**

* Free stories can be downloaded from my author website at PeterWachtBooks.com. My books are also available on Amazon and other online retailers.

YOUR FREE SHORT STORY IS WAITING

THE DIAMOND THIEF

This short story is a prelude to the events in my series *The Tales of Caledonia* and is free to readers who receive my newsletter.

Join Peter's newsletter and get your FREE short story.
PeterWachtBooks.com

SETTING THE STAGE

The Tales of the Territories continue the adventures of Bryen Keldragan and Aislinn Winborne as they travel across the Burnt Ocean to the Territories, what will eventually become the Kingdoms of *The Sylvan Chronicles*.

The events occur more than one thousand years before the happenings in *The Sylvan Chronicles* and take place in the lands far to the west of Caledonia that have been opened for colonization thanks to territorial grants from the deceased King Corinthus Beleron. There they will take on new challenges, make new friends and enemies, and continue to battle those who have turned to the Curse.

In the Territories, sometimes called New Caledonia, as in the other realms, the ability to use the Talent sets apart the person gifted with this unique skill. But being able to use the Talent is only part of the dynamic. For if a Magus chooses to follow a darker path, the Talent becomes the Curse.

The Sylvan Chronicles, The Tales of Caledonia, and *The Tales of the Territories* are a part of the larger world of *The Realms of the Talent and the Curse.*

1

ELIMINATING THE OBSTACLE

"Did you believe her?" The voice was quiet.

Cold.

Devoid of emotion.

Authoritative.

Lethal.

"I had no cause to disbelieve her." The Wraith Hunter worked hard to ensure that his voice didn't crack. Thankfully, he succeeded. The hesitancy that wanted to sneak into what he said never made itself known.

He was grateful for that.

While speaking with his master, he needed to appear strong, confident, under control.

Always.

"That's not an answer," the Wraith Lord challenged, his pure black eyes boring into those of his Hunter, his displeasure plain.

They stood on the long wall that encircled Stronghold. Once, the city had been the capital of Frisia. A thriving metropolis and the heart of a powerful kingdom.

The humans who had governed here were long gone, however. Courtesy of the Ten Thousand and the Wraiths.

Consumed by the Murk, Frisia had become the Wyld. The home of the Wraith Lord and his Horde.

Staring out into the grasping grey, the Wraith Lord allowed himself to indulge in a memory that he rarely had time for now.

The Dark Magus had sent him and his Wraiths into the kingdom and then Stronghold to decapitate the Frisian leadership. He and his assassins had done as ordered.

Just as they always did.

Silent and efficient kills.

The Ten Thousand had followed in the Murk, slaughtering the defenders.

Yet the Dark Magus had miscalculated, never believing that his Wraiths, beholden to him for their unique power, would betray him. Could betray him.

The Wraith Lord curled one lip, cracking the skin that already was stretched tightly across his skull. The most emotion he ever permitted himself.

The Dark Magus had been so consumed with his own perceived greatness that he never considered that the servants could one day become the masters.

And on that day, after they had conquered Stronghold, the Wraiths had done just that.

Under his command, the Wraiths had turned on the Ten Thousand, or rather what was left of them. The battle to take the city had reduced those fearsome warriors' numbers to a level that prevented them from standing against his Wraiths.

Those of the Ten Thousand who escaped the trap in Stronghold fled. They had no choice. They could not hunt in the Murk like his Wraiths could.

To this day, the Wraith Lord was proud of his hunters. Their discipline. Their drive.

They had hounded the Ten Thousand until not a single one remained alive in the smothering grey. Those who survived were lucky to break free from the Murk before his Wraiths killed them.

The Dark Magus, whose real name no longer held any significance and was now remembered simply as the Dread, did not realize what was happening until it was too late. Besides, he had been in no position to do anything about it because of the wound he had taken while killing the King of Frisia.

The Wraith Lord snorted. Their former master had been such a fool.

The Dread had been so intent on capturing the boy, so willing to take risks with the Curse to achieve his goal, that he never thought about the consequences of what he had done. Of where the path that he had chosen could lead.

The Dread created the Wraiths, the rulers of the Murk, but also creatures bound to the Murk.

A two-edged sword as the Wraith Lord well knew.

No one could challenge him and his Wraiths in the Murk.

Not the Ten Thousand.

Not the Dread.

Learning how to manipulate the Murk, stealing it from their master, the Wraiths had claimed the now-forgotten kingdom for their own thanks to the gifts granted to them by the Dread. The same gifts that allowed the Wraiths to free themselves from the Dread.

The Dread had made an error when creating the Wraiths, misjudging their will and their power. He paid a heavy price for that mistake.

Too bad for the Dread.

Excellent for the Wraiths.

And perhaps the worst blow to the Dread, the boy he had

hunted, the boy that he had to kill, the very reason for invading Frisia, had escaped him.

As his anger grew at the slights of the past, the Wraith Lord growled softly, a jarring rumble that reverberated from deep within him. For a thousand years and more the Wraiths had controlled the wisps of grey that nurtured them. Gave them their strength.

For the first time someone not of the Murk challenged them in their natural environment. And a human at that.

"That's the best answer that I can give, Lord."

The Wraith Hunter had learned not to waste his master's time. There was no point in speaking if he had nothing to say.

The Wraith Lord had summoned him to Stronghold.

The Wraith Hunter feared that he might never leave Stronghold alive.

He could think of no other reason for him to be called back to the home of the Wraith Horde if he had not made some error in the eyes of his master.

Those concerns running through his mind, the Wraith Hunter stood unmoving in the Murk, relishing the comforting touch of the threads of grey, even as he used every ounce of self-discipline to maintain his composure.

He had become his master's Hunter because none of the other Wraiths could stand against him. He was the best of the Horde. Yet, in the presence of his master, he felt insignificant. Small. Unworthy.

"Will the Magus touched by the Curse deliver what she has promised us?" whispered the Wraith Lord. He sensed his Hunter's unease. He had yet to decide if that discomfort was a sign of weakness or strength. "Will this Dark Magus give us the Wraith who is not a Wraith?"

The Wraith Hunter did not respond immediately. He knew that honesty was required. That to lie to the Wraith Lord meant a quick and certain death. Yet he understood as well that there could be a cost if his master didn't like what he had to say.

"Who can say, Lord? The Dark Magus is a human, just like the Dread. Those humans turned to the Curse are not known for keeping their word. They are known for breaking it."

The Wraith Lord considered what his Hunter said for quite a long time, the silence becoming heavier. He couldn't discount what his Hunter believed.

Because he believed it as well. The humans weren't trustworthy. They never had been.

The humans were nothing more than vermin that needed to be exterminated.

Eliminate the humans, and the Wraiths could expand the reach of the Murk. They could broaden their hunting ground. They could extend their rule.

"You are familiar with the Wraith who is not a Wraith." It wasn't a question.

The Wraith Hunter was reluctant to admit it, but he could not lie. "I am."

"He has bested you in the Murk?"

The Wraith Hunter struggled to answer, needing to tamp down the rage building within him as he could not deny the claim. "He did."

"You are supposed to be my best. You are my second in command. Yet a young man has drawn your blood. He has killed your Scouts. Has he not?"

"He has," the Wraith Hunter muttered.

Humiliation flooded through him. He should have killed the Wraith who is not a Wraith. That was undeniable. Yet he hadn't.

The human who moved like a Wraith, hunted like a Wraith, fought like a Wraith, still lived.

The Wraith who is not a Wraith now hunted in the Murk. That was not the way it should be. That was an abomination.

And the boy did it despite all that the Wraith Hunter had done to try to kill him.

"If I may, Lord, why are you so concerned about this boy? He is nothing. He will not be a problem for much longer. I promise you that."

"Why am I concerned about a human who has made my Hunter look the fool?"

"It was luck, nothing more," he replied, even though his protest sounded hollow in his own ears. He knew that luck had little to do with the boy's success.

"I doubt that." The Wraith Lord shook his head ever so slightly, clearly disappointed with his Hunter.

His Hunter should understand. But he did not. Or if he did, his anger and embarrassment were blinding him. "I am concerned because this boy not only fights in the Murk like he's a part of it, but also because he is giving the Highlanders the ability to fight with him. Does that not concern you? Does that not make your task more difficult?"

"The Highlanders cannot handle a blade as well as we can."

"Perhaps not," the Wraith Lord replied with a shrug of his own.

"We are faster."

"Yes, we are."

"We understand the Murk in a way that the Highlanders cannot. In a way that this boy cannot."

"We do."

"We are stronger."

"We are."

"We are smarter."

"We are."

"Then why are you concerned, master? This boy is nothing more than a temporary problem. Once I kill him, the Highlanders will become what they were before. Easy prey."

"I am concerned because the Wraith who is not a Wraith

has made all that we are, all that we use to our advantage in the Murk, less relevant," the Wraith Lord explained, disappointed that he even had to do so. "We are better with a blade. We are faster. We are stronger. We are smarter. We thrive in the Murk. Yet now we die in the Murk just like the Highlanders do. That is not supposed to happen. That is not the way of our world. And that did not happen until the Wraith who is not a Wraith entered the Murk."

"Do you believe this Dark Magus will give us this Wraith who is not a Wraith?" The Wraith Hunter knew that he was taking a risk by asking his Lord the same question he had asked of him. He couldn't help himself, however, his anger and annoyance freeing his tongue in a way that was becoming much too dangerous.

"I don't know," the Wraith Lord replied after pondering the question.

The Wraith Hunter sighed with relief when his Lord answered rather than simply slashing his throat for his perceived impertinence. "So it is worth the risk."

"What do we have to lose? We are not ready to conquer yet. If the Dark Magus succeeds, then that benefits us. If she doesn't, it still benefits us. Either way, we take what we want. We take everything below the Northern Peaks."

The Wraith Hunter nodded in understanding. "Should I leave the Wraith who is not a Wraith to the Dark Magus?"

The Wraith Lord turned toward him, staring, his pitch-black eyes boring into his Hunter's. "What do you think?"

His Lord's tone suggested that how he responded to the question would determine how much longer he drew breath. "I should kill him."

"You should kill him. Quickly. Before I kill you."

2

A NEW TARGET

"You two need to find some way to coexist."

"I'm not the problem," argued Lycia, her voice revealing not only how tired she was of this topic, but also her lack of interest in discussing it. "I've bent over backward trying to make that woman not see me as a threat."

"Why does she see you as a threat?"

Jakob walked a few more steps before he finally realized that Lycia was no longer by his side. When he turned back toward her, she looked none too pleased.

Lycia nodded knowingly. Either Jakob was incredibly dense, or he didn't want to acknowledge the obvious. She hoped that it was the latter, although she was beginning to think that it was a little bit of both.

She caught up to him quickly. She and Jakob hiked at the end of the long line of Highlanders who were making their way along the top of the ridge, their goal the valley that spread out before them more than a mile below. As was her habit, the other person who was the topic of their conversation walked at the front of the column, several hundred yards distant, the space between them increasing.

That was fine with Lycia. She didn't want to be anywhere near Saraa just as the Highlander preferred to stay as far away from the gladiator as she could.

"You really don't know?"

Jakob gave her a look of confusion.

"You really have no clue?"

"Lycia, what are you talking about?"

She heard the building exasperation in his voice. That made her think that he was telling her the truth. He really had no clue.

She didn't know whether to be amused by her discovery or even more intrigued with this reluctant rebel. So smart in so many ways and in others at a complete loss. She had no idea what to do with that.

"You're serious?" She still had a hard time believing that he could be so oblivious to the obvious attentions of a beautiful woman.

"Lycia!"

"Fine, sorry," she replied, lifting her arms to the sky, a sign of her own frustration. She was uncomfortable telling him this, but she needed to if they were going to move past it. And they needed to move past it, because Lycia didn't want it to get in the way of what they were trying to do. "Saraa views me as a threat because she thinks I came here not because I want to help you but because I'm interested in you."

Jakob's expression of irritation shifted back to one of confusion. Lycia couldn't stop herself from smiling.

Were all men so ridiculously inept at interpreting a woman's feelings? She didn't think so, although Jakob certainly appeared to be.

"Interested?" Jakob's bewildered expression deepened.

Lycia scrunched up her lips, not believing that she needed to make this even plainer for him.

"Romantically attracted," she forced out through clenched teeth.

Jakob allowed the uncomfortable silence to drag out between them before replying. "You're romantically interested in me?"

Lycia closed her eyes for a second and dipped her chin to her chest, her smile disappearing. She needed to gain control of the emotions roiling through her.

That wasn't the question that she had been expecting from him. She lifted her head, pinching the top of her nose between her thumb and forefinger.

"I didn't say that I was romantically interested in you. I said that Saraa viewed me as a threat because she believes that I'm romantically interested in you. Clear? There's a key difference that you need to grasp."

For a few seconds more Jakob stood there, staring at her. The longer he did, the more uncomfortable Lycia became. She feared losing herself in those flashing green eyes of his.

She felt a good bit of relief when finally he gave her a slow nod. He appeared to understand. They could move on to more important topics.

"So you're not romantically interested in me?" Jakob asked.

For a few heartbeats, Lycia didn't know how to respond. Was he really this thick or was he just being difficult?

Worse, before she could decide, she froze. She didn't know how she should reply. That sent an unanticipated spark of terror through her, because that indecision led to a conclusion that she did not want to consider.

"Sorry, just kidding," Jakob said with a small smile, giving her a wink upon seeing how his questions affected her. He felt a touch of remorse for putting her on the spot when she was being honest with him, but he couldn't help himself.

When he was uncomfortable, he tended to poke at others. Not a good habit, he understood, but a difficult one to break.

"You can't tell me that you weren't aware of Saraa's interest," Lycia challenged, not happy with Jakob's attempt at humor. She didn't want to follow that path, whether on her own or with him.

Jakob shrugged, then sighed, realizing that there was no way to escape this conversation. "I was. For some time, actually. I just wasn't aware of the extent of it. How it was affecting her and her judgment."

"You've never spoken to her about it?"

"No, I was hoping that her interest might wane."

"Hoping doesn't make it real," Lycia replied, giving him a disappointed shake of her head.

Jakob smiled then, seeking to soothe Lycia's ruffled feathers. "I know, I'm sorry. It's just that ..."

Lycia watched the several different emotions that played across his face. The strongest and most visible being the pain that, usually hidden deep in the back of his eyes, had pushed its way to the forefront.

He hadn't yet told her the cause of that pain, and it certainly wasn't her place to ask, although Duff had hinted at it.

A woman, the craggy Highlander had told her. A terrible thing what had happened.

He had said no more than that. Nor would he. Jakob's pain was his own, unless he chose to share it.

Pushing those thoughts down, Lycia realized as well that she had taken him by surprise with her line of questioning. That he hadn't been ready for this issue.

While they made their way along the ridge, he had been asking her questions about Declan. Having just met Lycia's friend and mentor during the battle of the broch against the Wraiths, he was still thinking about the Master of the Gladiators.

She couldn't blame him for that. She had an inkling as to

why that was the case, but she hadn't wanted to pursue that line of possibility with him.

Not yet.

Not until she knew him better.

Not until she knew how he might react if she revealed a few of her suspicions.

Although she preferred not doing that, hoping it wouldn't prove necessary.

Hoping that the truth would come out in another way.

Recognizing how Jakob was struggling, Lycia reached out with a hand, grasping his forearm gently. "You need to talk to her. This isn't good for her. It isn't good for any of us."

"You're right. I just don't know what to say."

"Do you care for her?" Lycia asked.

Jakob took a few seconds to gather his thoughts before replying. "I do. Just not in the way that she wants me to."

Lycia nodded. "That puts you and her in a difficult position."

"It does," he replied miserably.

"Can I offer you some advice?"

"Can I stop you?"

Lycia laughed softly at that. Even now, he offered her a hint of humor. "I've been in the same place as Saraa is now."

"Really?"

"Really," Lycia replied, a slight grimace playing across the hard set of her face. "It's not a good place to be. You don't know how Saraa is going to react, and I understand and admire your desire to not hurt her, but you need to tell her how you feel. She deserves to know. Because she needs to think about what to do next. Pining for you doesn't help her. It doesn't help anyone."

"Good advice," Jakob said.

"Then I've earned my keep for today."

Lycia's warm smile made Jakob smile, even as he worried

about the conversation that he needed to have with Saraa. A screech from the kestrel soaring above them saved Jakob from having to think more on those concerns.

Shading his eyes from the bright morning sunlight, he looked up. In addition to the very large raptor gliding above them, he identified several more in the sky. All the others, however, were congregating about two leagues to the west.

Jakob reached for the Talent, knowing from experience what the kestrel wanted him to do.

"What do you see?"

He waited until he had taken a good look before replying to Lycia. He was using the Talent to study the area around which the kestrels were flying and was in the process of incorporating into his examination what he was viewing through the eyes of the predators.

"They're taking a break." Jakob's smile broadened as he turned back toward Lycia. "Actually, they're making camp for the night."

"Just them? No prisoners?"

"No, no prisoners yet."

"That certainly will make it easier for us."

"It should. So long as we get there in time." Jakob started walking along the ridge, increasing his pace so that he could catch up to the Highlanders they had fallen behind. "Come on. The sooner we can get where we need to be to make this work, the better."

"So what did you do to him?"

The burly fellow with the ragged beard sitting on the other side of the fire, whip in hand, flicked his wrist. The sharp tip shot forward and burrowed into one of the logs. When he pulled back, large splinters of burning wood came with the steel spike.

"Exactly that," the man replied, his satisfaction obvious. "Right in the arse."

The men seated around the fire all laughed uproariously.

"Must have been painful," chuckled Reg, the lanky fellow who had asked the question.

"For him, yes," confirmed Dakar. "Dennison couldn't sit down for a week. Served the bastard right."

That earned another loud round of laughter from the men who were enjoying themselves that evening, the cool breeze that ran through the campsite making the bright flames of the fire dance to a private tune.

"And all this because he owed you some golds?" Anson asked. The water that he had spit out when he heard what happened to Dennison dripped down his beard.

"Some? He owed me ten golds," protested Dakar, who was cleaning the ash from the spike at the end of his whip. "He's lucky I didn't take an eye."

A final round of laughter followed before the men dug back into their stew. It was a good night. Quiet. And they doubted that there would be any trouble, which was a nice change.

During the last few months, many of these men had dreaded coming into the Highlands. The rebel lord had put a price on their heads ... quite literally.

At first, they scoffed at the bounty. That was until they realized that the Highlanders were making a special effort to collect.

And clearly not just because of the bounty.

Each of them had friends who had suffered a terrible end as a result of being caught by the very people who they were supposed to enslave.

Yet they still took the risk. They needed the additional

money that was paid out for engaging in this dangerous assignment.

Though their employer had given them an option, recognizing that some in the Highland Guard might have a weaker constitution, still he expected them to do this work, offering them a simple ultimatum. Find him his workers for the mines or take the place of the slaves themselves.

Despite the threat presented by the Highlanders, it had been an easy choice for all of them.

Even more so, none of them really wanted to get on the bad side of Captain Hippolates. Their commander had little patience for anything that he perceived as cowardice and insubordination. Better they face off against the Highlanders than him.

Besides, with the change in strategy, most of the men sitting around the fire and scraping at the last of their meal weren't too concerned about sharing the same fate as their friends who had been caught by the Highlanders.

Governor Sharperson had adopted new tactics as a result of the Kestrel's proclamation. The slavers now traveled in larger groups that dissuaded most of the Highlanders from attacking since they usually functioned in smaller squads.

In fact, in this party alone six slaver bands were traveling together until they got to their assigned positions closer to the Stone. Seventy-two men in all.

They doubted that the rebels would be foolish enough to attack so large a force as theirs.

When they reached the mountains that surrounded the road that ran from north to south through the Stone, they would break into their smaller groups and make their way to their hunting grounds. There, they could ambush any unwary travelers.

Once they made their quota -- for each band twenty slaves in total -- they would regroup and head to the mines.

It was a slower process than what was employed in the past, that was true, but hopefully a more effective one. Safer as well from the slavers' perspective.

Admittedly, the Governor wasn't so much concerned about the slavers' safety. Rather, he wanted to do all that he could to ensure that he got the workers required.

That was fine with them, because his desire matched theirs. They wanted to get paid, they didn't want to lose their heads, and they had absolutely no desire to work in the mines themselves.

"Where are Rennie and Robert?" asked Aden. The slaver sitting next to Dakar placed his bowl down by his feet and then licked his fingers to ensure that he didn't miss a drop of the stew. "They should have been back by now. They were supposed to dice with me tonight."

"They're probably off having a little fun. You know those two." Turkan, who sat on the other side of the fire, had a penchant for making fun of others so long as they didn't hear what he said, because then if confronted he could deny it.

Probably a smart move, Aden thought. Turkan wasn't the largest fellow. More skin and bones than muscle.

"Funny," Aden replied. "You know what Rennie and Robert would do to you if they heard you?"

"I'm well aware," Turkan replied with a gap-toothed grin. "That's why I said it while they weren't here."

Both Turkan and Aden laughed, as did a few others around them. Then Jonny, who sat not too far away from Turkan, piped up. "I'll let them know that you're looking for them. I'm supposed to spell them on the watch."

Jonny and several other slavers, leaving their bowls on the logs they had pulled close to the fire, rose from their places and prepared to march off into the darkness. They made sure that they had all their gear and their weapons before they did.

They weren't worried about the Stalkers. Those monsters would leave them alone.

They weren't worried about the Wraiths. The Murk wasn't anywhere near them that evening.

They weren't really worried about the Highlanders either. At least that's what they told themselves.

"You'll keep what I said to yourself?" asked Turkan, slightly concerned.

"What? You're worried about those two?" asked Jonny. "They can usually take a joke."

"Unless they're angry," Turkan muttered, wondering as Jonny and the other men headed into the darkness whether he should have kept his mouth shut. "And those two tend to be more angry than not."

~

"Where are those two bastards?" muttered Jonny. "It shouldn't be this difficult."

He should have found his friends by now. He should already be at his post. And he had no desire to be stomping around among the heart trees looking for the pair.

He could barely see anything as it was thanks to the small, pitiful torch that he grasped in one hand.

Jonny knew that having the torch affected his night vision. That had been drilled into him by the Sergeant who had trained him when he fought in the Roo's Nest Guard.

Nevertheless, he felt more comfortable with the firebrand in his hand. It gave him a sense of comfort, even though the rational part of his mind understood that it was ephemeral.

He had been looking for Rennie and Robert for the last five minutes because they weren't where they were supposed to be based on the assignments doled out when they made camp that evening.

Maybe Turkan was right. Maybe they were having a little fun.

It wasn't unheard of with those two. Although usually their fun never prevented them from meeting their responsibilities.

Then again, it could just be the darkness, which seemed to have settled heavily upon them thanks to the clouds that blotted out the moon. By dint of that, he assumed that the other men sent to relieve those on the first watch were having the same difficulty that he was.

When Jonny took his next step, seeking to pierce the darkness, hoping to catch a glimpse of his friends, he almost tripped. He put out his free hand, stumbling up against the tree root curling off the ground to his left.

Just in time. Otherwise he would have fallen flat on his face.

This was ridiculous. He didn't care what Rennie and Robert got into on their own time. But they shouldn't be doing that when they were on the watch.

Especially not here. They knew better than that.

Most of his friends didn't seem to be concerned about the Highlanders.

He was. Those bastards were hard men and women.

If they wanted to get something done, they did it. And he didn't want to be the latest slaver to lose his head because they decided that they wanted to do him.

Blast it!

Where had those two gone? They were supposed to be right around here.

Jonny pushed himself back to his feet, still holding onto the torch. He shifted the firebrand to his other hand so that he could blow on the scorched flesh of his palm where it had been struck by a few burning splinters that broke off when he ran into the root.

When he regained his feet, Jonny thought about what had happened.

It had been weird. When his foot got caught, it hadn't felt like he had wedged it beneath a root or a rock.

Strangely, whatever it was had felt softer. Almost squishy.

Jonny bent down, holding the torch out in front of him so that he could get a better look. His eyes went wide, his mind working furiously to comprehend what he was staring at.

Rennie!

He glanced to the side.

Robert as well!

One lying right next to the other.

Turkan had been right. They were together.

But they also were dead. Their throats cut.

Jonny pushed himself up, about to shout a warning, when he coughed out a gasp instead because of his shock.

A tall figure stood right in front of him.

Beyond that, he couldn't get a good look at who it was even with his torch, the flames of the brand preventing him from seeing more than a few feet in front of him.

"A gift from the Lord of the Highlands," Lycia said softly.

Jonny gasped, not really understanding what was going on even as he felt the cold steel slide across his throat. The last thing the slaver saw when he settled against the roots not too far from the corpses of his friends were the flames of the torch that dropped to the ground next to him.

"WHAT IN BLAZES is taking them so long?" demanded Aden. His fingers were getting itchy. That was good. Because that meant that his luck was with him. It would be a good night once he had those dice rolling around in his hand. "The watch should have completed the change by now."

"Like I said, probably having a little fun."

Aden was going to offer Turkan a sharp rebuke. He was

getting tired of the other slaver's comments. Instead, he held back.

The man was an instigator. That's what he was good at. There was no point in doing what Turkan wanted and get into it with him.

Still, even though he knew that he was wasting his time and only helping to make his own aggravation more acute, he couldn't stop himself.

"Turkan, shut your trap before I shut it for you," Aden ordered, turning toward the irritating fellow, a spark of anger in his eye.

Turkan smiled. Finally, he was getting the rise that he wanted out of Aden. It had been a boring night so far. Maybe he could rile his friend up more and have a little fun.

With most of the other slavers, he wouldn't have continued to push. Nevertheless, it was worth the risk.

If he could get under Aden's skin, it would help him when they started rolling the dice.

Aden won more than he lost. Every time. Sometimes he didn't stop winning.

Turkan knew that Aden didn't cheat. He and several others had tried to catch him, even weighing the dice.

But nothing. It was just Aden's luck, which ran good more than it did for most.

Understanding that, Turkan hoped that by distracting his friend, his own odds would improve at Aden's expense. Just one more comment should do the trick.

"I'd like to see you try, you ..."

Turkan froze, thinking that his eyes were playing tricks on him. A three-foot-long shaft had sprouted from Aden's eye, the slaver slammed backward by the power of the strike.

What was ...

Turkan ducked, hearing the much too familiar sound of

arrows whistling through the air followed by the sucking smack of steel barbs punching into flesh.

A strange silence fell over the camp for a few seconds, the slavers struggling to understand what was happening.

More of the steel-tipped shafts streaked out of the gloom, almost always finding a home in one of the men sitting or standing around the fire, their attackers taking advantage of their shock and hesitation.

When the slavers finally concluded that they needed to escape among the trees, before they could even begin to move, an explosion erupted right where the fire had been.

The powerful blast of light sent the flames and burning logs in every direction. Along with a few of the men who had been sitting too close to the blaze.

One of those flaming logs crashed right into Turkan's chest and sent him tumbling back into the darkness.

∼

"Were the few who were still alive able to provide any useful information?" Jakob asked.

He stood where the fire once burned and now was just a smoking mess. Bodies were strewn about the small clearing. Each one battered and broken, none of them a Highlander.

Only slavers.

Their surprise had been complete. The men who had entered these craggy, snowcapped peaks to enslave the weak and unsuspecting never stood a chance.

That didn't bother Jakob in the least. As his father had liked to say, "Don't fight fair. Fight to win." That was just one of Dougal's many adages that Jakob was applying to his strategy for freeing the rugged peaks that were now his home.

Of course, he might have used more of the Talent than was

required to blow apart the campsite. Yes, definitely a bit more than was necessary.

He had no regrets, however. It was quite cathartic actually. He did hold a grudge against the slavers after all, and with good reason, so he had found it difficult to resist the demand for vengeance.

"Nothing that we didn't already know," replied Lycia. "Most are just blabbering fools. They never expected to fall victim to the Highlander bounty with so many of their comrades with them."

She had managed the interrogations, all of which had been quite brief. None of the men really knew anything more than where they were supposed to go to make their catch and then where to deliver the condemned who fell into their net.

Beyond that, the slavers had no knowledge of the Governor's larger plans. Other than the fact that most of his soldiers were still positioned around the Stone. A detail that Jakob already knew for a fact.

"A bad decision that bit them in the ass," murmured Jakob.

"Indeed." A pity for the slavers, Lycia concluded. Not because so many had been killed. That didn't even make her blink. They deserved what fate had given to them. No, rather because they had nothing useful to trade for their lives. "Any more slavers we need to worry about?"

Jakob shook his head. He had used the Talent to search the wood and confirm that none in the large band had escaped. Just as he anticipated, his Highlanders had been exceedingly thorough in their work.

"None that are close. The only slavers that I can find now are by the road near the Stone."

"They're probably already trying to fill their quota."

"Probably," Jakob nodded. "We can worry about them later."

"Why later? Why not now?" After their easy victory over

this now decimated band, Lycia already was looking forward to the next engagement.

She hated the slavers with a passion. Almost as much as Jakob did. They reminded her of the men who had thrown her and her brother into the Pit.

"We have another challenge that we need to address first."

"And that would be?"

"Stalkers."

"Where?"

"The broch that Duff is working to complete."

"Really." She nodded her head thoughtfully. While she, Jakob, and the bulk of the Highlanders had left the broch where they had rescued Declan and his fighters, Duff had remained. He wanted to finish construction of the tower so that they could prepare for the settlers heading there in the next few weeks. "Coincidence?"

"I doubt it."

"The Stalkers believe that you're there."

"That would be my guess," Jakob agreed, "and I'd hate to disappoint them."

"How could those monsters have any idea where you are? I always just took them to be killing machines who were excellent hunters."

"You're not wrong about that last part," Jakob agreed. "As to how they might know where I am, I've been thinking about that."

"You're not going to make me drag it out of you, are you? After questioning slavers for the last hour, I'm not really in the mood."

Jakob smiled, appreciating Lycia's candor. "No, I'm not that much of a fool."

"Good to hear, because I was wondering about that after our previous conversation."

Jakob smiled, but he didn't fall for the bait that Lycia had set out for him. Instead, he focused on her original question.

"The Curse."

"What do you mean?" Lycia didn't understand.

"We know that these Stalkers are made with the Curse."

"I won't argue with you about that."

"Thank you, I appreciate it," Jakob replied with a larger grin.

Lycia motioned with her hand. "Spill it, Jakob. Like I said, I have little patience right now."

"Right, sorry. The Stalkers are crafted with the Curse. I'm assuming that whoever did the crafting is quite skilled in the application of Dark Magic. If I can use the Talent to find what I'm looking for, often searching for that corruption or taint that is associated with the Curse, then ..."

"Whoever made the Stalkers can do the same with the Curse," Lycia finished for him.

"Exactly," Jakob confirmed. "There are only a handful in the Territories who can use the Talent. That only makes this Dark Magus' search that much easier."

Lycia nodded, thoughtful, as she considered his reasoning. "Your theory certainly makes sense."

"I'm glad that you agree."

Lycia ignored his attempt at sarcasm. "But if this Dark Magus is tracking you with the Curse, then why aren't those Stalkers that were sent after you here instead?"

"That's a good question," Jakob agreed.

"I thought so. Now answer it."

"Just another theory, mind you."

"Let's hear it," prodded Lycia.

"This Dark Magus gives the scent or the sensation of the Talent affiliated with me to the Stalkers under his or her command and then sends them off to do their bidding."

"Kill you, you mean," Lycia clarified.

"Yes, kill me." Clearly, Jakob wasn't bothered by the harshness of her comment. He had been hunted as soon as he had set foot in the Highlands. Slavers first. Then the Wraiths. Now the Stalkers. "Because of the scent given to them, the Stalkers are following a trail."

Lycia understood now. "The Stalkers haven't reached the end of the trail yet, and they need to follow the trail to find you. They can't jump ahead. They'll come this way once they're done at the broch."

"Correct," Jakob replied, pleased and not surprised that Lycia grasped his reasoning so quickly.

"Unless we backtrack and catch them by surprise."

"Exactly what I was thinking," Jakob confirmed with a tempting lift of his eyebrows.

"How far?" asked Lycia, liking what Jakob had in mind.

"Five leagues. Maybe just a little bit farther than that. Just beyond the two ridges to the east and through the valley beyond that."

"How many Stalkers?"

Jakob searched again. He wanted to make sure.

"Twenty. Maybe a few more. I can't tell for certain because they're moving so fast."

"The Stalkers haven't attacked the broch yet?"

"No, they're coming through the forest now. They'll reach the green in a matter of minutes."

"Do the Highlanders know?"

Jakob nodded. "Yes, like I said, Duff is there. Those monsters won't be able to catch him by surprise. He's getting the last few Highlanders into the broch even as we speak."

"So we have some time."

"We do, although not much. If we can, I'd like to snare all the Stalkers in the noose."

"That works for me." With Duff at the broch and Jakob coming from the wood, they could catch the Stalkers between a rock and a hard place. A simple strategy and a good one in Lycia's opinion.

"Come on," Jakob said. "Let's get everyone going. We can leave the bodies for the vultures."

It wasn't long before the Highlanders were loping off into the woods, heading back in the direction from which they had come.

As had become her practice, Saraa ran at the front. Jakob and Lycia stayed closer to the rear.

"I hate this," muttered Lycia.

"Hate what?" asked Jakob, curious.

"Running."

"This isn't running," laughed Jakob. "For Highlanders, this is marching. We haven't even begun to run yet."

"I respectfully disagree," muttered Lycia. "If this is marching then I'm the queen of Caledonia."

Jakob laughed again. Lycia was a host of contradictions, but in one thing she was quite consistent. She never failed to speak her mind.

"We are the Marchers!" shouted Jakob, giving in to his good mood. "Enemies of the Highlands beware!"

The Highlanders running to his front answered him, roaring in agreement.

It had been a good night.

Eliminating so many slavers at a single time.

Now it was time to ply their trade against the Stalkers.

3

UNCOMFORTABLE SILENCE

"You all right?"

"Why do you ask?" Talia gave Davin a sideways glance, a slightly worried expression on her face, though she worked hard to conceal it. Could he really read her so easily?

"You seem a little lost."

"Please don't take this the wrong way, but I never took you for someone with a great deal of intuitiveness."

"A common mistake that most people make about me," Davin replied with a mischievous grin. "How do you take me?"

Talia didn't respond right away, biting her lip. She still hadn't gotten used to his frankness, and she knew that now was not the time for humor.

"I can handle it, Huntress." Davin offered her an amused smile. "Just spit it out."

"I see you as a weapon," she replied quickly, needing to get the words out before her natural hesitation stopped her. She didn't want to insult him, but she knew that he valued the truth and would settle for nothing less.

Davin nodded, mulling her response, Talia unable to interpret the expression on his face.

"I'm sorry, I don't mean to ..."

"It's all right," Davin replied, his smile now gentle. "Another common mistake people make about me. I assume a weapon because ..."

"Because you're dangerous. Both to those you're sent against and to yourself."

Davin closed his eyes as he thought about that. Wanting to disagree. Knowing that doing so would be a waste of his time. He nodded slowly. Then he chuckled just beneath his breath. "It seems that we both have a great deal of natural intuitiveness."

Talia snorted softly at that, then crinkled her eyes when she looked at him. "For a gladiator, you're not what I expected."

"You've said that before."

"I have," Talia admitted.

"I'm not just a weapon?"

"You are a weapon," Talia answered swiftly, probably too swiftly for Davin's taste. She tried to soften the blow. "But you're more than that. I see that now."

"I'm glad that your perspective has changed at least to a certain extent. How did you describe me again when we first met?"

"A lot of cocky piss and vinegar." Talia said it unashamedly, again hoping that she didn't offend the gladiator. She refused to be anything but direct with him just as he was with her. "Although it didn't take me long to figure out that it was more façade than fact with you."

Davin nodded. He couldn't blame her for that. A fair perspective based on his performance in the Colosseum. "There were many gladiators like that and worse. Much worse. More fact than façade."

"Were?"

"They tended not to live very long," Davin replied with a shrug.

"Why not?"

"Because those were the gladiators who thought they knew everything they needed to know before they walked out onto the white sand. They didn't feel the need to learn what was necessary to survive."

"A common failing, although not just common to the Pit," Talia agreed with a nod, "but not one of yours."

"No, I'm still alive. I learned everything that anyone was willing to teach me while I was in the Pit."

"A smart move on your part."

"One of the few, I readily admit," Davin replied, giving her a wink and a grin and wanting to get off the current topic. Him. "Now back to my original question."

Talia acquiesced resignedly. She had tried to move the conversation in another direction so that she wouldn't have to deal with the cause of her disquiet. Davin had allowed it, though only for a brief time. "Why I'm lost?"

"Exactly that." Davin settled back against the stern railing, one leg hanging over the side. "I'd really like to know."

"Well, with your newly revealed intuitiveness you should be able to decipher the answer all on your own, shouldn't you?"

Talia's statement was a test, and she looked all too pleased with herself having put the puzzle before him. That didn't bother him. Davin was happy to accept her challenge, because he needed a challenge right then.

He likened the current situation to fighting on the white sand. Although his current opponent wasn't hungry for his blood and didn't carry a sword or trident or whip, he still needed to figure out a strategy for breaking through her defenses.

"You just sank six pirate ships. You should be in a good mood after such an astounding success."

"I should, you're right, but I'm not." Talia enjoyed watching

Davin work the problem, although she wasn't going to offer him any help. That would remove all the fun.

"In fact, you should be in a great mood, because after your victory at Smuggler's Cove, there can't be more than a handful of pirate vessels left. You've almost achieved your primary goal of clearing those marauders from the Sea of Mist. And, perhaps most pleasing of all, you achieved it at the expense of your favorite person, Hakea Roosarian. Every pirate ship taken or sunk is a nice little jab right in her eye."

"True." Talia shrugged. Her expression didn't change. She was curious as to how long it would take him to get where he was going.

Davin was smart. Too smart at times. Occasionally dragging out things because he enjoyed the chase so much.

"But you're still not in a good mood."

"No, I'm not."

"Which suggests to me, because I'm so intuitive," Davin continued, offering Talia another wink as he said it, "that you're still dealing with the fact that you came face to face with your betrothed."

"He's not my betrothed. I never said that he was my betrothed."

There was some heat in Talia's voice now. Just as Davin wanted. Emotion could reveal a great deal. He had learned that quite quickly in the Pit. If he hadn't, he would have died not long after entering the Colosseum.

"You didn't need to. I could tell. My intuitiveness, remember?"

Talia snorted out another gentle laugh. It was very easy to get angry with Davin. However, it was very difficult to stay angry with him, even when he teased her or made her life more difficult than it needed to be.

He looked at the world in a way that she wished that she

could. Yet no matter how much she wished it, it wasn't going to happen. It wasn't natural to her.

He looked for the good. He looked for the fun.

She looked for the problems that she needed to solve.

Although they did both look for the challenge. That realization caught her by surprise when it came to her.

"Fair enough," she said. "However, it wasn't so much that I saw him even though I thought that he was dead."

"Right. That was a shock, I'm sure. Knowing you, however, it didn't last long." Davin leaned in, clearly pleased with himself. "It was because you were angry. With yourself. You failed to kill him the first time. And then when you had the chance again, you didn't kill him the second time. You achieved what you wanted to achieve with respect to the pirate fleet, an astounding success I repeat, but because of that intense almost obsessive personality of yours, you've decided to focus solely on your one failure. Hence, that sense of being lost that's plaguing you more than it should."

"You think that I'm obsessive?" Talia's hackles rose. Her tone hinted that she didn't know whether she should be insulted by his comment. She was leaning toward the former.

"I said almost obsessive," Davin clarified, as if the extra word mattered.

"That's not much better."

"But it's not far off from the truth."

"You really do think that you know what you're talking about, don't you?" Talia gave Davin a pointed look that he was more than happy to ignore.

Talia's attempt at sarcasm didn't stop Davin from continuing. "I do know what I'm talking about, which is why you're fidgeting right now. You only do that when you realize that you might have made a mistake or are not handling a situation as well as you would like."

"I am not fidgeting," Talia protested. At the same time, she clasped her hands together to prevent her dancing fingers from reaching for the dagger at her hip that she so wanted to flip from hand to hand.

The repetitive motion of the steel spinning through the air, Talia always catching it by the tip between thumb and forefinger and sending it back into the air just as Tennyson had taught her, always helped to calm her. It would also prove Davin's point, and she couldn't allow that.

"I hope you understand that failing to kill your betrothed …"

"Would you please stop calling him that?" demanded Talia, beginning to lose patience.

"Sorry," Davin replied amiably, understanding the cause of her irritation. Less with him and more with herself. "I am just a sharp blade after all." Then he ignored her grunt of frustration. "I hope you realize that failing to kill your betrothed really wasn't your fault. None of us could have known that the Stalkers would be there to help that pompous jackass."

"He's not my betrothed," Talia repeated with more force, shaking her head in irritation. She really wanted to reach for her dagger now, although not to flip the steel from hand to hand. Instead, she wanted to stab Davin with it. She knew what he was trying to do. She knew as well that no matter what she told him, he was going to continue down this path. To say that he was hardheaded at times would be a massive understatement. "We could have assumed that the Stalkers would be there."

"Why would we assume that? Especially where we were."

Talia started and stopped herself several times before replying. "All right, fair question. There was no good way to know that the Stalkers would be there."

Davin nodded, giving Talia a broad smile. He was impressed. She rarely acknowledged the truth so easily, at least when it was coming from him. "I'm glad that we can agree on that. Was that difficult?"

"Was what difficult?" Talia asked, not understanding anything other than the fact that the level of her annoyance with the gladiator sitting just a few feet away from her was increasing by the second.

"Admitting that I was right."

Talia almost responded immediately, several unseemly words preferred by many a sailor coming to mind. All of which she believed were appropriate for the situation and much deserved by the gladiator. She held back instead.

She was annoyed, that was true. But she was also amused.

Not wanting to give Davin the credit he believed that he deserved, she returned to the original topic of their discussion, even though she didn't want to do that either.

"Still, I should have killed Ronild. He deserves nothing less than a painful death."

"You're right about that. He does deserve it."

"How can you say that when I haven't really told you what happened between us?"

Davin didn't even need to think before replying. "Because I met him and because I know you. I told you once before, I see you."

Talia studied Davin, her eyes narrowing, brow furrowing, the silence stretching out between them. At first, she didn't know what to say to his pronouncement. She wasn't quite sure she understood his comment, just as she hadn't the first time he told her that, until she did. "Thank you."

Davin waved off Talia's gratitude. "Have no fear. You will kill your betrothed. Of that I have no doubt."

Talia almost snorted out another laugh, having to fight to hold it back. He just couldn't help himself.

No matter how much she might ask him to give over, he still

felt the need to poke and prod. Fine. She would simply need to do her best to ignore his efforts in that respect.

In this instance it was easier for her to ignore the urge to tell him for a third time that Ronild Magnison was not her betrothed.

"How could you know that?"

"Because, as I said, I know you, Talia Carlomin," Davin replied in a gentle voice. He leaned in even closer, his bright eyes capturing hers. "I know who you were. I know who you are. I know who you want to be, even though you might not yet know that."

"How could you possibly ..." Talia was at a loss, never expecting the conversation to head down this road. And she wasn't entirely certain that she wanted it to.

Because she was finding it harder and harder to dispute Davin's conclusions. Also because she didn't quite understand and certainly didn't want to acknowledge the feelings welling up within her that she had locked away for so long.

"I've seen what you can do," Davin continued. "When you set your mind to completing a task, you do it. Always. It's one of your most admirable traits."

"And one of my greatest weaknesses." Her mother liked to remind her of that whenever she thought that Talia was getting too big for her britches.

"Your words, not mine," Davin said with a shrug as he leaned back against the stern where the two railings met, that movement breaking his hold on her.

"You really can be aggravating, you know that, Davin?"

He waved Talia's comment away, just as he had done the other. "I've been told that many times, oh great Huntress. I'll be told the same many times in the future. I am what I am. I can't be anything else than that."

"If I had a blade handy, I'd stab you."

"Just to make you feel better, I'd probably let you," Davin replied with a grin.

"That's kind of you to offer," Talia chuckled, shaking her head. He never failed to lighten her mood.

"It's nothing. Now tell me about Ronild Magnison. Tell me why he continues to haunt you."

Talia hesitated. She hadn't spoken to anyone about what had happened with the Lord of Roo's Nest much less that fateful night in his manor. Not even her mother, despite Isana telling her multiple times that she'd be happy to share her burdens.

If she didn't want to speak with her mother about it, why would she open up to a gladiator she had accepted with a great deal of reluctance into her crew?

Yet for some reason that she didn't quite understand, she began to tell Davin about her relationship with the Lord of Roo's Nest. Maybe it was because she didn't think that he would judge her as someone else would. At least she hoped that he wouldn't.

"I need to give you some context first."

"I'm all ears for whatever you want to tell me," replied Davin, who settled back and made himself comfortable on the railing. He enjoyed a good story.

Talia smiled at his gentle prodding and his attempt to let her know that she could tell him whatever she liked. "In Roo's Nest, where my family comes from, where you live defines you. It confirms your social standing and your wealth."

"How do you mean?"

"You've never been to Roo's Nest?"

"No. I grew up in Tintagel. Fighting the Ghoules with Bryen and the Blood Company took me all over Caledonia and even into the Lost Land, but never to Roo's Nest."

"Roo's Nest is a harbor that dwarfs Ballinasloe many times over. A massive scarp rises above it. The rich live on the plateau atop the scarp. Everyone else lives on the crag's ridges based on what they've earned or what they hope to earn."

"Sounds risky. Living beyond your means."

"It is," Talia agreed. "My father refused to accept loans, not wanting to put our home or business at risk. Others are willing to take that risk. For some it works as they hope. For others ..."

"Not so much."

"Right."

"But from what I understand you and your family were doing well in Roo's Nest."

"We were," nodded Talia. "Very well. The company was growing. We were expanding our trade routes. We had begun to do business across the Burnt Ocean and even farther west."

"From your tone, you don't seem to think that was a good thing."

"It was a good thing, but hindsight and all that," replied Talia, a tinge of disappointment in her voice. "We were doing well but we wanted to do better. Some opportunities came our way that required an infusion of capital that we didn't have, and as I said, we didn't want to accept any loans."

"So your family looked for partners," Davin prompted, already understanding the direction the tale was going to take.

"We did our due diligence on several. We didn't do enough due diligence on the one we selected. Either that or the red flags were hidden too well."

"Ronild you mean?"

"Yes, Ronild Magnison, a Lord of Roo's Nest, twelfth removed from the ducal seat."

"Really? He told you that?"

"Many times. It was like he was afraid that I was going to forget it."

"Seems like he didn't want to forget it himself," mused Davin.

Talia snorted out another laugh, making Davin smile as

well. He really liked it when she did that, especially when she tried to hold it in. It made her seem more ... vulnerable.

"Probably so," she admitted. "Anyway, he and his family appeared to be the best option for expanding our business through a partnership. Of course, we didn't really have much choice. He lived atop the plateau with the richest and most powerful of the Duchy. My family lived down in the harbor. The lowest rung of society based on how those things work in Roo's Nest."

"Even with your family's success? You didn't try to move higher up the scarp?"

"I spoke with my mother and father about it once."

"What did they tell you?"

"That wealth and standing didn't matter so much in the world compared to how you treated the people important to you."

"Sage advice," Davin nodded. "I would have liked to have met your father."

"He would have liked to have met you," Talia said, a touch of sadness slipping into her voice as was common when she thought of Abram Carlomin. "You would have perplexed him. In a good way, though."

"I get that a lot," Davin admitted with a wink.

"Why am I not surprised?"

"Anyway, back to you," Davin said quickly, not wanting the conversation between them to go off on a tangent.

"Despite our success, my father wanted to stay close to our business, our ships, the people who worked for us and with us. That was why we were successful. He didn't want to do anything that could disrupt it."

"Then if initially it was just a business arrangement, how did you get mixed up with your betrothed?"

Talia shot Davin an angry look that he ignored completely, instead giving her that smile of his that said there was little point in taking life seriously all the time, because it was hard enough as it was. Not wanting to give him the satisfaction of knowing that he had gotten under her skin once again, she continued.

"It happened by mistake, or at least I thought it was a mistake. Thinking about it now, I realize that Ronild managed our relationship right from the start."

"How so?"

"I thought we ran into one another at the harbor by happenstance. He hadn't even been involved in the business negotiations. Actually, he didn't come across as someone interested in any aspect of running a business."

Davin nodded. Devious. "He and his family had learned of your family's success. Much like Roosarian, they thought that once they were in partnership with you they could take it for themselves. You were just a piece to be played."

"That's my assumption as well," Talia confirmed.

"So his marrying you makes it easier for the Magnisons to take Carlomin Trading Company as their own."

"A very simple strategy, yes," Talia confirmed again.

"Simple but cunning," Davin concluded, nodding not in appreciation but actually shaking his head in disgust, "and very cold and conniving."

"I thought so as well."

"And that's in part why you're still so angry. Not just that you failed to kill Ronild, but that you didn't see the Magnisons' scheme until it almost ensnared you."

"You catch on quick. Quicker than I did."

"Well, keep in mind that I wouldn't have fallen for Ronild's charms. He's not to my taste."

"No, I guess he isn't," Talia laughed. "Since you've tried to kill him twice already."

Davin nodded. "And I would have, both times, if not for some untimely intervention by unwanted third parties."

"Sounds like sour grapes, gladiator."

"Point taken," Davin confirmed. "Perhaps you should take your own advice."

Talia gave Davin a penetrating look, choosing to ignore his suggestion and focus on another of his comments. Curious. Also wanting to remove herself from being the focus. "Tell me, Davin Noname, what are your tastes?"

Normally, she would avoid this route. But since she had been feeling uneasy in large part because of Davin and his prodding, she wanted to see if she could return the favor and do the same to him.

"That's a topic for another day," Davin replied, deflecting her question with an unanticipated deftness. "Now returning to your betrothed's interest in your family's business, I learned a great many lessons in the Colosseum."

"You mean lessons that didn't necessarily involve the use of a piece of sharp steel?"

"Exactly so. For example, a lot of wealthy men and women visited the Colosseum regularly not just because they were interested in betting on the gladiatorial games, although they were, but also because they believed that it was to their advantage to do so. There were a good number of business deals worked out there. In the private suites a great many people increased their wealth and their power, usually at the expense of others."

"That's a very cold perspective on the world," Talia replied, knowing where Davin was headed.

"True, but it is accurate in my opinion. Those with power and wealth usually are seeking to increase both. They can't seem to help themselves. And few do as you and your mother are doing, investing what you've earned back into the people working with you and trying to build a community."

"It's the right thing to do," Talia said simply. "If my mother and I succeed, the people who have placed their trust in us need to succeed as well. It's only fair."

"I don't disagree," Davin confirmed. "But it's also uncommon. Because most others who are successful in business seem to view it as a zero-sum game."

"Meaning?"

"That they can increase their wealth and power not only by improving on their own success, but also by ensuring that those competing with them aren't successful."

"Very, very cynical, gladiator."

"Yes, but again, true, at least from what I've seen of the world."

"After my experience with Ronild, I won't offer much of an argument against your theory."

"So what was it about Ronild Magnison that caught your eye? Because he's really not much to look at now."

Talia smiled, appreciating his dry wit. She had assumed that Davin wasn't going to let that part of their conversation go, and she had been right.

Ronild wasn't bad to look at before I scarred him, she thought to herself.

When Ronild explained how life would be when she married him, how he would do as he wished and she would exist in a gilded cage, she was shocked. But not as shocked as when he attacked her after she told him that she was calling off their engagement.

The first few days after the assault happened, as she spent most of her time staring at the rolling swells of the Burnt Ocean, she felt terrible because of what she had done, believing that she had killed Ronild. The more she thought about it, however, the more she realized that Ronild had brought all that had occurred onto himself.

Tennyson had taught her that you didn't draw a blade unless you meant to use it.

It was either him or her. She just proved to be the better fighter.

After pulling herself back from those less than pleasant memories, she decided to answer honestly. "I guess it was because no one ever had looked at me the way he did." She threw her arms up in disgust. "The interest that he showed in me was all new to me. Unexpected. Pleasing." She clearly still wasn't happy with herself about that last. "I was a fool, I know. But he did have a great smile."

"Before you took that from him."

"Before I took that from him," she admitted, although she replied with very little emotion, not an ounce of regret to be heard.

She believed that Ronild had gotten what he deserved for attacking her the way he did. He was lucky to have survived the encounter.

And, if he had been smart, he wouldn't have followed her to New Caledonia. Because now he had given her the chance to finish the job.

"Dagger?"

Talia gave Davin a strange look. "Why would you ask that?"

"I was curious. When I saw him beneath the Rock for the first time, the scar looked like that kind of wound." Davin shrugged. "And you are quite good with those daggers of yours. Lethally so, in fact."

Talia nodded then, pleased by the compliment. "A dagger, yes." She pulled the blade from where she kept it in a sheath in the small of her back. It wasn't a large blade, but it was exceedingly sharp. She was embarrassed that there were several jewels embedded in the knob and along the grip. Gaudy, yes, though still effective. As she had demonstrated. "A wedding gift."

"He gave that to you?" Davin leaned in closer so that he could get a better look at the weapon.

"He did. I'm sure he regrets it now."

"He probably does. So besides his wealth, his status, and his formerly dazzling smile, what was it about him that caught your eye?"

"Why do you want to know?" Talia asked, wary.

Davin gave her another big grin, leaning in even closer than he had before. "Well, I'm hoping that I can learn something useful from you that I can use with the ladies."

Talia swiped at him playfully with the dagger, Davin pulling back swiftly. Just in case. She was laughing, but why take the risk?

"Now come on. Tell me. It couldn't have been just his good looks. You're not that shallow."

"Why do you believe that?"

"Because, as I said, I know you."

"You really are sure of yourself, aren't you?"

"I'm only sure of myself when I'm sure of myself."

Davin's last statement made Talia give the gladiator another hard look. It wasn't the first time his words had made her do so. "What does that even mean?"

"It means what it means," Davin said with a wink, enjoying how his response soured Talia's expression even more.

"You really are infuriating." Talia rolled her eyes. "I hope you realize that."

"You're not answering my question," Davin countered, ignoring her complaint.

Talia held back what she thought would be a stinging retort, which wouldn't have been helpful. Because Davin was correct. She couldn't deny that.

She was avoiding his question.

After almost a minute had passed, evaluating what had proven to be one of the worst experiences of her life, she finally responded. "Thinking back, I believe it was because no one else had ever demonstrated that kind of interest in me before. He treated me well, in a way that no one else ever had. I wasn't just a girl living down at the harbor. He made me see myself as something more than that. He made me feel special." She shook her head in annoyance. "And then he used that against me. I really was a fool."

"So you blame yourself for being taken in by Ronild. For being deceived and then making the mistake of falling in love with him."

"You really do speak bluntly, don't you?"

Davin shrugged. "Speaking bluntly eliminates confusion."

"It can also cause aggravation or worse," Talia challenged, "if that bluntness isn't tempered with discretion when discretion is called for."

"Point taken, thank you," Davin agreed amiably, unfazed by her comment. "Might I offer a word of advice, seeing as I've had to deal with people like you all my life?"

Images of Bryen, Declan, and Lycia immediately popped into his head. All three were much like Talia.

Confident. Focused. Driven. Never satisfied. Never willing to give in.

They were like forces of nature once they put their minds to a task that they believed needed to be completed.

"People like me?" She bristled at that a little bit, even though she was curious as to what he was going to say. She wanted to see if Davin would be able to pull himself out of the hole that he had dug for himself.

"People like you, yes. People who are so in thrall to the responsibilities that they've taken on that they never have the time to enjoy what they've earned. Even if just for a night."

Talia could have been angry with Davin for what he said, but she was finding it difficult reaching that necessary point on the scale that would tip her in that direction. With a great deal of reluctance, she had to admit that he wasn't too far off the mark. Instead of giving him a piece of her mind, she gave him a nod.

"What advice would you like to share, Davin Noname?" Talia asked in a tone heavily laced with sarcasm. "I would love to hear what wisdom the Crimson Giant has to offer."

"Death doesn't choose us. We choose our death."

"That saying really doesn't seem appropriate to what we're talking about."

"That's because you didn't let me finish."

"Then what were you going to say?" Talia motioned with her hand, wanting him to speed things along. She was beginning to lose patience.

"I was going to tell you, but you're not allowing me to ..."

"Just hurry up and finish, because you're taking way too long with your advice."

"Are you done?" Davin's tone suggested that he was irritated, even though he wasn't. He could see the spark in Talia's eyes. She was enjoying the give and take between them, and that's what she needed now, so he was happy to oblige her.

"I'm done. Sorry. Please finish what you were going to say. But quickly. It's taking you much too long to get to the point."

Talia didn't sound all that sorry to Davin, but he ignored her attempt to rile him up. "Death doesn't choose us. We choose our death. We also choose how we live. Regardless of the circumstances, the challenges, the good and the bad. We choose how we live. Before we choose our death."

"Insightful and macabre both at the same time."

"I try my best."

"Maybe if you had tried a little harder Ronild wouldn't have escaped."

Davin smiled at that, hearing the taunt in her voice rather than anger, taking the quip as she meant it. She had offered it in a teasing way rather than an insult. "Maybe. Still, it was a good day. We killed a good number of Stalkers. We eliminated the pirates and their ships we caught in Smuggler's Cove. We're both still alive despite being chased off a cliff by Stalkers and then having to evade them and then a Great Shark. So I'll sleep well tonight knowing that I did all that I could."

"You're going to bed already?" Talia was antsy. Her adrenaline was still flowing, and her conversation with Davin was helping her control it.

Also, although she wouldn't tell him, because she didn't want it to go to his head, she was enjoying speaking with him even though he was hitting the truth more often than she would have preferred.

"Yes, I'm tired. Fighting pirates. Fighting Stalkers. Escaping a Great Shark. It takes a lot out of you."

"You're really going to bed?" Talia didn't quite believe him. She didn't want to believe him.

She was enjoying their conversation. She was enjoying spending time with him. Talia didn't want it to end. She felt like there was more to say. Perhaps even more to do.

"As I said, it was a good day for us." Davin pushed himself up from where he had been sitting and swung his leg back over the railing. "It's all right to enjoy our successes. Until it's not."

"More words of wisdom from the Crimson Giant?"

Davin winked at her again. "Not mine. Declan's. If you had a good day, he liked to say that you should enjoy it. Then you should forget it. Because the next day would offer you a new challenge. What you did the day before would have no bearing on your ability to manage that new challenge."

"Which is why you survived on the white sand for so long."

"Exactly so."

"I like how you did that," Talia said, giving Davin a nod of appreciation.

"Did what?"

Clearly, Davin knew what Talia meant. His smile gave him away. Still, she knew that he wanted her to say it.

"How you brought this entire conversation full circle. I'm impressed."

"Glad to hear it." Davin began walking toward the helm and the hatch beneath it that would take him below. "And I'm going to bed."

"You said that before." Talia wasn't yet willing to end the conversation. "Yet you're still here."

"Good night, Huntress," Davin said over his shoulder as he walked across the deck. "Please remember that there's more to life than just what you want to get done. There's also just living. Enjoying what the world has to offer you. Making the most of what time you have. It doesn't have to all be about whether you win or lose."

"But it often is."

"It often is," Davin agreed.

"What does the world have to offer me besides blood and death?" she called after him, still not ready to let him go so easily. Hoping that he might come back. "I've seen little else for quite some time."

Davin turned before he ducked down the hatchway, catching the expectant look in her eyes that sent a not too unpleasant shiver through him.

"I used to think the same," he admitted. "Now, I realize that I'll never escape the blood and death. That the blood and death will always be with me. But I can escape it for a time if I choose to. So that's what I do."

"And that helps to keep you sane," mused Talia. "Another lesson from the Crimson Giant."

Davin smiled, then disappeared into the darkness, his voice drifting out from the hatch. "Who said I was sane? I like to dive off the crow's nest, remember?"

TALIA STARED for quite some time at the hatchway that Davin

had just disappeared through, lost in thought. Still lost as well, though not as she had been before she spoke to the gladiator.

Now she didn't know what to do. One part of her, the part that she tried to ignore, told her to go after Davin. That she wanted to continue the conversation with him, though in a slightly different way.

The other part of her, the more rational part, told her to move on to the next task. That giving in to a moment of temptation to fulfill an urge wouldn't serve her well in the future.

As always, the rational part of her won out. She remained where she was, near the stern railing, her eyes still fixed on the hatchway.

Nevertheless, that didn't prevent her from thinking about what had just happened. What might have happened if she hadn't exercised a remarkable level of restraint that chafed at her.

She hadn't wanted Davin to go. She wanted to keep talking with him. She wanted to spend more time with him.

Why was that?

She really wanted to understand, because this was so unlike her.

When Bryen Keldragan had asked that she take the slightly unstable gladiator aboard, she knew what the man responsible for the overthrow of the Beleron dynasty was doing.

They had reached an agreement after dispatching the small fleet of pirates. That was true.

Nevertheless, they didn't know each other well. And they needed to get to know each other better. They needed to be certain that they could depend upon one another going forward.

Davin working with Talia would help to build trust between them. That was to the benefit of both of them. Moreover, she couldn't deny that another capable fighter wouldn't hurt her in her efforts to eliminate the pirates haunting the Sea of Mist and unseat Hakea Roosarian.

Davin had proven Talia correct on that point almost immediately and many times after that. His escapades of the last couple days served as just one example of what he could do.

The Crimson Giant was a one-man wrecking ball when that was required of him. And Talia knew from experience that wrecking balls could be quite useful in certain situations.

Bryen's request to have the gladiator join her hadn't bothered her. It only made sense, after all.

Yet when she had taken a good hard look at Davin for the first time, she had hesitated. She had seen in that brief glance what Davin truly was.

Davin was a lost soul.

Just like her, even though she refused to admit that to herself or anyone else for that matter.

Hidden behind that grin of his, Talia could tell that the gladiator was trying to find himself.

That in itself didn't bother her. What worried her was that clearly he didn't know how to find himself.

She had taken on Davin as part of her crew primarily because she couldn't refuse Bryen Keldragan. Working with him, the Lady of the Southern Marches, and the Blood Company was too much of an opportunity to pass up. She also had allowed him to join her crew because she was curious.

About Davin.

About whether he would find himself.

About the type of person he would become if he did.

As she learned more about him, she realized that her initial assessment of him was incorrect.

Davin knew who he was. He knew what he needed.

It was because it was so strangely simple that it had taken her quite a while to figure it out.

He just needed the opportunity to be who he was.

Talia had given him that chance, and he had seized upon it.

Just as he had given her the chance to be who she was with him.

She didn't have to be Captain Carlomin with him. She didn't have to be the Huntress. She didn't have to be the owner of the most successful shipping and trading company in New Caledonia.

She could be Talia.

She doubted that Davin even realized what he had done for her.

Talia snorted softly to herself. Who was she kidding?

Davin knew. He just hadn't said anything. That wasn't his way.

That bloody intuitiveness of his.

That thought almost made Talia snort again with laughter. She held it in, hearing the boots coming toward her across the deck.

"All well, Captain Carlomin?"

Sirena Makarin, Captain of her Guard, emerged from the shadows on the port side. It took some effort for Talia to rip her eyes away from the empty hatch and shift her gaze to her.

"Quite well, Sirena, thank you."

The *Swift* was anchored in a narrow cove that sheltered a small fishing village. They were a good distance away from Smuggler's Cove and both believed that they would be safe for the night.

Sirena nodded. "I just wanted to make sure. You were speaking with Davin for quite a long time."

"That concerned you?" Talia tried to add a touch of levity to her voice and failed because of her continuing distraction.

"I know how the gladiator can affect you at times. That's all."

"Affect me?" She didn't know if she should be amused or worried.

Sensing Talia's discomfort, Sirena attempted to clarify. "I know that Davin can speak his mind at times in a way that can get under your skin." Sirena shrugged. "He speaks brusquely. What he says is usually on the mark. It's just that even though you might need to hear it sometimes he doesn't always pick the best time to say what he has to say."

Talia smirked. "That's one way to put it." She was impressed by how quickly Sirena recovered from her potential misstep. "The guard is set for the night?"

"Yes. The watch will change every two hours as you ordered."

"Good," Talia replied. She pushed herself up and headed toward the hatch through which Davin had disappeared. "I'm going to sleep for a few hours, then I'll be at the helm. I want to leave before dawn."

Sirena nodded. "We'll be ready, Captain Carlomin."

As she strode toward her cabin, instead of feeling confident Talia instead felt even edgier than she had before.

It could be because of her latest interaction with Davin. Sirena wasn't far off in her assessment with respect to that.

Speaking with the gladiator and having to wrap her mind around all his pieces of knowledge, and those distracting smiles and winks of his, had forced her to think in ways that she didn't really want to. Then again, the experience wasn't entirely uncomfortable for her.

For the most part, when he wasn't forcing her to acknowledge some truths that she might have preferred to continue to ignore, it had been an enjoyable experience.

Lost in thought as she walked down the corridor, she hesitated when she reached the door to Davin's small cabin. So small, in fact, that she had laughed when she discovered that he had to stoop so that he didn't knock his head on any of the beams and then turn sideways to move around in the tight space.

Yet he hadn't said a word to her about it. Not a single complaint.

For a brief moment, very brief, only a heartbeat, she considered knocking, her fingers inches from the door.

Instead, she pulled her hand back swiftly.

What was she thinking?

It had just been a conversation. No more than that.

She didn't want her speaking with Davin to become any more than that. If she allowed that to happen, it would only complicate an already complicated situation.

She knew that. She understood that.

Yet still she hesitated. Still she felt the desire to ...

Forcing herself to put one foot in front of the other, Talia moved silently down the corridor.

She shook her head ruefully. Her brief moment of insanity must have been because she was distracted.

Maybe the cause of her almost rash behavior was Ronild. Her believing that he was dead. She seeing that he was alive. Her missing the chance to kill him a second time.

Even after what Davin suggested, her failure still felt like a knife being twisted in her gut.

When Talia closed the door to her larger cabin that took up the stern of the *Swift*, she dropped down onto the bed that was cut into the far wall. She knew that no matter what she tried, she wasn't going to sleep very well that night.

She blamed Ronild and the Stalkers.

Yet when she closed her eyes, all she could see was Davin.

4

THE FINAL STEP

Hakea Roosarian clenched her fists so tightly to the wood railings running atop the gunwales that her fingers turned white.

The pain reminded her to relax her grip. She did. Only a minute later, however, she was back at it.

She was desperate for some outlet for her rage, yet she had nothing readily available to her as she stood in the bow of the launch that was taking her across the harbor to the Rock.

As she studied the monstrous fortress that rose above her, her fury threatened to explode once more. Her still to be completed citadel, languishing from neglect.

She couldn't stand the lack of activity that met her gaze. The stillness. The aura of ineptitude.

The city behind her was bustling. There was nothing but constant movement and noise, a buzz of activity reminiscent of a bee's hive.

Business was getting done.

Business that she should have been profiting from.

But she wasn't.

Even though this was her city. Her Territory.

She was the power in this land, yet as she moved with the waves pushing at the launch from the starboard side, she felt as if she had very little power that she could exercise even though she was the Governor of Fal Carrach.

She hated being in this position.

Enfeebled.

Undermined.

Just the thought of it made her want to puke over the side of the craft.

She didn't understand exactly how it had happened, although she certainly knew the cause.

Talia Carlomin.

That young woman had begun slowly, chipping away at her power. At her authority. At her standing.

In ways that at first were barely perceptible.

Then she evaded all the traps that Hakea had set for her.

Worse, after escaping all of those snares, that infuriating upstart had come out on the other side in a stronger position.

Hakea's fingers began to ache as she dug her fingernails into the wood even deeper.

She ignored the pain.

She deserved it.

She had allowed Talia Carlomin to do this.

Hakea had employed a more moderate response rather than crushing her adversary right from the start.

Hakea growled loudly enough for the sailors behind her to hear over the wind and the waves smacking against the launch's hull.

That was enough for them to increase the pace of their strokes, wanting to deposit the Governor at her destination as swiftly as possible. They knew quite well what could happen if she lost her temper.

Once again, Hakea forced herself to loosen her grip on the

wood railings. Allowing her anger free reign wouldn't help her do what she needed to do.

She needed to eliminate Talia Carlomin.

Swiftly.

Without fail.

With a great deal of prejudice.

All of Hakea's plans had been moving forward exactly as she wanted.

Until Talia Carlomin and her family arrived in the Territory.

Slowly but surely that young woman and her mother had started to pull apart all the strands of the web that she had been weaving to expand her power first here in Fal Carrach and then beyond into all of New Caledonia.

With every thread the Carlomins untangled, Hakea lost power and money.

She lost respect.

She lost more of the reputation that she had spent so much time cultivating.

That all had burned a hole in her gut that wouldn't be healed until Talia Carlomin was gone.

It was clear what was required. Once done, all would return to what it had been before the Carlomins stepped onto the dock at Ballinasloe.

But today ...

Today ...

Hakea was at a complete loss.

Now she wondered whether her belief in her success was more a dream than reality.

She still couldn't quite believe what had occurred.

She was the Governor!

She ruled this Territory!

She fumed thinking about it. This latest obstacle. This farce of a Council.

The conniving merchants who had allied themselves with the Carlomins actually had the nerve to request her presence before what they had named the Council of Fal Carrach.

Just thinking of that name made her shake with fury. Her fingers dug into the railings once again and with so much strength that she felt as if she could rip the wood apart.

The merchants of Ballinasloe said that they only wanted to discuss trade. That's why they met. To ensure that the business of the Territory was conducted without disruption.

Traitors! Every last one of them.

She knew the truth. The Council was just another of the Carlomin woman's cursed inventions that was designed to undermine her.

They had treated her well upon her arrival. Smiling. Even offering her a few bows of respect and kind words.

It was all a ruse.

They were playing her. Or at least trying to.

Hakea had to close her eyes and take a deep breath, attempting to control the almost uncontrollable urge to lash out.

If she was being honest with herself, the merchants and traders of the city had played her.

As soon as she walked into the warehouse that the merchants had transformed into a meeting house, she realized that she had made a mistake. That her very presence there legitimized the Council and its efforts.

However, she couldn't leave just seconds after she arrived. That would have been interpreted as a demonstration of fear, and she could never, ever appear weak or unsure.

Instead she had tried to gain control of the proceedings.

Hakea demanded to know why they had requested her presence when they had not paid the tariffs and taxes required of them. All of them were months in arrears. There was no discussion to be had until all debts were paid.

Hakea then offered every single attendee a condescending smile, locking eyes with each one. Searching for what had been there only months before.

Yet she hadn't seen the fear in the back of their eyes that she had anticipated. That she craved. That had served her so well in the past.

No, rather she had seen contempt. For her.

That discovery knocked her off her even keel.

"We have," one of the merchants had the gall to say. "Every last gold and silver required."

Hakea couldn't remember the woman's name, only recalling that she specialized in high-quality glasswork.

"But we decided that to ensure that those funds could be distributed more swiftly and specifically for the work that needed to be done," Hakea remembering the calculating look the woman had given her, a look of equivalence that immediately had rubbed her the wrong way and set her to grinding her teeth, "we've been putting those taxes into a fund managed by a smaller committee focused on the public works projects that need to be completed. The extension of the wall. The improvements that are required at the docks. The dredging in the northern section of the harbor."

"You did what?" Hakea had hissed, barely able to contain herself.

"We only thought it appropriate," the glassmaker continued, unperturbed by the murderous look Hakea gave her. "You have so much to deal with as it is, Governor Roosarian, that we assumed that was the reason for all the delays in the improvements that you promised us but had not yet begun."

The woman's pointed look told Hakea that she didn't believe her own words, but that she was going to offer them anyway. That she needed to say them in order to maintain the charade.

"Knowing that you were busy with so many other worthy

tasks," Hakea easily detecting the scorn barely hidden within the woman's voice, "we decided to remove that burden from your shoulders. All the businesspeople responsible for paying that tax agreed. All that was owed has been paid. All that we have collected is now being used as those funds are *supposed* to be used." Hakea didn't miss the glassmaker's insinuation based on the word she stressed.

"Why wasn't I informed of this?" Hakea had wanted to shout. She contained herself instead, remembering how the only thought that had been passing through her mind in that dreadful moment was that these fools were committing treason. That these thieves masquerading as merchants and traders needed to be exposed as what they truly were. Criminals.

Those funds were hers to do with as she deemed necessary. Not for some useless public works projects that did not benefit her directly.

"We did inform you." The spokeswoman had replied with an impressive calm, ignoring the murderous look that Hakea gave her. "When Captain Hippolates visited with us, we provided a note that he was to give to you. He did, did he not?"

That revelation had cooled Hakea's anger, if only a few degrees. They could have been telling the truth. They could have been lying.

Hakea wasn't certain, although the smug grin the glassmaker had given her suggested that the Council had done as she had said they did.

Captain Hippolates was notorious for ignoring details or tasks that he believed were beneath him or were less than interesting. If it required the use of a weapon, bullying, intimidation, or torture, then that was another matter entirely.

For a few seconds, Hakea had considered her next steps. She could call in the Fal Carrachian Guard and throw every one of these rebels and thieves into the dungeons beneath the Rock.

That would cow these fools.

That would show them that their doing anything that touched on the power that she exercised, that had been granted solely to her, would be met with an immediate, very final response.

That would have been the easy thing to do.

That would have been the most satisfying path that she could take.

Yet she had hesitated.

She had learned during her time as Governor of Fal Carrach that rarely was anything ever easy.

She wanted to destroy these merchants and traders. Utterly and completely. She wanted them to beg her for forgiveness, for the mercy that Hakea would never give them.

But she couldn't do that. Not yet.

If she did what her anger was telling her to do, then the flow of commerce through Ballinasloe would dry up. It would be weeks, if not months, before she'd be able to even restart a trickle of what was passing through the port daily.

As her gaze had swept over the expectant, pompous faces of those men and women opposing her from behind the pretense of looking after the business of Fal Carrach, Hakea realized that they had her over a barrel.

She'd have to wait for her revenge. She needed to play carefully for a time until she could crush these fools and take their businesses for her own.

The discussion after that had been meaningless, the members of the Council assuring her that they had nothing but the best interests of the city and the Territory at heart.

Once they were done giving her their promises, the members of the self-proclaimed Council of Fal Carrach had filed out, no longer feeling the need to speak with her now that they had completed their task.

Hakea still couldn't believe all that had occurred that morning.

Those merchants and traders who likely had never swung a sword in anger had been proud of themselves for standing up to her.

They thought that they had won. And they had known, before they had even called the meeting, that they would.

At least with respect to that single engagement.

Because they knew just as she did that she couldn't do anything to them. She couldn't throw them all into chains like she wanted to. She couldn't make examples of them by parading them through the streets beaten and battered. She couldn't use their disobedience to regain the power that she had somehow lost to them.

Yet.

But she would.

She just needed to do what she had failed to do so many times before.

She needed to kill Talia Carlomin.

Kill her.

Kill her mother.

Take the Carlomin Trading Company for her own.

Then all her problems with these merchants would disappear.

Then this so-called Council of Fal Carrach would understand what she would do if they disobeyed. In fact, she would do it anyway, they just didn't need to know that until it was too late.

These rebels and thieves would have no choice but to play by her rules. And then the wheels of commerce and governance within Ballinasloe and Fal Carrach would begin to turn as they had before those blasted Carlomins had arrived to ruin what she had been building here.

As they drew closer to the Rock, Hakea recalled her conversation with Torstan Sharperson when last they had met in Smuggler's Cove. What he had suggested she do to address her challenges.

Take a more direct hand.

Flex her muscles.

Use the power that only she could exercise that Talia Carlomin could not stand against.

Show those who challenge her what it means to take on the Governor. Show them the price they will pay for insubordination and outright treason.

Under most circumstances, she didn't listen to anything Sharperson had to say. She knew exactly what free advice was worth.

This time, however, she believed that what he told her held some merit.

Stone by stone, Talia Carlomin was destroying everything that Hakea had sought to build in the Territory.

Hakea needed to attack her nemesis directly. She needed to flex her muscles just as Torstan suggested. She needed to show those seeking to challenge her that any attempt to usurp her power or position would lead to a bloody and painful end.

Talia Carlomin first as the example. Then the others who proved to be too slow to toe the new line that she would draw across the pier.

But to do what she needed to do required help. Nothing that she had tried in the past succeeded. Except just once.

Acknowledging that truth, she would need to swallow her pride if she wanted to ensure her success.

She had been reluctant to test the tool that Ursina had given her. She hadn't thought that it would work.

But it had.

Surprisingly well.

If it had proven successful before in eliminating Talia Carlomin's father, then why not again?

It would be poetic in a sense. If her latest strategy for killing the upstart didn't work, then Talia Carlomin could die just as her father did.

Hakea didn't want to go back to Winborne and his wife for help. She hated the idea of being in their debt.

But she had no choice.

Removing the threat challenging her was more important than the respect and power that she would lose temporarily.

She would do what was necessary.

She couldn't afford any more mistakes.

Once this problem was solved, she could focus on retaking what she had lost.

That decision made, as the longboat approached the incomplete dock that jutted out from the island, she looked up once again at the Rock that towered above her.

It was designed to be a symbol of her power and wealth, this gargantuan citadel carved out of the stone rising on the island that was located in the center of the harbor.

Yet construction had stopped. All because of Talia Carlomin.

The cranes stood there lamely.

The scaffolding was bare.

The rocks, mortar, wood, and other supplies needed to complete the walls were nowhere in sight.

The stonemasons, carpenters, and other tradespeople who should have been finishing the fortress had found other work.

If the thought of what had happened hadn't enraged her so, she would have given Talia Carlomin credit for her clever maneuver. A tactic to be appreciated if her adversary hadn't applied it to her.

All the supplies and materials needed to complete the Rock were now being delivered to the Carlomin docks for the construction taking place there.

And that blasted woman had hired all the skilled craftspeople and put them to work on her almost endless projects. Every single one.

Even more surprising, instead of that massive expense putting her out of business, the Carlomin Trading Company was thriving.

That thought almost made her turn her gaze toward her challenger's docks at the far southern section of the harbor.

Enclave more like it. A city within a city.

She refused to give in to the urge. She refused to allow what was happening just across the harbor from coloring the decisions that she had just made.

She would reach out to Ursina. She would take whatever assistance the woman was willing to give her.

However, it would take time to put all the pieces of that scheme in place.

Knowing that, she would try another tactic while she waited.

If she was successful, it might make her attempt at seizing the Carlomin holdings that much easier.

And best of all, she wouldn't be in debt to the Winbornes.

5

A CONSTANT IRRITATION

"I can't believe that he made us both come out here," huffed Saraa, her irritation more than obvious both in her voice and her expression.

"He did it for a reason."

"I know he did it for a reason," Saraa almost shouted, fighting hard to contain her simmering annoyance.

"Then why allow it to bother you so much?"

"I can't believe he did this to me," Saraa muttered under her breath, not realizing that Lycia still could hear her.

"He wants us to play nice," Lycia responded, her voice even, devoid of emotion. She didn't want to give Saraa any chance to bite into what she was feeling.

She understood why Saraa was so furious. Although she believed that a good portion of her anger was misplaced.

"I have no problem playing nice so long as you stay out of my way," hissed Saraa through clenched teeth.

A silence finally settled over them as they kept watch. Saraa took several deep breaths, seeking a calm that refused to take hold.

She shook her head in irritation. She was maintaining the

decorum that she wanted. However, she was allowing this woman, this gladiator, this competitor to get under her skin. And for the life of her she couldn't understand why. Maybe it was because this was the first time she had been placed in a situation such as this.

One in which she had not gotten what she wanted.

Jakob Kestrel.

She had liked him the first time she had laid eyes on him, even with that horrific wound marring his features.

She didn't understand why he seemed to be immune to her charms.

He smiled at her. Treated her with respect. Yet she never succeeded in twisting him around her finger as she did so many others before she crossed the Burnt Ocean and settled in the Highlands.

There had been a spark between them when they first met. She was sure of it.

She had been taken with his stoicism. He had ignored the bloody wound that ran from his brow to his chin, not caring that with one stroke of a Wraith's dagger his handsome visage had been stolen from him.

She had been attracted to that sideways smile that always made her feel as if they were sharing a private joke.

Worse, she hadn't been able to get him out of her mind, and that was unusual for her.

She had never come up against a situation such as this, in which she and Jakob danced around one another, Jakob not once taking her up on the many hints that she offered him.

She didn't understand his restraint, even as it only made her want him all the more.

At first, Saraa had viewed Jakob as an enjoyable diversion. As time passed, he became more of a challenge.

She had tried many times to solve the riddle that was Jakob Kestrel. She was still trying, in fact. All with little success.

And now her efforts were proving more and more difficult because of the arrival of this tall, thin, red-haired gladiator who didn't seem to have an inch of visible flesh that wasn't marked by a scar.

Somehow, she had captured Jakob's eye.

He didn't make it obvious, his interest.

But Saraa could tell. She had too much experience in this area to miss it.

The spark that she saw in Jakob's piercing green orbs, that he tried so hard to hide, wasn't there for her. It was for this interloper that he had forced upon her.

Now Saraa had two problems. How to attract Jakob's interest with her competition always by his side and how to drive away this sinewy woman who seemed to have been born with those twin swords of hers in her hands.

Saraa didn't know what to do, because nothing she had tried had worked. Even now, she was failing miserably in her efforts to bait the gladiator.

In large part because Lycia refused to play her game. Even when Saraa was certain that the gladiator had several biting comments ready to go, she didn't bother to reply to much of what Saraa had to say, and that only served to rile Saraa up all the more.

She needed to find some way to get under Lycia's skin. To reveal what kind of person the gladiator truly was. And she would. Of that she had no doubt. It was just a matter of finding a chink in the woman's armor.

Lycia ignored the simmering Highlander as best as she could. Just as she had been trying to do since they took up their watch.

She knew full well that she had little chance of changing Saraa's opinion of her. Understanding that, she had little desire to try.

She sought only to take in what was a beautiful night. Not too chilly.

And it was quiet. She would have enjoyed the welcome solitude even more if her unwanted partner didn't feel the need to be right by her side.

Saraa grumbling under her breath ever louder, Lycia tried to stay focused on what was around them.

They were standing at the end of a narrow gap. Sheer rock walls rose up on each side to a height of several hundred feet. The opening between the cliffs led back to where the Highlanders had made their camp.

It was an excellent spot. Hidden. Defensible. There was no chance that the fire could be spotted.

A necessity, since Jakob was tracking more than a dozen Stalkers moving about in the darkness. Some several leagues away, some only a mile or two, so there was no reason to make it easy for the monsters to find their prey.

Jakob considered going after the Stalkers that night. With five squads of Highlanders at his back, they could eliminate several with little effort or risk on their part.

Instead, he decided that they could delay the hunt until tomorrow. After they achieved their primary objective. There were no settlements nearby. He didn't need to worry about the beasts attacking farms or villages.

Better to let everyone get some sleep. They had been on the move since before the sun was up. Heading back toward the broch. Wanting to reach Duff before the Stalkers attacked. The monsters' decision to wait until morning allowing Jakob to order a halt that would allow a few hours' rest. Besides, coming at the Stalkers during the day increased the chances of their success, denying the pitch-black monsters the advantage the night gave them.

Lycia approved of Jakob's approach. It was the smart thing to do.

And he needed to be smart, because Lycia knew that eliminating the Stalkers that were dogging them was just the first step in his larger strategy.

Once they were done with the Stalkers in their immediate vicinity, Jakob wanted to go after the slavers and put even more pressure on Governor Sharperson.

It was a hawkish move.

Bold.

Even a little risky.

That's why Lycia liked it so much.

When she fought on the white sand, she had preferred to seize the momentum right from the start and never let it go. Her aggressiveness had allowed her to walk out of the Pit every time. Her adversaries were never so lucky.

Upon meeting Jakob, she had sensed that he had the same perspective with respect to combat, and that pleased her.

Nevertheless, going after the slavers would have to wait a little while longer.

The Stalkers first. Then they could take the next step.

Lycia was looking forward to the challenge. Much like her brother, after spending so much time in the Pit, she had learned to thrive on the adrenaline required to survive such a demanding and usually lethal environment.

Soon after she had gained her freedom thanks to Bryen, she had devoted her energies to helping Bryen rid Caledonia of the Ghoule Overlord and his Legions. That had given her the fix she needed that she had grown accustomed to on the white sand.

The voyage across the Burnt Ocean had been difficult for her. Her brother had dealt with the monotony by diving off the crow's nest with a rope tied around his waist and surfing behind the ship.

Lycia shook her head at the memory, a small smile breaking free. Her brother acted the fool. Nevertheless, he did know how to keep himself on an even keel. Because just like her, he needed that adrenaline.

Unlike her brother, she struggled for a solution while aboard the *Freedom*. She had withdrawn into herself until Bryen sensed that she was struggling and had pushed her toward Arabella.

Flying above the ocean on the Griffon's back was the only activity that kept her sane until their battle against the Kraken in the Jagged Islands. That had proven to be a desperate fight. The Kraken almost breaking the Blood Company and taking the ship.

Even so, she relished the charge that surged within her while she was fighting for her life and those of her friends. She had felt more alive testing herself against those monsters from the deep than she had since leaving Caledonia.

Thankfully, since they had landed in the Territories, she hadn't lacked for challenges to keep herself occupied.

She needed to keep busy.

She needed to be helpful.

She needed to pull her own weight.

That's who she was, and Bryen understood that about her.

Yet, when Bryen had asked that she accompany Jakob Kestrel into the Highlands, she had thought at first that he was trying to get rid of her.

Yes, she understood that he needed someone that he could trust at this potential ally's side.

But why her?

It had only taken a few days for her to realize what Bryen was doing.

He was giving her what she needed.

He was giving her the chance to do what she was good at.

To fight for a cause.

To serve as a guide and advisor.

Perhaps most importantly, to protect Jakob Kestrel.

Because here in the Highlands, there were a great many enemies seeking to kill him. And there was no one better than the Crimson Devil to keep an eye on him. Just as she had done for Bryen.

Once she understood why Bryen had asked her to take on this task, she relished the challenge. Even though she didn't relish having to deal with someone like Saraa.

The woman had begun to mumble to herself again. Louder, more insistently, as if she were arguing with herself.

Lycia was used to it now, the buzz no longer setting her teeth on edge.

The Highlander probably was repeating the same grumblings that she had been spouting ever since they had started their watch.

Lycia knew that the relative silence wasn't going to last for much longer. Saraa would start up again in a stronger voice, just as she had been doing for the last two hours.

It was always different topics. Different concerns. Different worries that Saraa felt the need to share.

She even sought Lycia's input at times despite the Highlander's dislike of her, although she assumed that was only so that Saraa would have the chance to tear apart whatever argument she might offer in return.

What Jakob believed the next step would be in freeing the Highlands from the grip of Governor Sharperson. From all the other perils threatening the people living within these peaks. And then what would be required once that seemingly insurmountable task was accomplished.

Lycia barely listened to what the woman said. She knew that it was just another opportunity for Saraa to register her grievances with her. So she did her best to ignore the Highlander. She had faced worse distractions in the Pit.

Instead, Lycia concentrated on the darkness that spread out before them, which on this night was well lit by the full moon.

The narrow trail near where they stood guard led between the cliffs and wound down into the small valley below them. At the very far end, the ground had been cleared for several acres.

A new broch would rise there. Likely in the next few weeks. It was just a matter of getting the stone and the workers to begin construction.

Something of a challenge these days since so many brochs were being built all around the Highlands and so many Highlanders wanted to fight.

"We need to go directly after Governor Sharperson." Saraa had gotten to the topic that she liked to harp on the most. "That's the only way to end this."

"We can't," Lycia countered, fully expecting that she would come to regret opening her mouth. "Not yet."

"What do you mean not yet?" demanded Saraa, the timbre of her voice rising. She was pleased that Lycia finally was interacting with her again. It was exhausting trying to engage in an argument when the other person wasn't playing by the rules.

"It's really quite simple, don't you think?"

"Are you calling me simple?" Saraa replied with a touch of venom.

Lycia closed her eyes, seeking the patience that was rarely available to her, realizing that she had made a mistake. Although she did succeed in holding back the response that she wanted to offer to the more than aggravating woman. "No, I'm not calling you simple."

"Good, because if you had ..."

Lycia didn't allow Saraa to continue with whatever threat she was going to make. "I was saying that it was simple because at this moment the numbers don't add up. There are no other choices to be made but one."

"Numbers? What do numbers ..."

Lycia rode right over the Highlander again. "The numbers mean everything. Sharperson has a clear advantage in numbers. Two to one based on estimates. Perhaps even three. Haven't you been paying attention during dinner?"

"Of course I've been paying attention," Saraa responded sharply. She was going to say more in her defense, but she couldn't. Because she really hadn't been paying much attention the last few weeks, instead allowing her bad mood to sour her all the more.

The Highlanders discussed the larger world during their meals. As a part of that, Jakob always provided an update on what he had discovered with the Talent to ensure that everyone knew what was going on around them.

He had also begun extending his senses as far as the Stone so that they could get a sense of what they would face when they turned their attention toward the south. But for the life of her she couldn't recall what details he had provided in that regard, too consumed by her own concerns.

"Well, then, if you've been paying attention," Lycia continued, "you would recall that Sharperson has kept almost the entire Highland Guard within just a few leagues of the Stone. He has the advantage of several thousand soldiers. We could attack them directly, and I'm sure we would give them a good fight, even with Jakob using the Talent, but it would be a losing fight. We'd be playing to Sharperson's strengths rather than our own. For that reason, Jakob doesn't want to take the risk. At least not yet."

"I know that," Saraa grumped quietly, finding it hard to maintain her anger while at the same time she was chastising herself for allowing her aggravation to get in the way of her instincts.

"I thought you did," Lycia replied evenly, hoping to defuse the tension rising between them by putting forward a calm that she wasn't feeling.

She kept her eyes off of Saraa, instead peering into the darkness. There was little for her to see even with the moonlight setting the valley below them aglow. There was not a hint of movement. Not a sound to be heard that suggested they had anything to worry about.

Yet she felt on edge. Not because of the woman standing next to her. And not because of the clash she anticipated would come in the morning.

"We'll go after the Governor and the Highland Guard eventually. Just not yet."

"What do you mean *we*?" demanded Saraa, her fire returning in a flash. "You're not part of our *we*. You're not a Highlander. You never will be. For luck's sake, you shouldn't even be here."

For the next few minutes, Saraa continued with her diatribe. Several times the Highlander tried to draw Lycia back into the argument. Lycia ignored her.

She kept quiet, cursing her current circumstances.

Fighting on the white sand was bad enough. What had she done to deserve this kind of torture?

"Why are you here?" Saraa asked.

Lycia considered not responding to the Highlander, but at least with this question Saraa had spoken in a quieter tone. Lycia knew as well that if she didn't reply Saraa's temper would get the better of her, and then the annoying buzz would begin again.

"You know why." Lycia wasn't really in the mood for this conversation.

In part because of the topic, which Saraa liked to raise whenever they were forced together. Also, because Lycia's agitation was escalating.

The prickle along the back of her neck was working its way down her spine.

However, Saraa wasn't the cause of her agitation.

Lycia kept her gaze to her front. With not a cloud in the sky and the full moon, she could see quite a good distance down into the vale.

She didn't understand it. There was no reason for her to feel this way.

As if she were being hunted.

But she did. And that foreboding of an approaching doom was only intensifying.

She hated having a premonition like this. Even more, she hated not being able to identify the cause.

"You didn't have to agree," grumbled Saraa.

Lycia smiled thinly as she contemplated Saraa's comment, even as the hint of warning in the back of her brain sounded like a clarion bell. Aislinn had explained to her that sometimes you could find what you were looking for if you weren't really looking for it.

Strange advice she had thought at the time. Good advice, nonetheless.

Lycia did that now. Rather than trying to look for any signs that would give away whatever it was that was poking at her, she allowed her senses to drift. She swept her eyes slowly from one side of the vale to the other.

Not looking for anything in particular.

Not focusing on any one thing.

Because she didn't really know what it was that she was searching for.

As she continued with her new practice, she returned a small portion of her focus back to her conversation with Saraa. Lycia knew where it was going. She wasn't in the mood, but she didn't see how she could avoid it any longer.

"The Volkun asked me to do this. To help you and the other Highlanders." Lycia shrugged as if that explanation was all that needed to be said. "That's why I'm here. It's the only reason that I'm here."

"You couldn't have said no to the Volkun?"

Lycia smiled again, this time even more thinly. In fact, it wasn't much of a smile now. More of a disappointed stare. Remembering what she had been feeling when Bryen had made his request.

It wasn't that Lycia couldn't say no to the Volkun. It was that she had never had to in the past. Because he only asked something of her when it was necessary, and he had told her quite clearly that he believed that she was the only person who could accomplish the task.

She valued his trust. That was until he had asked her to shadow Jakob Kestrel.

Lycia almost refused, although she wouldn't admit that to Saraa. The Highlander would latch onto that like a dog with a bone.

Lycia didn't like the idea of functioning as a Protector. Doing as Bryen had done for a time for Aislinn Winborne. There was some negative residue attached to the concept that Lycia struggled to get past.

Before she had given Bryen her answer, she had told him her one demand.

She needed to meet Jakob Kestrel. She needed to make her own decision. She couldn't work with someone who she didn't respect.

Bryen had agreed to her requirement, Lycia knowing that he would. He would never force anything upon anyone, not after his own experiences in life.

She hadn't known what to expect from Jakob Kestrel. When Lycia met the Lord of the Highlands for the first time, her expectations hadn't been very high. That was in part because her standard for judging others was the Volkun.

She had seen a young man close to her own age. Yet there was one feature that really caught her eye.

He had a presence about him that she believed few could match. A quiet competence. A drive.

His green eyes blazed brightly, arrestingly so. And there, in the very back, she glimpsed the pain that he hid.

She believed she knew why it was lodged there.

A terrible loss. More than one, in fact.

She also recognized a determination that reminded her of one other person.

The Volkun.

Lycia could understand that pain and determination and how they worked off one another. Jakob's loss helping to buttress his resolve.

She hadn't said a word to Jakob Kestrel, yet right then she agreed with Bryen.

Here, in the Highlands, by Jakob Kestrel's side, was where she was supposed to be.

She knew it in her bones.

For the time being at least.

Once they were done with the work at hand …

That was a concern for another time.

"I could have, but I didn't," Lycia replied softly, her senses continuing to drift around her, seeking any anomalies that would offer her a hint as to the cause of her growing unease. "It just seemed like coming here was the right thing to do."

Saraa shook her head, barely able to contain her disgust, obvious that she did not trust Lycia. "I know what you are."

Lycia bit her tongue so that she wouldn't let out a laugh. "What's that?"

"A siren."

Lycia snorted at that. She couldn't help herself. She had expected something else. Something worse.

A killer, perhaps. That wouldn't have bothered her.

She killed, yes, but only when it was unavoidable. Only when it was necessary.

She wasn't prepared for Saraa's claim, and for some unexplainable reason it intrigued her.

"A siren? Really?" Lycia nodded and took the next few seconds to allow the moniker to play through her mind. "After spending so much time in the Pit, I'll take that as a compliment."

Hearing that, Saraa didn't know how to respond. She had meant the name as an insult, yet Lycia hadn't taken it as such.

That only made her angrier. She had wanted to get a rise out of the gladiator, and she had failed. Again.

She would need to try harder. No matter what it took she would get what she wanted.

"You're just here for Jakob," Saraa hissed.

Although Lycia understood that she meant it pejoratively, Lycia really couldn't dispute Saraa's claim. Because in part she was right.

Lycia was there for Jakob. Bryen had asked her to come here because of Jakob.

However, there was another aspect to her taking the assignment and working with the Highlanders. A factor that she only would admit to herself.

She liked Jakob.

He was similar to Bryen in many ways. Although not as hard as the Volkun, there was a steel in him. There was also a quiet confidence and self-deprecating humor that appealed to her.

That appealed to Saraa as well, Lycia knew. She would have had to have been a rock to have missed it based on the many looks the Highlander directed his way and how she tried to spend all her free time with him.

That didn't bother Lycia. That was just the way of the world. Often you didn't have much of a say in who you might be interested in. Much to her regret, she had learned that firsthand.

So, yes, she was willing to admit, at least to herself, that her motives for aiding Jakob went beyond her original reason for being there. Yet that wasn't relevant, and she wouldn't allow the burgeoning feeling within her to become any more than it already was.

While she was in the Highlands she would do no more than what was required of her. She was here for a specific purpose, and she wouldn't allow herself to be distracted from that purpose.

Better to protect herself.

Better to keep her emotions hidden.

Which she had been doing. She was certain of that.

That was why she couldn't understand why Saraa viewed her as a threat. Lycia had done nothing that could have given the Highlander cause to believe that she was there for any other reason than to help the Lord of the Highlands with his stated goal of removing the Governor of the Highlands from power.

She did have experience with rebellions, after all.

"I am here for Jakob," Lycia responded calmly, keeping the heat that was rising within her from her voice. She was really getting tired of Saraa challenging her on this same topic. Time and time again. "I believe in what he's doing. What you and the other Highlanders are doing here."

"You really expect me to believe that ..."

The rest of what Saraa wanted to say died in her throat, her expression shifting to one of concern. The gladiator's eyes had changed. They were as hard as stone.

Lycia didn't say anything. She didn't need to. The Highlander understood what was happening.

Lycia nodded subtly to Saraa's left, looking over her right shoulder.

Saraa didn't need to be told what was waiting for her there. She steeled herself for what Lycia was going to do, then nodded just as subtly as the gladiator.

Lycia moved with a shocking speed, reaching up and

pulling her twin blades from the sheaths on her back while in the same motion lunging right over Saraa's shoulder.

The Highlander remained frozen in place despite the terrible effort of doing so, her natural inclination to dodge to the side battling against the need for her to not get in the way of Lycia's lightning-fast attack.

Hearing the shriek of surprise and then the sound of steel sliding into flesh, Saraa ducked away from Lycia and pulled the sword from the scabbard she wore across her back.

She had less than a second to judge that Lycia had the Stalker that had been about to gut her from behind well in hand. The gladiator had stabbed the monster in the shoulder, disabling the use of one arm. Now she was forcing the beast back down the trail, giving Saraa the space that she would need to take on the other monster rushing at her out of the gloom.

Without really thinking, Saraa turned to her left and slashed in front of her from chest to ankle, cutting across the monster's thighs.

The Stalker, blood-red eyes burning in the darkness the only feature easily visible besides its claws, which flashed when they were caught by the moonlight, reared back in shock at being wounded so severely so swiftly.

The beast kept moving backward, unable to ignore its injuries, forced to evade the steel that swept toward it with a remarkable consistency. Saraa pressing her advantage, knowing that she couldn't afford to lose the momentum she had seized from the beast.

Lycia focused on the Stalker that she had wounded. She heard the other Stalker screech in rage behind her, and she assumed that Saraa could manage the beast on her own at least for a time.

Slicing and slashing with a devastating effectiveness, sprays of blood erupting in the space between them, Lycia allowed her thoughts to continue to drift, knowing that she had this combat well in hand.

Where had these Stalkers come from?

They hadn't come up the trail. She was sure of that.

Frustrated because she couldn't find the answer to her question, Lycia pivoted. She allowed the Stalker's claws to slide through the space in which she had been standing just a heartbeat before.

Before the monster could pull back, Lycia struck a ferocious blow. She cut down with both of her swords as if she were trying to split a log.

The finely sharpened steel sliced right through the Stalker's wrists. The beast's claws dropped to the rocky ground, spurts of blood shooting out from the stumps.

Lycia put the creature out of its misery with a swift stab through its waxy flesh and into its heart.

She spun around to help Saraa, not needing to confirm her Stalker's demise. Pleased that the Highlander didn't need her help.

Saraa had finished the beast with an alacrity to be admired. The Stalker lay on the ground, breathing its last, a dozen or more wounds crisscrossing its body.

"You didn't have to do that," Saraa grumbled, the two women standing on different sides of the gap, bloody swords held tightly in their hands.

"No, I didn't," Lycia replied. She had expected at least a thank you from the Highlander. She realized that this was the best that she was going to get for saving the woman's life.

As Lycia watched Saraa finish off the Stalker with a slice across the throat, her thoughts turned to the unanswered question that had plagued her just moments earlier.

The Stalkers hadn't come up the trail. Even with their natural camouflage, she would have seen them thanks to the brightness of the moon.

Then where had they come from?

She solved the puzzle when she heard a soft scrabbling above her.

A massive shadow fell through the air and landed right in front of Saraa, claws reaching for the shocked Highlander.

Lycia already was in motion. She drove the first two feet of one of her swords through the back of the Stalker's neck.

The monster froze mid-motion. Its spinal cord cut, the beast crumpled to the ground, its breathing slowing. The end near.

The cliff.

She should have assumed as much.

Sheer. Unless you were a monster with daggerlike claws.

That mistake had almost cost them both their lives.

When Lycia pulled her gaze up from the dying Stalker, she had a difficult time reading Saraa.

Usually she could. Usually the Highlander was angry. With her. With everyone else she had a smile and a kind word.

It seemed that the Highlander was coming to grips with what had just occurred.

Not that the Stalker had almost killed her. No, rather with the fact that the woman she hated had just saved her life. Twice. In only a few minutes.

"I didn't need your help," Saraa said with a venom that to Lycia sounded forced.

"We all need help from time to time."

Hearing the scramble of Highlanders rushing her way, drawn by the sounds of the clash, Lycia stared up at the cliffs. She didn't think any more Stalkers were climbing above her, but she would ask Jakob to check when he arrived.

"I could have managed the last Stalker."

"I'm sure you could have," Lycia replied.

She had no desire to get into another argument, and that would have happened if she pointed out that, in fact, Saraa could not have dealt with the second Stalker.

Her sword was down at her side. She never would have gotten the steel up in time to prevent the beast's claws from ripping into her chest.

Of course, rather than taking Lycia's comment as a peace offering, Saraa interpreted it as a veiled insult laced with sarcasm.

"Stay away from me." Saraa started walking down the path. Her body had begun to shake as she tried to deal with how close she had come to her own death. "Stay away from Jakob."

6

THE SEEKERS

Davin lay on his small bunk, or at least he was trying to given the tight space.

Even when he crammed himself against the back wall both his legs hung off the edge at an angle. It wasn't the most comfortable position, but it was the only one that didn't require him to sleep on the floor.

Supposedly, he had earned the small cabin because of his commitment and willingness to train the soldiers and sailors loyal to Talia Carlomin.

A sign of appreciation, the crew had said. Perhaps even a sign of respect.

At least that's what Sirena told him and what he chose to believe while they made a big show of granting him the cabin.

Davin knew the truth, however. The crew had taken it upon themselves to refit the small supply closet into sleeping quarters. When he actually slept, he had a habit of talking in his sleep – or more aptly described as shouting as he relived in his dreams many of his combats on the white sand -- and the rest of the crew had no desire to listen to him.

And of course there was the snoring as well.

Sven and some of the others had even said that he sounded like an elephant while he lay in his hammock in the crew's quarters, so loud that many of the sailors and soldiers feared that he might break the seal on the hull.

Thus, their decision to donate the time and effort that put him in a spot where he couldn't bother them.

He didn't mind.

Not really.

He didn't sleep much to begin with.

And when he did, if he wasn't snoring he was usually flopping about because of the nightmares.

He had ended up out of his hammock and on the deck more times than he cared to count because of that.

Now, he had his own space. The crew could sleep undisturbed. And if he did fling himself out of his small cubby, it wasn't as far a drop to the deck compared to a hammock.

A victory for both Davin and the crew. And as Declan had liked to say, those were the best kinds of victories.

Both sides won. Neither side bled.

After what had been demanded of him during the last few days, Davin should have been enjoying his time alone. As usual, however, he was finding it difficult to relax and recover.

His mind refused to turn off as he replayed over and over what had occurred in the cove and atop the cliffs.

Swimming into Smuggler's Cove. Twice, in fact.

First as a scout. Then to lead the attack. His fear of the great whites that might or might not have been swimming with him powering his strokes.

Challenging the pirates.

Taking on the Stalkers.

Eliminating a good number of both all on his own.

Heading up to the plateau atop the cliffs to hunt for Ronild Magnison, only to realize just in time that it was a trap.

Evading even more Stalkers with Talia in tow.

Escaping the Stalkers by leaping off a cliff and discovering much to his disappointment that the monsters had come after him, then benefiting from the timely intervention of a Great Shark.

Admittedly, if he had known that there was a Great Shark in the water with him, he would never have swum into Smuggler's Cove, much less jumped off the cliff. He would have preferred to take his chances along the ledge against the Stalkers.

Well, maybe he would have taken the leap. After all, he wasn't known for making the best decisions in the face of danger.

He probably would have just thought about it a little longer before jumping because it would have given him more of a rush.

Then, finally, getting Talia Carlomin back aboard the *Swift* safe and sound, although quite angry and frustrated despite her recent successes as he had confirmed during their rather lengthy conversation.

Talia Carlomin.

She was the reason he was where he was rather than with Bryen or Lycia.

She was why he couldn't get to sleep. Why he couldn't calm his mind.

He knew it. He just didn't know what to do about it.

Talia Carlomin.

The Huntress.

The thought of the name given to her by the pirates made Davin smile. That smile quickly twisted into a frown.

Why couldn't he get Talia Carlomin out of his mind?

It was so incredibly irritating to have her residing there. Then again, it wasn't all bad.

That's what was so frustrating.

He didn't want her there, but then he did.

It was the strangest thing, and he didn't understand it.

He didn't like it when he didn't understand something, particularly about himself.

Even more, he didn't want to think too much about it, worried where his thoughts would take him.

Because maybe it was less about not understanding and more about him not wanting to admit the truth.

She had given him a few looks at the end of their conversation, hints perhaps, that only made it more difficult for him to settle his mind and fall asleep.

Not bad hints, of course. Unsettling would probably be the best word. Maybe even enjoyable. Exciting even.

Davin scrambled around in his small cubby, trying to find a more comfortable position. When he was done, he ended up right where he had been before.

A useless effort. It might have to be the floor for him tonight.

Maybe he was just restless.

That was likely it.

Because he was always restless.

His mind never turned off, just as was the case now. The best way to make use of his almost manic energy was to employ it.

That had been a problem for him in the Colosseum. He would wake at all hours because his brain would pull him out of his light slumber.

Bryen usually would be up as well. He was the same way.

They rarely slept well, which only made sense considering where they resided at the time and what fate held in store for them, because only one man had escaped the white sand alive … until the rebellion.

Instead of lying there, wasting time, stuck in their own heads, he and Bryen would leave the barracks and make their way into the Pit. They were supposed to stay in their cells until the sun began to rise, but the guards atop the wall never bothered them.

Their habit of crossing the training ground and then walking through the gates that led into the Colosseum had become a part of their routine. Moreover, it gave the bored soldiers assigned to the Colosseum something to watch other than the shadows that played across the white stone.

Davin and Bryen would train in the moonlight and the torches. When they tired of that, they would talk.

He missed the time he spent on the white sand with Bryen. He missed their conversations.

His friend always had a way of making him feel better about himself when he was down, or he offered a new perspective for looking at a dark situation that made it seem as if it really wasn't as bad as Davin thought it might be.

He understood that it was inevitable that things would change between them. Initially, Davin had assumed that the stimulant for that would be one of them dying. Likely him, actually.

Instead, the shift began when the Duke of the Southern Marches took Bryen from the Colosseum. Just as it should have, Davin would be the first to admit. Just as it continued after Bryen returned to the Colosseum and the gladiators of the Pit became the Blood Company.

Change was difficult for most. It was difficult for him. He readily conceded that.

Still, despite his current struggles, he was glad that his life had changed. Because if it hadn't, he probably would have bled out on the white sand.

Every gladiator did. Eventually. Unless you were the Volkun.

Maybe it wasn't all that had happened since his time in the Pit that was making him uneasy. Maybe it had nothing to do with the Stalkers and the pirates and the Great Shark.

That was all old hat to him.

Rather, he feared that the strange, almost pleasant tension he felt when he was with Talia Carlomin was what was putting him on edge.

Talia Carlomin!

Why did everything this evening seem to drift back toward her? Why couldn't he get her out of his mind?

No, what he was experiencing now couldn't be because of her.

Maybe it was just that he missed his friends. He even missed his sister, despite the fact that more often than not she did her best to aggravate him.

Maybe it was because right now the only person he felt that he could really talk to was the Huntress.

Talia Carlomin!

Again!

No matter what he thought about, no matter where he was, no matter what he was doing, she popped into his mind.

Always!

He couldn't prevent it. And he didn't know what to do about it because a very small part of him, if he was really being honest with himself, didn't seem to mind.

That knowing smile of hers. That smirk that suggested that she knew more than he did. That she knew better than he did.

Those eyes that ...

Davin pushed himself up too quickly in his close quarters, grunting quietly as he smacked his head on the roof of the cubby that served as his bed. He rubbed gingerly at the knock on his forehead, the sudden pain giving him a much-needed clarity.

His focus shifted in an instant. He became the Crimson Giant in a heartbeat, feeling as if he was back on the white sand.

He could sense that something wasn't right. It was worse, actually.

The atmosphere aboard the *Swift* had changed from one breath to the next.

A miasma of evil had draped itself across the ship.

Understanding that every second counted, he pushed himself out of his bunk. He ignored his clothes and his boots, grabbing his spear and quietly sneaking out into the corridor in just his underclothes and his bare feet.

He stepped slowly and carefully, not wanting to make a sound, not wanting to reveal himself, as he walked down the hallway.

He was trying to track the almost indescribable feeling that taunted him. That told him that some unknowable and unstoppable doom fast approached.

No, he was wrong in that respect.

The doom already was aboard.

He needed to find it.

Destroy it.

Davin didn't get far before he found what he thought was the source of his disquiet.

He stood right in front of Talia's door.

He knew it in his heart. That feeling of wrongness was centered in her chamber.

Why that would be, he didn't know. Nevertheless, he needed to find out, because a loud voice in the back of his head was telling him that Talia was in danger.

Feeling the press of time, Davin reached for the knob, spear held at the ready.

He stopped himself, taking just a second to think. A rare occurrence for him, since when he decided to do something he usually moved forward with it immediately.

Better to do than think, he liked to say, much to Declan's

chagrin. Since his friend and mentor had tried so many times to teach him to think first then do.

Should he be doing this?

He could be making a terrible mistake.

Davin shook his head to clear it.

Listen to your gut.

Another of Declan's frequent maxims. And right then his gut was telling him that he was doing the right thing. He just needed to move faster.

Davin reached out again, turned the knob, and pushed open the door without making a sound.

The moon streaming through the windows created a variegated design of darkness and shadow. But that wasn't the only reason Davin's eyes were drawn toward the stern wall.

One of those windows was slightly ajar. All the others were closed and locked.

Talia might have wanted the fresh air. Then again, maybe she hadn't.

Davin kept his eyes focused toward the front as he walked on silent feet into Talia's cabin. Sweeping his gaze through the darkness, he relied on his peripheral vision to catch any movement to either side that might not fit with the stillness of the chamber.

With each step he took his belief that he was in the right place, that there was some presence aboard the *Swift* that shouldn't be, only got stronger.

Davin could just make out the shape on Talia's bed. However, it wasn't very well defined because of the gloom. Probably just sleeping, he hoped, but he needed to make sure.

In a flash of movement the blankets on the bed went flying and a figure materialized right in front of him. He didn't move his head, just looking down with his eyes.

Talia held a dagger against his throat.

"What are you doing here?" she demanded. Although she

knew that it was Davin who had entered her quarters, she still kept the blade against his throat, wanting to make the point that she didn't appreciate his entering her cabin without her permission. "And why aren't you wearing any clothes?"

Not having the time to explain, Davin used his forearm to none too gently push Talia out of the way, sending her tumbling head over heels back over the bed.

Just in time too.

Davin brought his spear up in front of him, both hands on the haft as he angled the steel to block the long dagger that sliced through the gloom toward his throat. And then again, twisting the haft in the other direction to counter his attacker, the assassin pivoting and cutting with the long dagger in his other hand.

The next several seconds played out much like the first.

The shadow that attacked him barely made a sound. Gliding through the darkness streaked with moonlight, the intruder slashed with long daggers, sometimes scraping across Davin's spear, just as often missing entirely as the gladiator twisted and turned to avoid the many stabs interspersed with cuts and slices.

Davin didn't bother to attack. Instead, he concentrated on forcing the assassin closer to the door and away from Talia, who was pushing herself up from where she had gotten stuck between the cabin wall and the bed.

Davin cursed himself for not thinking more clearly, his concern for Talia getting in the way of his preparations. Talia's quarters were the largest on the *Swift*, although still not very large. It was certainly no place for a long weapon like the one that he preferred. He should have grabbed his daggers instead.

Yet there was nothing that he could do about that now except think of how Declan would have laughed at him if he was watching the combat.

Davin had brought a spear to a knife fight.

Nevertheless, he remained focused on his task even as he tried to identify who it was who had slipped through the back window intent on killing Talia in her sleep.

He couldn't really see much of his opponent. The darkness and the distracting beams of moonlight didn't help, nor did the fact that whoever it was blended into that darkness and shadow like the Wraiths did the Murk.

The most logical explanation was that it was one of the crew. But he knew without having to give that hypothesis much thought that it was also the wrong explanation.

He knew every member of the crew, had known them for quite some time. He diced with them. Worked with them. Trained them.

If any of the crew could fight like this, he would have sensed it in the practice ring.

As Davin continued to move with a speed that matched that of the assassin, neither he nor the shadow making any noise other than the scrape of steel daggers across the haft of his spear, he began to understand. What he concluded shocked him.

Because of all the assassins he could have interrupted, this one was the most dangerous. Also the most expensive.

That last part actually made sense.

His adversary had to be a Seeker.

It was the only answer based on what he had glimpsed and what he was experiencing.

Just a moment before they had both stepped through a ray of moonlight. The assassin had been gliding backward, Davin forcing the attacker back toward the door.

His opponent was wearing all black, a black balaclava as well to hide his face, which really wasn't all that surprising.

His adversary was using a pair of long daggers. Again, not very surprising based on the assassin's assignment. The weapons that Seekers chose to use were based on skill, personal preference, and the environment.

What confirmed it for Davin was the assassin's eyes. Those unique, perhaps magically made, dark purple eyes that allowed the Seekers to see almost as well in the dark as they did in the brightest sunshine.

If Davin was right, then it seemed that Declan was wrong. And that pleased the gladiator a great deal.

Seekers were considered the deadliest assassins in all the realms. There was a strong belief that if a Seeker was sent after you, then you were living on borrowed time.

Because you would never see their steel. Not until you were just about to breathe your last.

Davin had seen the Seeker, he was very much alive, and he was doing his best to keep it that way.

He had never come up against a Seeker before, which stood to reason since he spent so much of his early life in the Colosseum. But Declan had told him what Seekers were and what they did. Although Declan hadn't been able to tell Davin how a Seeker's eyes were transformed into a deep purple.

He had pestered the Master of the Gladiators with that question many a time, Declan only able to give him an educated guess. The Talent had been employed, but no one had ever been able to confirm that supposition.

Davin shifted his thoughts back to his current predicament, understanding that he couldn't allow himself to become distracted.

This Seeker was incredibly fast. So fast that only a few of Davin's previous opponents could match this assassin.

Actually just two. Lycia and Bryen.

If Davin was going to stay alive, then he needed to end this fight, because if he didn't, eventually his opponent – he still couldn't tell if it was a man or woman – would get the better of him.

Not surprisingly, even as he was looking for the chance to attack rather than defend, just as his mind had a tendency to do, he asked himself a question that he found quite interesting and worthy of consideration.

Why would someone send a Seeker after Talia?

Davin brought his spear up again on an angle, allowing the Seeker's steel to scrape across the haft. This time, however, rather than preparing for the next slash, Davin pivoted and lowered his shoulder.

He rammed it into the Seeker's midsection and sent his smaller opponent stumbling back against the far wall.

Davin smiled. Finally, he had gained some breathing room.

While the Seeker pushed off the wall, Davin turned his body sideways, spear to his front, ready to resume the combat.

The Seeker hesitated, however.

Davin assumed that the assassin never had anticipated being discovered by someone with the skill and experience to prevent what should have been an easy kill.

While the Seeker stood there, deciding on a new strategy for killing Talia, Davin answered his own question. Because it was so obvious that he really didn't need to think much at all to reach the conclusion that made the most sense.

Hakea Roosarian.

Who else would have such a strong desire to eliminate Talia? Who else would have the money required to contract with the Seekers?

No one.

That question answered, two more immediately came to mind.

How did the Seeker find the *Swift* and then get aboard?

And, perhaps even more important, was there more than one Seeker?

Recognizing that the assassin was about to attack again, Davin nudged those questions to the side, not willing to give up the small amount of momentum that he had gained by forcing the Seeker to change his strategy.

Davin really would have liked to know who he was fighting. But that would have to wait. Assuming that he survived the combat.

Before the Seeker could come at him again, Davin closed the distance between them in two swift steps.

He kept his movements tight and economical. Not lunging with his spear, rather just moving his wrists and his shoulders as he stabbed, using the steel in a similar fashion to what the Seeker had been doing with the long daggers.

For the next few breaths, it was the Seeker's turn to focus solely on defense, not having a chance to attack because of Davin's skill. Grimacing from the effort of having to parry the powerful jabs that came with a speed reminiscent of a hornet's sting.

Davin smiled at the Seeker's frustration. Enjoying the reaction that he earned.

He kept the assassin fixed in place. He refused to allow the Seeker to break away from where Davin had forced his opponent up against the wall.

It proved to be a fairly simple task for him, actually, because unlike the Seeker, who needed to kill him to get to his target, Davin didn't need to kill the Seeker to achieve his objective.

Not after catching out of the corner of his eye the hint of movement along his right side.

Finally, Talia had extricated herself from where she had fallen between the bed and the wall.

She was furious. At Davin for knocking her out of the way. At herself for never realizing that an assassin had snuck into her quarters.

She released her anger with a cold precision.

Before the Seeker even realized that Talia had joined the

combat, she slid her dagger into the assassin's exposed side, in between the ribs, piercing the heart.

The combat ended at exactly that moment.

Davin watched as the Seeker's dark purple eyes flashed once before they glazed over. He thought of cutting the assassin's throat, just to make sure, then realized it wasn't necessary as the body slumped back against the wall and then slid down to the floor.

Talia stepped up next to him then, and they both looked down at the corpse at their feet.

"An assassin," Talia said unnecessarily.

"More than that," Davin replied.

"What do you mean?"

"Not just an assassin. Apparently someone really wants to make sure you die."

"Davin, what do you mean?" Talia's voice contained the hint of fire that he was accustomed to, especially in circumstances such as these.

That pleased him. Most everyone else would have pissed their pants at having come so close to dying at the hands of an assassin. For Talia it was no more than another challenge to be addressed.

"Someone sent a Seeker after you."

"A Seeker?" Talia scoffed at that possibility. "There aren't any Seekers. They're just stories now. There hasn't been a Seeker in centuries."

"That we know of," Davin countered.

"They're just stories, Davin."

"You mean like Stalkers and Wraiths," Davin replied, giving her a meaningful look and not bothering to offer her several other monsters that were supposed to be no more than myths but that he had discovered were all too real, images of Ghoules and Kraken playing unbidden through his mind.

"Good point," Talia grumbled reluctantly, acknowledging the truth in his words. "How could you tell?"

"The eyes," he replied.

Talia nodded, taking a closer look at the assassin's glassy expression. Dark purple. She had never seen anything like it, and from what the stories said, those eyes confirmed that Davin was correct.

"Hakea Roosarian?"

"That would be my guess."

Talia nodded. "We really need to kill her."

"We will," Davin replied quietly, his words sounding like a promise to Talia.

She pulled her eyes from the Seeker and focused on him. He was quite a sight standing there in the moonlight, spear in hand, wearing nothing but his underclothes.

She was about to make a joke, something suggestive before she thought better of it, when she heard a thump on the deck just above them. A few seconds later, another thump followed.

"It seems that more than one Seeker was sent to kill me."

Davin nodded. Both of his questions had been answered. The fact that he was standing in Talia's cabin in his underclothes didn't bother him in the least, his mind already turning to what he needed to do next.

"Come on." He headed for the door.

Talia followed right after him, glimpsing the many scars marring his broad back as he passed through the moonlight then losing them in the darkness of the corridor beyond.

The Seekers were formidable adversaries, she knew. But those on the deck had yet to come up against the Crimson Giant.

DAVIN AND TALIA stepped quietly out onto the main deck, slipping into the shadows draping the helm, weapons at the ready.

What greeted them was, unfortunately, what they expected to see.

Three bodies slumped against the gunwales. Two on the port side. The one on the starboard side was leaning over the railing and likely wouldn't remain there for long.

Davin nudged Talia in the shoulder, gently this time, pulling her eyes toward the port side where he was looking. Two shapes that were barely visible in the gloom were sneaking toward the helm.

Two more Seekers. Wanting to go belowdecks to confirm that their partner had completed the contract before all three escaped through the open window in Talia's quarters, a rowboat likely waiting for them below.

Davin and Talia nodded to one another. There really was little need to discuss strategy based on their current circumstances. There was only one option available to them.

Talia rushed out from the shadows, aiming for the Seeker on the right. Davin was right behind her, sprinting on bare feet toward the Seeker on the left.

Talia allowed the fury that was boiling within her, placed there by her attempted assassination, to drive her. She attacked the black-clad Seeker with a vengeance, her daggers slicing toward her adversary with a dangerous yet controlled freneticism.

The Seeker's purple eyes flashed angrily. The assassin wasn't used to fighting in this way. Usually, it was a single slice and then the combat was over.

Because of Talia's remarkable aggression, the assassin had no choice but to move back across the deck, struggling to avoid the steel that was coming closer and closer. Slicing through the black fabric of his shirt. Soon to cut into his flesh.

Davin attacked the other Seeker with more thought than Talia exhibited. Just as he had done in her cabin, he kept his movements controlled and efficient as he directed the assassin away from the other Seeker and toward the railing.

He wanted to limit his adversary's options, because he wasn't in a rush.

Just as had been the case with the first Seeker, Davin understood that he didn't need to be the one to kill this assassin. He could leave that to someone else as the advantage initially enjoyed by the Seekers faded away just as they faded so easily into the darkness.

"Carlomin Guard!" the gladiator roared. "Rise and fight for the Huntress! Assassins on the deck!"

Davin saw the look that flashed across his opponent's eyes when he issued his order. Shock followed by concern and then perhaps even a touch of fear.

The Seeker's goal changed abruptly. Escape now took precedence over murder.

Davin assumed that the other assassin had reached the same conclusion.

They just hadn't realized yet that they'd never get the chance.

Just seconds after Davin's cry, he heard the pounding of dozens of boots racing up from belowdecks. Then Sirena was there, emerging from beneath the helm and leading the charge.

With a single command, the soldiers and sailors at her back split into two groups, each one focused on a different Seeker. They rushed right into each combat, allowing Davin and Talia to step back as the first squad forced the closest Seeker up against the mainmast and the second hemmed the other assassin against the portside railing.

The Seekers were deadly assassins. They were skilled. They were fast. But they stood little chance against so many determined and angry fighters at one time.

"Don't kill them unless you have to!" ordered Talia.

Talia's command didn't change the soldiers' tactics. It just meant that they couldn't take the combats all the way to the inevitable end unless they had no choice.

The soldiers and sailors were patient. They didn't need to rush. They just needed to wait for the right opportunity.

Because the chance that they were waiting for would come.

The squad that took on the Seeker challenging Davin got the first break. The assassin overextended while trying to defend against a stab that unexpectedly turned into a slash across the ribs.

The Seeker hissed in pain and then again. Sven made the most of the momentary distraction and lunged, punching his spear into the assassin's gut and using his momentum to take the Seeker to the deck.

He held the assassin there, pinned against the wood, the Seeker moaning, unable to move without shuddering from the almost indescribable pain.

The other Seeker glimpsed what happened on the other side of the deck. Not wanting to suffer the same fate, the assassin crafted a web of steel right in front of his attackers, forcing them back, gaining the space to try to leap over the side.

The assassin only got so far. Sirena anticipated just such a play and shot the Seeker through the leg, the crossbow bolt punching through flesh and bone and then into the gunwale, pinning the assassin against the railing.

Two highly trained assassins thwarted in only a few minutes.

Talia was quite pleased with the skill demonstrated by her soldiers and her crew. It appeared that once again her decision to have Davin train the Carlomin Guard was the right one.

Taking several deep breaths as she turned her boiling rage down to a simmer, Talia went first to the Seeker bleeding out on the deck, Sven holding the rather smallish figure – the assassin wasn't much taller than she was – in place.

She took a moment to study the assassin, not feeling the need to remove the mask. A man. Or a woman.

Talia couldn't tell for sure because all she saw were the purple eyes. Regardless, definitely soon to be dead.

"Is it worth trying to make them talk?"

Davin walked up next to her. "No, they won't talk. They only know who they're supposed to kill. No more than that. And we know already the answer to the only question worth asking."

Talia nodded. "Sven."

"Yes, Captain." The bulky sailor, who had been the first fighter behind Sirena, looked up. His eyes were calm, focused, as he gave the spear a twist and earned a groan of agony from the Seeker as the steel cut deeper inside the assassin's belly. His working with Davin in the practice ring clearly had paid off for him and for her.

"Over the side please." Talia knelt down and cut the assassin's throat, believing that she was performing a mercy since the Seeker was already close to death. "Let the sharks have their fill."

"Yes, Captain." Sven pulled his spear free with a loud squelch, then started walking toward the Seeker stuck to the side of the Swift. "The same for the other, Captain?"

"Yes, Sven, thank you."

"Not a bother at all, Captain."

That done, Talia turned her attention to Davin. "We need to have a conversation. But first, put some clothes on please. You look ridiculous."

Talia stood at the helm of the *Swift*, finally feeling the calm that she had been searching for after the Seekers' attack.

It was the middle of the night. Nevertheless, the deck of the ship was abuzz with activity as she guided the sleek craft out toward the Sea of Mist.

She didn't expect any more attacks in the cove. Still, it was safer out on the open water, and there was no reason to take any unnecessary risks. She didn't want to invite on board any more assassins who might be lurking in the fishing village.

Davin stood behind her, although not too close. He had climbed the ladder, then leaned back against the railing and stayed out of her way as the *Swift* got underway. And, as she had ordered, he had gotten dressed before he came up from his cabin.

"I'm not going to bite, Davin."

"What do you mean?"

"You seem a little nervous. Is that why you're staying back there?"

"It has been an interesting evening."

"That it has," Talia agreed, a small smile playing across her lips as she kept her eyes on the bow, wanting to make sure that she adjusted course if the sailors standing on each side of the prow and charged with identifying sandbars told her that she needed to change direction quickly.

"I'm not nervous. I'm just enjoying the view."

Talia briefly looked back over her shoulder, catching the grin that he hid as soon as she locked eyes with him. There wasn't much for Davin to look at other than her in a darkness that was infrequently illuminated by the moon battling with the clouds above.

"Be careful, gladiator," Talia said with an arched eyebrow before she turned her attention back to what she was doing. The sailor on the port side called for her to turn the wheel just a few degrees in that direction, and she did so promptly. "You're swimming in dangerous water."

"That seems to be a fairly common occurrence thanks to

you, Huntress," Davin replied. Talia heard the smile on his lips. "I'm just answering your question."

"You're doing more than that and you know it." Talia allowed a few seconds to pass before continuing. She breathed a little easier. They were past the sandbars that lined the entrance to the cove. The deeper water beckoned. "Maybe you're nervous because I had my dagger at your throat. You didn't realize just how fast I could be with a blade."

"That was probably the case," Davin agreed amiably.

Talia snorted, certain that he was just humoring her. "So what's on your mind, gladiator?"

"How do you know there's something on my mind?"

"I know," Talia replied confidently, "because I know you."

It was Davin's turn to chuckle softly. She was using his own words against him. And she had said that she wanted to have a conversation, so no reason to delay.

Not wanting to dance around the issue, he decided to be direct, which he tended to be anyway if only because he didn't have the capacity to handle most matters delicately. "I was wondering what you were thinking when you found me in your room."

"What do you mean?"

Talia sounded slightly flustered to Davin, her keeping her back to him strengthening his suspicion.

Davin nodded, expecting just such a reaction. "You had that look in your eye."

"What look would that be, gladiator?" Talia's voice didn't crack this time, regaining the strength Davin was accustomed to hearing within it. "The one that told you I didn't want you there and that I had everything under control?"

Davin ignored Talia's attempt to extricate herself from the topic that he had raised. "The look. You know the look I'm talking about."

Talia was glad that she was holding onto the wheel, because

her knees were feeling a little unsteady. She wasn't ready for this conversation. That wasn't why she wanted him up on the helm.

"The only look that I was giving you was one associated with my trying to decide whether or not to slice your throat. You were lucky the Seeker was there, gladiator. If not for that, I would have given you another scar to remember me by."

Davin laughed at that, appreciating Talia's bravado. He expected no less from her. It wasn't long before she was laughing with him.

"You know what we need to do next, correct?"

The lightheartedness drained away from both of them at Davin's question.

"I do."

Hakea Roosarian had sent the Seekers after her. They had failed.

But Hakea Roosarian wouldn't stop trying to kill her. Her success depended on Talia dying.

If Talia wanted to survive, then there was only one solution to the dilemma.

She needed to kill Hakea Roosarian first.

7

THE STORY DEEPENS

"How far are we from Shadow's Reach?"

"About five leagues, Lady Winborne," Benin replied. He pointed to the saw-toothed, snow-capped mountains that were blocking their way. "Once we're farther along the trail and on the other side of those peaks, you'll get a better glimpse of the city. It really is a sight to behold."

Aislinn nodded, curious as to what awaited her when she finally had an unobstructed view. Even from this distance and the mountains impeding her gaze, she could make out the jagged, cloud-shrouded shape of Shadow's Peak rising well above all the other mountains in the range.

Shadow's Reach, her uncle's capital, rested right beneath that monstrous massif. The town that had quickly grown into a city had earned its name because of the perpetual twilight in which it existed.

"You were saying that Shadow's Reach had changed in just the last few months, Sergeant. How so?"

"Some of it is obvious, Lady Winborne. Some of it less so."

"What are some of the obvious changes?"

"More soldiers on the walls. More soldiers in the streets.

Curfews. A requirement that those of a certain age, men and women, serve in what your uncle is calling a militia."

"A militia?"

"Yes, Lady Winborne. It's to allow the Northern Guard to focus on defending the walls." Benin shrugged, clearly not believing that such a measure offered much value. "A declaration of martial law as well, giving the Governor the authority to do whatever he deems necessary in the interest of the city and the people of the Territory."

"That is concerning," murmured Aislinn. On the one hand, such actions could be viewed as those of a leader seeking to use a potential crisis to become a despot. On the other hand, it could all be no more than what would be expected based on the current challenges besieging her uncle. "Then again, that would make sense if the Wraiths are becoming more of a threat as you say they are."

"Agreed, Lady Winborne," Benin nodded. "I certainly won't dispute your reasoning." He shrugged. "How all this will balance out is yet to be determined. Nevertheless, there's more to it than that."

"Explain," Aislinn said in the commanding tone that she had used while conducting her responsibilities in the Southern Marches and then during her forced captivity in Tintagel. Recognizing what she was doing, she reached out a hand and patted Benin gently on his arm to apologize. "I'm sorry, Benin. Old habit. Would you be able to provide more detail?"

"No apology necessary, Lady Winborne," Benin replied with a warm smile. "Let me offer just one example, and one in which I am intimately familiar. The soldiers serving in the Northern Guard and loyal to your uncle."

"What of them, Benin?"

"Your uncle has argued that the militia that is being trained is supposed to defend the town, leaving the walls of Shadow's

Reach and those of the Shadow Keep, the fortress that your uncle is building, to the soldiers of the Northern Guard."

Aislinn nodded, understanding why Benin had raised this issue. "If the Northern Guard could perform its primary responsibility of defending the city and the citadel, then what purpose does the militia serve?"

"Exactly, Lady Winborne. That's the question that needs to be answered."

"I assume that you already have an answer, Benin? You wouldn't have pinpointed the issue otherwise."

"I do, Lady Winborne. It's not an answer that anyone wants to hear."

"The Northern Guard can't perform its most important function."

"That's my assumption as well, Lady Winborne."

He nodded to the two squads of soldiers hiking with them through the mountains. Not seen were the scouts who were up ahead and on the flanks charged with spying out any potential threats.

Benin knew the scouts really weren't needed. Not with the Lord Keldragan and the Lady Winborne using the Talent to ensure that there was nothing around them that could give them any cause for concern. Still, the Blademaster had taught Benin well, and old habits die hard.

"All of my mates are of the same mind as I am," Benin continued. "The Northern Guard isn't up to the necessary standard for fighting the Wraiths. Please keep in mind, I don't say that as a criticism. It is simply a theory based on facts. The Guard has an excellent Captain. She knows what she's doing. Many if not all of her soldiers are experienced and well trained. Rather, it's that little can stand against the Wraiths when they come in the Murk."

"Which is why my uncle is worried."

"Aye, he is," Benin confirmed with another nod. "For that and other reasons."

"The Northern Guard can't protect the town or the citadel," Aislinn said in almost a whisper, not quite believing that such a conclusion was possible.

From what Benin had told her, her uncle had more than two thousand soldiers serving in the Northern Guard. That should be more than enough to defend Shadow's Reach.

Yet apparently it wasn't. Why else would her uncle go to the trouble of forming a militia if not to provide a last line of necessary defense?

"That is our belief, Lady Winborne," Benin replied. "The Blademaster believes it as well."

"Do you have any evidence, Benin?"

"Pieces here and there that lead to one inescapable conclusion. In speaking with the soldiers and officers in the taverns, many of whom also visit the smithy in which the Blademaster works, they're worried. They know what they can do, and they know what the Wraiths can do. Because of that knowledge, they're actually more worried than the people living behind the walls. But that's only because they know more than the average person on the street. They're privy to information that is being withheld by your uncle to help ensure that he can maintain order."

"Why do you believe that my uncle is withholding information?"

"Because from what we've determined, the rumors that are running rampant through the city are true. Too many have confirmed it with their own eyes. Besides, no matter what restrictions might have been placed on them, soldiers will talk when that information relates to the safety of their families and their loved ones."

"What rumors would those be, Benin?"

"Governor Winborne continues to tell the people that the Wraiths have yet to breach the walls."

"But they have, haven't they?" Aislinn prompted.

"They have," Benin confirmed. "Almost every time the Murk comes in now to blanket Shadow's Reach, the Wraiths attack the wall. Most of the Wraiths, but not all. A few are always sneaking past the defenders and murdering people in their homes."

"They're testing the defenses," Bryen suggested, having no doubt that he was correct. "They're preparing the way for a larger attack. And while they're making a point, they're sowing terror within the populace. That will only aid them when they come in force."

"You've hit the nail on the head, Lord Keldragan. The Wraiths have already determined that they can breach the city's walls. They have already proved that they can break into people's homes, focusing their attention specifically on residences that are supposed to offer a modicum of protection since they're designed to keep the Wraiths out."

"They're scouting," murmured Bryen, hating the Wraiths' success but appreciating their strategy, both of which were more than just concerning for the residents of Shadow's Reach.

"They are," Benin agreed with another of his preferred nods. "It only makes sense. As you said, Lord Keldragan, their scouts are preparing the way for a larger force. Your uncle, Lady Winborne, knows this. He has no choice but to form a militia. If the Northern Guard can't hold the Wraiths at the walls – and clearly they can't through no fault of their own – then the only option for the people living within the walls is to defend themselves. Because the Wraiths will get through."

"And what are the chances of the people in the town surviving a larger fight with these Wraiths?" Bryen believed that he already knew the answer to his question.

"Slim to none, Lord Keldragan," Benin replied softly. "Sad,

but true. Even with the Northern Guard, even with the militia, the only reason that the people of Shadow's Reach remain alive is that the Wraiths have yet to attack with the goal of conquering the city. It's as simple as that. The soldiers know it even if they don't want to acknowledge it. The rest of the people living in Shadow's Reach will come to the same conclusion, although at the worst possible time."

"And we have no idea when the Wraiths will attack in greater numbers?"

"Correct, Lord Keldragan. All we know is that they will. It creates something of a pickle, doesn't it?"

"It does, Sergeant," Bryen agreed, smiling at the Sergeant's word choice even as his mind turned to what might need to be done, if anything could be done, to provide the people of Shadow's Reach with a better means for defending against the monsters in the mist. Several ideas already were working their way through his mind thanks to what he had learned from Jakob Kestrel.

"And this is true, Benin? Not rumor? The Wraiths have breached the walls?"

"Unfortunately it is Lady Winborne. Besides the ill-starred homes in which more than a dozen families have been slaughtered, the Blademaster fought one of those monsters in the street not too far from the wall."

"Why would he do that?" demanded Aislinn. "What was he doing out in the Murk?"

Benin chuckled, expecting just such a reaction from the Lady of the Southern Marches. She and the Blademaster had grown close during her forced residency in Tintagel. "You know the Blademaster. He always needs to see something for himself when he has questions that require answers."

"He wanted to test himself against the Wraiths," Bryen nodded, not surprised. "I'm assuming the Wraith regretted challenging him."

"I assume that the monster did, Lord Keldragan. The Blademaster received just a scratch. When we returned to where the combat took place once the Murk cleared, we saw a trail of blood leading back to the wall."

"Good for the Blademaster."

"Indeed, Lord Keldragan. The Wraiths bleed. It's just a matter of killing them. That's the hard part. Because there are none in the Northern Guard who can match the skill of the Blademaster."

"Are the people beginning to doubt my uncle, Benin?"

"They are, Lady Winborne." He shrugged, not wanting to sugarcoat what might be a difficult conclusion for her to absorb. "It's only natural. Everything that is happening because your uncle fears the loss of control is not unexpected either."

"The harsher measures that are being applied," nodded Aislinn.

"Yes, Lady Winborne. The presence of more soldiers in the streets. Not just because of the Wraiths, but also because of concerns about unrest among the populace. Hence, the curfews as well. Although there is more that is concerning than just the curfews."

"What do you mean, Benin?"

"Anyone speaking inappropriately about the Governor, or being said to have done so, is taken off the streets and imprisoned."

"Just because of what they are saying?"

"Because of what they are being said to have said," clarified Benin.

Aislinn's expression hardened, her eyes narrowing. "That is not the mark of a good ruler, Benin. Moreover, that is not the uncle who I knew growing up."

"Drastic times often require drastic measures. There is more, Lady Winborne."

"I was afraid of that."

"Prisoners are being sentenced without trial. Work crews are being formed and sent off into the mountains to perform supposed public works projects, although none have yet to return, the first having been gone for more than three months. Contracts for indentured servitude are being rescinded, those people being forced into the work crews. I hate to say it, Lady Winborne, but it all points to one inevitable conclusion."

"It does." Aislinn couldn't deny it.

The Governor, much like a Duke, was supposed to rule based on the law. When the Governor chose not to do that, no matter what excuse offered, that led to a dangerous, slippery slope from which there was often no hope of backtracking.

The Governor would no longer be a Governor. The Governor would become something more since that individual applied the law at his or her discretion.

The risk being that Governor would be interested first and foremost in maintaining his power. He would be working to better his own interests first rather than taking into consideration the interests of the people.

"Benin, how does all this fit into the talk of slavers coming this far north?"

Bryen walked right next to Aislinn, never very far away from her. He had begun as her Protector and then had become so much more. Yet even with the power of the silver Protector's collar broken, still he played that role.

Willingly now even though Aislinn was more than capable of taking care of herself. All because of an emotion stronger than the magic that had bonded him to the Lady of the Southern Marches in the first place.

"I'm sorry to say, Lord Keldragan, that it's more than just talk."

"The slavers are not satisfied with the Highlands?"

"Not anymore. Not with the Highlanders making things so difficult for them now."

"Yet still they need workers for the mines," Bryen mused.

"That they do, Lord Keldragan. Although not for the Highland mines. Trying to lead groups of prisoners across the Northern Steppes, especially with the increasing frequency of the Murk sliding down from the Wyld, would be asking too much of them."

"There are mines in the Northern Peaks?" asked Aislinn. "I hadn't heard about that."

"A new discovery, Lady Winborne," grumbled Benin, "and not a good one in my opinion."

"I take it, Benin, that Governor Winborne has control over the mines?"

"Not officially, Lord Keldragan ..."

"But in reality, yes," Aislinn finished.

Her disappointment in her uncle continued to grow the more she learned of what was occurring in the Northern Territory. Still, although the picture that Benin was painting was quite clear, she would reserve judgment until she could see it all for herself. And she wouldn't have to wait much longer for that.

"Unfortunately so, yes. Nothing happens in the Northern Territory without the permission of Governor and Lady Winborne."

"Lady Winborne," mused Aislinn. She had learned that her uncle had gotten married, although that information had never made its way across the Burnt Ocean to her father. "When did she first appear on the scene?"

"Mind you that I and my mates weren't here then. Fighting Ghoules and all with you in Caledonia."

"And for that we thank you, Benin."

"From what we've been able to piece together, not too long after your uncle arrived. They've been inseparable ever since."

"Do you know much about this woman named Ursina?"

"Very little, Lady Winborne. My apologies, but there is little information to be had."

Aislinn gave Benin a sharp look. She could tell that he was holding something back. "Out with it, Benin. I can take it. My opinion of my uncle already has soured, so you have nothing to fear in that regard."

Benin shrugged. "Again, I have no way to confirm. This is just what we've heard from others."

"And?"

"And many say that the real ruler of the Northern Territory is Lady Winborne. That your uncle rules in name only. The real power rests with her."

Aislinn thought about that for almost a minute. Her memories of her uncle were incomplete, having been formed when she was a child. She had some sense of the man he was before he left the Southern Marches and no real sense of the man he had become upon arriving in the Northern Peaks.

"I can't wait to meet my aunt," Aislinn finally said. "I have so much to learn about her."

"I take it that you've come across these slavers, Benin?"

"Just once, Lord Keldragan." A very satisfied expression shifted Benin's usually friendly face to the one he offered during a clash. Hard. Exacting. Menacing.

"I assume that you made the slavers see the error of their ways?" Bryen had fought with Benin. He would have been a worthy addition to the Blood Company if he had ever been forced into the Pit.

"We did," Benin affirmed with a nod. "They got what they deserved."

Before Bryen could ask his next question, a soldier emerged from between the trees on their left side. The scout trotted over toward the Sergeant.

Benin called out before the woman had gotten more than ten yards beyond the wood. "How many?"

"Ten. Maybe one or two more."

"A threat?"

The scout shrugged, her expression hinting that she really wasn't all that concerned. "Probably not. It's a makeshift affair. More pitchforks than blades."

Benin nodded as they continued along the trail, the scout falling in next to him. He wasn't really all that surprised, as what he assumed they were hiking toward was becoming all too common these days. All because of the many reasons that Benin had given to Lady Winborne as to why the Northern Territory had changed so swiftly in the last few months.

"You're sure on the number, Aimee?"

"Yes, Sergeant. We watched them for a while and then skirted around them. They're all massed on the trail. There were no skirmishers or scouts hidden in the surrounding forest. I really don't think that they know what they're doing."

"We'll want to check again. Not that I'm doubting you, Aimee. Just in case circumstances have changed by the time we approach."

"Of course, Sergeant," Aimee replied. "Surila is watching them now. She'll be able to give us an update once we get closer."

"Well done, Corporal," Benin said with a hint of pride in his voice. "How far?"

"Two miles."

"Where the trail forks I assume?"

"Yes, Sergeant."

"Do they know we're here?"

"I don't believe they do. At least not yet. Before we came back this way, we did see a few of them start to head off down the path, walking through the wood to stay out of sight. They'll find us here in twenty minutes or so if we don't take appropriate action."

"And that we will do, Aimee. Anything else?"

"They set up a barricade to block the trail."

"A barricade? Really?"

Aimee shrugged. "As I said, they don't really seem to know what they're doing, Sergeant."

"That's what I was afraid of," muttered Benin. "Why don't you take the squads here with you. You know what to do."

"Yes, Sergeant," Aimee replied, smiling broadly. She was pleased. Both with her assignment and by the fact that Benin had entrusted her with it.

Benin then turned toward Bryen and Aislinn. "I hope you don't mind if we continue this conversation later. We've got some business to attend to first."

8

INTO THE SHOALS

"How long until we catch up?"

"Less than an hour." Talia stood on the helm of the *Swift*, enjoying the strong breeze gusting across the deck. The gentle chop they cut through played to their advantage. It would allow them to overtake their target faster than they might have otherwise.

"You're certain it's one of the pirate ships?"

"Yes, I'm certain, Davin," she sighed, a hint of exasperation in her voice. They already had been over this. "It's hard to miss the black sails. Besides, we've come upon this ship before. The side was repaired quickly, and they haven't had a chance to cover it up."

"I was just asking," Davin replied, not offended by the sharpness of her tone. He could understand why it was there. "Spiked?"

It really was one of Talia's and Master Hari's more ingenious inventions, the row of steel prongs that slammed into place when one of the Carlomin ships came alongside a marauder. An effective and efficient way to send it to the black depths without having to board. Sven had told him that Captain Aaronson had sunk one and badly damaged another ship, unable to finish the job because he lost the limping frigate in a storm.

"Just so," Talia confirmed with a sharp nod. "That vessel has been living on borrowed time."

Davin smiled, having no doubt that Talia was correct. That by the end of the day the ship fleeing them would be at the bottom of the ocean.

Another important step in the almost complete task that Talia had set for herself and her captains.

After the Huntress' latest victory in Smuggler's Cove, the pirates plaguing the Sea of Mist had almost run their race with only a few remaining.

If all went to plan, it wouldn't be long before the marauders were no more than a memory.

In their last battle they had sunk six vessels in a single night. This frigate seeking to escape them had to be one of only a handful of ships left that Hakea Roosarian had outfitted as part of her strategy to gain control of the shipping along the New Caledonian coast.

Yet Davin couldn't quite understand why Talia was so tense after her recent success. This was the opportunity they had been waiting for. That they had been working toward.

Well, actually, Davin nodding to himself as he thought about it, he could understand why Talia seemed anxious with just one target in her sights. It was her natural state.

Whether good or bad, she tended to be tense most of the time. Slightly on edge. Her anxiety increasing as she drew closer to achieving the goal she had set for herself after her father's murder.

Rid the Sea of Mist of the pirates and she would eliminate one of the primary levers that the Governor of Fal Carrach was using to exercise her power. Roosarian would be weaker than she already was, likely to a point where Talia could take more direct action against her.

"You seem like a kettle about to boil," Davin offered. "Why so worried?"

He thought that talking about it might help her relax. Clearly, he was mistaken, because she wasn't in the mood.

"You ask a lot of questions," Talia replied sharply, keeping the spyglass fixed to her eye. The vessel sailing just ahead of them knew that they were there, yet the captain had yet to engage in any of the evasive maneuvers that she would have if she were in the same position. Odd. "Not all of them are useful or wanted."

"I'll keep that in mind," Davin replied quietly, deciding to take a different approach to try to lighten the mood.

"What are you doing?" Talia demanded.

Davin stood right behind her. So close, in fact, that she could almost hear him breathing.

When she moved in any direction to get away from him, he shifted with her as they watched the *Swift* gain on the ship that was growing ever larger with each passing second.

"What are you doing, Davin?" She was in no mood to play games. She elbowed him to gain some space, earning a grunt and a laugh for her efforts.

"You told me when I first joined you that it was your ships, your rules," Davin replied as he stepped back a few feet, rubbing his hand where she had hit him in the ribs.

"I remember telling you that, yes. Even so, that doesn't explain why you feel the need to shadow me like you are doing this very second."

"You didn't want me going off on my own. You told me to stay close to you at all times. As you said, your ship, your rules. I'm just doing as you ordered me to do."

"What's your point, Davin?" Talia demanded, the heat in

her voice unmistakable. "I really don't have time for this child-ishness."

"I'm not making a point, Huntress."

"You always have a point, Davin, even when you think you don't. And you only call me the Huntress when you're trying to irritate me."

"You give me too much credit on both counts. You seem to believe that everything I do, I do for a reason."

"I probably do give you too much credit, yes. But I'm still right." She faced him, scowling, hands on her hips. "What's your point? We need to move on to more important matters."

"You really want to know? You might not like what I have to say."

"I wouldn't have asked otherwise, Davin. Now out with it before I stab you with a dagger instead of elbowing you in the ribs. You're wasting too much of my time as it is."

Davin had to work hard not to laugh at her comment. She probably would stab him anyway based on the look that she was giving him. "I'm just trying to point out that sometimes you become so focused on trying to control every little thing around you, manage every little detail that's right in front of you, that you miss the broader picture."

Talia bit back the sharp reply that was immediately at the very tip of her tongue. She understood what he was doing now.

She was beginning to think that he knew her much too well for someone who had sailed with her for only a few months. It seemed that she would need to adjust her initial take on the gladiator, because he was much too perceptive.

"You really can be irritating, you know that?"

Davin shrugged, grinning, pleased that some of her stress had dissipated. You couldn't head into a fight filled with tension. You needed to be relaxed if you were to think clearly and make good decisions.

"You certainly aren't the first person to have told me that," he replied with a wink.

"And that doesn't bother you?"

"Why would it bother me?"

"Fine, I release you from that original requirement. Just give me some space, all right?"

Davin stepped farther back from Talia, nodding her an apology. "Do you mind if I offer you one additional thought?"

"Is it related to what we've just discussed?" The sharpness in Talia's tone suggested that she was still irritated with him and had no desire to continue with whatever game he was playing. "Because I've had enough with just one lesson from you today."

"It is, in part, but it isn't."

"Davin, what does that even mean?" Talia sighed more heavily. She realized that she asked that very same question quite frequently of the gladiator.

"It means what it means," he replied with another shrug. "It is relevant to what I told you before. That you spend so much time looking at the specifics of a situation that you sometimes miss the larger picture."

"And what is it that I'm missing now, Davin?" she growled, growing tired of this conversation.

"You might want to take a look at our stern."

Talia stared at Davin for several seconds. She wanted to yell at him. She wanted to tell him that he needed to stop annoying her. But she couldn't, not with the sick feeling that was slowly taking up residence in her stomach.

Raising the spyglass to her eye, she studied the water to their south. A flush of heat ran through her.

She realized that her anger didn't result from what she saw, although that was concerning, but more from the fact that Davin was correct. Talia had focused so much of her attention on the ship fleeing them that she missed the signs that hinted at the situation into which she had sailed with one blind eye.

Davin hadn't. He had sniffed out the trap before she did, and that fact didn't sit well with her.

Three ships approached from the stern, and they were coming fast.

She released a stream of curses that only widened Davin's smile.

"You couldn't just tell me this?" she demanded. "You needed to make me work for it?"

"I didn't want to aggravate you any more than I already had," Davin replied quietly, even though the expression he gave her didn't match his words.

"Is that so?"

"It is. Declan always liked to say that a lesson learned was more effective than a lesson taught. Better chance of it sticking with you."

Talia scrunched up her face, not knowing whether to scowl, smile, or scream. Why did this gladiator have such a confounding effect upon her?

"You know where you can stick all those sayings of yours, Davin?"

"I can guess," Davin replied. "Shall I find Sirena and bring her to the helm? I'm assuming that we're going to want to discuss strategy now that we're the ones caught in the snare."

Talia didn't bother to reply, nodding instead. That was enough to send Davin sliding down the ladder and bounding across the deck toward the Captain of the Carlomin Guard, who was standing near the prow.

Talia brought the spyglass to her eye once again. The ship to their front was trimming its sails to reduce its speed, while the three vessels coming at them from behind had adjusted their positioning. Their pursuers were taking the necessary measures to ensure that she couldn't use the *Swift's* greater pace to escape the trap.

Not with the marauders coming up on their stern and now starboard side.

They were going to have to fight their way free.

Davin was right again, blast it! There was no other option.

And all because she had focused too much on what was in front of her rather than giving credence to the possibility that the pirates left in the Sea of Mist might still have a trick or two up their sleeves.

She had hoped that with just a few more seizures she could hammer home the final nail in the pirates' coffins.

Now she hoped that the clash to come wouldn't be the nail in her coffin instead.

~

"WHY DIDN'T YOU WARN ME?" Talia barked.

"I did warn you."

"You didn't warn me, Davin. You tried to give me a lesson when all you had to do was shout out that there were three pirate ships coming up on our stern."

"Does it really matter now?" He lifted his arms to say that in his opinion it didn't. "What's done is done. Besides, we have them right where we want them."

"What do you mean we have them right where we want them?" Talia was at a loss for words. She gave the gladiator who stood by the helm, spear in hand, a broad smile curling his lips just as was usually the case, an incredulous look. "We have one ship to our front that's blocking us in. Two at our stern doing the same. And then the last coming up on our starboard side. With what's running below the water on our port side, we have nowhere to go."

"Exactly," Davin replied pleasantly. "We have nowhere to go

and neither do they. They're committed. They're coming for us. That means they can't get away from us."

"That may be so, but we can't get away from them either. It's four against one, which means four times as many soldiers as we have on board. If they catch us, we have little chance against them."

"Of course we have a chance," Davin challenged. "We just need to turn the odds in our favor."

"And just how are we supposed to do that, Davin?" Talia's exasperation was plain.

"They want us just as badly as we want them, correct?"

"Correct," answered Sirena Makarin, who stood at the back railing of the helm.

She was curious as to what Davin had in mind. Although he was prone to taking risks that others might not, in the short time that she had known him the risks that he had taken had paid off. Every single time.

"Then we use that against them. They know that if we sink them, the Sea of Mist will be empty of pirates. Something Roosarian will want to avoid at all costs, especially after the last beating we gave her."

"Davin, I don't see how ..."

"And they know that if they sink us, Roosarian will be quite pleased," Davin continued right over Talia's protest. "From what I understand, there is quite a price on the head of the Huntress."

"How much now?" asked Sirena.

"Sirena, this isn't the time to encourage him," Talia chided.

"One thousand golds from the rumors I've heard."

"That's quite a lot of money," murmured Sirena.

"It is, indeed, Sirena," Davin agreed, his smile somehow growing even wider.

Sirena smiled and then laughed. She had figured out what Davin had in mind. "They won't break off the pursuit now.

They think they have us right where they want us. And with the pressure Roosarian is applying and the bounty available, they'll take risks they wouldn't take otherwise."

"Exactly, and that's why the ship to our front was willing to serve as bait," Davin explained.

"Would you just tell me what you have in mind, Davin?" Talia had lost patience with the gladiator for what seemed like the hundredth time in just the last few minutes.

"Before I first met you, we ran through the Floe."

"What does that have to do with ..." That's when it hit Talia.

Davin had told her what had happened during his passage from the Burnt Ocean into the Sea of Mist. His captain had taken the ship through the channel of icebergs drifting from south to north with several pirate ships right behind them.

Two of the pirate ships pursuing them hadn't made it through, sinking because they were so desperate to catch their prey that they ignored the risks associated with navigating the treacherous Floe.

She nodded to herself as she thought about Davin's unsaid proposal. It was a risky idea. It was also a good one.

Talia turned toward the helmswoman, her eyes flashing brightly as she thought about what she was going to do next.

"Take us into the Shoals."

Most likely a death sentence for her and the entire crew. But would that really matter if the pirates caught them?

At least this way they had a chance to control their own fate.

～

"I can't believe you convinced me to do this."

"You're loving every second of it," Davin challenged with a soft chuckle and wink.

Talia didn't reply. She just smiled.

He was right. She was loving every second of what she was doing.

However, she refused to tell him that. She didn't want to give him the satisfaction of knowing that he was correct.

"Off the starboard side!" Davin shouted.

Talia had seen the hazard and already adjusted the *Swift's* course with just a light touch on the wheel. In response, the frigate cut neatly toward the port side. Then with another delicate touch on the wheel the cutter curled around the underwater reef.

If she hadn't corrected their course at the very last second, the razor-sharp coral would have ripped through their hull, leaving them foundering on the reef or sinking. Either way, they would have been an easy target for their pursuers.

That was the danger of the Shoals.

Monstrous reefs rising up from the sea floor.

A graveyard for many a ship, a few masts even poking up above the waves to note where a craft had met its disastrous end.

Nevertheless, that's the risk Talia was willing to take. A run through the Shoals usually didn't end well, but she didn't have any other options.

The question now was whether her decision would pan out as she hoped that it would.

That's why she had taken the wheel as soon as they entered the hidden maze of hazards. If the *Swift* ended up at the bottom, it was going to be because of a mistake that she made and not one made by someone else.

So far, thankfully, she hadn't made any mistakes. How long that would continue she couldn't say.

Because most sane mariners avoided the Shoals at all costs.

There was no single path through the reefs that lay just off the New Caledonian coast only a few leagues north of the Strand. There were many.

Some would think that was a good thing. In some instances, it was.

The problem was that those paths kept changing.

The reefs expanded or died depending on the health of the corals, the temperature of the water usually the determining factor. When the temperature of the water warmed, the planktonic larvae of the corals migrated, sometimes as far as ten or more miles, forming new reefs and adding to the maze that ran beneath the waves.

Over time, as one path closed another opened. The trick for getting through the Shoals was understanding how to read the water.

Those who knew what to look for stood a chance of making it through the Shoals. Those who didn't found themselves at the bottom of the Sea of Mist, their ship often becoming a part of the coral that ended their run through the maze.

On a day like this, when the sun was shining brightly, there was no fog, and you could see how the color of the sea changed, revealing where the coral was and where it wasn't, you stood a chance of making it through the Shoals without meeting a tragic end.

Assuming you could navigate your ship through the maze. Success demanded a nimble touch at the wheel and nerves of steel.

If it had been a grey day, when the color of the sea matched the clouds above, well ... better to fight it out with four pirate ships than attempt the perilous underwater labyrinth.

"Davin, port side!" Sirena yelled.

The Captain of the Carlomin Guard stood by the railing on the starboard side, keeping an eye on the ship that had cut in toward them.

The pirates sought to close the distance so that they could attack. Finding their avenue of approach blocked, they had to turn away for the time being as Talia cut along the narrow reef on the west side while the pirate ship tracked them on the east side.

As soon as the reef came to an end, and assuming there wasn't another reef up ahead that would force them to turn again, Sirena would have a fight on her hands. Of that, she had no doubt.

Several dozen pirates stood at the port rail of the chasing cutter. Their expressions grim, cutlasses gripped tightly, ready to leap onto the *Swift* when the chance arose.

Davin realized that he would have his hands full as well as he slid down the ladder and ran over to the port railing. There was no reef on this side that they had to worry about at least for the next several miles.

Instead, they had to worry about the black-sailed frigate that was angling in toward them from that direction and at the end of its curl would have a straight shot at the *Swift*.

Talia had nowhere to go so long as she ran along the reef on their starboard side.

Of course, this wasn't the first time their pursuers had tried this maneuver. So far, they had enjoyed little luck, never quite getting into a position from which they could attack successfully.

Until now.

Either Talia got them out of danger with some deft maneuvering or a reef came into play at the worst possible time for the pirates.

Even so, now that it seemed likely that the pirates would finally get their chance, Davin wanted to make sure that they paid a heavy price for their aggression.

"Sven!"

"We stand ready, Crimson Giant!" roared the huge sailor.

"Shield wall on the port railing!"

Sven and the sailors and soldiers on that side responded immediately, pulling shields up from where they had been strapped against the inner hull. These shields were different from those that Davin was most familiar with.

They weren't the scuta of the gladiators. Rather, they were a refined version. Another of Master Hari's innovations.

These shields were more than a foot smaller in length. They still were curved, though not as much as the scuta with which the Blood Company had fought their way across Caledonia.

They also fit into grooves carved out of the railing, which allowed the sailors and soldiers to lock them into place. Once set in position, the shields increased the height of the railing by four feet, adding to the level of difficulty for anyone seeking to board with ill intent.

That also meant that rather than having the traditional shield bearers, then spear, then swords, maybe even archers behind the swords to defend against any attack, there were just the spears right behind the shields and then a mix of archers and cutlasses.

The same tactics that had proven so effective when employed by the Blood Company, though requiring fewer fighters. A key distinction that gave the *Swift's* crew an advantage they knew how to make the most of.

Sven and the soldiers and sailors with him got the shields in place right before the frigate slammed against the side of the *Swift*.

Talia, unable to avoid the blow because of the reef running on the other side, used all of her strength to turn the wheel toward the port side at the very last second so that the *Swift* pushed back against the frigate right before the collision. Her quick thinking kept them off the coral hidden beneath the waves just a few yards away on the starboard side, but not by much.

With the two ships scraping against one another, no more

than a few feet separating the vessels at any time, the first wave of pirates tried to climb over the shields.

That didn't go as planned for the overconfident boarders.

With the help of their comrades crowding around them, three men swung a leg over the steel barricade.

Their success was short-lived. Stuck atop the shields, the rolling motion of the ship hindering their efforts, they were easy targets for the spears waiting for just such an opportunity.

A fourth pirate avoided the stab in part, taking it in his thigh instead of his chest when he dodged out of the way at the last second. However, at the exact moment that he was trying to make his escape, the *Swift* hit a trough.

Rather than falling back onto the deck of his ship as he intended, thrown off balance by the severe dip, his testicles smashed down onto the sharp rim of the shield. Gasping out a silent scream, he slid off the top of the shield, clutching at his nether region, barely able to draw a breath as he gazed at the blood staining his pants.

When the badly wounded pirate hit the deck of the *Swift*, Sven finished him before the man even realized what had happened, stabbing the marauder through the heart with a quick thrust of his sword.

Despite that first attack's lack of success, as the two ships ran through the water, their hulls scraping and slamming against each other, more pirates tried to force their way aboard.

None were willing to take the risk that their dead friends had. Rather than trying to climb over the shields, they attempted to push their way through instead.

A more cautious approach to be sure. Also, one doomed to fail.

The shields held strong, the pirates unable to do much against the steel barrier with their cutlasses. Moreover, they unwittingly placed themselves in a vulnerable position, now having to worry about what might come at them from above.

Sven and his fighters did their best to dissuade their attackers, spears shooting down over the tops of the shields.

The first few thrusts stabbed into flesh, earning cries and groans of pain. That was quickly followed by roars of anger as the pirates spent more time dodging the spears than trying to break through the shield wall.

Davin watched it all with a grim expression of satisfaction. He didn't feel the need to involve himself in the skirmish. Sven had the clash well in hand.

Nevertheless, he sensed an opportunity that he didn't want to lose. One that also would allow them to test another of Master Hari's innovations.

The shields were proving quite effective when locked in place, but they didn't need to be all the time.

"Sven! Alternating spears!"

"As you command, Crimson Giant!"

The change was instant and jarring for the pirates, who stood dumbfounded when a shield in the center of the wall of steel was pulled back on a hinge, a soldier with bright eyes appearing and jabbing her spear through the gap. She caught the pirate standing right across from her in the throat, the man stunned by the sudden attack.

Before the man collapsed to the deck, clutching at the mess where his throat had been, choking on his own blood, the shield was back in place, the barrier running along the railing intact once more.

Though only for a few seconds.

Farther down the line another gap appeared when a shield was pulled down. Once again a spear shot through, another pirate falling to the deck in agony, clutching at his groin.

Just as quickly as that gap had appeared, it closed. The wall whole once more.

And so it went for the next few minutes. Sailors pulling

shields back, those shields locking back in place as soon as the spears did their bloody work.

Only Sven knew the rhyme or reason of the attack, and that kept the pirates on their toes. Acknowledging the precision of this lethal tactic, none of the marauders were willing to risk a spear in their groin or their gut, so they stayed farther back from the shield wall.

That decision, although certainly the smart one in terms of keeping themselves alive, negated their ability to continue their assault with any hope of boarding the *Swift*.

Davin was pleased by the crew's success. Nevertheless, he knew that the fight wasn't over. There was still one more way that the pirates could attempt to cross the narrow gap between the ships.

"Archers!" he yelled. "Free to fire!"

Shooting at a target with a crossbow in rough seas was a massive challenge. Hitting anything was more luck than skill. And it still was.

Although not to such a degree for the sailors perched in the rigging of the *Swift*.

Because unlike on other vessels, the men and women charged with ensuring that not a single pirate swung across from the yardarms need only concern themselves with aiming their weapons. With their crossbows fixed to the *Swift's* yardarms, and the sailors strapped into small seats that allowed them to maneuver their weapons on a broad arc, they benefited from a previously unattainable stability.

They didn't have to worry about falling to the deck below. They didn't have to worry as much about the movement of the ship. They could worry solely about their accuracy.

That innovation from Master Hari, almost an afterthought while he was talking to Davin about his desire to set the shields along the railing on hinges, proved its worth in a matter of seconds.

Two pirates had climbed the mainmast of their ship and scurried out onto the end of the yardarm. Grasping tightly to the ropes tied there, they swung through the space between the ships when they judged they had the best chance of landing on the *Swift* rather than in the water between the two surging vessels.

They didn't get very far. Several crossbow bolts punched into them – chest, thigh, neck, gut -- the jolts and the bloody wounds knocking them from their ropes and dropping them on top of their comrades below, who still were seeking some way past the shield wall while trying to avoid a spear to the gut.

The other pirates up in the rigging who wanted to follow after the two failed trailblazers decided that it was best to get down from their positions as fast as possible when they saw how quickly the sailors across from them reloaded their crossbows and turned the wicked weapons toward them.

Coming under a withering fire, the pirates enjoyed just as much success as their two comrades. None made it back to their deck.

All of them died in the rigging, their bodies hanging grotesquely, three or four crossbow bolts sprouting from each one, as they went through the last spasms of death.

"Fire on the helm!" Davin roared.

The archers on the yardarms shifted their focus immediately, turning their weapons toward the wheel.

Before the pirate manning the helm knew what happened, a bolt punched him back against the railing, the steel shaft skewering him through the chest.

Collapsing to the deck on his back, for just a second no one controlled the vessel until the captain jumped over the dying sailor and grabbed the wheel. Desperate to keep the ship on its course despite the bolts streaking down toward him, he ducked beneath the helm, the steel shafts smacking into the wood around him.

Davin watched the last of the brief fight above him with a touch of pleasure. The innovations that he and Master Hari had worked on together had proven their utility in just seconds.

He grunted in satisfaction when he heard Sven's call. The sailor pointed toward the destroyed helm of the pirate ship.

The captain, though still alive, was wounded, a steel shaft sticking out of his arm. Having had enough of the archers' assault, he turned the wheel hard to port and curled the frigate away from the *Swift* so that he didn't crash into the reef that was coming up on them from the north.

A respite earned, and one that they deserved. But only for a brief time, because Davin saw from his vantage point that the channel opened up for quite a long ways once they got past the reef bracketing them in on their starboard side.

Instead of congratulating the crew and soldiers on their success, he turned his mind toward preparing them for the next round of the battle. That was until he heard the shout from his own helm.

Talia had watched the fight on the port side as much as she could, but in glimpses only. She needed to focus on the way ahead to ensure that they stayed clear of the reefs lurking just beneath the surface.

They were doing well so far. That was true. They remained free of the pirates.

However, with the channel opening up around them, even Master Hari's enhancements that had proven so effective against the attack on the port side wouldn't be enough to prevent the pirates from boarding the *Swift* when the two other marauders bracketed them past the reef.

It was a numbers game. They would be stretched too thin to defend on both fronts at the same time.

Understanding that, Talia believed that they needed to change their strategy. It was as simple as that.

And, unfortunately, the only possibility she could think of

that gave them even a glimmer of hope of slipping free from the noose that was tightening around them required that a desperate risk be taken.

"Davin!"

The gladiator hesitated before responding to Talia's call. He wanted to ensure first that the frigate on his side of the *Swift* wouldn't be coming in on them from that direction again at least for the next few minutes.

Satisfied that they had nothing to worry about for a mile or more because of the reef running along the port side, he climbed back up to the helm.

"I need you to do something for me, Davin."

Talia noted the gladiator's bloody spear. She breathed a little easier.

It seemed like none of the dark splotches on his leather armor were his own blood, although she couldn't be sure, and she didn't have the chance to confirm that he wasn't wounded. She needed to concentrate on guiding the *Swift* past the last reef.

Once through this narrow channel, she would have to shift course again. The color of the sea changed a few hundred yards ahead.

To follow the edge of the crescent-shaped coral, she needed to turn sharply to port and then curl more gently back to starboard. Then they would enjoy smooth sailing for several leagues before they were back in among the reefs.

Under other circumstances that would be a good thing. Not now, however.

That open channel would give the pirates pursuing them the chance to finally come up alongside them. And, if the ship they had been chasing got into the right position, the pirates would box them in.

Then, despite all of Master Hari's innovations, despite the courage and tenacity of her soldiers and sailors, the death knell would ring for the *Swift* and all aboard. It was only a matter of time.

"As you command, Captain."

Talia was about to offer him a sharp reply, but an even faster glance told her that he wasn't teasing her. He was just treating her with the respect that she deserved as the commander of the ship.

She appreciated that immensely. And she hated what she was about to do next. But she didn't have any choice.

She couldn't think about one man's life. She had to think about all the lives aboard the *Swift* who depended on her judgment.

If one man needed to risk death to give all the others a better chance at living, so be it. That was the burden of being the captain.

"I'm sorry to do this, Davin, but ..."

He listened attentively as Talia explained what she required from him, even as he tracked the pirate ship off the starboard rail that was preparing to make another run at them.

Davin wasn't worried, however. Sirena had everything on that side well in hand. The shield wall already was locked in place along the railing and the archers were in position on the yardarms. The pirates would have a difficult time boarding from that direction.

"You said that I shouldn't do that, Captain," Davin said after Talia finished telling him what she wanted him to do. "You were quite specific, in fact. Multiple times. That if I did what you want me to do, you'd cut the rope and leave me in the deep water."

"Yes, I know that," Talia admitted, her eyes remaining fixed to the front. She turned the wheel gently to the starboard side, beginning the curl that would take them along the western side of the reef. "But you can belay that order. I need you to do it now. If you're willing to take the risk. I know that I'm asking a lot of you. That I'm asking for the impossible. But I wouldn't ask if I didn't think it ..."

"It's the only way," Davin interrupted, understanding that she had no choice but to put him at risk. He could read the battlefield just as well as she could. "I'll take care of it."

He stepped up close to her then so that he was standing right at her side. She didn't look at him even though she was desperate to do so. She couldn't without risking a devastating crash against the reef.

"Once this is over we're going to reevaluate all these rules you set for me," Davin said, his voice firm. "They seem to be more guidelines than rules. If we're going to work together in the future, then we need some clarity. About more than just what I can and can't do out on the water."

"Agreed," replied Talia, even as her heart clenched. Because of what Davin was about to do. Also at what he was suggesting. She knew that conversation, if it ever occurred, would touch on matters beyond her original agreement with the gladiator. "If you're going to do this, you need to do it now. We'll be in the channel when we're past this reef. Once there, you'll have ten minutes to do what you need to do. No more than that, and probably less if I can pick up a few more knots with the wind."

"Maybe we should talk about this now," Davin suggested. "There is no guarantee that I'm going to survive this."

"Davin, would you just do what I need you to do rather than doing your best to make my life difficult? We're losing time. I wouldn't ask you to do this if I didn't believe that it was absolutely necessary."

"As you command, Captain," Davin replied.

He saw the look of fear that passed behind Talia's eyes as he walked past her and toward the ladder that would take him down to the deck. Davin assumed that she believed that he was worried about the assignment she had given him. That she was sending him to his death.

Most others if given such a task probably would be. But most others were not him.

Actually, he was excited. He hadn't had the opportunity to do what he was about to do for quite some time, and he would be the first to admit that he had missed it.

Reaching the mainmast, he drove the blade of his spear into the deck and then started pulling off his armor.

"Sven!"

"Yes, Crimson Giant!"

"Bring me the longest rope you have. As fast as you can!"

9

FROM THE CROW'S NEST

Davin gripped the railing of the crow's nest, his fingernails digging into the wood. The wind, which had picked up in just the last few minutes, seemed intent on throwing him from his perch. The mast swayed so violently as the *Swift* soared over the crests of the waves that he was having a hard time keeping his feet.

He didn't mind the rough handling. The additional burst of speed that Talia was making the most of would help him with the task that he had agreed to.

He did feel a bit exposed, however.

The battle was about to begin again. The two pirate ships on each side of the *Swift* were curling closer so that they could renew the assault.

And he was standing one hundred and fifty feet above the deck in his underclothes with nothing but a dagger strapped to each calf.

If his sister could see him now, he knew exactly what she would say. Not wanting to hear Lycia in his head, he took a deep breath and prepared himself for what he was about to do, visualizing his next steps and his ultimate goal.

Talia was about to guide them beyond the reef and into the open water. The very tip of the crescent-shaped reef streaking by at exactly that moment.

She was doing exactly as she said she would. She was attempting to milk just a few more knots from their already incredibly fast vessel with the hope that they could slip the noose.

If Talia succeeded, Davin's unique services wouldn't be required.

A good effort on her part, but he could tell that it wasn't going to work.

Even with the additional speed Talia didn't have enough room to maneuver around their hunters with the reefs limiting their possible paths in this part of the Shoals.

The pirates were tracking them closely, intent on their prey. The ship on their port side giving them a little more distance after the captain botched his initial attack and learned the true depth of the challenge he faced.

The pirates on those two vessels demonstrated little interest in trying to board them now. Rather, their goal had shifted. They just wanted to keep the *Swift* in place.

Davin couldn't argue with the strategy.

A strategy, actually, that he had forced upon them.

The third ship was swiftly coming up on their stern now that the captain of that vessel had sighted the break in the Shoals. The pirate knew just as Talia did that the next few minutes of open water would give him the chance that he had been waiting for.

The fourth vessel worked hard to stay in front of the *Swift*. Blocking their path.

The captain cut from side to side erratically, preventing Talia from using the *Swift's* speed to shoot out of the trap and leave the pirates high and dry.

Davin had to give the marauders credit where credit was due.

It was a surprisingly good plan. And it was proving successful ... so far.

The pirates had a lot to gain if they killed the Huntress. Even more to lose if they didn't. And the change in their watery battlefield favored them now.

Understanding that their current predicament was only going to get worse, Davin needed to get to work. Because it wouldn't be long before the trap closed completely.

Focusing on the ship that was closing on the *Swift* from behind, he judged that the distance soon would be just about right.

It was time to make sure that all was ready.

Davin tugged on the rope a few times, confirming that it was tied tightly to the mast. He then checked the knot that fastened the rope around his waist. Secure enough so that it wouldn't slip off but not so tight that it would break his ribs when he hit the water and the drag began.

Satisfied, he pulled himself onto the railing of the crow's nest.

His toes curled around the wood.

He studied the pirate ship coming up behind them one more time.

He nodded to himself.

His target was exactly where he wanted it to be.

With a devilish grin and a whoop of joy, he jumped from his perch. The ship's momentum sent the *Swift* well past him, giving him a clear path as he dove into the sea.

The shock of the freezing water when he went below the surface knocked the air from his lungs.

He fought to keep his mouth closed.

He couldn't afford to give in to the natural impulse to suck in the seawater.

Instead, he focused on grasping the rope so that he could exercise some manner of control over his movements as he was pulled behind the *Swift*.

Once he got a good grip, he felt better. More under control.

His preliminary success allowed him to relax just enough so that he could give in to the drag of the ship.

Best to save his energy now and allow the work to be done for him until he was in position.

He hadn't done this for a while, and he had worried for just a few heartbeats that he had forgotten how.

Thankfully, it all came back to him quickly.

He couldn't fight it.

He had to go against his nature.

He just needed to surrender to what was happening, understanding that the forces in play around him were stronger than he was.

When he felt the sharp tug at his waist, he realized that it was time.

Although it had seemed like an eternity, after less than a minute below the water, he kicked for the surface. Seconds later he pushed his head above the waves.

He took a deep breath, desperate for the air. When he did, he got just as much froth, a wave smacking him in the face.

He blamed that on the fact that he was out of practice.

Coughing out the water, he took another deep breath, but only after he turned his head to the side so he didn't go through the same experience again.

Better. Now for the hard part.

Davin drew his knees into his chest, at the same time pulling himself a few feet farther along the rope.

Now that he had some slack, he tried to flip over so that he was getting pulled on his back. Once he did that, he would turn so that he could see the *Swift*. From there, he could pull himself up so that he was surfing on his feet.

He failed the first time. Losing control of his body as he was dragged behind the *Swift*, he crashed back down onto his face and belly before he could even place a foot atop the water.

He chalked up that miscue to his lack of practice.

Understanding that time was running out, he began the same process again. As he had done before, he pulled his knees into his chest.

This time, he felt more comfortable in his actions. He turned himself around so that he was on his back. An easier task, the movement coming back to him. And then he was facing the direction he wanted.

He attempted once again to set his feet into the surf so that he could pull himself up.

For just a second, he succeeded, his eyes widening in delight. They closed with disappointment just as quickly.

A rogue wave that was several feet higher than the chop he had been fighting through slammed into him.

Catching him by surprise, he lost his balance and crashed face first back beneath the surface.

Davin didn't allow his second failure to bother him, his determination becoming an unshakable stubbornness. He was getting closer each time. He just needed to keep trying.

Working his way through the same process as he had done before, the motions more natural now, he got up faster on his third attempt.

And he stayed there.

In seconds, he was surfing on the balls of his feet behind the *Swift*!

He was about to yell out in triumph, almost unable to contain his exuberance.

He stopped himself just in time.

He was running right next to the bow of the pursuing ship, and he didn't want to give himself away, fearing he might be heard over the rush of the wind and the frigate surging through the sea.

A quick glance up and to his left told him that he had little to fear. The pirates on the main deck and scrambling about in the rigging hadn't seen him.

They were focused on the *Swift*. No shout of warning given. Not a crossbow in sight.

Good. So long as they didn't see him, he stood a chance.

Not having any time to waste, and not wanting to risk another fall as the chop in the Shoals increased because of the strengthening wind, he tilted his left knee down just a few inches.

He was careful not to dip so low that he disrupted the fragile balance that he had achieved. He had no desire to taste the seawater again or, worse, smack his head against the hull.

If that happened, he was dead.

As he glided skillfully across the surface of the ocean toward the hull, he reached down and carefully pulled the dagger free from the sheath on his right calf.

When the hull was no more than a few feet away, he stabbed as if he were trying to gut a Ghoule. Thankfully, he didn't miss, plunging the sharp steel into the wood.

Gripping the hilt tightly, he tugged on the slip knot, the rope unraveling from around his waist.

He was free from the *Swift*.

He was on his own.

Hanging from the hull by just a single dagger, he ignored the waves that slapped at him. Acknowledging but not giving in to the ever-present peril that if he lost his grip he'd drown in the Shoals even if he didn't get caught beneath the pirate ship first.

To belay that concern, he focused on what he needed to do. He reached down and pulled free the dagger sheathed to his other calf.

With a controlled jab, he drove the steel of that blade into the hull.

Success!

He wanted to shout.

He growled instead.

He was firmly in place now. He had made it to the ship with the pirates none the wiser. Just thirty or so feet below the deck railing.

Now he just needed to climb the hull of a frigate crashing through fifteen-foot waves. Sneak on board. Fight his way through the fifty or more men standing above him. Then, finally, somehow, disable the ship.

And after that?

If he actually proved successful?

He had to get back to the *Swift*.

Slim odds at best that he was going to make it all the way through that progression. But there was nothing for it.

Pulling free the dagger he had first driven into place, he reached up and punched the steel into the wood higher up on the hull.

The deadly consequences didn't faze him in the least. It couldn't be any harder than fighting a giant scorpion on the white sand.

Then Davin grinned, relishing the challenge before him. Knowing that he was exactly where he was supposed to be.

Because if he somehow survived, he'd have quite a story to tell.

FREE OF THE reef that had been running on the starboard side, open water in the wide channel that beckoned to her for the next few leagues, Talia kept a firm grip on the wheel.

Her concern now wasn't staying free of the reefs. At least not for the next few minutes.

Rather, it was on keeping the *Swift* exactly where she needed her to be.

Talia had to give Davin the chance to do what she had asked him to do.

That meant allowing the ship chasing them to draw closer than she would have preferred.

However, there was no point in making that concession if Davin wasn't in place.

If he wasn't where he was supposed to be in the next minute, she needed to assume the worst.

Then, no matter how much it pained her, she had to think about what other options – those very few if any at all that were available to her – she had for escaping her pursuers while keeping her ship and her crew intact.

She really didn't want to think about that possibility.

Davin had to succeed.

He had to!

She glanced back over her shoulder.

No sign of him.

Talia tightened her lips and bit her tongue. Maybe it was too early.

Yet she had thirty seconds at most before she needed to decide her next step.

Where was he?

Blast it, Davin, you need to make this work! Don't make me leave you to your fate.

She had heard of his exploits. About how he had mastered this skill.

It had been a while since he had last attempted it, but he wouldn't have agreed to her request if he didn't believe that he had a good chance of success, would he?

She shook her head in anger. At herself most of all.

Who was she kidding?

She should have thought about this some more before asking.

This was Davin.

The gladiator had a penchant for taking risks that others wouldn't. Of course he would agree to what she had asked him to do even if he didn't think he had a good chance of surviving the experience.

He thrived on taking extreme risks.

Talia cursed herself and Davin for being fools. If he didn't make it, then she promised that she would kill him herself.

The bile rising in her throat as her worry intensified, only a few more seconds remained before she needed to decide.

She glanced quickly over her shoulder once more.

Stars be praised!

He had done it!

He was hanging from the hull. Even better, he was climbing the hull.

She smiled broadly as she turned back around, relief flooding through her.

She really shouldn't have doubted him.

Nothing seemed to faze Davin. Not even the threat of imminent death.

What frightened most people was just another task to be completed in his mind.

Whether Davin made it through the next few minutes was in his hands now. Probably just how he preferred.

She had to trust him now.

And she needed to turn her attention to the other threats they faced so that if he did, indeed, achieve his objective, she was in a position to get him back aboard the *Swift*.

Assuming that even proved possible.

That thought driving her, she watched dispassionately as the frigate came up on their starboard side.

"They're going to know what to expect this time," Sirena called. The Captain of Talia's Guard stood right at her shoulder, having to raise her voice to be heard over the wind. "They saw what we can do. How hard it will be to take us."

"They did," Talia agreed. "That's why they're going to change their approach. And just when they think they have us, we're going to give them a surprise that makes them crap their pants."

"Spearguns?"

"Yes, it's time to test Master Hari's most recent invention."

Sirena smiled wickedly. If this worked, then the pirates were going to get what they so richly deserved. She shouted from the helm before she slid down the ladder. "Sven, spearguns behind the shields!"

Talia watched as two teams of sailors hustled to the storage lockers just below the tiller. The men and women pulled open the doors and emerged with the modified ballistae and their stands.

More sailors appeared and, working with Sven on one side of the *Swift* and Sirena on the other, they locked the weapons in place using the steel rings bolted into the deck that ran at regular intervals along the gunwales.

Talia glanced to her front. She remained right on course with several more minutes of open water remaining to her.

She looked back over her shoulder for just a heartbeat. The pirate ship at their back was still hounding them.

Most important, the frigate had not drawn any closer nor fallen any farther back. That was important.

"Ready, Captain Carlomin!" Sirena yelled from the starboard side railing.

Talia's smile matched Sirena's. Their attackers were not going to enjoy what happened next.

Now that all was in place, there was just one more thing that Talia needed to do to improve the odds of their next play.

"Trim the sails!" Talia ordered.

The sailors waiting in the rigging obeyed instantly, scampering across the yardarms, adjusting the cloth.

The *Swift* began to slow ever so slightly.

The slower speed put the *Swift* at greater risk. Nevertheless, Talia believed that her decision would pay off in the end.

Sirena wondered about the wisdom of putting themselves in such a vulnerable position for this one chance. She pushed that thought from her mind immediately.

Captain Carlomin knew what she was doing. The Huntress had yet to lose a fight on the water, and clearly she wasn't worried about defending the port and starboard sides at the same time.

Gutsy, Sirena thought. If Captain Carlomin wasn't worried, then she wasn't either.

"Make sure they're right next to us, Sirena," Talia called down from the helm. "It won't take them long to wise up. Focus on the helm as we discussed."

"Of course, Captain Carlomin."

Sirena surveyed the sailors standing ready behind the ballistae. The weapons stood as tall as a man and had been built to function specifically aboard a ship.

Seeking to increase the effectiveness of the ballistae, Master Hari had modified the traditional firing mechanism so that each weapon could shoot three steel spikes that were almost as long as harpoons before needing to be reloaded. Not just one.

All of the weapons were ready to fire. All of the sailors stared at her expectantly, just as anxious as she was to pay back the pirates for their depredations.

"On my command, Sven."

The two ships racing alongside crashed against the *Swift* at almost the same time with an incredible force.

The captains of the two vessels had only one objective with

their current strategy. To eliminate Talia Carlomin's greatest advantage. The speed of her ship.

With a good strike, they hoped to disable the *Swift*. Then the Huntress and her crew would be easy pickings.

The two pirate captains, standing on their helms, waited with bated breath to determine the extent of the damage that they had caused. With the force of the blow that each had given, the *Swift* might already be taking on water.

To find out, they ordered their helmsmen to turn their ships away just a hair and continue to run alongside so that they could examine the *Swift's* hull.

Both men spewed a host of curses when they saw the result of their well-planned assault.

It hadn't worked out as they hoped it would.

True, there was a good bit of cracked and splintered timber because of the collision, but it was their own vessels that had absorbed most of the damage.

They never considered the possibility that the Huntress' Master Shipbuilder might have used fire in a unique way to harden the *Swift's* hull. Strengthening it. And thus the reason for the darker color of the wood used for each Carlomin vessel.

Instead, they allowed their rage to rule them.

They had one goal, and they were going to achieve that goal, no matter how many blows it took.

The Huntress was going to the bottom of the sea.

Despite the significant damage to their own ships, the two captains ordered their vessels turned back into the *Swift* again. Not quite believing that they had failed so miserably the first time. Hoping that a few more hard smacks would do the trick.

With the shields fixed in place along the gunwales, the pirates didn't even bother to try to cross over. They didn't want to go through that useless and deadly exercise again.

Instead, they hoped that their ships would do the job for

them. They held onto whatever they could so that they didn't tumble to the deck when the next collision came.

Once again, the two ships crashed into the *Swift* in another explosion of shattering wood.

And, again, there was little harm to the *Swift*.

The two frigates absorbed the bulk of the damage.

The second collision ripped several long pieces of timber free from both hulls. A long crack also appeared that ran from below the waterline all the way up the gunwale on the ship sailing along the starboard side, and it appeared to be expanding.

Disappointed that the *Swift* had barely been affected by the knocks, the pirates concluded quickly that their current tactics were of little use.

In fact, they were beginning to believe that if their captains smashed into the *Swift* again, another collision would send them to their doom instead.

As their ships pulled away once again, before the pirates could assess the true extent of the damage and determine how much water they were taking on, they had a more immediate and shocking threat to worry about.

The captains never anticipating that the Huntress had set a trap for them while she herself was caught in the trap of their own making.

"Gunners, free to fire!"

Sirena's timing was perfect.

At the exact same time, a block of shields on each side of the *Swift* dropped down on their hinges.

Large ballistae appeared in the gaps.

The pirates stared in disbelief, frozen in fear as they realized much too late the true nature of the danger they faced.

They had made a terrible mistake.

They had believed that they could take on the Huntress and win.

They were learning much to their regret that they didn't stand a chance against the woman who had rid the Sea of Mist of so many of their comrades.

Screaming in rage and excitement, the sailors aboard the *Swift* pulled the levers, three long steel bolts shooting from each of the five weapons set on each side of the ship.

Because of the proximity, each harpoon slammed into a target. Never missing. Helms, masts, pirates ... it was a devastating and overpowering attack.

The helmsmen and the captains never stood a chance. Neither did the wheels, which were destroyed in an instant.

The impact of losing the rudders was immediate. The badly damaged frigates curled away, caught by the wind and the waves.

The pirates had no chance of regaining control of their ships. They would continue to flounder until they crashed into the reefs that were only a few hundred yards away on each side.

Talia watched it all out of the corner of her eye.

She was quite pleased.

Master Hari would be as well. In fact, he would be ecstatic to know how well his new creations worked.

She had no time to enjoy her success, however.

Two down. Two to go.

Much better odds now that the channel she was sailing through was beginning to narrow.

Yet her focus remained on keeping to her course.

Davin had only a few minutes left before she would need to change direction. If he didn't complete his assigned task before she turned the *Swift* to the west, then he was consigned to a watery grave.

Davin worked as rapidly as he could to climb the hull, but he couldn't go as fast as he would have liked. Not with one slip meaning his death.

He needed to be careful.

So he didn't rush.

He made certain that each time he drove his daggers into the hull they were stuck fast.

One above the other, usually no more than one foot higher than the next, slowly pulling himself up toward the railing.

His muscles burned.

His feet dangled more often than not, unable to keep a good grip on the slick wood.

That made his climb all the more difficult.

The pitch of the ship only complicated his efforts. The natural rise and fall of the vessel through the rough chop almost threw him off several times, his daggers holding fast to the wood, but his hands slipping off the wet hilts despite the extra leather he had wrapped around the grip.

Thankfully never both at the same time.

If that happened, he was done for. Simple as that.

That very real possibility didn't bother him.

He was used to it.

Five years on the white sand helped to negate the fear of his own death, a reality that could so greatly affect others who never endured the experiences that he had.

What truly bothered him was the possibility of failing to do what he promised Talia Carlomin.

Talia Carlomin!

Even now, climbing the side of a ship as it surged through the Shoals, knowing that several score pirates waited to greet him on deck, assuming he even made it that far, his thoughts drifted toward the Huntress.

Shaking his head in a mix of amusement and annoyance, he continued with his climb. He managed to keep his grip as slowly, ever so slowly, he pulled himself higher up the side of the cutter.

He stopped when he reached a point just a few feet below the series of portholes that ran along the side of the ship, the railing just a few feet above them.

As he hung there, he realized that once again he had allowed his impetuous nature to rule his decision making when he agreed to take on this foolhardy task. He really should have given more thought to his method rather than his madness upon reaching the ship.

He had focused most of his attention on actually getting to this point, not really believing that he would make it this far. Now he needed to decide how to speed things along, because his timeframe for returning to the *Swift* was closing quickly.

He could continue his climb and pull himself onto the deck. Maybe with the *Swift* running just in front of him the pirates above wouldn't pay him much mind. All their attention focused on their quarry.

He doubted that, however. He assumed that if he did suddenly appear on the main deck that he'd be challenging a large number of pirates to a massive melee with just a dagger in each hand.

The simplest choice, true.

Still, that option didn't appeal to him.

It seemed the most likely way to hasten his own death.

Moreover, it gave him little chance of completing his mission.

That's what needed to guide his thinking now. Because the lives of everyone on board the *Swift* depended on what he did during the next few minutes.

Discarding that first idea, he looked to his left.

He could try to work his way along the hull with his daggers and, if all went well, pull himself up onto the deck near the helm, which was located closer to the stern of the vessel and away from where, judging by the noises he was hearing over the wind and the crashing sea, most of the pirates had congregated on the deck.

Assuming that he didn't fall from his perch, of course.

And assuming that no one noticed him clinging to the side of the ship as he worked his way farther along the hull or when he flung himself over the rail, likely flopping along the deck like a floundering fish, unable to defend himself effectively because his arms shook and burned with the strain of his efforts.

But getting past all that, then he could make a try for the captain.

Kill him.

Kill the helmsman.

Destroy the wheel.

Simple.

Just like the first plan.

And perhaps one that offered him a greater chance of success.

Could he do it?

Maybe.

There was a lot that would need to go right. That's why he hesitated.

Davin felt as if he had used up most of his luck just reaching the place where he hung from now. Besides, climbing his way along the side of the ship would require valuable minutes that could be spent on other more effective diversions.

Yes, this second strategy gave him a better chance at success than the first. Still, it was fraught with potential risk.

The most obvious was that as he tired the likelihood only increased that he was flung into the sea when the ship dropped into a trough or crested a wave while he had only one dagger punched into the hull.

Having seen out of the corner of his eye just how effective

Talia had been when she used the spearguns to destroy the wheels of two of the frigates, making for the helm so that he could give it a try certainly appealed to him.

Nevertheless, he was still wary of that approach. The odds remained heavily against him.

Deciding to go against his nature, which often directed him down a path that required him to take the highest risk, Davin chose to take a more cautious approach. One for which his sister probably would be proud of him.

The plan that formed in his mind might work.

It might not.

But he liked the associated odds better.

And he really wanted to get off the side of the ship, the progressively rougher waves making it much harder for him to keep his grip on his daggers.

Decision made, Davin punched into the wood with his daggers, climbing a few more feet up the hull until he was hanging right beneath a porthole.

He pulled himself up so that he could peek through the glass.

He couldn't see much, the cabin dark except for the few streams of light that flashed through the porthole he was staring through as well as the several others that ran along the wall to his left.

A large space, then. Maybe even the captain's chambers.

He couldn't tell for sure.

However, he was certain that the cabin was empty, which was exactly the way he wanted it.

Pulling the dagger in his right hand out of the wood, he used the hilt to break the glass, grateful that the pounding of the sea and the shouts just above him drowned out the noise that he made. Knocking away the few remaining pieces that might slice into his flesh left him with an empty, circular window frame.

Reaching into the porthole with his right hand, dagger leading the way, he began to wriggle through the opening.

He was half in, half out when he realized it was a tighter fit than he had anticipated. His shoulders were caught in the gap, the jostling from the ship rising and falling in the waves not making it any easier for him.

Davin spent the next few seconds trying to free himself from his predicament. Finding it difficult to get any leverage, it was taking longer than he would have liked to get into the chamber. Nevertheless, he tamped down on the urge to just force himself through.

He reminded himself that he needed to be careful. After all the work to get where he was, his end goal in sight, he didn't want to give himself away now.

He continued to squirm in the porthole, punching his daggers into the inside wall to give himself more leverage as he tried to pull himself into the cabin. The primary impediment, his broad shoulders, finally made it through the broken window.

He realized that he had been correct. He was breaking into the captain's quarters.

That was good, since the captain was quite busy at the moment, and he was still hanging in the porthole.

"Who in the blazes are you?"

Davin looked up, not noticing when the door to the cabin opened on silent hinges. More interested in forcing his way through the tight space.

A pirate stood across the cabin from him, cutlass in hand.

Davin reacted with barely a thought, flicking the dagger in his right hand in an underhanded motion.

He returned his focus to pushing his way through the port-hole, breathing a sigh of relief as the pirate who had discovered him struggled to breathe. The man crashed back against the door frame, dropping his cutlass, reaching feebly at the hilt of the dagger sticking out from his throat.

Davin nodded to himself, impressed by his effort. It seemed that Talia wasn't the only person with some skill at throwing daggers.

Talia Carlomin!

Why couldn't he go more than a minute or two without her pixielike face coming to mind? This was really beginning to aggravate him.

For just a second, he wondered if she had the same problem that he did, only in reverse.

Did she think about him as much as he thought about her?

He snorted out a silent laugh, unable to give that thought any credence.

Why would she waste her time thinking about him?

She was one of the most powerful women in New Caledonia. He was a gladiator. He was with her only because Bryen had asked her to take him on.

To think that there was anything between them, or that anything could develop between them, was absolutely ridiculous.

Finally touching the floor with his hands, Davin rolled the rest of the way through the porthole, back on his feet again in a flash.

He shook out his arms, wanting to get rid of the burning sensation caused by his tired muscles.

Finally getting some feeling back, he flexed the muscles in his shoulders as he watched the pirate die. When the man took his last breath, his blood-covered hands dropping to his chest, Davin remained in place, standing there for several heartbeats, listening.

He didn't hear anything that he didn't expect to hear, and certainly nothing that gave him any cause for concern.

Shaking his arms out a final time, he reached down and

pulled free his bloody dagger, wiping it on the dead man's shirt before sheathing it again.

Keeping the dagger in his left hand, he grabbed the back of the man's collar and dragged him into the cabin. Once the body was out of the way, he pulled the door shut as he stepped out into the narrow corridor.

Davin had considered taking the man's clothes, thinking that he might be able to blend in with the crew. He decided against that almost as soon as he thought of it, realizing that it was a foolish notion the instant it crossed his mind.

Davin was too tall and too broad in the shoulders to fit into the much smaller man's clothes. Not only would he look ridiculous – well, more ridiculous than he already did running around in his skivvies -- but the pirates would see right through his attempted deception.

A ship's crew was a tight-knit bunch. They knew each other better than they wanted to. His walking out onto the deck as if he belonged there was a fool's choice.

Better just to move swiftly and decisively and use against his enemies the half second of hesitation before they realized who he was.

That decided, now he just needed to locate what was so critical to his plan.

It had to be somewhere aboard this ship. That was a given.

He worked his way slowly down the passageway until he reached the ship's ladder.

Every so often he glimpsed flashes of movement just above him.

Those didn't worry him. They were entirely in line with what he expected to see.

Most important was that none of the crew came belowdecks. Not with them so intent on catching up to the *Swift*.

That single-mindedness on the part of the captain and the crew would work in his favor.

Satisfied that he didn't have to worry about being taken surprise by another errant pirate, Davin climbed down the ship's ladder to the lower deck.

He hoped that what he wanted was on this level, because he was running out of time, and he knew that only the hold and the bilge would be below him.

He had only gone halfway down the corridor before he struck gold. It was the smell that gave it away, Davin following the smoky odor to its source.

Davin pushed open the door. The supply locker.

Just as he thought would be the case, a barrel of sealed pitch was tied down to the deck and sat against the far wall.

Pitch was a resource critical to every ship. It was used to seal the wooden planks and offer some level of waterproofing. It was essential to making quick repairs that were required on most any voyage, a fact that he had discovered during his journey across the Burnt Ocean aboard the *Freedom*.

He had learned as well from Declan during his time in the Pit and then the Blood Company that the substance could be employed in another way as well, and that's exactly what Davin intended to do.

Using a crowbar he found propped up against the wall, Davin ripped open the top of the barrel and then grabbed several buckets he found off to the side. He filled them with pitch and placed them out in the hallway and a good distance away from the door.

That done, he sliced the rope with his dagger and tipped over the barrel, the pitch spilling all over the room and seeping through the boards to the deck below.

Davin used the beams above his head to climb over the spill and out into the hallway, not wanting a drop of the sticky substance on him, the rocking and rolling of the ship sending the pitch sloshing out into the corridor after him.

That unanticipated development would make his next task much easier.

As the pitch streamed toward him at the speed of molasses, he stopped and listened, just to be sure. He didn't want to be rushed or interrupted.

Nothing but silence other than for the usual creaking of the ship, the shouts of the pirates on the main deck muted.

Davin reached down toward the sheath on his right calf. Instead of the blade, he pulled free a thin length of steel that resembled a file but was a piece of flint.

He knelt down over the spill of pitch that was flowing out into the hallway toward him. It didn't take more than a few strikes from his dagger.

When the sparks dropped down onto the tarlike liquid, a gentle whoosh and a bright flash followed, the highly flammable substance burning brightly and swiftly. The flames rushed back toward the source of the pitch, engulfing the storeroom in a flash.

Davin stepped back, shielding his eyes. He smiled broadly for just a few breaths. That was all the time he had to relish his handiwork.

He picked up the two buckets of pitch and started running down the hallway, tilting the one in his left hand so that a thin stream followed behind him along with the flames licking at his heels.

He dropped the bucket when it was empty. Dashing up the ladder, he tilted the bucket in his right hand as he made for the deck. All the while the flames that burst into an inferno belowdecks raced after him.

Davin was beginning to worry that he might have been too successful. That he might not have given himself enough time to escape.

Pumping his legs even faster, he realized that there was nothing to do for it now other than to stick to the plan and hope for the best.

When he burst out of the hatch below the helm, he was pleased to see that all the pirates were distracted by what was happening to their front.

The stern of the *Swift* couldn't be more than fifty yards ahead of them, the captain and his men intent on catching their prey after a long and difficult chase.

Standing in the hatchway, feeling the heat intensifying at his back, he flung the last of the pitch and the bucket up and onto the helm, a few splatters covering the wheel and even the helmsman.

"What's the meaning of this?"

Davin heard the cry from just above him, grinning all the while. The captain and the helmsman had no idea what was about to happen, and Davin didn't feel an ounce of regret or sympathy.

Knowing that he only had a few seconds to make his escape, Davin burst into motion, sprinting across the deck. He didn't look back when he heard the much louder whoosh, the fire building below the main deck, exploding out of the hatchway and reaching up to the helm.

The blaze gained an even more powerful life when it came into contact with the open air, the flames licking up the helm, following the path of the pitch, and then blasting up into the sky.

With just that single brief touch, the fire ate hungrily into the sails of the mainmast, the greedy beast's appetite insatiable. What had started as a flare-up controlled by the space of the corridor became a full-fledged conflagration in just a few heartbeats.

Davin didn't bother to look behind him. He didn't worry about being struck down by a crossbow bolt or the steel of a cutlass as he raced past the men so focused on killing his friends.

The pirates were only now beginning to realize that they faced a graver threat than the Huntress or the reefs bracketing them on both sides.

Because of that, Davin was just an afterthought.

In fact, several of the pirates who stood in front of him actually moved out of the way when they saw him coming. They couldn't quite understand why their ship was on fire, nor why a man with hair the color of the flames at his back and wearing nothing but his underclothes was racing toward them.

Sprinting right through the shocked group, Davin jumped onto the prow and ran toward the very tip.

He heard the next whoosh, this one much, much louder. A crash followed right after. Probably a yardarm or two coming down if not the mast itself.

He really wanted to see that, maybe even admire his work.

Instead, he forced himself to keep his face forward, focusing on where he placed each foot as the stem narrowed.

He was stuck on a dying ship, and he really didn't want to be.

He began to feel the heat of the flames, which already had leapt to the foremast, when he dove off the prow, the rough seas beckoning to him.

He hoped that his luck held. Because if it didn't, he was dead.

Simple as that.

～

"Did he make it?" Talia asked, the tension in her voice plain.

She had seen the flames beginning to lick at the sails of the ship pursuing them, that single glance confirming for her that the cutter was finished, even if the captain and his crew hadn't yet realized that horrifying truth.

When she looked back again, she couldn't believe how swiftly the blaze had engulfed the frigate.

Davin certainly was thorough when he took on a task of destruction. A unique and somewhat worrisome skill of his.

Sirena didn't reply right away. She had been watching what was happening at their rear for the last several minutes. Her delay in responding only increased Talia's angst.

Yes, Davin knew what he was getting himself into, and clearly, he had taken risks like this before. Dealing with Ronild and his friends beneath the walls of the Rock coming to mind.

Each time he had survived, yet now ... now, she was worried. Very worried. Because she was certain that he had never taken a risk like this before.

"Sirena, do you see him?" she demanded, her voice tight and now tinged with fear.

Talia didn't understand why she was beginning to get upset. They had destroyed three pirate ships in just a quarter hour. They needed to sink one more frigate.

If they did that, the Sea of Mist would be free of the pirate scourge.

Then she could finally challenge Hakea Roosarian and make the witch pay for the death of her father.

And all that possibly at the sole cost of one brave, obnoxious, humble, annoying, funny, irritating, gracious gladiator.

Almost anyone else would have seen that as a fair trade.

She didn't.

Davin challenged her in so many different ways and so frequently. Yet despite all that, she wasn't ready to give him up just yet.

"Yes! Yes, I see him." The relief was obvious in Sirena's voice. "He's got the rope. I don't know how he did it, but he's got the rope."

"Get a squad to the stern to help haul him up."

Sirena started shouting a series of orders, Sven and a handful of sailors racing toward the back deck.

That terrible worry mitigated, and finally breathing again, Talia turned to her last task.

The captain of the pirate vessel to their front had just realized that the odds that favored him only minutes before had turned against him. He was alone.

No longer the hunter.

Now the hunted.

The only question was whether she could catch him before the open waterway came to an end. Once they reached the reefs again, there was a good chance that the captain could navigate away from her and use the Shoals to make his escape.

"Unfurl the sails!" Talia commanded, refusing to allow that to happen.

The sailors in the rigging responded immediately, the *Swift* jumping forward as the additional sailcloth caught the wind.

The distance between the two ships lessened just as the pirate captain started to curl toward the northwest, making for a narrow passage between the two reefs that were visible thanks to the change in the color of the sea just a few hundred yards to their front.

Clever and risky. Talia had to give the man that.

Of course, he didn't really have any choice. He couldn't expect to win a fight against her, not after she sent three of his allies to the bottom.

However, if he made it into the channel before she reached him, she would have to slow her pursuit, perhaps even end it, or risk crashing.

Still, that didn't mean that she didn't have a chance.

For just a second, she feared that her plan wasn't going to work. She shook her head, clearing it, needing to focus on what she was about to do.

She was committed now. Just like Davin had done with his scheme, she needed to take this risk. There was nothing to do but see it through to the end.

"Lower the battering ram!"

A team of sailors at the bow did as ordered, releasing the lever and working the winch. The thin piece of steel that extended thirty feet beyond the prow slid into the water.

Talia turned the wheel ever so gently, changing the angle of her approach as the reefs became more visible, the rush of rough water across the top of the coral revealing the entrance to the gap her prey was making for.

She was only going to get one chance, so she needed to make it count. Especially since she couldn't manufacture the strike that she wanted originally. What she had in mind now would have to do.

With the entrance to the narrow channel fast approaching, she was only a hundred yards behind the ship, cutting toward the pirate on a right angle.

The innovations to the *Swift* came into play then, allowing the craft to surge through the water. The hull barely touching the waves, Talia sought to close the distance.

Fifty yards.

The captain at the helm didn't bother to look back, not wanting to see how close the Huntress was. He concentrated on beginning the turn to starboard that would allow him to take his ship in between the reefs.

Forty yards.

Talia kept on her course, having eyes only for the spot on the cutter's stern that she had picked as her target.

Thirty yards.

A slight adjustment to the wheel.

Twenty yards.

"Brace for impact!" Talia heard Sirena yell.

Rather than the anticipated crash and the sound of

breaking timber, the touch of the battering ram felt more like the brief moment of resistance before a bubble popped. Because just as quickly the steel extending from the prow of the *Swift* was free of their quarry.

Exactly as Talia wanted.

The strike nudged the ship even farther starboard, the stern of the vessel swinging around so that the bow of the ship came farther forward than it should have on its curl.

Talia didn't bother to watch, knowing what was going to happen. Instead, she listened as she guided the *Swift* into the channel between the reefs with a quick turn of the wheel, her ship responding effortlessly to her command.

She realized that if she slammed into the stern of her quarry dead center as she had planned, she would be sentencing herself and her crew to a watery doom. Both ships would be wrecked on the reefs.

Talia only wanted that for the pirates, adjusting her positioning just enough so that the razor-sharp ram sliced across the back corner of the stern of the fleeing ship just below the surface and opening a long gash.

Water immediately surged through the widening slice as the timbers weakened, and that gentle nudge was just enough to knock the ship out of the channel and toward the reef on the eastern side of the gap.

Talia smiled viciously when she heard the crash and the sound of shattering wood, the frigate smashing into the coral with a devastating finality.

She had killed her prey just in time. More important, her crew and her ship were healthy and whole.

Even the waterlogged gladiator who walked slowly across the deck toward the helm wearing only his skivvies.

10

THE BARRICADE

"Where are they?" Dari didn't want to be there. None of them wanted to be there. They didn't have any choice, unfortunately. Not if they wanted to stay alive. So they were where they were. "They should have reached us by now."

"Maybe they went around."

Dari gave Elias a look that revealed his utter disbelief at such a proposal. "Around where? Beyond the trees on both sides the land drops away a thousand feet or more. There's nowhere else to go, Elias!"

"It was just a thought," Elias explained, rolling his eyes, not understanding why his friend was in such a sour mood. They had done this before, and it had worked exactly as they wanted. There was no reason to think that the same wouldn't happen again for them now. "It seemed like you wanted an answer to your question, so I gave you one."

"It was a rhetorical question, Elias," Dari replied, already tired of the conversation thanks in large part to his nerves. He was on edge and for good reason. Yet there was little to do other than to go forward. He wouldn't be able to relax until all this was over.

"A what kind of question?"

"A rhetorical ..." Dari stopped himself, then closed his eyes for a second, needing to take several deep breaths before he lost his temper with Elias.

There was no point in engaging with Elias on this topic. It would only bring his already high level of aggravation to an even greater extreme, and Dari wanted to avoid that. His anxiety mixed with his rapidly increasing annoyance was making him feel ill, tasting the acid from his stomach in the back of his throat.

And that was just the half of it.

His hands were shaky. He was having a hard time taking a deep breath. His heart was beating much too fast. He was sweating even though the weather was crisp, and he wasn't doing anything more than standing behind a barricade constructed of fallen tree limbs and a few cut logs they had dragged in place.

In short, he felt like he was going to pass out ... if he didn't puke first.

Dari knew the cause, but there was nothing to be done about it except to suffer through the next hour or so. Hopefully, it wouldn't take any longer than that.

He closed his eyes again and shook his head in frustration. He really didn't want to be here. He really didn't want to be doing this.

Yet, he didn't have any other options. He and his friends had been reduced to becoming brigands because of what was happening in the Northern Peaks.

"It's a question that doesn't need to be answered, Elias," Dari explained once he had opened his eyes again, still irritated, still sweating profusely, still feeling lightheaded, though just a bit calmer.

"If you didn't want the answer to the question, then why would you ask the question in the first place?"

Dari opened his mouth to reply, then closed it just as quickly.

Elias was a good friend. He was honest. He was trustworthy. He would risk his life for Dari's. But he wasn't the sharpest tool in the shed.

Understanding that, Dari decided to drop the topic and move on to his primary concern. "How far away were they when last you saw them?"

"They were less than half a mile away, Dari." The farmer turned bandit who held a rusted hoe in his hand gave his friend a big grin, clearly pleased with himself. "They didn't see me, I can tell you that. I was too well hidden within the wood. I was like one of those Wraiths who haunts the Murk. You can't see them. You can't hear them. You can't tell until the very last second that they're about to ..."

"How many again?" Dari asked, not wanting to give Elias the chance to continue down the rabbit hole he had fallen into. Not really wanting to hear about what a Wraith could do in the Murk, speaking of a slaughter seemingly inappropriate based on what he and his friends were doing that morning.

"Just four," Elias responded quickly. "One woman and three men."

"And you're certain that they weren't soldiers?" Dari couldn't hide the trepidation in his voice.

All of them were nervous. Just like he was. All of them except for Elias, who didn't seem to be affected by the tension that had settled over Dari's small band.

True, he had fifteen men and women standing around him in small groups. All of them armed.

Well, at least as well armed as could be for people who were used to working in the fields. Pitchforks and sharpened hoes were their primary weapons.

Even so, he wasn't a fool. Despite their greater numbers, trained soldiers wouldn't be dissuaded from taking them on.

"They didn't look like soldiers, Dari," Elias replied excitedly. "Really. Not from what I saw. Just four travelers. But ..."

"But what, Elias?" Dari caught the hitch in his friend's voice.

"The three men could be guards for the woman." Elias shrugged, arching his eyebrow for just a heartbeat. "They seemed quite protective of her, and she was quite well dressed. Maybe a well-off merchant. It was hard to tell. I didn't get too close. I didn't want them to suspect that they were being watched."

Dari shook his head for what seemed like the thousandth time in just the last few minutes. He could only expect so much from Elias. And he did have to give his friend credit where credit was due.

He was the only one in the group willing to risk a scouting mission to see if anyone was coming their way so that they could be prepared. The others wanted to stay together. After their experience with the slavers and then the Murk, they believed in safety in numbers. And he really wasn't in a position to argue with them.

Why was he still there?

Dari had asked himself that question many times since they escaped the slavers.

He had come to the Northern Peaks based on a promise that for payment of his passage, after seven years of labor he would own the land that he worked. During those seven years, after giving Governor Winborne a contracted portion of his crops, he was free to keep for himself what he needed and then sell whatever was left over in the marketplace.

Based on his prospects in Caledonia, it had appeared to be an excellent bargain. Particularly since Governor Winborne had developed a reputation for fairness.

During the first three years his indenture had worked well and exactly as it should. It was only recently that the world around Dari had changed drastically, just as it had for the men and women standing with him behind the barricade, and certainly not for the better.

It was just in the last few months that the slavers had come to the Northern Peaks.

When he heard the stories from the south, Dari believed that being forced to work in the mines was a threat that only the Highlanders would have to face. Governor Winborne would protect them from such a fate.

He had learned otherwise and much to his regret that his naive assumption was incorrect.

After he escaped the slavers, he could have tried his luck in the Highlands. He had heard that the new Lord of the Highlands hated the slavers and did everything in his power to protect the people living within those peaks. But he had worried about surviving the journey across the Northern Steppes.

With good cause he believed now that the Wraiths were coming south so frequently in the Murk. There was no place to hide on the Northern Steppes.

Still, making the attempt seemed less risky to him now than staying where he was. Not too far, in fact, from where the slavers had taken him. Shadow's Peak was just off to the east.

So why was he still here?

Dari shook his head again, not quite comprehending the decision he had made.

That wasn't true.

He did understand why he was still here. He was here because he felt some kind of responsibility to the people with him.

They were his friends. Until they were ready to attempt the journey to the south and into the Highlands, then he would stay here with them. Come what may.

And, because of his desire to ensure that his friends remained alive, he had become a criminal.

Dari didn't want this. Not any of it. He wanted to go back to the life he had before the slavers came.

However, thinking that way was useless.

None of them could go back to their farms. If they did, they'd probably end up back in the hands of the slavers.

Right now their primary concern needed to be their own survival. They could hunt, and they were. But better weapons certainly would increase their chances of success. Coin would help them acquire some other needed supplies as well.

So waylaying a few travelers with whom they crossed paths was a necessity for the time being, no matter how much they might dislike the act.

"Are we doing this?" Elias, recognizing Dari's far-off expression, realized that his friend was distracted once again.

A fairly common occurrence for Dari these days. It didn't bother Elias. As their appointed leader, Dari had a lot on his mind. He needed to think.

"Only four?" Dari returned his focus to Elias, locking eyes with him until his friend nodded. "Yes, we're doing this. We have to do this. How else are we going to survive if we don't?"

"Dari!"

Annisa called to him. She stood in the center of the barricade, a pitchfork in hand. To make the weapon more manageable, she had sawed off three feet from the handle.

She hadn't had to use the weapon yet. She didn't really want to.

She adopted a vicious expression, nevertheless, as did all the other farmers standing with her. She wanted the travelers coming down the trail to think that she would use the weapon if they forced her to.

When Dari turned toward her, she nodded down the path.

In an instant, Dari's nerves became more frazzled. He could feel the sweat dripping down his back. For a moment, he couldn't breathe, and he had the almost uncontrollable urge to race into the trees and empty his bowels.

He began to feel better when he saw who was coming his way.

Just the woman and one man.

Elias was right. She was well dressed. She did look like a merchant. She might even be of noble birth, although he had no way of knowing.

Dari's eyes widened when he studied the fellow walking by her side. His hair was almost completely white despite his youthful appearance. And those grey eyes. Harder than the black stone of Shadow's Peak.

He sensed immediately that both the man and the woman were dangerous. He was certain as well that they weren't just travelers, and not just because of that wicked looking double-bladed spear that the man carried.

Still, it was too late to step back from what had already begun.

"You can stop right there," Dari called out. His friends spread out along the barricade, although none yet moved around the flanks to encircle the two travelers. They, too, sensed the coiled violence that radiated from the pair.

"Right here?" the man asked in a quiet voice that carried a hint of menace. He and the woman halted just a few yards from the pile of roughly cut logs.

The woman smiled brightly, seemingly trying to put Dari at ease. However, the man ...

"Yes, right there." Dari stared at the man, those eyes of his making it feel like a spike of ice shot down his spine. He had no doubt that the looming fellow knew how to use that weapon of his to deadly effect. Even more frightening, he didn't seem to be too worried about what he had walked into or the number of adversaries he faced. And that worried Dari. "Are you trying to be funny?"

"I'm just trying to do what you want," the man replied calmly. "I'd prefer that no one got hurt. I'd like to avoid any mistakes on both our parts if possible."

Dari didn't know how to respond to that statement. Primarily because the tall fellow was calm as could be despite so many people brandishing weapons just a few feet in front of him.

It made him think that the man standing before him was more worried about Dari and his friends rather than himself and the woman with him.

Dari realized then that he had made a mistake. He should have listened to his gut. Trying to rob these two was a bad idea.

Still, there was nothing to do but go forward with the plan. Better just to be done with all this as quickly as possible.

Having reached that conclusion despite his misgivings, Dari nodded to his friends. Elias and several others trotted out from behind the barricade and surrounded the man and the woman, neither of whom made any effort to stop them.

"Where are the others?" Dari asked.

"What others?" the man replied.

"I was told that there were a few more with you."

"No, just the two us," the woman answered amiably.

The man leaned on that dastardly spear of his, giving Dari a predatory smile.

Dari gulped. Not able to hold the man's gaze, Dari turned and looked hard at Elias, who stood behind the man and the woman. "You said four."

Elias shrugged. "I could have been wrong. I didn't get very close. Like I told you, I didn't want to give myself away."

"You were supposed to get an accurate count!"

"I'm not a soldier, Dari. I'm a farmer!"

"No names, Elias! We talked about this!"

"You just used my name, Dari!" Elias threw his arms into the air. "I did the best that I could, all right. No one else was willing to go with me, and I was scared. I saw what I saw and then I came back. I can't help it if I didn't get close enough to get a good count."

"Gentlemen," the woman said softly, though in a commanding voice that grabbed the attention of everyone standing on the trail, her interruption silencing both Dari and Elias. "Do you mind if we get on with this?"

"Yes, of course," Dari finally said after he knocked himself out of the shock that had settled within him for just a moment.

Before turning his gaze back to the woman and the man, he gave Elias an angry look. His friend ignored him, offering a frown in return.

"Surrender your weapons and the supplies that you're carrying," the leader of the ragtag band ordered. "Also, what ever golds and silvers you can spare. We'll leave you with enough coin so that you'll still be able to make your way when you get to Shadow's Reach."

"That's very kind of you," the woman replied with a broad smile.

"We need what you can give us so that we can survive in the wild. That's true. Even so, we're not trying to rob you blind." Dari nodded to the woman. He almost offered her a small bow because of the confidence and command with which she presented herself.

Dari was beginning to think that this might work out exactly as he wanted. An easy score with no bloodshed.

He and his friends go on their way. These two travelers go on theirs. Nothing more happening than a one-sided exchange.

"I don't think so."

That response from the dangerous looking young man shot a bolt of fear straight through Dari's heart. "You don't think we'll let you go if you do as I say?"

"No, we believe you," the man said with a smile that never reached his eyes. "You're not thieves or murderers. Or at least if you are, you don't have much experience with either profession. That much is clear. What I meant is that we're not going to do what you want us to do."

"Why not?" Dari demanded, not understanding how he had lost control of this situation so swiftly.

"Because you've got a bigger problem than just us." The man nodded, suggesting that Dari look behind his back.

The farmer didn't want to do as the cold-eyed fellow urged, because he feared that he knew already what he was going to see.

But he knew as well that he couldn't avoid it forever. So he turned slowly, reluctantly.

"This isn't good," Dari mumbled to himself.

More than a dozen men and women emerged from the trees at the same time, encircling Dari and all of his friends. Clearly, they were the very kind of people who he was trying to avoid at all costs.

They weren't farmers.

They were soldiers.

Seeing the man's wild-eyed expression, the woman focused her attention on Dari and spoke in a soothing tone. "I would suggest that if you want to avoid bloodshed, your blood being shed more specifically, that you and your friends drop your weapons. If you do, I promise you that no one will be hurt."

"Are you slavers?" whispered Dari, although what he asked was clearly heard by all on the trail because it had gone so quiet so quickly.

"No, we are not slavers," the woman replied, a touch of indignation in her voice. "We seek only to speak with you and then we will be on our way."

Dari gulped, mimicking the action of several of his friends. They still held their weapons, their eyes locked on the hard-eyed soldiers who had yet to reach for theirs. In his opinion, that was both a good and bad sign.

Good because maybe they really didn't want to kill or enslave him and his friends. Bad because they were confident enough in their skills to believe that they could get their weapons free before Dari and his friends placed them in any real peril.

"Why should we trust you?"

"I, Aislinn Winborne, give you my word as the Lady of the Southern Marches. No harm will come to you if you drop your weapons."

Dari stared at the young woman who demonstrated an admirable assurance. He didn't really know who the Lady of the Southern Marches was, although he was certain that the Southern Marches was on the far eastern coast of Caledonia.

Even so, she seemed trustworthy. Besides, he didn't have much choice. The story of his life these days.

Dari nodded then and released his pitted and rusted sword. His decision made it easy for his friends, all of whom dropped their weapons as well.

"Good decision," Benin grumbled, the Sergeant standing at the back of the small group and having no desire to harm anyone.

With a nod, his soldiers stepped forward, herding the farmers together and then up against the barricade. They didn't bother to tie the farmers' hands or restrain them in any way. However, they did ensure that none of them carried concealed weapons.

"I admire your restraint, Benin."

"It's necessary, Protector," Benin replied. "These people aren't doing this because they want to. They're doing it because they need to."

For a few seconds more, Bryen studied their opposition, now huddled together.

Benin was correct. They were poor, bedraggled, obviously desperate.

"Dari, please come here," Aislinn said.

The farmer hesitated, fearing that he was about to be made into the example of what would happen if any of his friends failed to heed the commands of their captors. Yet instead of being dragged from the group as he expected, two of the soldiers stepped out of the way so that he could walk past and approach the Lady Winborne.

"I'm sorry, my Lady," Dari stammered. "Truly, we're all sorry. We don't want to be doing this. Truly. And we wouldn't have hurt you. I promise you that. Truly, my lady, I ..."

"Dari, please take a breath," Aislinn said, fearing that the terrified farmer was going to hyperventilate, "and maybe focus on me rather than the scary looking fellow standing next to me."

Dari hadn't been able to take his eyes off the intimidating man. His weapon, the blades on both end razor sharp, was frightening enough. One swipe from that spear and Dari would lose his head.

However, it was the hard, cold eyes that he feared the most. Even worse was the scar on his cheek and neck.

Dari guessed that it had been made by a claw, but from what kind of animal he didn't know. In fact, he didn't really want to know, because he couldn't understand how the man standing before him was still standing after a swipe like that.

Yet what was most intriguing with respect to that horrendous scar was the very thin streak of black that ran through it. A burn that never healed, maybe?

"Dari, focus on me please."

Dari nodded, finally turning his attention back toward Aislinn when the man gave him a nod and a wink.

"Where are you from, Dari?"

"Sharston, my Lady. Born and raised."

"You were a farmer in Sharston?"

"I was, my Lady. That's all my family before me knew."

"Then why did you decide to come to the Northern Territory if you were a farmer in Sharston?" Aislinn wondered.

"I didn't have a choice, my Lady."

"How so?"

"I lost my farm," Dari replied sadly, the pain in his voice obvious. "It had been in my family going back eight generations. Then one day, just out of the blue, it was taken from me and there was nothing that I could do to prevent it."

"What happened, Dari?"

"The Duke of Sharston increased the taxes. We sought to appeal to his better nature, but he wouldn't see us. We sent him a petition, telling him that we couldn't pay the taxes and continue to run our farms."

"I take it he didn't respond?" Aislinn asked in the form of a statement, not surprised.

She had met the Duke of Sharston once. He exemplified those rulers who she detested. Only out for themselves, more than willing to ignore their responsibilities toward the people who relied upon them so long as they got what they wanted.

"I and most everyone else living near me couldn't afford the taxes. We gave what we could, but it wasn't all that was demanded of us." Dari shrugged, a tear forming in his eye. "We did all we could, Lady Winborne. Truly we did. And we sent another petition, explaining our circumstances and how we were trying to meet his demand, but still the Duke of Sharston ignored us. It wasn't long after that when the Duke sent soldiers to claim the land as his own."

"That must have been terrible, Dari," Aislinn said softly, her compassion helping to put the farmer more at ease.

"It was, Lady Winborne, it was," Dari confirmed. "I was kicked off my own land even though it had been in my family for eight generations. Eight generations! So were all the other farmers near me. We lost everything. All in a single day."

"It was Talus Sharperson who took your farms?" asked Bryen.

Dari nodded. "He did, Lord ...?"

"Bryen," the scary looking soldier answered.

"He did, Lord Bryen."

"Just Bryen, Dari. I'm not a lord and have no desire to be one."

Dari smiled at that, nodding his appreciation. Maybe this scary fellow wasn't so bad after all. "Me neither. Just a waste of space." His eyes widened when he realized what he had just said. "Present company excluded, of course, Lady Winborne."

"You have nothing to fear from me, Dari," Aislinn replied, hoping to assuage the terror that had formed once again in the back of his eyes.

"I'm even more glad now that I killed him," Bryen said, nodding his head in satisfaction and giving the farmer a wink.

Dari examined the imposing man again, the one who so obviously looked like a lord but had no desire to be called a lord. He then glanced down, still finding it difficult to keep his eyes on the fellow whose expression shifted from cold to frigid then back to cold, with nothing in between.

"You killed that bast ... I mean, you killed Talus Sharperson?"

"I did, Dari. I took his head in the Colosseum."

That brought a broad grin to Dari's sad face, finally finding the courage to look Bryen in the eye. The Colosseum. Now that made sense.

Maybe this man was one of the gladiators he had heard of who had played a role in overthrowing the Belerons.

"Thank you, Lord ..." Dari nodded and bowed slightly to hide his embarrassment. "Thank you, Bryen. He deserved it."

"You're welcome. And you're right. He did."

"And that's why you came here, Dari?" asked Aislinn.

Dari nodded. "We all did. We're all from Sharston." He motioned to the group of farmers standing behind them who were all quite terrified.

"How did you afford the passage?"

"Indentured servitude," Benin explained.

The Sergeant stood not too far away from the farmer, listening. He had heard this story much too often since he had arrived in the Northern Peaks in search of the Blademaster.

"Yes," Dari confirmed. "Seven years of work with passage paid."

"And after seven years?" asked Aislinn.

"Then we own the land that we work. And during those seven years, once we paid what we owed to Governor Winborne, we could keep what we had left for our own use and sell whatever we didn't need."

"It was going well for you?" asked Aislinn.

"It was," Dari nodded. "It was a fair deal. Until just recently."

"What happened?"

"Slavers."

"A much too frequent occurrence," Benin interjected. "I hadn't realized that they were working in the Northern Peaks until just recently."

Dari nodded. "They weren't until just recently, you're right. The Highlanders have learned how to defend themselves, so the slavers have come looking for easy pickings here now that Governor Winborne has opened several mines and there are few willing to work them."

"Why not?" asked Aislinn.

"The work is too dangerous, and the pay is a pitiful sum. Most of what little is earned goes toward food and lodging near the mine."

"Governor Winborne had to rely on other means to find his

workers," Benin explained. "Since those workers were reluctant to begin with, he adopted the approach that many have said Governor Sharperson has employed in the Highlands, although with a much more limited effect now that the Lord Kestrel is haunting those peaks."

"So these slavers picked you, Dari?"

"They did, my Lady. They came for all of us on market day at our small village not too far away from here. They said the terms of our indenture had changed."

"But you got away."

"We did, Lord Br ..." Dari caught himself just in time. "We did, Bryen." He said it with a not undeserved satisfaction regarding his escape.

"How did you succeed in doing that? From what I've heard, evading the slavers is a difficult task."

"The slavers came out of the wood and surrounded the village when the market was in full swing on the green. They herded us all into a pen where we keep the draft horses. They were getting these long chains and manacles ready for us because none of us wanted to go."

"You fought your way free?" Benin was having a hard time figuring out how this lot of farmers stood any chance whatsoever against slavers who likely were or had been soldiers at one time.

"We didn't, no. We're not soldiers."

"Then what happened, Dari?" Aislinn asked.

"The Murk," Dari replied, his voice cracking when he said it, the terror of that moment still with him.

"It must have come in fast," prodded Benin.

"It did," Dari confirmed. "Faster than we'd ever seen before. Like it was coming for us." Dari shrugged. "I guess you could say we got lucky. The slavers stopped what they were doing. The mist wasn't even very thick yet, but even then at the very edge we could see these tall shapes lurking within."

"The Wraiths," murmured Benin.

"Yes, the Wraiths," Dari confirmed, proud of himself for being able to name those monsters without his voice cracking. "The slavers ran. We ran."

"The difference being that you had somewhere to run to," suggested Bryen.

"We did, Bryen," Dari said with a sad smile. "Almost all of us made it. The slavers ran in the wrong direction. We found their bodies afterward."

"How did you and your friends escape?"

"We were on Elias' farm on the other side of the pen and a good distance away from the Murk that had yet to settle all around us, Lady Winborne. He took us to a crevice in the cliff behind his farmhouse." He shrugged as if there really was nothing to it. "We slipped in there before the Murk blanketed the dale, and he had a makeshift steel door that slid down. We locked it in place. The Wraiths probably could have broken through if they really wanted to, but I think they got their fill of slaughter with the slavers."

"Very clever on Elias' part," nodded Benin.

"It was," Dari agreed. "If not for him, we'd be dead. When the Murk cleared, we came out from the crevice. We saw the slavers. Or at least what was left of them."

"But you couldn't go back to your farms?" asked Aislinn. "Even with the slavers gone?"

"No, my Lady."

"Why not?"

"You said you were the Lady of the Southern Marches, my Lady?"

"I did."

"You truly are a Winborne, my Lady?"

"I am, Dari. I spoke the truth."

"You can tell us, Dari," Bryen said. "We won't harm you. If we were going to, we already would have." Bryen nodded over his shoulder, Dari watching as the soldiers who were suppos-edly guarding his friends actually shared bread and rations with them, having seen how thin they were. "The Lady Winborne is not like her uncle."

His words brought Dari's surprised gaze back to the scarred fighter. Staring at his grim visage truly was frightening, but Dari could sense within him an honor that he had learned much to his disgust was all too often lacking in those who were supposed to use their power for the betterment and protection of those in need.

"Why not plead your case to Governor Winborne?" asked Aislinn. "He is supposed to aid you rather than make your life more difficult."

"The men who seized us were his men, Lady Winborne," Dari replied, taking Bryen at his word that he had nothing to fear. "They weren't dressed like the Northern Guard, but we had seen several of them before. They had accompanied the tax collectors. We had little doubt as to who sent them."

"You haven't tried to go back to your farms because you fear another group of slavers will come for you?"

"That's correct, Lady Winborne."

Bryen and Aislinn shared a look. They were both thinking the same thing.

"I believe we need a few squads of the Blood Company here," Bryen said. "I'll reach out to Declan."

"They can supplement the Blademaster's efforts," Aislinn agreed. She then turned her attention back to Dari. "From what I can tell, your foray into thievery as a way to survive isn't going well for you or your compatriots."

"It is not, Lady Winborne. As I said, we're farmers. That's all we know. That's all we want to be."

"And if we can give you a place safe from the slavers, Stalk-ers, and Wraiths, would you be interested?"

"We would," Dari confirmed, his eyes brightening with a spark of excitement.

"Then let's talk a little longer, Dari, because I believe my friends and I might be able to help you."

11

DEFENDING THE BROCH

"What do you say, Duff?"

"What do I say to what, Tommie?"

The bald Highlander, the thin, white scar wrapping around his scalp, stood atop the broch. The petite archer, her bow almost as tall as she was, stood next to him.

Neither bothered to look at one another. They stared out at the forest to the west instead.

"To my proposal, Duff," Tommie continued. "What do you say?"

She smiled knowingly. His fingers were tapping the hilt of the overlarge blacksmith's hammer he favored. He was nervous and trying to hide it.

She didn't know why he was hesitating. Neither of them were getting any younger. She wanted to start making plans that didn't always involve traipsing through the Highlands in search of monsters and men to kill.

Although on this gloomy morning, the sun having just risen over the peaks at her back, visible only because the dense clouds had taken on a dim reddish hue, it seemed that she wouldn't have to hunt the monsters plaguing her home. Rather, those monsters were hunting her.

Her smile widened just a bit. Duff was looking at her now. Just a brief glance. Thinking.

Good. Now he just needed to confirm what she knew he had decided already.

Tommie kept her eyes on the trees so that he could study her for a few seconds more. Then he shifted his focus back toward the wood ringing the tower.

Duff had to give Tommie her due. He admired her persistence, even though it frightened him on occasion.

When Tommie knew what she wanted, she went after it.

And for some strange reason that Duff didn't quite understand, she wanted him.

She already knew his answer. She just wanted to hear him say it.

He could understand that desire, and he was ready to tell her.

Just not at that moment. Rather at a time better suited for the purpose.

Because at that moment, their attention needed to be directed toward the clash that was about to start.

Duff snorted softly in amusement. Tommie was wearing her spectacles now.

It wouldn't be long before she placed them in the leather pouch that hung from her neck rather than keep them perched on the end of her nose. She was better with her bow when she relied on instinct.

Duff didn't really understand it. In fact, he had given up trying to understand it.

The only thing that mattered to him was that she never missed.

"What proposal, Tommie?" he asked distractedly, a slight

curl twisting his lips. He was enjoying the game that they were playing. A game with which they were both quite familiar.

There. The first hint of movement along the edge of the wood.

Nothing more than a slight shift in the shadows.

The beasts had arrived. Waiting at the fringe. Not yet ready to reveal themselves.

And right on time according to his scouts' calculations.

While Jakob had gone off with most of the Highlanders to hunt for the slavers he had identified, Duff and a handful of squads had finished building and then mounting the main door to the broch. That critical task had been delayed when they all stopped what they were doing to help Declan and the Blood Legion.

Just in time too.

As he surveyed what was about to become a battlefield, Duff was glad that he had put most of the Highlanders with him to work clearing the last of the trees so that they had a rough green with a circumference of several hundred yards centered around the tower. Or rather it would be once the grass started to grow.

That last part wasn't important, however. The open field and the excellent sightlines were.

The cleared space ensured that the Highlanders had a killing ground to their front in every direction. Moreover, it prevented the Stalkers hiding in the wood from sneaking any closer to the broch before being discovered.

Duff grinned. A vicious look. More shadows gathered at the edge of the wood. He knew what that meant.

Just then the Stalkers chose to reveal themselves.

The towering beasts, their charcoal-colored skin resembling melted wax, as if their flesh had been held up to a flame when these creatures had come to be, stepped free from the gloom. They stared hungrily at the tower and the men and women standing atop it.

Duff grumbled under his breath. Four fists of the monsters. Maybe even a few more still lurking in the wood, not yet showing themselves.

He had never seen so many of these beasts together at one time. Just one fist at most. And even that had been rare.

When these Stalkers had first started hunting in the Highlands, they had been solitary killers. That had changed in just the last few months.

If his memory served, these monsters began to coordinate their attacks when Jakob Kestrel became the Lord of the Highlands.

Curious?

Not really.

Not based on the theory that he and Jakob were working under.

But this many? And all of them willing to attack a strong fortification?

That suggested that their theory was more than just a theory. That the monsters' purpose was exactly as they suspected.

A frightening thought. Also one that couldn't be ignored. Because he agreed with Jakob that they could put this new knowledge to use.

Not just against the Stalkers, but also against the one commanding them.

Of course, that all depended on whether he and his Highlanders survived this fight and whatever other challenges Jakob might be dealing with that morning deeper within the mountains.

"About us rooming together," Tommie replied amiably. Completely unaffected by the monsters below.

She gave him a nudge on his shoulder that failed to move

him. He was positioned there like a rock, projecting a calm that the Highlanders standing atop the broch with him appreciated.

Duff only had twenty fighters. A one-to-one ratio was not good odds when facing Stalkers.

He couldn't allow that obvious fact to affect his bearing in any way. Confidence in battle, whether the odds favored you or your opponent, was essential to surviving that battle.

He had learned that from both Declan and the Blademaster. The only way to keep his soldiers calm and focused was for him to come across as calm and focused, even if he was anything but.

"I know you didn't forget," Tommie continued, "because you know what I'd do to you if you did."

Even as his guts squirmed just a touch because of the topic that Tommie refused to let go, Duff couldn't stop himself from smiling. Tommie had that effect on him, even when she was threatening to stab him.

"You mean living together," he corrected.

"Rooming together. Living together. Is there really much of a difference, Duff? The arrangements between us would be the same. We're practically living together now as it is."

Tommie understood that this was a difficult topic for Duff, so she was trying to approach it delicately. Perhaps even give him a different perspective than the one that had been dominating his thoughts since she first proposed the idea to him.

The Highlander was a devil with that hammer of his, taking on any man or monster without fear. When it came to matters of the heart, however, not so much.

"There's quite a difference between the two," Duff challenged, his eyes never leaving the Stalkers that still stood, unmoving, at the edge of the wood. "One suggests that we're just friends. The other suggests that we're more than friends."

"Aren't we already more than friends?" Tommie asked in a suggestive tone.

Not knowing how to answer, he hoped that the Stalkers would choose that very moment to begin their attack.

Beneath his breath, he cursed in disappointment. The monsters remained in place, standing still as statues.

"Well, I guess that depends on ..."

"Duff," Tommie's voice was sharp, just like the tip of the arrow that she had nocked to her bow. Before she did that, she removed her glasses and placed them carefully in her pouch. "Will I need to use this against you rather than the Stalkers?"

"No, of course not," Duff protested, his face turning a bright red that affected most of his head, which only made his white scar stand out even more. When he heard the quiet laughter coming from behind him, he flushed a deeper scarlet. He assumed that he resembled an overripe tomato, because Bertie and Martin obviously were enjoying his discomfort. "It's just that ..."

"Is there anyone else you want other than me, Duff?" Tommie already knew the answer. Otherwise, she wouldn't have asked the question.

"No, you know that, Tommie. It's just that ..."

"They're coming!"

Duff closed his eyes for just a few heartbeats and breathed a sigh of relief, silently thanking Martin for the interruption. "Tommie, we'll talk more when this is over."

"That we will," Tommie agreed. Although she refused to let him slip away easily. "We're going to need to decide where in the Highlands we want to settle specifically. That's what we'll be talking about next, Duff. Just so we're clear. Just so you understand where things stand between us."

Tommie pulled back on her bow as the streaks of black raced across the open ground toward the tower. Deciding on her first target.

He realized that now wasn't the time to contradict her.

"Lasses and lads, it looks like we have a fight on our hands,"

Duff called out in a loud voice that traveled across the top of the broch to every ear.

"No different than any other," replied Bertie with a shrug.

"You've got that right, my friend. Let's see how long we can keep these beasties off us."

If necessary, the Highlanders atop the broch could slip back through the trapdoor. However that tactic didn't appeal to Duff.

Such a maneuver suggested defeat, and it put them all at greater risk.

The main door was fortified just as it should be, because that was the most obvious avenue of attack. They had taken on that project first. He doubted that the Stalkers were going to break through that foot-thick piece of oak that they had wrapped in steel bands.

And even if they somehow did, the Stalkers would have to fight their way through the narrowing entrance that allowed a single Highlander to hold the passageway at the far end while spears and lances shot through the murder slits carved into the walls.

The broch's only real weakness was where Duff stood now. They hadn't had time to finish building the trap door in the roof, which when completed would resemble the one fixed into the stone at the front entrance.

When the Stalkers gained the top of the broch – and with this number of beasts racing toward them that was more than just likely -- they stood a good chance of forcing their way into the tower.

Duff and the Highlanders with him needed to prevent that at all costs, because if they didn't, it put the families hiding within in grave danger.

"Archers to the wall!" Duff roared.

The monstrous beasts were halfway across the space that would eventually become the town green. Thanks to their frightening speed, the Stalkers appeared to be no more than blurs at times, although a few of their features were still visible.

Their razor-sharp claws unmistakable and perfect for climbing stone. And those blood-red eyes that never failed to send a chill down his spine.

"Tommie has command!"

Tommie smiled at that as she stepped to the parapet. Ten Highlanders moved with her, bows drawn, arrows nocked.

"Focus on those closest to the tower!" she ordered. The archers with her adjusted their aim down toward the ground beneath the broch. "Release!"

The steel-tipped shafts shot from the Highlanders' long bows. All of the archers had experience shooting at these dangerously fast beasts, and they put it to use with a calm resolve.

All of the arrows found flesh. One of the Stalkers collapsed to the ground, pierced by three of the bolts, the shaft through its eye the one that killed it.

Unfortunately, none of the other strikes slowed the monsters. One of the Stalkers stumbled, pierced through the thigh. The beast simply reached down with its monstrous claw and snapped the wood, pulling the shaft through and throwing it to the ground.

The other Stalkers just kept coming, not slowing, ignoring their wounds, several of the creatures simply snapping the shafts in half so that the arrows wouldn't impede their efforts, maintaining their pace, intent on their prey.

"Nock!" Tommie commanded.

The Highlanders atop the tower did as she commanded.

"Draw!"

"Release!"

Tommie would continue the coordinated attack for as long as she could. Maybe one more flight of arrows, Duff guessed, before the Stalkers dug their claws into the stone and began to climb.

Then the spears and swords waiting behind the archers would come into play.

Duff was ready. He was confident. He gripped the haft of his hammer gently, enjoying the weight of his weapon in his hands.

Despite the numbers, he believed that he and the Highlanders with him stood a good chance against these Stalkers. Three more of the beasts were down now, writhing in the grass, peppered with shafts.

If Tommie and her archers could take a few more out of the fight, even for just a few minutes, and the Highlanders kept to the tactics that had proven successful in the past, then they could hold their own against their attackers.

Duff's heart dropped into his stomach. Three more fists of Stalkers appeared at the edge of the wood, not just the one that he had anticipated.

The Stalkers at the border of the green didn't wait, sprinting toward the tower, eager to join the fight.

Duff's eyes hardened as he let loose a stream of curses. Their chances of surviving this encounter had just dropped dramatically.

Without the trapdoor atop the broch, it was only a matter of time.

They were trapped.

And they were on their own.

"Saraa, have everyone stop at the edge of the wood. We don't want to give ourselves away before time."

Saraa, who had been running just in front of Jakob, nodded. She sprinted off without saying a word.

She was angry with him for spending so much time with Lycia. For not heeding the many warnings that she had given him. So much so that her displeasure was almost palpable.

Jakob ignored it. He had more important matters to deal with that morning.

He and the several squads of Marchers with him had been running through the Highlands for much of the night. In that time, they had covered almost six leagues.

You could never get to where you wanted to go in the Highlands as the crow flies. There were always inclines, declines, and curling paths that they needed to navigate, and that had increased the distance and the time that it had taken them to reach the broch.

He had been using the Talent to search among the heart trees to ensure there weren't any Stalkers hiding from them. Waiting to strike when they least expected it.

There hadn't been.

All of the creatures were focused on Duff and the Highlanders atop the tower.

That confirmed, he had watched the battle develop as they approached from the southwest, connecting the Highlanders with him to the Talent as he did when they fought the Wraiths in the Murk so that they could see what he could see. So that they all knew what they were racing toward.

He also relayed his plans in the same way. Simple and effective. Eliminating any possible confusion from the start.

Just the way he liked it.

Just the way it needed to be with them going into battle against so many Stalkers at one time.

"You all right, Lycia?" Jakob asked over his shoulder.

"Why wouldn't I be?" Lycia grouched. She gave his back a brief frown before returning her gaze to the forest floor. She needed to be wary of the thick and curling roots of the heart trees that ran across the ground and had an annoying habit of trying to trip her whenever she wasn't paying close enough attention. "I said I didn't like to run. I didn't say that I couldn't run."

"Noted," Jakob replied with the hint of a smile. "I'll keep that in mind. She can run, but she doesn't like to run. When she does run, she tends to get grumpy."

Jakob heard the snort of laughter from behind him, glad that he had been able to lighten Lycia's mood. Either that or she was preparing to stab him in the back with one of the swords with which she was so competent.

He wasn't quite sure which, because he was still trying to figure out the gladiator. But the puzzle that was Lycia could wait.

Now, less than a quarter mile from the broch, he needed to decide on the tactics that would give him what he wanted.

A chance to reduce the pressure on Duff and the Highlanders atop the broch while not putting so much pressure on the fighters with him that the large number of Stalkers overwhelmed them.

A tricky balance to be sure, yet one that he believed he could attain.

The archers had already had their say. A handful of the Stalkers, all of them resembling pincushions, littered the green. Too few, unfortunately.

Because as soon as the rest of the beasts scaled the tower the nature of the fight changed.

The Stalkers were pressing the Highlanders hard, putting their many advantages into play.

Duff, as expected, was right in the middle of the clash, swinging his hammer with a controlled abandon, the Highlanders with him demonstrating an admirable tenacity.

But the stalemate could last for only so long.

Now there was only one option for preventing a slaughter of the Highlanders.

Clear the top of the tower.

Fast.

Jakob saw that the trapdoor had yet to be put in place. That was the key weakness.

Once the Stalkers forced their way into the broch, the Highlanders were done.

Lycia came up next to Jakob with the trail widening to allow more than one person passage at a time. She gave Jakob a nod. "What are you thinking? By that look of yours, it's risky."

"Why do you think that I'm thinking of something risky?"

"I can tell. I can read you pretty well now," Lycia replied, not bothering to tell him that he reminded her of someone.

"I don't know if that's good or bad," murmured Jakob, glimpsing the bright rays of sunlight beginning to break through the forest canopy, the clouds finally clearing. They were just a hundred yards from the edge of the green. No more than that.

"I don't know either," Lycia admitted with another snort of muted laughter. "I do know that whatever you're thinking, it's probably risky."

Jakob didn't reply, just giving her a grin and a wink instead. Because she was right.

He did have an idea. It might not be a good one, but it was an idea. And what it entailed of them was indeed quite risky.

Of course, he really didn't believe that he had any other choice.

Time was running out. He couldn't expect Duff and the Highlanders with him to last much longer atop the tower.

He nodded to himself a few times as he considered what he was about to do.

Twenty Highlanders to join a fight between just as many Highlanders and an almost equal number of Stalkers.

Not good odds. Not good odds at all.

"It is risky, you're right," Jakob finally admitted. He didn't bother to share how he planned to adapt the plan they already had discussed. He would do that in just a moment. "Give me a second. I need to speak with Duff."

"*We're here,*" Jakob said, reaching out with the Talent to connect with his friend.

"*What are you doing here?*" Duff swung a powerful blow with his hammer that struck a Stalker full force in the chest. He succeeded in knocking the beast back against the tower wall, earning himself a brief respite. Very brief, because the monster was already pushing itself up off the ground. Dazed and, not unexpectedly, scarcely hurt. "*I thought you were going after the slavers?*"

"*We did. We're back here because I thought you could use some help.*"

"*That we could.*" Duff didn't bother to tell him where things stood atop the broch. He knew that Jakob could review the tactical situation with just a glimpse of the Talent and likely already had. "*What did you have in mind?*"

Jakob offered him a very brief synopsis of his plan.

"*Are you mad?*" Duff demanded, forcing back the same Stalker with another bone-crunching swing.

After feeling the full force of Duff's hammer a second time, the Stalker was wary. The beast chose to seek easier prey, reaching for Tommie's back with its razor-sharp claws.

Duff stopped the monster cold, reversing his motion and bringing the head of his hammer down on the monster's right knee.

The sounds that Duff heard, the kneecap shattering and then the Stalker's shriek of pain as it tried to hobble away from him, was music to his ears.

"*On occasion, though not now. At least I don't think so. It's the best chance that we have.*"

"*All right, lad,*" Duff agreed reluctantly. "*If you're willing to take the risk, so am I.*"

JAKOB STEPPED out from the wood, sword still strapped to his back, the daggers he had acquired from one of the Wraiths that had failed to kill him still sheathed.

What he planned to do next didn't require steel. That would come later.

Lycia emerged with him on one side, a sword in each hand, Saraa on the other, her favored steel in one hand and a dagger in the other.

The Highlanders with them followed, forming a wedge with each side anchored against the trees at their backs.

The Stalkers didn't pay them any mind, unaware that they were there. Seeking to slaughter the Highlanders atop the tower.

"We are the Marchers!" Jakob shouted at the top of his lungs to ensure that he was heard above the clash. "We will stand fast! We will stand strong! We will stand free!"

Jakob waited for almost thirty seconds, expecting, hoping, that many of the Stalkers would turn in their direction at his proclamation.

His play didn't work.

None of the monsters did, continuing their assault on the square of Highlanders fighting for their lives one hundred feet above him.

He would need to get the monsters' attention in another way. Jakob was about to amplify his voice with the Talent when he felt a hand on his arm.

"Why don't you try this," Lycia suggested. She handed him a curled horn that she had pulled from her small pack.

"Where did you get this?" Jakob asked. The craftsmanship confirmed that it was old, several centuries at least, and based on the scrapes and dents the horn likely had survived more battles than he and all the Highlanders with him had survived combined.

Yet the finely wrought steel shined brightly, Lycia obviously taking good care of the artifact. It was important to her, and this was the first time that she had shown it to him.

"A gift from my father before he died. I've kept it with me ever since. From the streets of Tintagel to the Colosseum to here."

"I appreciate the gift, Lycia, but are you sure you want me to use this? Perhaps since it's yours you should …"

"Blow the horn, Jakob," Lycia ordered, cutting him off. "I promise you. It will bring the Stalkers to us."

Jakob smiled. "As you command, gladiator."

He turned back toward the tower, impressed by how the Marchers continued to hold, keeping the Stalkers beyond the shield wall set around the open trapdoor.

Lifting the mouthpiece to his lips, the steel gleamed brightly at the touch of the rising sun. He didn't look up when he heard the screech of a kestrel, the massive raptor soaring above the battlefield at exactly that moment.

A sign of things to come perhaps.

On this day and beyond.

Taking a deep breath of air into his lungs, Jakob blew a clear, strong note that blasted off the mountains surrounding the small valley and echoed among the peaks.

Lycia was right.

The fighting atop the broch stopped, the Stalkers disengaging from the Highlanders and staring down at Jakob and his small force standing at the edge of the wood.

Stopping was all well and good, but Jakob wanted more than that. He wanted the Stalkers coming to him.

He was the reason they were here, after all.

Hunting him.

Jakob blew the horn again. The clear note echoed once

more off the encircling mountains and traveled deeper within the Highlands, continuing to reverberate among the snow-capped peaks.

That second blast knocked the Stalkers from their stupor. Jolted into motion, a good number of the monsters scrambled down from the tower, focusing on what they perceived to be easier prey as they sprinted across the cleared field, clawed feet digging into the ground and leaving deep gouges in the dirt and mud.

With shrieks of ravenous hunger they increased their pace, focused now on the reason that they were there in the first place. They had located the source of the magical scent that had been infused within them.

The young man with the horn was the one they needed to kill. That magical scent pulling them toward him, a compulsion that they couldn't ignore.

Jakob's expression hardened, green eyes flashing.

It seemed that his plan might actually work.

Before placing the horn on his belt, he blew one more time. Just because it seemed like the right thing to do.

Three clear, resounding notes.

The symmetry of what he had just done made him think of the writings of an ancient general that Dougal had made him study when they lived in Roo's Nest.

"We hear. We come. We conquer."

Those were the words that the general had used before crossing the Gallish River to battle the barbarian tribes that had never before been defeated.

Until he had brought his Legions to the field.

What was the general's name?

It was on the tip of his tongue, and even though the Stalkers raced toward him, his inability to recall the appellation irritated him.

Kaisari.

That was it. A man who was loved by his soldiers, who was loved by his people, but in the end was betrayed by his friends and colleagues because they viewed him as a threat to their power.

A sad conclusion for a man who sought to bring back glory to a dying empire.

Yet now wasn't the time to allow his thoughts to wander. It was time for Jakob to finish this clash with a lethal finality before it really began.

Reaching for the Talent, he studied the Stalkers sprinting toward him.

Their blood-red eyes burned with delight.

Hungry for the kill.

Hungry for the one they had been sent after.

Jakob knew the truth of it. These Stalkers were here for him. They had followed the scent given to them by their master.

If he had not come, once the beasts had finished here, they would have continued to hunt for him. Following his magical scent until they found him. They had no choice, the power of the Curse too demanding to be ignored.

In one sense, Jakob had made it easier for the Stalkers by coming to them. Reducing the time they would have to wait before they could try to kill him.

In another sense, he had made it much more difficult for the Stalkers. Because he knew what they were about.

He had the beasts right where he wanted them.

He was very, very angry.

And since he couldn't yet go after the one who created them, he could exact his vengeance on these monsters instead.

"Marchers, we make our stand here!" Jakob shouted, the beasts now no more than twenty yards away. "Let the Stalkers come to us! It is on this field that they will understand what it means to feel the wrath of the Highlanders!"

Jakob usually wasn't one for speeches. He tended to avoid them like the plague unless Duff forced him into it.

But his decision to say something, much like his decision to blow the horn three times, just seemed like the right thing to do based on the current circumstances.

With the Stalkers now only ten yards away, Jakob raised his arms until they were parallel to the ground, holding them there for just a heartbeat, before whipping them down to his sides.

The Stalkers didn't have time to scream. To evade. To flee.

They only had time to die.

Bolts of lightning blasting down out of the clear sky.

Ripping apart the ground.

Ripping them apart.

~

"Blasted beast!" Duff roared.

He ducked the Stalker's swipe, then shifted his feet carefully, bringing the haft of his hammer parallel to the stone and catching the Stalker's other claw right before it tore into his skull.

If the blow had connected it would have given him a scar worse than the one that already marred his visage, a result that he preferred to avoid. Assuming he survived the wound to begin with, which was unlikely.

The Stalker strained to push Duff's steel down so that it would have a clear path to stab him in the chest.

Duff fought to keep his hammer in place, but the monster was too strong for him. Adapting quickly to that reality, Duff used the beast's momentum against it.

Dipping his shoulder, Duff allowed the Stalker's claws to slide across the steel.

The Stalker didn't respond to the adjustment fast enough.

Duff's shift in positioning caused the monster to lean out

over the battlements, a hundred-foot drop just inches away as it strove to maintain its balance.

As the Stalker struggled to avoid the call of gravity, Duff pivoted and then kicked backward with a boot. He connected with the Stalker's knee, the joint bending at an unnatural angle.

Duff didn't see the result of his efforts. He did hear the crack and the hiss of pain that followed.

Spinning back around with a remarkable grace for such a large man, Duff advanced toward the Stalker, which was performing a strange dance as it tried to keep its place atop the wall with its one good leg, a clawed foot digging into the rock while the useless appendage dangled out over the parapet and threatened its balance.

The Stalker swung its claws wildly, its shoulders and hips losing their usual fluid movement, the herky-jerky motion reminding Duff of a marionette.

Because of its struggles, the monster had lost interest in Duff as it desperately tried to prevent a back-breaking fall.

Duff hadn't lost interest in the Stalker.

With a short, compact swing, Duff slammed the head of his hammer into the Stalker's one good knee. The sickening crunch could be heard over the other sounds of the battle, the Stalker shrieking in agony as it fell backward off the wall.

Duff would have been pleased by his success if not for the faint scratch that he somehow heard above the sounds of steel and claw meeting behind him. He thought that he had finished the Stalker when it disappeared over the side.

Not so.

Somehow the Stalker grasped the top of the wall with just a few of its daggerlike fingers. And, despite the terrible injuries to its legs, the beast was attempting to swing its other claw up and over its shoulder.

If the Stalker could gain purchase atop the wall with both claws, it could pull itself back over and rejoin the fight.

A valiant effort, Duff admitted reluctantly. A doomed one as well.

Duff looked over the edge, locking eyes with those of the Stalker.

The beast was a horror.

A killing machine.

The Stalker deserved to die.

Yet those eyes.

Those all too human eyes held Duff in place for just a few heartbeats.

But no longer than that.

With a powerful stroke, Duff brought the full force of his hammer down atop the monster's skull.

The squelch of steel smashing bone was loud enough to be heard over the larger battle. The dead Stalker slipped silently from its place along the wall and fell to the ground far below.

Duff stared over the side, transfixed by the body crumpled at the base of the tower.

Strangely he felt a sadness at having to kill the Stalker. He had never experienced that emotion before in a combat such as this.

Maybe it was because of what he glimpsed in the back of the Stalker's eyes.

Not anger.

Not fear.

Rather relief.

It was as if Duff finally had given the Stalker the peace that it so desired.

A strange feeling indeed. Then again, perhaps there was some validity to it as well if his and Jakob's theory about how Stalkers were made was accurate.

Shaking off the feeling of gloom that threatened to consume his thoughts, Duff pulled his eyes away from the edge and back to the top of the broch. He searched for Tommie first.

He sighed with relief. She was out of arrows and her short sword was streaked with blood. Even so, she had survived the fight with no more than a few scratches marring her forearms.

He watched her clean the blade with a rag before sheathing it. Picking up her bow from where it lay near the trapdoor, she walked over to where the physick who had stayed in the tower during the fight had set up an aid station.

Not to gain care for herself, Duff was certain. No, she had gone over there to see how she could help.

That was Tommie's way.

Always looking out for others before she looked after herself.

That was one of the reasons he loved her.

His eyes sharpened and a grin broke his grim expression when that realization struck him.

He loved her, and she knew that he did. She wouldn't have wasted her time on him otherwise.

He had been a fool about their living situation.

He knew what she wanted. He knew what he wanted.

They both wanted the same thing.

Yet he had been difficult just for the sake of being difficult. Just because it was an uncomfortable topic for him to discuss.

Truly he was a fool.

No longer.

Their next conversation would be the one that Tommie had been pushing for. Where they were going to live together.

Although he was thinking that perhaps they should think about doing more than just living together.

That was a musing for a later time, however.

Duff swept his gaze across the top of the broch. Thankfully, despite the Stalkers' overwhelming numbers, only a few Highlanders had been killed.

The loss of any Highlander was a terrible thing, yet he felt good about the results of this battle, because it could have been much, much worse.

A massacre.

And it was.

But not for the Highlanders.

Although if Jakob hadn't arrived when he had that probably would have been the result.

Thanks to the Lord Kestrel's excellent timing instead of Highlanders littering the top of the tower and the killing ground below, it was the Stalkers.

That fact shifted his gaze to the space that his fighters had finished clearing just yesterday. Not a single Highlander had been killed at the base of the broch.

The same couldn't be said for the Stalkers.

Their bodies, strewn about the open space that was pockmarked now by holes that were ten feet wide and just as deep, looked like they were no more than rag dolls after having experienced the tremendous power that the Lord of the Highlands had brought to bear against them.

"You're a crazy one, lad," Duff called down when he saw Jakob walking toward the broch.

The young man looked up at him then. His eyes were sad while his posture and expression were confident.

A good sign, Duff believed.

Because there was still a great deal more killing that would be required for them to free the Highlands from the monsters and the men terrorizing those living within these rugged peaks.

"Yes, but you knew that to begin with."

"I DON'T MIND you using one of the sayings preferred by the Blood Company," Lycia said. She sat atop the broch, munching on a piece of bread, watching the sun set in the mountains to the west. Jakob sat by her side.

It was the first time that day that they had a chance to relax. The dead Highlanders needed to be buried. The wounded Highlanders cared for. The Stalkers burned. And Duff insisted that the trapdoor atop the broch be completed before darkness fell.

"Standing fast and all that," she continued. "It's a good saying. So that makes sense. But why the Marchers? We ran through the night. We didn't march."

"It's what came to mind," Jakob replied with a shrug, staring at the burnt orange and red coloring the clouds as the sun sank in the west. "Besides, Duff has been using it, and it kind of stuck on me."

He smiled when he heard the screech of a kestrel, a quick glance confirming that the raptor was circling high above him.

At first, he had not known what to make of the fact that there always seemed to be one of those large predators flying in the sky above him. Now, it didn't bother him in the least.

Actually, it gave him a sense of comfort, almost as if he were being watched over.

"Did you want me to call us the runners?" he asked. "That doesn't sound right."

"I agree with you about that. But the Marchers?" It was Lycia's turn to shrug. "I just thought you'd be more creative."

"I was caught up in the moment, all right, and I was a little busy," Jakob replied with just a touch of defensiveness. "Nothing else but what Duff has been using came to mind. It just seemed like the right term. Besides, several of the High-landers already view it as a badge of honor."

"All right. But if it sticks, it's your fault."

"I wouldn't have it any other way," Jakob replied. He then reached down, pulled the horn free from where he had slipped it onto his belt right before he attacked the Stalkers with the

Talent, and handed it back to Lycia. "Thank you for allowing me to make use of that. Our strategy wouldn't have worked without it."

"It likely wouldn't have, you're right." Lycia took the horn from him, staring at it wistfully.

His fingers lingered on hers a touch longer than they needed to. She didn't mind.

"What we're doing isn't sustainable. It doesn't give us the victory that we need."

"You mean running around in the Highlands as if it's a pasture filled with gopher holes and trying to whack a gopher on the head when it pops up and then having to move on to the next and the next, never stopping?" asked Lycia. "And by gophers I mean slavers, Wraiths, and Stalkers."

"You're just irritated because you don't like to run."

That comment earned Jakob a punch on the arm, his soft chuckle covering the pain of her knuckle digging into his muscle.

"I told you before. I don't like to run, but I can if I need to."

"I know. I was just teasing." He tried to rub some life back into his arm. "You've given us a good description of what we're dealing with right now." He sighed, trying and failing to release the stress that was building up within him.

Lycia gave Jakob the silence that he wanted for a few minutes more before offering him a thought. "Declan taught me a great deal in the Pit. He also has a great many sayings."

"And one of those sayings applies to our current circumstances?"

"It does," Lycia replied confidently. "If you don't like the game you're playing, then change the game."

Jakob thought about that. Duff was doing an excellent job of ensuring that the brochs were being completed at a rapid pace so that more and more Highlanders would have protection from the perils plaguing them.

The Highlanders also were doing well against the Stalkers. The tactics they had put in place specifically for eliminating those beasts were proving quite successful. Even when there was a larger group of Stalkers moving through the mountains, the brochs were just as effective against them as they were against the Wraiths and the slavers.

The slavers. That enemy immediately brought to mind Governor Sharperson. Those two threats were inextricably tied together. Perhaps there was a way to unravel that knot and make the lives of the Highlanders a touch easier.

"You're telling me to narrow my focus."

"I am," confirmed Lycia. "Focus our full attention on one threat. Once we eliminate that threat, we move on to the next. That way we don't waste time and energy running around the Highlands."

"You just don't like running," Jakob countered, trying to inject some humor into what had become a serious conversation.

"That's beside the point. You know I prefer fighting. Give me a target and point me toward it."

Jakob nodded, agreeing with Lycia's perspective. "That I can do."

12

NIGHTTIME VISITOR

"Always trying to save everyone," murmured Aislinn. She gave Bryen an arched eyebrow and a knowing smile as she said it.

She sat next to him on a log that they had pulled up in front of the small fire they had built. Benin and one squad of soldiers were curled up in their blankets on the other side of the flames. A loose skirmish line made up of the other squad was set at staggered intervals out in the woods to a distance of one hundred yards.

Even though Bryen and Aislinn used the Talent to search around them regularly, ensuring that the small company had little to fear from what might be lurking in the dark, just like the Blademaster, Benin was exceedingly thorough in how he approached his work. The habits he had learned while serving under Jurgen Klines were deeply ingrained and never ignored.

"Only those who deserve saving," Bryen replied softly, not wanting to wake the sleeping soldiers.

Benin had sent a third squad of soldiers with Dari and the other farmers who had been evicted from their steadings toward the northwest and a small dale that was five leagues distant. Apparently, this wasn't the first time that Benin, during his wanderings through the Northern Peaks, had sent people in need to that hidden hollow.

The Blademaster had set several other squads of soldiers to fortifying the entrance to the dale he had discovered before he arrived in Shadow's Reach. The valley was concealed within the peaks of some of the most intimidating mountains of an already rugged range. And, once through and on the far side, the drop-off of several thousand feet was unscalable.

Most important, the dell only could be accessed through a narrow crevice. A natural chokepoint that the Blademaster's soldiers put to good use, helping to ensure that those living there would be protected from roving bands of slavers.

The Wraiths were another matter entirely, and one that the Blademaster had yet to solve. Thankfully, those monsters in the mist had yet to demonstrate any interest in the hidden valley, their attention still focused on Shadow's Reach.

Of course, that wasn't surprising. Why waste your time reaching for the fruit high up in the tree when you can cut the tree down instead?

Aislinn had been impressed though not surprised by the Blademaster's initiative. When Jurgen Klines saw a problem, he addressed it as quickly and efficiently as possible. She had learned that about him right from the start, and she thought it was one of his most admirable qualities.

"I've yet to see you make that distinction yet. In your mind, you seem to think that everyone deserves saving."

"Yes, well, one of my weaknesses," Bryen replied with a noncommittal shrug.

Aislinn smiled, pleased by how uncomfortable she had made him. She hadn't done it intentionally, although she was enjoying her success since it was so difficult for her to do.

His desire to help those in need was one of the reasons she loved him. When she first met Bryen after her father had taken him from the Pit and made him her Protector, she had some difficulty understanding how he could seek to help others first rather than himself after all the blood, pain, and death of his previous existence.

Then, as she had learned more about the gladiators and spent time with them during her forced residency in Tintagel, she had begun to comprehend how Bryen had obtained his perspective on the world. Why he focused more on the needs of others rather than on his own needs and desires.

"You know what's going to happen, don't you?" Aislinn's question was really a statement.

"What would that be?" Bryen asked.

"As soon as those squads from the Blood Company reach the Blademaster's hidden valley and find those farmers, they're going to start training them so that they can do a better job of protecting themselves. Then they're not just going to be farmers. They're going to be fighters as well."

"That's not necessarily a bad thing, is it? They need to be able to defend themselves. Relying on others for that would be a precarious decision."

"You just can't help yourself, can you?"

"What do you mean?"

"You did it in Caledonia," Aislinn said, giving him a gentle nudge with her shoulder. "You're doing it here. It's a pattern with you."

"Doing what?" Bryen asked innocently. He had a sense as to where Aislinn was going with her argument, but he didn't feel the need to help her get there.

"Recruiting for the Blood Company. Before we left, Declan already had begun doing it with the refugees. You're doing it here as well. I agree that having a few squads of gladiators in the Northern Peaks could prove useful, but there's an underlying reason for sending for them, isn't there?"

"I'm not recruiting," Bryen protested, "but you are right.

Having a few squads of the Blood Company here with us to add to the soldiers loyal to the Blademaster likely will prove useful to our larger efforts with respect to your uncle and your aunt."

"Yes, you are," chuckled Aislinn, amused at how meekly he was defending himself, his sparkling eyes revealing the truth even as his words didn't. "And she's not my aunt."

"If she's married to your uncle ..."

"Stop trying to change the topic. I know she's my aunt if my uncle married her. But I won't accept her as my aunt until I've gotten to know her better. Although it's proving hard to keep an open mind about her. My uncle as well after speaking with Dari."

"And what if she doesn't want to get to know you better?"

"Meaning?"

"I know you've already thought about it." Bryen poked at the fire with a stick and earned some sparks for his efforts. "If the stories of her hold on your uncle are true, then she ..."

"Likely won't want me around," Aislinn replied. "She'll view me as a threat."

"Just so."

"I won't argue with you about that, Protector," Aislinn replied, trying to use her authoritative voice and finding it difficult to do while speaking softly so as not to disturb those with them. "We will deal with my uncle's wife when we meet her. Now back to trying to expand the Blood Company into the Blood Legion."

"I am not trying to create a Blood Legion," Bryen replied, a hint of exasperation creeping into his tone. "Although a name like that could prove quite useful as well to our efforts."

"Bryen," cautioned Aislinn.

"Sorry, I was just kidding." Even though he smiled as he said it, he doubted that Aislinn believed him. "I am not trying to create a Blood Legion. Just as Declan and Rafia are doing on the Isle of

Mist, I am just trying to help these folks. Yes, the Blood Company will offer some training because they'll need to learn how to protect themselves. And until they're ready to do that, the squads that Declan sends will take on the slavers if they become a threat."

"What do you mean by taking on the slavers?" Aislinn shook her head, though not in annoyance. She should have assumed that his thoughts would turn in this direction.

"Just like Jakob Kestrel, we might want to teach the slavers that farmers and other people trying to survive in the Northern Peaks are not fair game. That there is a price to pay for their efforts. There's a simple way to do that."

"Something else that I won't argue with you about."

"That doesn't worry you?"

"Why would it worry me?" Aislinn didn't understand his concern.

"If your uncle is involved with the slavers ..."

"If my uncle is involved with the slavers, then he will answer to me," Aislinn stated coldly. "The grant for this Territory was given to my father. My uncle is serving in his place here. As the Lady of the Southern Marches I have the authority to remove him if I deem such an action necessary."

"Authority and capacity are two different things," Bryen replied quietly, though he gave her a lift of his eyebrows.

Aislinn smiled then, realizing that Bryen had maneuvered their conversation in this direction from the very start.

"You want to make sure that if I choose to take that action, I have the capacity to do so."

Bryen nodded. "I read the charter as well." He shrugged again. "I just want to make sure that if you decide that something drastic needs to be done, it can be done without any threat to you."

"Always playing the role of Protector," murmured Aislinn, her eyes flashing brightly, a touch of warmth flowing through her as she gazed at Bryen, the fire in front of them having nothing to do with it.

"It's a role that's grown on me," Bryen replied simply.

"It's grown on me as well," Aislinn admitted. She pushed to the side what she wanted to do next, knowing that this was neither the time nor the place. Instead, she returned to the topic that had started this conversation between them. "Bringing a few squads of gladiators to bolster the Blademaster's soldiers helps to address that concern."

"It does," Bryen replied.

"And in that mind of yours, you're thinking that by bringing a few squads of the Blood Company here to protect Dari and the other people who might be residing in that valley that some of them might want to join the Blood Legion after your gladiators have trained them to fight."

"That thought had crossed my mind."

"Very devious of you."

"Not devious, just practical. As Dari said, most of the people with him are farmers. That's all they know. That's all they want to be. A few might choose to stick with the blade, but I got the feeling that they preferred the hoe, pitchfork, or scythe to the sword or dagger."

"In the hands of a skilled fighter, those three implements can prove to be just as lethal as a blade."

"That thought had crossed my mind as well."

"Was this your plan all along?"

Bryen smiled, giving Aislinn a nudge with his shoulder. "My only plan was to help these people learn how to defend themselves. What happens after that is beyond my control."

Aislinn shook her head in wonder. She thought she knew her Protector. Yet every day she seemed to learn something else about him.

Such as right then his ability to put several pieces into motion that once connected would offer a cohesive strategy for addressing a larger challenge in the future that might or might not become a larger challenge. Truly impressive ... and endearing.

"You know, next time you can tell me what you have in mind," Aislinn said with a broad smile, giving Bryen another nudge with her shoulder, "rather than making me have to figure it all out on my own."

"Yes, but you enjoy puzzles."

This time Aislinn gave him a much harder nudge with her shoulder that almost sent him tumbling from the log, setting them both laughing softly.

"It's no different than what we've done in the past," Bryen replied once he had found his seat again.

"Though on a larger scale," countered Aislinn.

"Likely so, but that's not necessarily a bad thing."

"You mean creating a counterweight to my uncle or any of the other Governors."

"Your words, not mine."

"True words, though."

"True words," Bryen admitted. "Shouldn't there be a counterweight? Based on what we've learned in the short time that we've been in New Caledonia, it seems that a counterweight is necessary. Since there is a lack of oversight from Caledonia, there is little to stop the Governors from doing what they want, such as becoming more than Governors."

"A valid concern." Aislinn knew that most who got a taste of power often wanted to take as large a bite as they possibly could. "Still, what you've already set in motion is risky."

She doubted that her uncle or any of the Governors would look kindly on a free fighting force a thousand or more strong that answered not to them but to the man who led the revolt that toppled a Caledonian dynasty that had existed for three hundred years.

"Risky, yes," Bryen agreed, "and apparently necessary. If the

Governors aren't doing what's required of them, then someone has to help these people."

"And now we're back to where we started," Aislinn said with a gentle chuckle.

"You enjoyed that, didn't you?"

"I did, yes," Aislinn confirmed. "I like the fact that I know how your mind works."

"So you can use that to your advantage going forward?" Bryen gave her a wink when he said it.

"Absolutely," Aislinn confirmed with another soft chuckle. "I understand why you and Declan are building the Blood Company into the Blood Legion. There is a great deal of value in the work despite the risk. But do you think we'll really have need of them?"

"Who can say?"

"But ..." prompted Aislinn.

"But I have a feeling."

"A feeling?"

"Yes, a feeling," Bryen replied. "I know, it's hard to base decisions on feelings. That you prefer hard evidence before moving forward with a particular strategy."

"You're so certain of that?" Aislinn cut in, arching her eyebrow at him.

"I am," Bryen replied confidently.

"You think you know me so well," Aislinn chided.

"I do know you. Just as you know me." He reached up with his hand, his fingers sliding across the silver collar he still wore around his neck. "The Protector's collar told me a great deal. Spending time with you even more."

"All right, Protector. I get the point." Aislinn felt slightly flushed when she gazed into Bryen's eyes. She enjoyed the feeling.

"And I don't disagree with you about the need for hard

evidence to make crucial decisions. In fact, I favor the use of hard evidence. But ..."

"But just like Noorsin Stelekel you don't like not knowing what you don't know," Aislinn finished for him, so you want to be ready for what might happen."

"Exactly so," Bryen confirmed with a nod. "Duchess Stelekel's saying couldn't be more true. Until we connect with the Blademaster and gain his perspective on what's going on in Shadow's Reach and the surrounding environs, we have only what we have learned ourselves to make decisions. And, to be honest, all that we have learned since reaching New Caledonia has been disappointing and troubling. In my opinion, it just seems like the right thing to do. Your uncle and aunt might not be involved in the plays being made by the Governors of Fal Carrach and the Highlands. Then again, they might be. Besides, you said it yourself."

"I'm a threat," Aislinn said softly.

"You're a threat."

Aislinn stared at Bryen for quite a long time. She had reached the same conclusions as he had. And though he hadn't said it, she knew as well what he was doing.

He was trying to help those who couldn't help themselves. That was undeniable.

He was also trying to protect her. Just because they had broken the magic that had bonded them through the Protector's collar didn't mean that he had stopped trying to serve as her Protector.

Another spark of warmth shot through her as she turned the full weight of her gaze on him. This warmth not because of the fire that blazed in front of them.

She worked hard to push what she was feeling to the side, this time finding it to be more of a struggle. Her examination of him wasn't meant to challenge his decision making. Rather, she was trying to figure out if there was anything that Bryen was leaving out since he didn't always share with her everything that he was thinking.

"I agree with your strategy," Aislinn finally said, making it sound as if Bryen had proposed it to her rather than just moving forward with it without first getting her permission. "I willingly admit as well that I believe there's a good deal of substance behind this feeling of yours."

"That there's some game in play here just beneath the surface that we have yet to identify."

"Exactly that," Aislinn confirmed. "With what we've learned from Talia Carlomin and Jakob Kestrel, the efforts by the Governors of the Highlands and Fal Carrach to seize even more power are quite obvious. My uncle as well if Dari is correct that the slavers are being drawn from the Northern Guard, and I have no cause to disbelieve him."

Bryen nodded, mulling what Aislinn said. It really wasn't all that complicated. And, as Declan liked to say, sometimes what it looked like was exactly that.

"As we discussed before, everything seems to be pointing to Shadow's Reach. I get the sense that we might be able to find whatever is lurking beneath the surface there."

"And if we do, having the Blood Legion at our backs wouldn't be a bad thing, now would it? Particularly since the Wraiths likely will continue to be a problem."

"Exactly. I'm glad you thought of that."

Aislinn snorted softly, appreciating Bryen's dry humor. "I would simply ask that we go slow at the start. We don't want to build an army unless we absolutely are certain that we need to."

Bryen nodded in agreement. "Of course. I would argue, however, that we're not building an army. We're just helping people learn how to defend themselves."

"Now you're just playing with words," Aislinn accused.

"I am, you're right. In large part because I don't think we

want your uncle to assume automatically that we're seeking to turn the Blood Company into a force that could challenge his Northern Guard."

"Good point," Aislinn admitted. "Although I do agree with you that you never know when we might need an army, so better to have one than not."

"My thinking as well," Bryen said with a smile that froze on his face. "Do you sense it?"

Aislinn nodded, her eyes narrowing, expression grim. "It's similar to an Echidna."

"That was my thinking as well."

"Behind us," Aislinn murmured. "Just ten yards or so."

"Yes, it got past the guards with little trouble. Benin is not going to be happy."

"He won't be, but you can't fault the pickets. There's no way that you could see it without the Talent."

"You ready?" Bryen asked in a whisper. "It's just five yards behind us now."

"Ready," Aislinn confirmed.

At the same time, Bryen and Aislinn shot up from their seats and spun around. Neither could see anything in the darkness that greeted them other than the gloom of the night. Thanks to their use of the Talent they didn't need to.

Not knowing exactly what they faced, Bryen infused the Spear of the Magii with natural magic so that he was prepared if necessary. Yet with Aislinn there with him, there really was no need.

Aislinn was quite thorough with her attack, a bolt of white-hot energy blasting from her palm and slamming into the invisible assassin.

They both heard a hiss and then a bone-snapping crunch, whatever had sought to kill them quietly in the night smashing against one of the heart trees at their backs.

"What in blazes?" roared Benin. He was up from his

bedroll, intricately braided beard askew, sword in hand. The soldiers who had been sleeping on that side of the fire were on their feet as well, weapons held at the ready.

"An assassin," Bryen explained quietly.

He stepped in front of Aislinn and walked toward the slumped shape just a few yards distant. Aislinn's use of the Talent had ripped free the Curse that had been used to conceal the assailant.

Certain that the assassin was dead because of the smoking wound where its chest had been, Bryen used one of the blades on the end of his spear to shift the body onto its back so that they could all get a good look at what had come for them out of the shadows. Aislinn aided their efforts by crafting a small ball of energy that illuminated the glade in which they had been sleeping.

"There are no more of these nasties waiting for us in the darkness?" asked Benin.

"No, just the one," Bryen confirmed, nodding toward the dead creature.

"It was camouflaged?"

"It was," Bryen replied. "Whoever made this creature concealed it in the Curse. That's why the sentries never saw it."

"Only someone with the Talent could identify it."

Bryen nodded. "And only then because Aislinn and I have faced a situation such as this before. Creatures crafted from the Curse able to use that Curse to hide in plain sight. Otherwise ..." He shrugged, not wanting to go into detail as to what could have happened if they hadn't discovered their hidden attacker.

"What is the bloody thing?" Benin had never seen its like before.

"I don't know," replied Bryen.

"It kind of looks like a Stalker," Benin said, "but a malformed one. As if the maker of these creatures only had so much time to work on this one before sending it off on its way."

"That's a good way to put it, Benin," Aislinn said, kneeling to get a better look. "I think as well that this confirms that the Stalkers are made."

Bryen and Benin both nodded, agreeing with her conclusion. The creature crumpled against the tree trunk was human, or what once had been human. The sightless eyes were a pure black, fangs had replaced his incisors, and his hands were twisted into claws.

Similar to a Stalker, but not a Stalker. Perhaps a Stalker not yet fully transformed.

"It's ingenious, really," Benin murmured. "If one of these nasties wasn't hidden by the Curse, from a distance it would appear to be nothing more than a man."

"The perfect assassin," Bryen agreed.

"Coming for you, Lord Keldragan."

Bryen shook his head. "No, not for me."

"For me," Aislinn said quietly.

When the creature approached out of the darkness, its focus had been on her. Not on Bryen.

"Any thoughts on who might have sent this monster?"

"A few, though nothing that can be substantiated," Bryen replied. "At least not yet."

"Building the Blood Legion might not be such a bad idea," Aislinn murmured when she pushed herself back to her feet.

"It might not," Bryen agreed.

"On to Shadow's Reach?"

"On to Shadow's Reach," Bryen confirmed, "but carefully. Your uncle might not be the man you remember him to be. And we have no idea who his wife could be."

13

OUT IN THE OPEN

"Will they do it?"

"They will."

"When?

"Three days' time," Talia replied, striding down the pier, increasing her pace to match her companion's long strides.

"Can we wait that long? Roosarian will have found out by now that she no longer has a pirate fleet. She might feel the need to take more drastic action and much more quickly than we might expect. She knows just as well as we do that there's only one course she can follow now that she's lost her best weapon for gaining control of the Sea of Mist."

"I had thought of that as well, Davin. Believe me." Talia did her best to contain the frustration that had surged through her ever since her partners had decided to delay. Arguing they required the additional time to prepare. To grow backbones more like.

Revealing all that to Davin would do little to help her. In fact, she wouldn't be surprised if Davin decided to pay her allies a visit, seeking to prod them into action sooner with a few pokes of his spear.

"I can only push so hard," she explained. "It's as simple as that. You know how long it took me to get the other members of the Council to believe what we've been telling them, or rather to finally act on the evidence we were providing them, because I have no doubt that they were of the same mind as we were months ago. They're just afraid. They need to get past that."

Her voice was sharp, unavoidably so. Talia shook her head in annoyance. This time at herself rather than at Davin as was usually the case.

She was taking out her irritation at the other merchants' unwillingness to act swiftly on the gladiator, and that wasn't fair. Even so, she needed a target for her anger, and he was the closest one.

Whether the delay the Council was forcing upon her was because of their indecision or fear or both, she didn't know for certain, although she could guess.

She did know that Davin was correct.

If they were going to have any chance of success, they needed to move faster than Roosarian did.

"Do you trust them?"

Talia thought about his question rather than dismissing it out of hand, because clearly based on Davin's tone he didn't.

"No, not all of them," she admitted after having to think about it longer than she would have preferred. "Most understand what needs to be done if this Territory is to thrive. A few will go as the wind blows. We can trust them to do what they think is best for themselves."

"Such as talking to Roosarian? Perhaps trying to work out a deal for themselves?"

"You think they would do that understanding what the likely consequences of such an arrangement would be?"

"I think that some of them would do exactly as you said. They'll do whatever they believe is best for themselves. And I'm sure there are a few who are just arrogant enough to believe that they could get away with it without getting stomped on by Roosarian like all the others."

Talia stopped then. Davin continued a few yards farther down the main dock that extended out from the Carlomin compound and led to the shipbuilding facilities before he realized that he was on his own.

He turned back around and waited, recognizing that the Huntress was deep in thought.

He left her to it. He took the time that she was using to deliberate to get a better feel for their surroundings.

It was a quiet night, the moon peeking in and out of the clouds that drifted lazily above them. The men and women who had been working beneath the sails at the end of the pier had passed them as they returned to their homes, Master Hari offering a brief greeting.

Hari had been in a good mood. He had just completed the hulls of two more ships that would be joining the Carlomin fleet by the end of the month.

The carpenters and shipwrights would be going to their beds after a good meal. He wished that he was doing the same.

He was tired after his escapades of the last few days. Yes, he had helped to remove the last of the pirates from the New Caledonian coast, but he hadn't gotten a chance to rest.

As soon as they returned to Ballinasloe, he had been put to work, helping Talia make the final arrangements for what could only be described as a coup.

The risks that they were taking didn't bother him. He had some experience with rebellions.

No, what bothered him was that he was mildly agitated. And his agitation wasn't being caused by the woman he was escorting, as was usually the case.

There was some other aspect to the evening that wasn't sitting well with him.

He didn't know what.

That's what was worrying him.

He didn't like not knowing what he didn't know.

Declan had begun to use that saying, picking it up from Aislinn Winborne, who had in turn learned it from the Duchess of Murcia. Now that same saying was worming its way through his own head.

An appropriate one, he thought. Still frustrating, to say the least.

In an attempt to assuage his rising concern, he turned on the dock in a slow circle, taking in everything around him. Looking for anything that might be out of place.

Nothing caught his attention.

No strange noises.

No stealthy movements.

Maybe that's what was getting under his skin. It was too quiet for his tastes.

He heard the water lapping against the posts of the pier. Nothing more than that.

There wasn't a boat to be seen on the water.

The lights of the boardwalk lining the harbor gleamed brightly.

The low rumble coming from those frequenting the taverns, bars, and houses of ill repute created the regular backdrop that was no different than what he was used to on any other night.

Normally, all that would have put him at ease. But it didn't.

It only increased the feeling of nervous anticipation that had settled in the pit of his stomach.

Davin's thoughts returned to the Council. They were afraid. Understandable considering the risk.

But they couldn't wait.

Because Roosarian wouldn't wait.

Davin shifted his attention to the Carlomin compound.

After a thorough perusal, nothing in the direction from which they had come gave him any cause for concern.

He had been at the main gate just minutes ago. Sven had been right where Davin had asked him to be.

The soldiers stationed there had been alert.

He and Talia had nodded to the guards lining the pier at hundred-yard intervals, the men and women keeping their eyes and ears open. Wary, suspicious, and exactly where they were supposed to be.

All seemed safe.

All seemed well.

All seemed ... too quiet.

What was it? What could it possibly be?

He felt as if he were about to walk out onto the white sand for a combat.

The answer hit him like a fist across the jaw.

Roosarian wouldn't wait. She couldn't wait.

"Speak your mind, Davin. You always do anyway."

Talia's words drew Davin out from his dark thoughts, lifting his head up from where he had been staring at the rough timber of the pier.

He knew what it was now. He could sense it.

A threat coming toward them.

But from where?

And what could it be?

He shook his head as if to clear it.

Maybe he was just tired.

Maybe he just should have been in his bed like he wanted to be so that he could recover from his exertions of the last few days.

"You said it yourself, Talia," Davin answered finally, his eyes not focused on her. Rather they were drifting from side to side, looking for anything untoward. "People do what's best for them. You've been leading the fight against the pirates. You wiped them from the Sea of Mist. You've proven incredibly successful, deservedly so, and most of your Council love you for it."

"But some don't," she replied softly.

She listened intently to what he had to say, because he only called her by her name when he was worried. Usually about her. She had learned that about him very quickly.

He had joined her to provide what assistance he could. At the behest of Bryen Keldragan, true, but also because he needed to prove something to himself.

She understood that. Because she was trying to prove something to herself as well.

And in just the few months that he had been with her, he had proven his worth time and time again. Not just in his actions. Also in how he looked at the world.

He saw things that others didn't ... or didn't want to.

"Some don't," Davin confirmed with a nod. "It's only natural, isn't it?"

"Jealousy. Greed. Probably a bit of both."

"Yes. Some of your supposed allies are probably wondering what they could get if they did a deal with Roosarian. I wouldn't be surprised if more than just a few had thoughts of supplanting you."

"That's a harsh way of looking at the world, Davin."

The gladiator nodded, not disagreeing with her. Because she was right. He also believed that it was a realistic way to look at the world.

He shifted his gaze toward the bay on the northern side of the pier. He waited a few seconds before saying anything else.

During that time, he listened.

He watched.

He thought that he heard a disturbance moving through the water. Perhaps even caught a shadow of movement.

There was nothing there now.

Probably.

"You think I could look at the world in any other way?" he asked almost to himself. "A jaundiced eye certainly has proven useful."

"Do you really think some of them would stoop so low?" wondered Talia, still finding the possibility that Davin had raised difficult to accept. Or perhaps she simply didn't want to because that would require speeding up her plans and reassessing several of her supposed allies. "After what we've done for them?"

"After what you've done for them, yes, but a few will believe that all you've done, you've done for yourself. The fact that all you have done has weakened Roosarian only plays to their addled beliefs and their fears. You've put yourself in a position to overthrow Roosarian. Better the devil you know ..."

"Than the devil you don't know," Talia said, completing the age-old saying that Davin had started to offer her.

Talia was about to protest, her natural inclination to not want to believe what Davin was telling her. Instead, the logic in Davin's words looped through her mind.

He was right. She hated having to admit that, but he was right. Again.

A few of the merchants on the Council had wavered throughout their discussions. They only had moved forward because the majority of their peers had dragged them along with them.

Every man and woman on the Council knew Roosarian was a threat because of the power she exercised. To say nothing of the additional power that she could exercise if they gave it to her.

With Talia's success, some of them might view her as a threat as well. Some of them would consider playing Roosarian against her then wait and see who was still standing when the inevitable confrontation occurred.

If they believed that they could profit from it.

And they likely could.

They could try to fill the vacuum that was left over or negotiate a better deal for themselves.

Distasteful. Deceitful.

But as Davin had said, it was only natural.

These men and women survived and thrived because of the deals that they made.

"What would you suggest?" Talia asked, realizing that if she discounted his argument she put at risk all that she and her mother had accomplished since her father's murder.

Davin didn't give her the grin that he usually offered her when she was forced to concede that he was right. The grin that always irritated her. The grin that also always made her smile.

Now, he was all business, having given this some thought.

"Double the guard at the gate and along the docks. Sven is already there with some of his friends, but a couple more squads wouldn't hurt."

"You think Roosarian would be foolish enough to attack our docks? Now?"

"Yes, I do. She has more fighters than we do. If she beats us, then there is no one else who can stand against her. Your Council will disappear, and all your friends will forget you. Or rather your memory, because Roosarian wants you and your mother dead. That's the easiest play for her."

"You already put measures in place without my approval?" demanded Talia.

Finally, Davin gave her the grin that she expected. "Of course, not," he protested. "I just suggested that Sven and a few of his dicing friends might want to conduct their game near the main gate. That's all. It's a good spot ... for a lot of things."

"Davin, you can't ..."

"I know, I'm sorry," he said, raising his hands in apology.

"It's just that I'm worried about you, and I didn't have a chance to talk with you about it since you were in with the Council."

That statement stopped Talia in her tracks, what she had been about to say lost to her. She stared across the space between them, beginning to see Davin for who he was, not for who she thought he was.

He was more than just a gladiator. More than just an incredibly accomplished fighter.

Her eyes widened as the realization struck her.

He was a man. And he was interested in her not because she was the Huntress.

He was interested in her as a woman, even though he had never said as much to her.

Despite the tension of their current situation, Talia's lips curled into a teasing smile. Because she didn't quite know what to do with this new knowledge. "You're worried about me?"

Davin was about to respond. He held back instead. He gave her a look that she found difficult to interpret.

Talia assumed that he was going to offer her a flippant remark. What he said next warmed her heart.

"I am worried about you," he replied in a strangely defeated voice, as if he had been fighting the truth and didn't want to anymore. "Very worried."

"You think Roosarian might try for us directly?" Talia realized that the discomfort she believed that she sensed in his voice was hiding an entirely different emotion.

"She's out of options," Davin replied, thankful that Talia had released him from the trap that he had set for himself. Although he got the feeling that she had only done so for a time. "If you were in her place, what would you do?"

Talia thought about what Davin said. What he had revealed as well.

She was impressed. This was a side of the gladiator that he

rarely revealed. A political acuity and strategic perspective that only came out when he believed it was necessary.

She was also a little frightened. Not because of the threat presented by Roosarian. She could deal with that.

Rather because of the emotion that she glimpsed in Davin's bright eyes.

With a great deal of effort, she pushed those distracting thoughts out of her mind. She needed to concentrate on their most immediate concern.

Davin indeed was right. She was tired of admitting that to herself, but she couldn't avoid it.

That meant that she needed to respond accordingly. She needed to assume that Roosarian would make a direct play against her.

And she wouldn't wait.

Talia was about to issue a series of orders on what she wanted done next when Davin's expression bottled up her words in the back of her throat.

Davin's eyes had changed in just a heartbeat.

They were hard now.

Cold.

Focused.

The Crimson Giant stood before her.

Before she could utter a whisper Davin stabbed with his spear right over her head.

Her eyes widened in shock. Both at what he did and the sound that she heard from behind her.

She pivoted. So fast that she almost slipped off the pier.

The keen point of Davin's spear had punctured a Stalker's eye and continued through the socket into its brain.

With a sharp twist, Davin pulled his steel free, already turning around, spear at the ready, prepared to meet the next threat as she watched the monster collapse to the dock.

She hadn't even known the Stalker was there.

If not for Davin, the monster would have driven its claws right through her back. She would have been dead, and she wouldn't have seen it coming.

A shriek of pain pulled Talia's eyes away from the corpse. On the north side of the pier, another Stalker was climbing out of the water, reaching for the post.

Davin prevented the monster from getting a handhold. Literally.

With one swipe of his spear, he removed the Stalker's claw at the wrist, the monster splashing back into the water.

Davin's quick action pulled Talia free from the shock that threatened to take hold of her. She pulled her sword from the scabbard across her back and reached for one of her daggers with her other hand. At the same time she swept her gaze along the pier, sizing up what was fast becoming a dire situation.

Several more Stalkers were pulling themselves out of the water, the only noise revealing their location the sound of the water dripping down their bodies and splashing onto the pier. Otherwise, if the Stalkers didn't stand near the torches fixed to the posts, they appeared to be nothing more than large shadows in the night.

A few of the guards near where she and Davin stood on the dock already were dead, their bodies floating in the water or crumpled in unnatural poses on the pier.

Those closest to them were luckier. They had seen and heard the brief combat Davin had engaged in, alerting them to the danger they now faced.

The soldiers fought well. Desperate to defend themselves. Their steel swords clattering against the Stalkers' armored flesh and claws.

Despite their tenacity and their skill, it was a losing proposition for most. Only a very few stood any chance at all fighting on their own against a Stalker, and one of those few stood next to her.

"We need to get out of here." Davin held his bloody spear out in front of him as he searched for his next opponent.

"But where?" Talia wondered.

Stalkers were pulling themselves up onto the pier both to the east and west of them. When she glanced toward the main compound, she glimpsed the beginning wisps of flames licking out from the windows of several of the buildings lining the pier.

Their attackers were already in the enclave, and they appeared to be everywhere.

Davin was right, although he had been wrong about the timing. It was happening much sooner than either of them anticipated.

Roosarian was coming for them directly just as Davin said she would. Only Roosarian was using tools that Talia never thought she would see employed openly in Ballinasloe.

But why wouldn't the Governor?

Roosarian had everything to lose if she failed. Therefore, she would do all that she could to ensure that she didn't.

Davin stabbed with his spear, driving the steel through the throat of the Stalker that was pulling itself out of the water and onto the deck right in front of them.

The monster gagged, reaching toward the ragged wound, that motion sending the dying monster back into the water beneath the pier.

"Come on," Davin said, reaching for Talia's arm and pulling her after him. "We need to find a position where we can defend ourselves, and it's not here. It's too open."

Talia nodded, staying right on his heels.

She sliced with her sword as they ran down the pier toward the drydock at the end. Her steel cut across the throat of another Stalker that was just about to gain the pier, the soft gurgle suggesting to her that she had killed the monster.

And again, slicing across the knee of another Stalker before the beast got its clawed feet beneath it. Not an incapacitating wound, but one that would slow down the monster.

Yet despite her success, she knew that it wasn't enough. There were too many shadows pulling themselves up onto the pier.

As their footsteps pounded in her ears, Davin's roar, which was loud enough for everyone in the compound to hear, made her ears ring.

"Rise Carlomin Guard! Stalkers on the piers!"

"It's a good run tonight, lads and lasses," Sven said amiably. "My apologies, but you know how it is. When the luck is with you, you have no choice but to sail with it and see where it takes you."

"Would you just roll the dice, Sven," muttered Ari, the sailor shaking his head in disbelief and irritation. "You can't keep rolling sevens. Your luck will come to an end soon enough."

"We'll see, Ari. We'll see."

Sven complied, kneeling down in the street that ended just in front of the main gate to the Carlomin compound. The dice rattling in his hand, after a quick shake he let fly.

"Seven! Again! How is that possible?" demanded Ari. "That's nine times in a row!"

"Are you questioning my integrity?" The hulking sailor pushed himself to his feet and towered over the much smaller Ari. They were good friends, but even the bonds of friendship were tested when one was making good coin and the other was losing it.

"No, Sven," gulped Ari, trying to step away from him and finding his way blocked by the brick wall at his back.

"Do you think the dice are weighted, Ari?" Sven held the bones right out in front of him. "You're welcome to check if you like. They're the same pair with which you were throwing snake eyes time after time. So it's not the dice, Ari, no matter what you might think."

"No, Sven, that's all right," Ari mumbled. He was beginning to sweat, and his voice cracked as if his balls hadn't dropped yet.

Usually, Ari could push Sven without any repercussions. His friend had changed, however. In just the last few months, in fact, after spending so much time with the Crimson Giant in the practice ring.

It was like Sven was trying to adopt as his own the code of honor that Davin had employed since his time in the Pit. So now, rather than laughing off Ari's jibes, he took very seriously anything that he perceived as an attack on his honor.

Ari sought to calm his agitated friend as fast as he could, because he didn't stand a chance against the sailor who was just as tall and just as broad as the gladiator and several stone heavier. "Just a bad run of luck for me and a good run for you."

Sven stared at Ari for a little while longer, studying him, making the smaller sailor's knees shake. Then he stepped back with that amiable smile of his. Rubbing the dice with his hand, he gave them to Ari.

"Maybe some of my luck will rub off for you. Why don't you have another go."

Ari nodded his thanks and then bent to his task, promising himself that he would watch his tongue for the rest of the night so that he kept himself out of trouble. He was grateful that the gentle giant had returned.

Sven watched Ari's roll from just over his shoulder. He smiled. Sevens.

It seemed that some of his luck had rubbed off on his friend, who was now reaching eagerly for the dice to make another throw while looking back over his shoulder to give Sven a grin and a nod of gratitude.

Sven was about to congratulate Ari on his change in fortune when a quick flash at the back of the alley caught his eye.

He was about to walk down the lane to investigate, reaching for the dagger he kept on his belt as well as the truncheon that always felt so right in his hand, when the smell of smoke stopped him.

Before he could identify the source, several streaks of movement pulled his attention to the square just beyond the main gate.

He didn't know what had caused the shadows farther down the path that led to the main pier. He did know what had caused the shadows just on the other side of the entrance to the Carlomin compound.

Davin was right to have placed him and his friends there tonight.

Just then, Captain Makarin strode up to him. She appeared to be a bit on edge. And he couldn't fault her.

"Sven, what are you doing here? This isn't your usual haunt."

"A request from the Crimson Giant."

"What kind of request, Sven?" Sirena asked, not understanding, her worry increasing because of that.

"He said that he had a bad feeling about tonight. I'm beginning to think that he was right."

"Why do you say that?"

Sven nodded toward the main gate. More flashes of moonlight off steel could be seen on the other side.

When Sirena turned in that direction, her response was immediate. "Sergeant, close the gates and the portcullis!"

The soldiers manning the entrance responded immediately, although not fast enough. Several score black-clad soldiers wearing the colors of the Fal Carrachian Guard rushed out of the darkness, fighting and pushing their way past the first row of defenders.

Sven and the sailors with him didn't hesitate, charging into the clash right on Sirena's heels. Stabbing with their daggers, pounding helmets and heads with their truncheons, they buttressed the strong effort made by the Carlomin Guard, halting the invaders' initially swift advance. Then as more sailors and soldiers rushed into the mix pushing Roosarian's soldiers back.

They barely needed to give any thought to their tactics. All of them had spent time in the practice ring with the Crimson Giant. All of them put what they had learned to immediate and good use.

They eliminated the few soldiers of the vanguard who managed to set foot on Carlomin property. Sending the rest fleeing back into the square.

"Carlomin Guard, shield wall!" Sirena shouted.

Soldiers posted farther along the wall responded to her call, climbing down from their position atop the parapet and forming up behind their comrades to stand against the next push by the Fal Carrachian Guard. Stopping it cold before the advance could gain any traction.

Still, the soldiers loyal to the Carlomins faced a real challenge. They had not been able to close the gate or drop the portcullis, the entrance to the compound the ground for which the two groups of combatants vied.

If the soldiers loyal to Hakea Roosarian gained a foothold there, then the soldiers loyal to Talia Carlomin were doomed.

That couldn't be allowed.

Sirena judged that the Carlomin Guard would hold their position for now, but not for much longer. Not without reinforcements.

Understanding that reality, Sirena turned toward Sven. Her eyes widened in shock when she saw the flames flaring off the roofs behind them. Some of Roosarian's soldiers must have gotten over the wall to set the blazes.

"Sven, go to the barracks. Right now. All companies but for one are to report to the main gate at double time."

"And that one company, Captain?"

"You're in command of that company, Sven."

"Me? You can't be ..."

"No questions, Sven," Sirena said harshly, needing to get into the fight at the gate, the shield wall beginning to bend as it fought to hold its position. More of Roosarian's soldiers had joined the push from the other side with another phalanx racing down the main boulevard to join them.

"Yes, Captain."

"With your company, get everyone in the compound out of the buildings and fighting those fires. That needs to be their priority."

"Yes, Captain."

"Once you've done that, you take your company and you sweep through the compound from here down to the drydock. Clear it of anyone who shouldn't be there."

"Prisoners, Captain?"

"No prisoners, Sven. We don't have time or the resources for that. Kill them all."

"Yes, Captain," Sven replied unfazed, giving Sirena a sharp nod. Agreeing with her assessment, he started to run off to do as she had ordered. His friends went with him. Sirena's call pulled him back for a moment.

"Sven! Be smart! Captain Carlomin is with the Crimson Giant. They're on the dock."

"Stalkers?" he asked, thinking that dark shadow that he had seen just a few minutes before could have been one of those monsters.

"Assume so. Clear the docks. Make sure that Captain Carlomin is safe."

Sven nodded before sprinting off with more than a dozen sailors at his back.

Sirena watched him disappear into the darkness. She wanted to go after Talia herself, but she needed to focus on this larger crisis that unchecked could become a catastrophe.

If the Fal Carrachian Guard made it into the compound in mass, then it wouldn't matter what happened to her friend and employer.

Besides, she assumed that Talia's best chance of surviving this surprise attack was with Davin. The gladiator rarely left her side when she was outside her office, and she trusted completely in Davin's ability.

His commitment as well.

He would give his life for Talia without a second thought if that was required of him.

Almost pitying whatever might attempt to kill Talia Carlomin while the Crimson Giant guarded her, she turned toward the gates. Roosarian's soldiers were trying to push through the shield wall, but they were having a difficult go of it. And now more of her soldiers were beginning to stream toward her from the barracks.

If she was smart and quick, she could gain control of this battle in just a few minutes. And, at the same time, perhaps exact a little revenge of her own.

If she was lucky, she might come across the Captain of the Fal Carrachian Guard, and she could kill that bastard herself.

Grinning viciously, Sirena drew her sword and raced toward the battle at the main gate.

"She's going to pay for this. I promise you that."

Davin ignored Talia, leaving her to her rage, understanding how it was aiding her in her combat against the Stalkers that were rushing toward them from both directions on the dock.

He had wanted to get to the drydock. If they had made it

there, they could have put one of the hulls against their backs and limited the monsters' potential lines of attack.

It would have made their task of staying alive somewhat easier. Or at least it would have allowed them to buy some additional time with the hope that help would come.

No such luck, however. They had only made it another hundred yards down the pier before they had to stop and focus on nothing more than defending themselves.

Back to back.

Doing whatever they could to prevent the Stalkers from cutting through their defenses with their claws. A handful of the monsters surrounding them while a few more were climbing onto the pier.

Their odds, bad to begin with, would have been even worse if not for the company of soldiers mixed in with sailors that had rushed out onto the pier from the direction of the Carlomin warehouses.

Davin glimpsed Sven at the far end. He was glad for the man's efforts and the fighters with him. Their risking themselves on the pier had drawn the attention of a good number of the Stalkers.

Stalkers that would have been focused on them instead.

But not enough of the monsters to give Davin and Talia the opportunity to find a stronger defensive position.

Davin stabbed with his spear, realizing that as soon as he did that the Stalker standing to his front was going to dodge out of the way and evade his attack.

That was fine with him. That's what he wanted actually.

Because that Stalker wasn't Davin's primary target. Rather, it was the monster standing right next to that beast.

While pulling back his spear, he turned the blade slightly, the angle just enough to cut across the unsuspecting Stalker's throat.

As the monster brought its claws up to the wound, Davin

kicked out with his front foot. He caught the Stalker full in the chest and sent him flying backward into the bay with a loud splash.

One less Stalker to worry about. Still, there were plenty more to deal with.

Shifting his attention to a Stalker on his far right, Davin slashed down with his spear.

The Stalker tried to scratch across Talia's back as she faced off against another of the monsters. Davin's quick thinking prevented the beast from striking true.

The distracted Stalker reared back, failing to avoid the deep slice across its forearm.

Talia sensed the movement behind her, but she wasn't worried.

She was never worried when Davin was close to her.

The gladiator would do as he needed to do. And he would always protect her back.

That thought buoying her, she focused on what she needed to do. That meant she had to kill the Stalker that was slicing for her face with a speed that she could barely follow.

Dodging to the side, she brought her sword up just in time. She caught a claw with the blade, taking some satisfaction when she felt the beast's flesh dig deeply into the steel without her having to do a thing.

The Stalker screeched in pain as the steel cut between its thumb and forefinger all the way to the bone. Nevertheless, that didn't stop the monster from continuing its attack, the bloody and painful wound only serving to enrage the beast.

Ripping its claw off her steel with another shriek of pain, then drawing the claw that was dripping blood close to its chest, the Stalker kicked at her with one of its clawed feet. Missing by no more than a hair, the monster roared in rage while slashing at her with its other claw.

Talia was ready, anticipating the attack.

Not needing to move, she simply raised her blade so that it was vertical to the pier.

The Stalker's claw slashed across the blade, a streak of blood splashing between them.

The Stalker's blood-red eyes widened with shock, staring at the terrible wound it had just inflicted upon itself.

Taking full advantage of the Stalker's distraction, she punched with her dagger right beneath the Stalker's lower ribs. Hearing a satisfying grunt, she gave the blade a nasty twist as the Stalker tottered back.

She didn't know if she had killed the beast. She hoped that she had.

She couldn't be certain, because even though the wound she had given him would kill most other adversaries, these Stalkers were incredibly difficult to send to the other side.

If nothing else, it was one less Stalker to worry about for the time being.

Yet that might not be good enough. Their fight to stay alive was becoming more and more desperate.

For every Stalker they killed or maimed, another stepped in to take its place, the beasts continuing to pull themselves out of the water and scramble onto the pier.

"Davin, this isn't sustainable," Talia growled. She lunged with her sword. Her swift attack forced back a Stalker that was little more than a shadow but for its eyes before she swung around, keeping a back foot in place to steady herself as she parried a stab from another beast that thought to catch her while she was occupied. Clever, but not clever enough. She had been ready for exactly that play. "There are too many."

"I know," he grunted as he slashed with his spear, earning a hiss of pain from the Stalker that had just cut at him wildly with its claws.

The beast had only succeeded in ripping off several large

splinters of wood from the post rather than digging out large chunks of flesh from his body.

Davin hadn't missed, his slice well placed. Right across the top of the Stalker's knee and thigh.

The monster stumbled back, unable to put any weight on the injured limb. Desperate to maintain its balance, the hobbling monster knocked into another Stalker that had just pulled itself up onto the pier and was about to join the combat.

Instead, they both fell back into the harbor, the water around the pier now churning wildly.

Not only because of the many Stalkers seeking to gain a clawhold on the dock, but also because of the great whites that were drawn there by the commotion and the blood.

The massive sharks were biting indiscriminately into whatever they found in the water, not caring if their powerful jaws bit into a dead or dying Stalker or one desperate to get out of the water or even one of their brethren.

To them, it was all just meat.

"Then what are we going to do?" Talia demanded, because she didn't have a single good idea.

She was angry. She hated the hazardous straits that she and Davin faced, knowing that the Stalkers were there for her. She hated even more the clash taking place near the main entrance and the smell of the fire that was raging through the compound.

"This," he replied, giving her a wild grin.

"What are you …"

Before she could finish asking her question, Davin grabbed her forearm and pulled her off the pier, having just cleared the space that he wanted by stabbing a Stalker right in the groin, the monster crumpling to the dock with a terrible groan.

Falling through the air, a bolt of fear ran down Talia's spine.

Did Davin actually believe that they could swim to safety with all the sharks and Stalkers in the water?

That was absolutely ludicrous.

They were simply jumping out of one terrible situation and into one that was even worse.

Before she hit the water, her knees buckled against the deck of a longboat. She reached out with one hand, sword still in her grip, preventing herself from slamming into one of the sides at the very last second.

When she righted herself, sword held at the ready, Davin was already on the bench across from her, pulling hard at the oars and trying to take them away from the pier as swiftly as possible.

"Keep them off us," Davin grunted, throwing his back into his work. He dipped the oars into the water, working hard to put some distance between them and the Stalkers that stood at the edge of the pier, hissing and shrieking at the prey that was escaping them.

Talia didn't bother to reply, knowing that the Stalkers would not be giving up the chase. She swung her sword through the air and cut across the side of the first Stalker that tried to jump into their craft.

The monster shrieked in rage as it splashed into the water instead, its ribs a bloody mess.

Before the beast could get its head back above the water, it was gone. A massive great white, at least thirty feet in length, clamped down on the Stalker's midsection and dragged it beneath the waves.

But that didn't stop the other Stalkers on the pier from jumping into the water and swimming toward them.

Talia did her best to fight them off, cutting and slashing at wrists and claws, understanding that she didn't need to kill the beasts to keep them out of the longboat.

As the seconds turned to minutes, it became more and more difficult.

Claws reaching up and over the gunwale in every direction.

The beasts not caring about the great whites that were now gliding along the side of the craft and yanking them beneath the surface with an increasing regularity.

Davin ignored it all, trusting in Talia, focused only on rowing. On getting away from the pier. Believing that if he could gain just a little more space and pull the longboat into the current that ran through the harbor, the Stalkers wouldn't be able to catch them.

But as the claws continued to dig into the sides of their craft, he realized that his hope was never going to become reality.

Not in their current circumstances.

Even with the sharks aiding them, there were too many Stalkers.

Talia couldn't handle them all on her own.

Having no other choice, Davin released the oars and reached for his spear. He stabbed a Stalker right through the eye when the monster, both claws gripping tightly to the side, peeked above the gunwale and shrieked in hunger.

From that point forward, there was nothing but steel, blood, and flesh, Davin and Talia engaging in a desperate battle to keep the Stalkers from boarding their small craft that bobbed precariously in the choppy, shark-infested water.

14

HOSTILE TAKEOVER

Hakea Roosarian stood atop the unfinished southern wall of the Rock. Her wicked grin made her look like a cat that had just caught a mouse.

She was quite pleased with herself. More than pleased, in fact.

She was ecstatic.

She had been stalking this mouse for the better part of a year, although her prey really wasn't a mouse.

Her prey had claws.

Not for much longer, however.

By the end of the night, Talia Carlomin wouldn't have anything at all. She'd be no more than an aggravating memory.

The flames burning through the buildings closest to the docks warmed her heart.

The antlike figures racing through the shadows, desperate to put them out, gave her a little burst of excitement.

The chaos playing out before her sent a shiver of pleasure down her spine.

The shouts and screams were music to her ears.

Beyond that, however, she was too far away to have a good sense of all that was happening across the harbor.

All appeared to be playing out as it should.

Still, she had expected more and larger fires by now. More destruction.

She had anticipated more black-clad figures racing through the walled off compound as the Fal Carrachian Guard broke through the main gate and onto the Carlomin property.

Perhaps it was too soon to have such expectations.

Hakea was certain that she had taken Talia Carlomin by surprise.

She was certain as well that her Guard would force their way past the wall.

How could they not? Her soldiers greatly outnumbered those fighting for the Carlomins.

And she had absolutely no doubt whatsoever that with the number of Stalkers Ursina had given her, all of them tasked with killing her nemesis, that in the end all would work out exactly as she believed it would.

The mouse would be no more. Slaughtered. Ripped open with a single swipe of the cat's sharp claw.

It was just a matter of time.

Besides, the attack had just begun. There was still a great deal more to do.

She just needed to be patient, which, admittedly, was not one of her strengths.

After watching for a few minutes more, the flames not as high, the fires not as many, the chaos not as complete as she had hoped, Hakea turned away from the scene developing in front of her. She needed confirmation. She needed to be sure that all was progressing as it should.

"Find Captain Oselnik. I want you back here with his report in less than an hour," she ordered.

The figure standing farther along the parapet shifted uncomfortably. Lifting his leg with a good bit of effort, he walked stiffly out into the light provided by the torch fixed to the wall, a large bandage wrapped around his right knee, a crutch under his right arm.

"I'm not a messenger, Hakea."

"Too badly wounded to get down to the harbor? Is that it?"

"I didn't say that, Hakea," he replied with a good bit of heat. "I may be wounded, but I'm not an invalid."

"Then do as I ordered, Ronild. Find Oselnik and bring back a report on where things stand at the Carlomin wharf. I need to be striding triumphantly through that gate in the next few hours if we're to have any chance of success."

"As you order?"

Roosarian stared at Ronild Magnison for quite some time. Her gaze hardened. Then she nodded.

Not only did he believe that he was better than she was, more capable, but he was also a believer that a woman was the weaker sex. She could see it in that cocky expression of his.

Not a surprise. Not even a disappointment for her. She had known that about him since they were children. It just meant that her pleasure increased when she had the chance to put him in his place.

"As I order," Roosarian replied slowly, biting off the words so that there was no mistake to be made. "You don't seem to understand your place here, Ronild."

"I am a Lord of Roo's Nest, Hakea. I am a …"

"You are nothing here!" Hakea shouted, her words silencing Magnison. "And you forget yourself."

"I do no such thing," protested Magnison.

"You do," Hakea replied sharply. "You like to tell people that you're twelfth removed from the Duke of Roo's Nest."

"It's only the truth, Hakea."

"And I'm the niece of the Duke of Roo's Nest. In Caledonia, I had a higher position than you. Here, in Fal Carrach, I have a higher position. I am the Governor. You are not."

"Hakea, it's just that …"

Hakea stepped down from the stone she had been using to look out over the parapet and placed herself right up against Magnison's chest.

Ronild took two stumbling steps back, uncomfortable not because of her proximity but because of the fire in her eyes.

"I rule here, Ronild. Not you. You are here at my pleasure."

"Hakea. I am simply trying to prepare you for …"

"If I decide to have you thrown from the battlements, there's nothing you can do to stop me."

At that very moment, two soldiers stepped out into the light from their positions along the wall. Their expressions showed no emotion, although their eyes suggested that might be a sight that they'd like to see.

"Hakea, please …"

"There is no please with me, Ronild. I order and you do as I say."

"Yes, Hakea," Ronild sighed, the fire that had been in him just moments before quenched by her ferocity and the two men waiting to see if he would give them the chance to act as they desired.

"Good," Hakea nodded, stepping back toward the parapet. "Now you will go to the Carlomin compound and get Oselnik's report. You will then return here. Do you understand?"

"I can do more than just that for you, Hakea," Magnison offered, seeking to reclaim some of his usual bravado.

"Really?" chuckled Hakea. "And if you come up against the Crimson Giant again, you'll be able to stand against him? Maybe hit him about the shoulders with that crutch of yours?"

Magnison's face sparked a bright red, spittle accompanying every one of his words, as his rage, never far from the surface, broke free. "Hakea, I am more than capable …"

"If you were capable, Ronild, you would have killed the Crimson Giant by now. If you were truly capable, you would have killed Talia Carlomin when you had the chance. But here we are."

Hakea shook her head in disappointment, not surprised that she had beaten him down so easily. He had so much more fire when they were children. Now it seemed that with every scar that he took, every wound, a part of him was cut away. His anger no more than a mechanism to mask his many deficiencies.

So be it. She would use Ronild for as long as she could. Then she would discard him when he was no longer of any value to her. "Now get out of my sight, Ronild. Do as I have commanded."

Ronild bit back the sharp words that were at the tip of his tongue, realizing that now wasn't the time for any more displays of defiance. "As you order ... Hakea."

Ronild turned to go, beginning to walk stiffly and slowly past the two soldiers, when he was forced to stop.

"Governor Roosarian, Ronild. To you, I am Governor Roosarian."

Ronild didn't bother to turn around. "As you order ... Governor Roosarian."

Hakea watched Ronild hobble away until he was lost in the darkness that played across the battlements. He was properly cowed at the moment, although she had no doubt that this confrontation would come up again soon.

She was already looking forward to it. She enjoyed putting Ronild in his place.

And she was hoping to receive a good report from Oselnik. She wanted to walk through the gates of the Carlomin enclave while there was still some fighting on the dock. It would burnish her reputation and ensure that everyone in the city, everyone in the Territory, knew what would happen if they decided to challenge her in any way.

But before she did that, she needed to know what was going on.

And in the meantime she could do what she could to speed along the hostile takeover that she had begun against the Carlomin Trading Company.

15

TO THE SOURCE

Talia stabbed with her sword, piercing the armpit of the Stalker that had pulled itself half out of the water.

The monster's fang-filled grin of anticipation as it reached with its claw for Davin's back swiftly turned into a choking rictus of agony as the steel sliced through muscle and shattered bone.

Davin had his hands full. One Stalker succeeded in looping a leg over the side of the longboat. Another was attempting to roll itself over the gunwale, bleeding profusely from several slashes across its chest yet unwilling and unable to give up the fight.

Davin slashed blindingly fast with his spear, slicing across the throat of the Stalker perched on the side of the craft.

The monster gurgled softly before tumbling back into the water, clutching at its ravaged throat.

He continued the motion, bringing the blade down along the back of the other Stalker's calf, almost severing the leg completely below the knee.

The wounded Stalker reared up, shrieking in rage and pain, swiping wildly at its tormentor with its razor-sharp claws.

Davin ducked the swing then kicked out with his left leg. Catching the beast in the shoulder, the monster splashed back into the bay.

Davin didn't think either of the Stalkers would be a threat any longer. He doubted that they'd even get their heads back above the surface.

Not with the great whites that tracked the combat across the harbor.

He had gotten lucky. Catching the edge of the current before he released the oars, the flow pushed the longboat away from the dock and toward the north. The long trail of blood, bodies, and body parts that he and Talia had no choice but to create proved irresistible to the maneaters.

When Talia pulled her blade free, the steel the only thing keeping the Stalker slumped against the gunwale in place, the dying beast slid from the railing and slipped beneath the waves, several large fins already cutting through the water and moving toward the latest offering.

"It's done," Talia huffed. She was exhausted. Her muscles burned from the exertion of the fight. Her clothes clung to her as if she'd actually fallen into the harbor.

Davin nodded, catching his breath as he leaned on his spear for balance. He didn't say a word. He was just glad that they had escaped the Stalkers that had come for them on the dock.

Neither had any idea how many Stalkers they fought as their longboat drifted through the harbor. Although the churning in the water behind them, the fins of the great whites occasionally slicing through the waves, told them that the very large, dim shadows gliding by right along the sides of their craft certainly appreciated their efforts.

After quickly examining Talia to make sure that she wasn't badly wounded, identifying just a few scrapes and cuts on her forearm, one on her neck, and another on her brow, Davin worked his way carefully around the longboat.

He used his spear to dislodge several clawed hands that still gripped the gunwale despite their former owners now residing in the bellies of the beasts that were fighting over the last of the remains floating atop the waves.

The sound of those severed limbs plopping into the water only served to bring closer several of the sharks, a few of which were longer than their launch. The great whites swept by in their deceptively lazy motion, investigating, wanting to determine if there were any more easy meals to be had.

Certain now that Talia was correct, that they had escaped the Stalkers sent against them, Davin swept his gaze around the harbor.

All was as it should be. Just another late night in Ballinasloe.

Except to the south.

Fires continued to burn along the front of the Carlomin wharfage. It was a terrible sight to behold, several warehouses ablaze, thankfully none of the residences.

His careful eye told him that it should have been worse. There should have been more damage. Because Roosarian had caught them completely by surprise.

Yet there wasn't. Only a handful of buildings were on fire, and even from a distance it appeared as if those blazes were under control.

He reached the same conclusion with respect to the fighting after listening to the sounds of the battle that drifted across the water, as he really couldn't see much unless it was illuminated by the light provided by the burning buildings.

There should have been a great deal more screaming and shouting.

More cries of pain, anguish, and terror.

The unmistakable clash of steel striking steel or steel striking claw.

But there wasn't.

Based on his very unscientific assessment, Davin believed that the Fal Carrachian Guard had yet to break into the compound. What he was observing in fiery glimpses was the last of the work of a few arsonists who had snuck in before the fight at the gate began.

Davin smiled then for the first time since their flight had begun. He realized why the Carlomin Guard had not capitulated to the larger Fal Carrachian Guard. Why the soldiers loyal to Hakea Roosarian had failed to get past the wall.

"Sirena."

"Likely so," agreed Talia, smiling as well. Her Captain was competent to a fault. And there was no way that she would ever surrender to soldiers who also masqueraded as pirates.

There was bad blood there, Sirena losing her husband to the marauders. The bad blood would always be there, until there wasn't any more blood to be had.

"Roosarian's strategy has not worked as she wanted," Talia mused. "The Governor is going to be less than pleased."

"That she will be," Davin agreed, his voice revealing his pleasure at that finding. He sat down on a bench and leaned his forearms along his knees, spear still close at hand. Just in case. "I almost feel sorry for the Captain of the Fal Carrachian Guard -- I can't remember his name other than that it's a mouthful – because someone is going to pay a price for their failure, and he's the most likely target. If Sirena doesn't get to him first."

"A pity indeed," Talia replied with a snort, the dread that had plagued her since the attack on the pier finally beginning to shift to a few other emotions.

Hope.

And the desire for revenge.

She could almost see it in her mind's eyes. The popinjay Vanion Oselnik standing just beyond the main gate to the Carlomin compound cursing and growling in frustration. Sirena standing atop the wall and giving him one of her challenging stares as his soldiers failed time and time again to breach the gate.

Talia sat down next to Davin, taking stock of their current situation. The gladiator had removed all the severed limbs, although there was nothing that he could do about the pools of blood scattered about the bottom of the longboat.

They needed to get back to shore. Unfortunately, they were down to one oar.

They had lost the other one when she smacked the forehead of a Stalker seeking to kill Davin from his blind side while he was engaged with another of the monsters.

Her strike had been enough to knock the Stalker back into the harbor. But she had lost her grasp on the implement, bashing the creature with one hand, reluctant to let go of her sword.

She hadn't killed the monster. However, she hadn't needed to.

The great white lurking right next to the craft had taken care of that for her.

Though the implement proved quite useful during the clash, only having one oar at hand was going to make navigating the harbor and getting back to the dock more of a challenge.

They would need to find a solution to that, because they were approaching the Rock. No more than a few hundred yards offshore, in fact, the current pushing them closer to Roosarian's headquarters and away from the safety of her compound.

"Get down!" Davin hissed. He ducked beneath the gunwale, at the same time wrapping his arms around Talia and taking her with him so that she was curled up on top of him.

"You're doing this for a reason, I hope," grumbled Talia, her face pressed against his sweaty, bloody, and torn shirt. "Because this isn't the time for games."

"Doing what?" Davin asked in a whisper.

"Holding onto me like you're never going to let go," Talia replied. She turned her head so that she could breathe again and also look up into his blood-smeared face, giving him a big, teasing grin. "I never knew you felt this way about me."

Davin stared at Talia for a few seconds, not understanding what she was implying. When he realized the position that they were in, his eyes widened, not so much in shock as fear, a rare occurrence for the gladiator.

He tried to extricate himself quickly, unwrapping his arms as carefully as he could. However, the tight quarters of the longboat and his desire to keep their bodies below the side of the craft made his efforts more difficult than he would have preferred. His struggles only brought Talia closer to him, their bodies pressed together, their faces less than an inch apart.

For just a heartbeat, he stared into her eyes. He saw a spark there that he had never seen before.

A strange urge rushed through him, his lips, almost of their own volition, slowly moving toward hers. And rather than being nervous or afraid, he felt as if this was what he was supposed to do.

He saw how Talia's eyes widened, first in surprise, then in some other emotion that he couldn't identify, that he didn't want to identify. Not then.

At the very last instant, he regained control of himself. Not understanding what had come over him with so much at risk. He pulled back slowly, reluctantly, his face turning bright red as he heard Talia's soft chuckle just below his chin, her reaction confusing him.

"Did you see that?" he asked when they finally worked themselves free from one another. Feeling flushed, and not because of the fight across the harbor, certain that his face was redder than his flame-colored hair, Davin locked away the emotions that had rushed up on him by surprise.

He nodded over the gunwale, and they both peeked at the same time. They were so close to one another that they could feel each other's breaths on the other's cheek. By silent, mutual agreement, they each shifted an inch to the other side so that they could focus on the task at hand.

The Rock was coming up on them fast, the current sweeping them toward and then along the rocky shore.

At first there was nothing but darkness to be seen on the isle, the black stone of the Rock fading into the gloom. The only light came from the torches set on the unfinished walls of the citadel that towered above the beach.

Talia pulled back and covered her mouth with her hand to prevent a gasp from escaping when she picked out three dark, very large shapes, only their blood-red eyes easily visible in the night, slide out from a crevice in the rocky outcropping near the southeastern tip of the cay.

Stalkers.

Her expression hardened. She watched as the monsters raced through the sand and out into the water. As soon as they were waist deep, they dove into the surf and began to swim across the harbor toward the Carlomin docks.

Whether they reached their destination wasn't a given, what with all the great whites waiting for them in the deeper water. Yet if even one made it across it was one too many.

"That proves it, doesn't it?" murmured Talia. They had suspected the source of the Stalkers in Fal Carrach. What they had just seen confirmed it. "Although there was very little doubt left to begin with."

"It does," Davin replied. "Although you really don't need any more evidence after Roosarian's attack. I'm sure Sirena will keep a few dead Stalkers there so that we can use them as needed."

"That she will," agreed Talia. "She knows what to do."

"Now it's a matter of what we need to do. Or rather what we can do."

"What do you mean?" asked Talia, not quite understanding.

"Hakea Roosarian played her hand," Davin said, his eyes locked onto the crevice as he searched for any more Stalkers that might be exiting from beneath the Rock. Only seeing the three who were already well past them in the water. "At the moment, it doesn't look like it was a good one. We've countered every play that she's made, assuming Sirena can hold the gate."

"Sirena will hold the gate. Of that have no doubt."

"I don't doubt it," Davin replied calmly, lifting his eyebrow as he noted the heat in her voice.

Talia nodded, glad to hear him say that. They waited almost a minute more as their longboat continued to drift toward the Rock. They didn't see any more shadows with blood-red orbs racing out from the crevice. Perhaps those were the last of the monsters.

"We need to ensure that the Council is aware of what we've learned."

"I doubt that matters now," Davin replied. "There's plenty of evidence with dead Stalkers scattered across your docks all coinciding with an attack by the Fal Carrachian Guard. The proof is quite damning. Irrefutable."

"I guess you're right."

"I am," Davin replied confidently. "Besides, Roosarian probably won't care about that now. She's going to need to figure out what her next move is. And she only has so much time in which to make it. Because if she doesn't, she's done for."

"We already know what her move is," Talia countered. "It's the same play that she's failed at so many times in the past."

"Killing you," Davin said softly.

"Killing me," murmured Talia, almost beneath her breath. "We should try to head back. Provide what assistance we can to Sirena and then figure out how we can marshal our forces and those of the Council so that we can deal more effectively with Roosarian."

"We could," Davin agreed, although he didn't sound convinced.

"That would be the smart thing to do," Talia continued, hearing the hesitation in his voice. "Ensuring that we have the resources to unseat her."

"It would. I can't disagree with you about that."

Talia gave him a questioning look, her mind moving down the path that his had traveled already. "But still you do."

"I wouldn't call it a disagreement."

"Then what would you call it?" Talia's irritation rose again as the full weight of their current situation, along with the decision that she needed to make, hit her square across the jaw.

"A difference of opinion. No more than that."

"There's a distinction between a disagreement and a difference of opinion?" demanded Talia, not quite believing that she was getting into an argument over semantics while the fate of all that she had been working toward hung in the balance.

"All right, maybe a difference of opinion is the wrong term," Davin admitted. "Let's call it a different perspective."

"What perspective would that be, Davin?" Her tone suggested that she was losing patience with him.

"That we have more than one choice to make."

"Just spit it out, Davin. We're almost to the beach beneath the Rock. We only have one oar to get us back across shark-infested waters. And we don't know if any more Stalkers are going to pop out from beneath the fortress."

"We could head back toward the docks with one oar, although that would be quite a challenge. It would take a good bit of time and effort."

"Or?" Talia prodded.

"Or, assuming that Roosarian is here at the Rock, not yet ready to grace us with her presence until the Fal Carrachian Guard breaks into the compound – and we know that's not going to happen, so she's going to be here for a while -- we could try to finish this ourselves," Davin suggested, turning toward Talia and giving her a feral, expectant grin.

It didn't take Talia long to figure out what he was suggesting. She mimicked his smile when she did. She liked that idea. "We could."

Using the only oar they had as a rudder, Davin more guided than rowed the longboat up onto the rocky shore.

He was quite pleased with himself.

Not because he got them to the island. That was inevitable. The current would ensure that.

Rather that he brought them in right where he desired. A few hundred yards away from the crevice from which the Stalkers had emerged, wanting some distance from the gap to start.

When the hull scraped against the sand, he and Talia both leapt out and grabbed a side, pulling the craft farther up the rocky shore so that the tide didn't take their ride back out to sea.

They couldn't afford to become stranded there. They needed a way off.

Because if they succeeded in what they were about to attempt, there was still a great deal more that they would need to do to have any chance at all of seizing control of Ballinasloe.

Davin recognized where he was. The door in the Rock that opened up onto the shore was right in front of him, no more than a few dozen yards farther up the beach.

This was where he had fought Ronild Magnison and his three friends the first time. It seemed like ages ago that he had engaged in that combat, although actually it was only a few months in the past.

He had killed one of them. The big one who was much too overconfident with his sword.

A common occurrence, he had discovered in the Pit. And as he had done on the white sand, Davin had been more than happy to use that overconfidence against his adversary.

Unfortunately, Davin didn't kill Ronild when he had the chance. He wished that he had, especially now that he knew who he was and how he was connected to Talia.

That was a failing that he hoped to remedy in the future since there was little that he could do about it now.

Although the door hidden within the wall provided one option for entering the citadel, that wasn't their initial objective. Rather, it was the crevice that was farther down the beach.

From where they stood, they could barely see it, the gap masked by the rocky outcropping from which the southern wall of the Rock had been carved.

Davin was about to head in that direction when his heart almost leapt out of his throat. A shadow detached itself from the wall not too far away from the door and streaked across the sand, its blood-red eyes fixed on Talia.

There was no way that Davin could put himself in front of her with the longboat in the way. The monster was too fast. She would need to meet this attack on her own.

"Talia ..." Davin warned in a hiss, fearing that he had been too slow to identify the shadow and that it was already too late.

It wasn't.

Talia became aware of the threat at the same time that Davin did. She took two quick steps forward to meet the attack.

Ducking a hurried and clumsy swing by the Stalker, the monster slipping at the worst possible moment where the sand, rock, and water met, Talia slashed across the creature's thigh and knee with a clinical efficiency while the beast's claw passed through the air above her head.

The Stalker crashed into the surf, choking on the water that rushed up onto the shore at the insistence of the incoming tide. Before the beast could pull its head out of the froth and screech a challenge that might catch the attention of anyone above them on the wall, Talia positioned herself behind the beast.

She drove her sword through the Stalker's heavily muscled back, the bloody point sticking through its chest. When she pulled the blade free, she twisted to ensure that she shredded the monster's heart.

The Stalker remained kneeling in the surf for just a few heartbeats more before falling face first into the gentle waves. Dead.

"That was quite impressive," Davin told her, his heart almost beating normally again.

Talia turned back toward Davin. He stood behind her, spear at the ready in case she needed assistance. Her expression said quite clearly that she did not.

"I'm not just a pretty face," Talia said, giving him a wink. "Worried about me, gladiator? Since you didn't want to let me go just a few minutes past."

Davin opened his mouth to reply, then closed it just as quickly. Thankfully, and perhaps even surprisingly, he realized that the first thing that he was going to say probably wasn't the best thing to say.

Likely it would just get him into a good bit of trouble with Talia, and that was something that he didn't need after what had just happened between them on the longboat.

"Why did you risk yourself like that?" he demanded in a whisper, hoping that the flintiness of his voice would counteract the teasing nature of her words.

"It was necessary," Talia replied with a shrug. She realized that she needed to say more because even though she had just replied to Davin with one of his own favorite explanations when she asked him much the same question, he expected more from her. Just as she did when their positions were reversed.

"I saw the Stalker when we beached the longboat. It snuck out from the crevice and worked its way along the wall, hoping to catch us when we least suspected an attack. But I was ready for it. And, as you saw, I dispatched it exactly how you taught me. Fast. Efficiently. No wasted movement or decisions."

Davin opened his mouth to reply, then closed it just as quickly. Once again he realized that the first thing that he was going to say probably wasn't the best thing to say, and that it would just get him in trouble with Talia. So he kept those thoughts to himself despite the strong urge to share them.

Besides, he couldn't argue with her. She was correct.

She had done exactly as he had taught her to do when fighting a Stalker. And she had done it with a competence and skill that was truly impressive.

"If we're going to do this, then I take the lead," Davin said as he began walking along the beach toward the crevice, knowing that there was no point in continuing the conversation because he had little chance of coming out on top.

"Why do you take the lead?" protested Talia. She believed that her recent demonstration of skill more than qualified her to be at the front of their risky expedition. "The Stalkers want to kill me after all. Why not give them the chance?"

"Because you're more important than me, Talia. You know that just as well as I do."

At first, Talia didn't know what to say as the gladiator strode past her. In large part because he had called her by her first name. He rarely did that, and only when he really wanted to get her attention.

Nevertheless, she did feel the need to argue against his claim. "That's not really ..."

"It is true, and you know it," Davin cut in, not wanting to give her the chance to build up a head of steam. He knew that once she got going it was hard to slow her down. "You're a leader in this Territory, all of New Caledonia actually. Thousands of people depend on you. If this works the way we want it to, then you're going to need to deal with all of the challenges associated with Ballinasloe and then all of Fal Carrach. Not me. You. You lead."

"But Davin, I ..."

"I'm a gladiator," Davin continued as he stepped up to the side of the crevice and peered in, Talia right behind him.

It was pitch black for the first hundred yards. Then a dim glow appeared where it looked like the tunnel curved to the west. He didn't see any of the blood-red eyes waiting for him in the darkness or rushing at him out of the gloom, so he assumed that now was as good a time as any to put their plan into motion.

"It's that simple. There's really no need to have this conversation at all." Then he glanced at her quickly and gave her a grin before he turned his eyes back toward the tunnel. "Besides, if I allowed anything to happen to you, Sirena would skin me alive. I'd really like to avoid that if I can, because that woman scares me."

Slowly, Talia's sour expression turned into a fleeting smile. She nodded. She couldn't challenge his argument.

Well, she could. But then she'd just be wasting time. No matter how much she hated having to admit it, he was right.

Davin nodded as well, then he slipped into the crevice, Talia following on his heels.

~

Davin and Talia crept through the gap, wary of what they might discover once they navigated around the jagged rocks that made it seem like they were walking into the maw of a monstrous creature. Thinking of what had emerged from the slice beneath the Rock just minutes before, they both believed that the imagery that came to mind was more than appropriate.

After just a few feet, they found themselves in a rough natural passageway. It was several yards wide and twice as tall.

The beginning section of the tunnel that was closest to the beach was pitch black. Here they had no choice but to move by touch. To do that, they both kept one hand on the rough wall to guide their way, weapons in the other.

More than willing to sacrifice speed for silence, they placed their feet carefully, not able to afford a stumble, worried about what might find them in the darkness if they gave themselves away.

Davin in the lead, he kept his spear out to his front.

He didn't think that he would actually see a Stalker if there was one waiting for them in the craggy tunnel. The only tell-tale sign that might offer a hint that one of those beasts was hiding in the darkness would be its blood-red eyes.

Rather, he hoped that even if he didn't see the Stalker sneaking toward them, he might get lucky, and the monster might run onto his spear by mistake.

A foolish hope, perhaps. But he didn't care. It was all he had.

They were taking a risk.

A big one.

He couldn't afford for it to go bad.

Not with Talia at his back.

Nevertheless, with each slow step they took as he and Talia worked their way farther down the tunnel, he became more and more nervous. His reservations growing, becoming louder.

This had happened to him before. An edginess, a prickling

all across his skin, that warned him that he was moving toward evil. Toward a danger against which steel would offer little in the way of an effective defense.

The source of his rising unease wasn't the Stalkers. As he had demonstrated more times than he could recall, Stalkers didn't faze him in the least.

He could kill Stalkers.

He couldn't kill with his spear what he was creeping toward. Filling the tunnel with its suffocating presence.

Whatever peril was down here with them, it was more dangerous than a gaggle of Stalkers.

That's what worried him.

Although not so much for himself. Rather for Talia.

He had faced difficult odds in the past. That wasn't to say that he could do so in the future without paying a cost, but as he had explained to Talia, she was more important than he was.

If he fell, then the world continued to turn.

If she fell, all that Talia and her mother had been doing to create a Ballinasloe and Fal Carrach that offered more than just what Hakea Roosarian was willing to give the people living here would come to nought.

Davin breathed a little easier when they reached the very end of the passageway. The darkness began to recede, the dim glow of a torch lighting the way where the tunnel curved to the left.

Davin looked behind him, catching Talia's sharp gaze, wanting to make sure that she was still good with the plan.

She nodded, answering the question in his eyes.

Talia and Davin continued down the corridor, which now revealed the work of stonemasons who had sanded down the rough-hewn walls.

Based on where they had entered the crevice, Davin judged that they were close to the very center of the Rock, even as the tunnel upon turning to the left had led them down beneath the citadel's walls a good fifty feet.

Every few steps, Davin stopped, Talia mimicking his actions. The tunnel was well-lit here, and they could see that in another twenty yards the corridor opened into a larger chamber.

"I can't believe this," Talia whispered.

Talia right next to him, Davin knelt down next to the stone balcony that circled around the hall, peeking through the stone slats. The hollow below them had been carved out from beneath the citadel.

"Why not?" Davin whispered, shaking his head in anger. "Nothing about Hakea Roosarian or what she'll do to achieve what she desires surprises me anymore."

Looking down into the circular chamber, their eyes were drawn immediately to the cells that had been cut into the far wall. Steel bars prevented the small crowd of Stalkers waiting there in the shadows from slipping free.

They weren't surprised by what they saw. Rather, they were surprised that they had never considered this possibility before.

Talia and Davin were beginning to understand. They had assumed that the Stalkers were being sent here to Roosarian by whomever it was who was using the Curse to create them.

They were wrong.

The Stalkers were being made here. In this very room.

That was the source of the evil that Davin sensed as they moved deeper beneath the fortress.

Right next to the cell that held the Stalkers was another cell, stuffed as tightly as a barrel of fish to the point where none of the men and women imprisoned within could lie out on the floor.

Probably criminals and some unfortunates taken off the streets of Ballinasloe who Roosarian didn't believe would be missed.

"We need to do something," Talia whispered into Davin's ear.

Before she could move along the balcony toward the stairs at the far end that led down into the hollow, Davin grasped her wrist and held her in place.

"Wait a moment."

He had caught a flash of movement coming out of the gloom on the far side of the small chamber.

16

THE TRANSFORMATION

"**S**hould you not be out on the wharf to proclaim your great victory?"

A petite woman with a bewitching voice, face hidden behind the folds of a cloak, walked next to the Governor of Fal Carrach into the light created by the torches burning brightly in the wall sconces lining the chamber.

"I will get there soon enough," Hakea Roosarian replied. "There is nothing to fear. Our victory is assured. I can proclaim it whenever I desire."

"Of course, my dear. My mistake."

Hakea gritted her teeth, fighting hard to not offer the biting response that would only serve to make an already difficult situation more difficult.

This woman upon whom she currently relied so heavily had an innate skill. She knew exactly what to say, how, and when to ensure that Hakea was continually on edge. Every other word was an insult, or at least it felt like it.

She consoled herself with the fact that this arrangement between them wouldn't have to continue for much longer. Hakea would make sure of that.

When the time was right. Just not now. Which meant that she would need to suffer the woman's presence for a few minutes more.

"You've been doing well, Hakea," the cloaked figure said in a tone dripping with condescension. "Soon you won't need my assistance at all."

"Sooner than you might think, you treacherous hag," Hakea thought, smart enough to keep what passed through her mind to herself. She understood the danger in which she would have placed herself if she had uttered those words.

Her unwanted partner liked to present herself as the kindly aunt.

Hakea knew that would change in a heartbeat if the woman sensed even a speck of disrespect.

So she needed to be careful. Very careful. Having already gotten a taste of what could happen when the woman lost her temper.

With a sharp nod from Hakea, the squad of soldiers that followed them into the chamber spread out along the wall.

The beasts stared expectantly at the humans from which they were separated by only a few thin steel bars. The soldiers stayed well clear of the cell, having no desire to become the target of those monsters' intense, hungry interest.

Once her men were where they were supposed to be, she closed her eyes for a few seconds and took several deep breaths. Hakea seeking to gain control of the anger that had been building within her. Finding the task more elusive than she would have preferred though knowing why.

Hakea hated the woman. For many different reasons.

If she was honest with herself, the primary cause of her fury and intense dislike was that the woman was all that Hakea wanted to be.

The composure. The self-assurance. The confidence. The potency.

Yet there was nothing that Hakea could do to reverse their roles, because there was nothing that she could do to the woman. She was too strong. Too canny. Too aware.

Not yet anyway, she mused. Hoping that a chance to balance the scales might come her way, though knowing as well what that was worth.

Perhaps never after seeing the power that the woman exercised. The power that they were about to put into play once again.

Her partner walked over to a small shelf hidden in the shadows that was carved out of the stone. She pulled free a small vial of black liquid from a wooden box, the inside wrapped in velvet. The five other vials nestled there were all empty.

"It seems that tonight you are well on your way to eliminating the primary threat to your rule and our prosperity. You should be proud of yourself, my dear. You've done a much better job than that bullheaded young man in the Highlands."

"I know what needs to be done and I do it," Hakea replied coldly, absolutely certain that the woman was offering her another veiled insult. "I am nothing like Torstan Sharperson."

"No, you certainly are not. And for that my husband and I are grateful."

"Why do you say that?" The comment surprised Hakea.

"It's quite obvious, isn't it my dear?" the woman replied, motioning to two of the soldiers waiting along the wall. The men walked over toward the cell filled with prisoners. "My husband and I can't hold your hand or Torstan's forever. Sink or swim is the saying, isn't it? Apparently we won't have to worry about you after tonight. We'll be able to focus our full attention on Torstan so that we can finish righting the ship."

"Are you suggesting that I couldn't manage my part of the deal without you?" Hakea's voice became even colder as she seethed at the obvious insult.

"I'm suggesting nothing," said the cloaked woman.

Her partner hadn't bothered to turn toward Hakea. Instead, she faced the cell from which the soldiers were pulling out a tall, scrawny fellow with a matted beard who wore nothing more than rags. The pair brought him right up to the woman.

She studied the man for a time. He stood there complacently, his eyes unfocused, his mind perhaps somewhere else.

All the fight had left him long ago. Whether beaten out of him by life in general or his experiences here beneath the Rock, she didn't know and didn't care.

She only cared if he was a worthy specimen.

Once she was satisfied, the cowled woman nodded.

The two soldiers worked quickly, clearly having done this many times before.

They dragged the unfortunate victim to the wall. While one soldier held him there with a meaty hand on his chest, the other looped leather straps around his wrists and then his ankles, ensuring that he couldn't move more than an inch in any direction.

"Then what are you suggesting?" demanded Hakea. She continued to struggle to control her temper. She was trying to adopt the woman's supercilious tone, but she knew that she was failing miserably.

"I'm simply telling the truth, my dear," replied the cloaked woman as she walked over toward the man. "You can be as angry as you want, but you know it as well as I do. If not for me and my husband, you'd be in a much worse position than Torstan Sharperson. In fact, you might not even have your seat, the Carlomin woman stealing it right out from under you."

"Do not compare me to Torstan Sharperson," hissed Hakea, the first hint of her anger apparent in her voice, "and Talia Carlomin will never take Fal Carrach. I rule here. I will always rule here. Best to remember that."

Hakea cursed herself for a fool for her minor explosion in temper. She was allowing the woman to do it to her again.

The woman who was her most important ally knew exactly what to say to get under her skin. It was one of her unique skills.

For just a few heartbeats, Hakea wondered if the woman enjoyed picking at scabs, because that's what she was doing now. Picking at Hakea's scabs and quite effectively.

"I would never dare to do such a thing, Hakea," the woman replied in a somewhat placating tone. "You know that. I was simply stating the truth. That's what you prefer, isn't it? What's the point if we can't talk plainly to one another? You know as well as I do that without me, all that you've tried to build here in Fal Carrach would be at risk. When the Carlomin woman is gone, so too will be that risk. You will rule freely here, which means that you will no longer require my services so frequently."

"And what will you do when you're no longer aiding me as you're doing now?" Hakea asked with a sickly sweet smile that did little to hide her underlying contempt and hatred.

"I have my own challenges to deal with now, my dear. While you regain control over your Territory, as I'm sure you will, I will be managing the difficulties we face to the north." The woman shrugged, the only sign of the movement a faint ripple along the edge of her cloak. "Before that, however, based on how matters stand in the Highlands, I have a feeling that I will be spending a great deal more time there as soon as I'm done with you."

"It's good to know that I'm the lesser of the problems that you must rectify."

"Quite right, my dear," the cloaked woman said with a gentle laugh. "That's the right way of looking at it."

For several seconds, Hakea stared at the woman, unable to hide her loathing, yet at the same time strangely impressed by how her partner turned Hakea's sarcasm against her so deftly.

"Now let's get on with this so that I can return to the north and you can enjoy your victory on the wharf," the cloaked woman suggested, ignoring Hakea's expression.

"As I said, I know what I'm doing," Hakea growled. "I've done this many times now. I doubt that I will have need of your services after tonight."

"Good, I'm glad to hear that, because Torstan needs all the help that he can get," the cloaked woman replied with another musical laugh.

She handed the vial of black liquid to Hakea. She then explained to her once again what needed to be done despite Hakea having indeed managed the transformation on her own many times before.

"Remember that only one drop is required. To give more than one ensures the death of the creature or perhaps creates a monster worse than a Stalker. Something that you learned the first time you attempted this when you didn't follow my instructions. Better that we don't find out again, don't you think?"

Hakea nodded reluctantly, not seeing any point in stopping the woman because she was going to continue with the lecture whether she liked it or not. She had done so each time that Hakea prepared to use the noxious liquid.

"It won't happen again. I promised you that."

Another reason she abhorred the woman. How she so liked to focus on Hakea's failures.

Still, Hakea did agree with her ally. She had no desire for a repeat of what happened the first time she had managed the transformation, and at that poorly.

Only months before actually. Hakea had been anxious. Also excited. Too excited, in fact.

Her hand wasn't steady, and she wasn't careful with the

dosage. She had sent an entire stream of the cold, boiling liquid contained in the vial down the throat of the prisoner rather than just a single drop.

She had been utterly intrigued and horrified by the transformation that occurred. What had resulted from her error was both exhilarating, revolting, and terrifying.

She had wondered if what she created wasn't so much a mistake as the next step in the process that she had been engaging in. When the beast shot a claw toward her face faster than a snapping whip, she realized just how foolish it was for her to play with such a thought.

If you were going to create a monster, then you needed to be able to control it. Otherwise, you were only ensuring your own death.

It had taken six men to hold off what had resulted from the overdose, the monster not heeding any of the commands she had given to it. Instead, seeking to kill everyone around it.

Only the cloaked woman had been able to finish the creature. And even then, she didn't succeed until three of the soldiers fighting the beast had been badly wounded, two of those men dying from their injuries later.

"Let's hope so, dear," the cloaked woman said. "Remember as well that as soon as this one begins to turn, you have one minute to bond with him. Do not waste that time. Otherwise, doing this to him will be a waste."

"I understand," Hakea replied. "I made one mistake, and that just the first time. Since then I've turned the last fifteen with little trouble. You have nothing to fear."

"Of course, dear. I just like to be careful. For your sake as well as mine since I will be leaving what's left of the solution here with you. I would hate to hear of another mistake occurring when I'm not here to save you."

"You have nothing to worry about in that regard," Hakea replied firmly, realizing that there was no point in trying to defend herself or argue with the woman. Anything she said would be turned against her in a way that only made her appear more foolish.

Better just to grin and bear it for a little while longer. Better to do what needed to be done here with her ally.

And then finally she would be gone. Hakea would be free of her incessant insults, some veiled, most not.

"Good, I'm glad to hear that, my dear," the woman replied with a nod. "Now one more time, just to be certain."

"You still don't trust me despite what I've shown you?" Hakea asked, shaking her head more in amusement than disappointment now, beginning to realize that she had just identified one of this woman's few weaknesses. Her need to exercise control. Over everything and everyone.

"I trust no one, Hakea," the cloaked woman replied calmly. "Try not to take it personally. And I would suggest that you adopt the same approach to your relationships. Perhaps if you did, we wouldn't be in the position that we're in now."

Rather than engaging in another argument that Hakea knew that she had little chance of winning, she nodded. Not in agreement with what the woman had said. Rather as a confirmation of what she had just discovered.

The need for the woman to exercise control. Hakea was certain that at some point in the future she could use that failing to her advantage.

Not wanting to delay any longer, eager to be rid of the woman, Hakea stepped up to the haggard prisoner, his chin resting against his chest. Those large eyes of his stared down at her.

He was terrified.

Of her.

Of what she was about to do to him.

That didn't surprise her, because her victim had seen what was about to happen many times before. And he knew that there was little point in trying to resist, not with the leather straps and the two soldiers standing right next to him.

Hakea smiled then, unable to stop herself. She had defeated her victim without saying a word. Without doing anything.

Now that was a power to be savored. And she did, an enjoyable rush running up and down her spine.

"Open up, sweet one. There is much I need you to do."

Instead of fighting her, the man allowed Hakea Roosarian to grasp his chin tightly and lift his head. She then spilled one drop of the roiling black liquid down his throat.

Hakea released her grip and stepped back quickly. Unable to take her eyes away, completely enthralled, just as she was every time she did this.

The change began instantly. In just seconds, the man's body was broken and remade.

His bones cracked and reformed. His frame elongated and widened. His muscles exploded beneath his flesh, taking the place of the gristle that had been there before.

His skin assumed the color of the liquid Hakea had dripped down his throat and became waxy in appearance. His hair fell out.

His hands and feet became longer, his fingers and toes turning into claws. His teeth narrowed and then sharpened into fangs. And his eyes, once a piercing blue, darkened to a blood red.

Through it all the man screamed. In the first few seconds, what came from his throat was an ear-splitting shriek that swirled around the circular chamber. As the transformation progressed, it became a silent scream, the man's sanity leaving him as he was forced to surrender to the animal that he was becoming.

When the conversion was complete, Hakea stepped up to the Stalker and spoke to the beast in a very quiet voice.

Earning a deep rumble of acknowledgment in return, Hakea stepped back and nodded to the soldiers. They released the Stalker from the leather straps.

In a blur, the Stalker was gone, streaking up the steps leading out of the hall and down the dark tunnel on the far side of the balcony.

"Well done, my dear," the cloaked woman said. "Remember, do not waste the liquid. I have no more for you. But, as I said, after tonight, I doubt that you'll have need of it."

With a satisfied nod, the woman turned away from Hakea. Then with a flick of her wrist, a spinning black mist appeared before her.

The woman stepped through without a word. Just as quickly as the portal had formed, it vanished.

Silence descended within the chamber. Hakea, the soldiers, the prisoners, the Stalkers in their cell, not making a sound.

17

HUNT THROUGH THE ROCK

They couldn't take their eyes from the scene that played out before them.

An aberration.

An abhorrent twist of nature.

Davin and Talia watched with a horrified fascination, a single drop of the black, virulent liquid transforming the unfortunate victim into a perverted creature.

A Stalker.

In just seconds.

Through it all, they barely remembered to breathe.

Shocked.

Frightened by the power of the display.

Bound even more tightly to their purpose.

They were not surprised by what they witnessed. They just never anticipated what it would be like to watch the change occur with their own eyes.

Both fought the urge to race down the steps and try to save the man. Only succeeding because they understood that there was nothing that they could do for him.

That they would only be placing themselves in even greater danger.

They understood as well that they needed to remain focused on their more important task.

The many before the one, as Declan liked to explain it to Davin. His friend and mentor had used that phrase more times than he could count while they were training in the Pit.

Just thinking about it helped Davin settle down. A new resolve filled him. His grim expression became even grimmer.

Davin had never understood why Declan tried to teach him that. Why it seemed to be such an important concept for the Master of the Gladiators.

Now he understood the utility of that saying. The necessary coldness of it as well.

There was nothing that he and Talia could do for the man selected to become a Stalker.

However, there was something that they could do that might derail Roosarian's plans and ensure that the atrocities that she was committing here beneath the Rock were never committed again.

Angry at what they had observed and determined to put a stop to this heinous practice, controlling the urge to intervene, they waited in silence until Roosarian was done and her soldiers headed back the way they had come. Even then they waited for several more minutes, wanting to ensure that the Governor of Fal Carrach didn't come back unexpectedly and catch them in the act.

"We need that liquid," whispered Davin, his eyes focused on the nook at the far end of the chamber.

"I want Roosarian."

"I know you do," Davin replied calmly, hearing the hate and determination in her tone, hoping to quell the outrage and desire for revenge that pulsed from Talia, "and I understand why. You'll have it. I promise you." He turned to face her then, making sure that he caught her eyes, wanting her to understand what he was telling her because he knew how emotion could get in the way of rational thought in a situation such as this. "The liquid is more important."

Talia was about to offer a protest. Davin cut her off.

"The liquid first. Then Roosarian. Fair enough?"

"Fair enough," Talia finally grumbled, finding it difficult to pull her gaze away from her partner's. Davin was right, but that didn't mean she had to like it. "When do we go?"

"Give it a few more minutes. We're not doing this until we're alone, and I want to make certain."

The cloaked woman disappearing through the portal confirmed for Davin without a doubt that she was a Magus. He had seen Bryen make use of the Talent in a similar way. Although he was certain that the woman hadn't used the Talent to take her leave.

She had employed the Curse, which confirmed for him as well how the liquid in the vial had been made. What it contained.

That discovery didn't surprise him. Not after what he had seen upon escaping the Pit and falling in with several Magii. Not after fighting the monsters that the Ghoule Overlord created and had sent after them. Not with that essence of evil teasing him ever since he began his hunt beneath the rock.

Nevertheless, he would be the first to admit that it frightened him.

He knew how terrible the power of the Curse could be. He knew as well that he didn't have any defense against it. Because of that, he preferred to be cautious when he came up against an adversary or an obstacle against which he had little to no chance of success.

Davin wished that Bryen or Aislinn were with him. Even Rafia despite the Master of the Magii making him distinctly uncomfortable with the intensity of her stares and her questioning looks. As if she could see all that he was thinking.

But he didn't have his friends with him. Therefore, he would take his time and not rush into what could easily become an even more perilous situation.

As each minute passed, Davin sensed that Talia was getting more and more antsy. She could barely stay still as they hid behind the balcony railing.

He was going to tell her to settle down, that she was just making him nervous. He didn't.

There was no point in wasting his breath. When she was like this, whatever he told her would just rile her up even more.

Thankfully, it wasn't too long before the chamber was clear except for the Stalkers locked away in their cage and the men and women condemned to become those monsters in theirs.

Unable to sit any longer, Talia began to push herself up. Davin reached out gently and placed a hand on her shoulder, keeping her in place with a strong grip.

He shook his head.

She was about to tell him that there was no longer any reason to delay and to get moving when she caught a flash of movement down below. She dropped back down to one knee, shrugged off Davin's large hand, and peered through the stone slats.

Two soldiers marched out of the darkness at a fast clip. To Davin's experienced eye, he interpreted their rapid and nervous movement as having been given a task that they didn't want. Therefore, they were going to complete it as swiftly as they could and be done with it.

The pair approached the cage filled with Stalkers, one with the keys in his hand, the other drawing his sword and standing back a few feet.

Davin shook his head in amusement. That really was a useless gesture on the part of the soldier.

If the fools were going to release a Stalker and the beast wanted to kill them, it would do so with little trouble. The ragged swings of a single blade would have little effect.

Talia nodded an apology to Davin as he leaned in closer to her, peering through the stone pillars in the railing to watch the soldiers.

It proved to be a surprisingly simple, innocuous process.

The first soldier unlocked the cell door and stepped out of the way. Instead of the mad rush that both Davin and Talia had anticipated, only one Stalker stepped out of the darkness.

The other monsters stayed exactly where they were. Not trying to escape. Waiting. Almost docile.

Talia observed with a great deal of interest, believing that she knew why.

Those other Stalkers had not yet been released on their assignments. Until they were, they would remain here.

The Stalkers were killing machines. That was undeniable.

For the most part, however, they were controlled killing machines.

Assassins.

Just another reason why Talia felt the desperate urge to gain her vengeance on Hakea Roosarian.

The Stalker glided right past the two soldiers, ignoring them completely, then sprinted up the steps and was gone, off to complete whatever task the Governor of Fal Carrach had given it.

The soldier with the keys, clearly anxious if not outright terrified, slammed the cell door closed and then locked it, earning a few low rumbles of displeasure from the Stalkers in the cell, although none of them made a move toward him.

The soldier behind him sheathed his sword. Then they both walked out of the chamber and back down the hallway at what was more a trot than a walk.

Davin didn't blame them for being frightened. The Stalkers were nasty beasts.

Quiet once more, again Davin settled back against the stone railing. Talia did as well.

He came across as completely at his ease. She aimed to imitate him, although she had to remind herself multiple times to stop tapping her fingers on her knee.

Another ten minutes passed before Davin finally shifted his position and looked back through the slats.

"Can we go down and …"

Davin shushed Talia, waiting, wanting to make sure. He allowed his eyes to roam around the chamber and into the gloom of the hallway below.

He wasn't looking for anything in particular. Rather, just for anything that might catch his eye or ear.

A motion. A flash. A sound that shouldn't be there.

Nothing.

No movement.

No noise.

Finally, Davin nodded.

"About time," grumbled Talia, which brought a smile to Davin's lips.

They pushed themselves up from their hiding place and walked on silent feet along the balcony to the steps that took them down into the chamber.

Davin held up his hand. Waiting again. Listening. Allowing his gaze to wander all around them.

Nothing.

They walked down the stairs slowly, not daring to make a noise.

When they set foot on the tiles of the chamber, Davin stopped again, Talia right behind him.

Listening.

Watching.

The prisoners demonstrated no interest in them whatso-ever, lost in their own miserable worlds, understanding what fate held in store for them.

Davin could only liken it to what it must be like for those sentenced to the gallows, withdrawing into themselves before the fateful act.

The Stalkers stared at them intently. Their blood-red eyes tracked their movements as they walked across the chamber toward the shelf in the wall.

Yet the monsters didn't make a noise. They didn't make a move toward the bars.

They appeared to be curious. Beyond that they offered no other reaction.

Talia couldn't look away from them. Barely visible in the darkness except for those blood-red eyes.

A shiver of fear ran down her spine. The steel bars keeping them there didn't look very strong.

An irrational fear blossomed within her, and she needed to fight to keep it under control.

If the Stalkers wanted to get out, they probably could.

Needing to do something, even though she knew that it was a useless gesture, she kept her hand close to the hilt of one of the many daggers secreted about her body as she followed on Davin's heels.

Davin ignored the Stalkers entirely, having eyes only for the reason that they were there. He hadn't been in a rush to walk down into the chamber, but he didn't have any desire to be there any longer than he needed to be now that he was there.

With that thought guiding him, he reached in carefully and grabbed the one glass vial that still contained the roiling black liquid. Turning back toward the hallway that led out from the chamber, he handed the vial to Talia. She placed it carefully in the small pouch on her belt.

"Back out the way we came?" Talia asked quietly. "Then

once we get the liquid somewhere safe, we can focus on dealing with Roosarian."

"Back out the way ..."

Davin stopped in his tracks. He should have expected as much. It all had been just a little too easy.

He could see them in the passageway through which Hakea Roosarian and then the two soldiers had entered and exited.

Definitely more than one. Barely a hint of movement. Just a whisper, really.

As usual, it was their eyes that gave them away.

One set of blood-red orbs peered at him out of the darkness that masked the corridor.

Then another not too far behind the first.

And one more.

Davin stepped back from the hallway, reaching out with his hand and pulling Talia behind him. He brushed her chest by mistake as he did so, not wanting to take his eyes away from the monsters waiting for him in the dark.

"What are you ..." Talia began to demand, shocked by Davin's behavior, not understanding the cause ... until she watched with wide eyes as the three Stalkers emerged from the tunnel. Working to control her burgeoning fear, she concentrated on what they needed to do next. "Can we kill them all? Make a break for it afterward?"

She already knew the answer, yet she still felt the need to ask. With the three monsters staring hungrily at them, she needed some hope, faint though it may be.

Davin shrugged apologetically. "One, yes. Two, maybe. Three ... that's asking a bit too much. And if there are three, there are probably more."

Talia nodded. She had assumed as much. "Then you must have some idea as to how to get us out of this."

"Why do you think that?"

"Because you always have ideas. Not all of them good ideas,

mind you. But right now, I would agree to any idea that you might have." She glanced at him expectantly. "So do you have an idea?"

"I do," he replied softly, never taking his eyes away from the monsters blocking their path.

Talia gave Davin a sardonic look that he missed. "Would you care to share that with me?"

Davin nodded toward the Stalker on their left. That monster was farther ahead of the other two by a good ten feet. The pair still standing by the entrance to the hallway. They appeared to be more interested in preventing their escape rather than attacking, leaving that task to the one closest to them.

"That one first to even the odds."

Talia nodded. "That's a good plan."

"I do have my moments."

"Few and far between, however."

Davin snorted softly. "Riding me even now?"

"Sorry," Talia replied quietly, acknowledging that the cause for her barb was her nervousness, her face beginning to flush at the initial response that she had been about to offer but quashed before she could embarrass herself. They were facing desperate straits, yes, but she still had her standards. "When do you want to ..."

Davin launched himself at the Stalker before Talia could complete her question.

Cursing in aggravation, sword held at the ready, she followed him. She could talk to the gladiator about his communication skills, or lack thereof, when they got out of this mess. If they got out of this mess, she corrected.

The Stalker was incredibly fast, knocking to the side the spear that Davin thrust toward his hip.

However, the monster wasn't fast enough to stop both

Davin and Talia, who hid behind the gladiator, not revealing herself until the moment was right.

The Stalker concentrating on blocking Davin's steel with its claws, Talia came out from behind his broad back and slashed across the beast's exposed left hip. Her blade scratched against the bone and cut away a large chunk of flesh.

The Stalker dropped to one knee, clutching at the bloody gash.

Davin took full advantage, bringing the blade of his spear back around and slashing across the monster's throat without a second thought.

Both he and Talia stepped back then, not stopping until they were in the center of the circular chamber.

The two Stalkers set to join the fight stared at their dying brethren. Then they shifted their cold gazes toward Davin and Lycia. As one, they glided toward them across the tile floor.

"You ready?" Davin asked.

"Ready as I will be," Talia murmured. "We don't really have much choice, do we?"

"We don't," Davin replied. "Just one piece of advice."

"What would that be?" Talia asked, finding it incredibly difficult to pull her eyes away from the harsh gaze of the Stalker that seemed to have eyes only for her.

"Don't die," Davin replied quietly.

"Useful as always," Talia grumbled with her own snort of quiet laughter.

"I do what I can," Davin replied, glad that she hadn't lost her sharp wit.

He wasn't concerned about her. At least not overly so.

The thought of facing off against a Stalker would have terrified most people. Not Talia.

He had no doubt that she could handle herself. She had tested her skills against him so often that he would rate her as just as good with a blade as the majority of the gladiators in the Blood Company.

Talia appreciated Davin's humor. It helped to relax her as she prepared herself for the combat. Thinking about how she could apply her strengths. Considering the Stalker's weaknesses – although admittedly there were very few – and how she might be able to take advantage of them.

"Maybe think about doing a bit more in the future," Talia offered in return.

"I'll keep that in mind," Davin chuckled. Then he brought the blade of his spear to his forehead, turning ever so slightly and nodding to Talia. A sign of respect between warriors. "I'll see you on the other side."

For just a breath, Talia was speechless, understanding the importance of the moment. She didn't know what to say, never expecting Davin to do what he just did. Without really thinking, she raised her blade to her forehead and offered him a nod in return. "I'll see you on the other side."

Davin smiled broadly and then leapt away from her. He lunged with his spear for the Stalker standing across from Talia.

The monster responded as expected, scrambling back, his clawed feet scratching across the tile.

Talia recognized Davin's attack for what it was even if the Stalker didn't. A feint.

Instead of continuing his assault, in the same motion Davin moved with a remarkable fluidity toward his left, slashing at the Stalker that stood right across from him, hoping to take his opponent by surprise.

Unfortunately, he didn't. But he did earn Talia the opportunity to get in the first strike, and she did with a brutal precision.

With the Stalker directly in front of her still focused on Davin, Talia did as she had to the first Stalker, slicing across the beast's hip. Once again, her aim was true, cutting all the way to the bone and shattering the joint.

The Stalker hissed in pain, tottering backward and slipping not only because of its wound, but also because its clawed feet failed to gain much purchase on the tile floor.

Talia didn't hesitate at the Stalker's obvious and worsening struggles. She feinted a backhanded slash toward the Stalker's throat, the beast dipping away from her to avoid it.

The beast shrieked in pleasure as it dodged the blow despite the limitations of its injuries. Yet in doing so he only succeeded in giving Talia an even better chance of striking her real target.

The Stalker's other hip.

Stopping her slash mid motion, with all the power that she could muster, she sliced into the Stalker's leg at the top of the thigh all the way to its pelvic bone.

The Stalker's shriek of pleasure quickly became one of agony. The beast fell back onto the slick floor made worse by the puddles of blood forming beneath its clawed feet.

Talia tugged at her sword, desperate to free it. She failed, the steel wedged too deeply into the monster's bone. She had no choice but to let go of the hilt when her adversary fell away from her.

That didn't stop Talia from finishing the combat, however. Wary of the Stalker's claws, she pulled a small dagger from the sheath on her right hip and in the same motion flicked it through the air.

Talia grunted in satisfaction, mirroring the Stalker's grunt of surprise that was followed swiftly by a soft gurgle, her dagger lodged in the monster's throat.

As the beast died slowly, its body twitching as it gasped for the breaths that wouldn't come, Talia planted one boot on the Stalker's ravaged thigh and pulled with all the strength that she had.

Finally, after three tries, her sword came free.

She turned away from the Stalker, hearing the growl of anger on the other side of the chamber, fearing that she would have another beast to fight.

She breathed easier when she realized that Davin was enjoying a good bit of success against the last Stalker.

The monster bled from several nasty slashes across its chest and thighs, and there was a deep puncture that revealed bone on the left side of the beast's back.

Davin must have punched his spear right through the beast's shoulder, which would explain why the Stalker was attacking the gladiator now with just its right claw.

Yet even with only one working appendage, the Stalker forced Davin back toward the chamber wall not too far away from the nook that had held the vial of black liquid.

Davin didn't know what was happening with Talia. He wanted to help her, but he couldn't. The Stalker refused to die easily, so he didn't have the chance. All he could do was hope that she survived her own combat.

Because he needed to concentrate on the enraged, one-armed Stalker, the beast attacking him with a ferocity that was impressive if not for the fact that it was directed toward him.

His spear was a blur as he defended himself. He didn't bother to think about attacking. Rather, his focus was on keeping the monster away from him and waiting for the best opportunity to finish the beast.

Davin realized that he would never get that chance when he saw the sharp steel tip slide through the Stalker's chest right where his heart was. The lost opportunity didn't bother him in the least.

The monster stood stock still, not quite comprehending what was happening, even as the steel disappeared and then reappeared just a heartbeat later in almost exactly the same place. And then again. And then one more time just for good measure.

Davin watched with a mix of satisfaction and regret as the Stalker's blood-red eyes, once burning with a lust for blood and death, slowly faded to black, the monster crumpling to the floor right at the gladiator's feet.

"Two Stalkers," Davin nodded. "Really impressive. My sister is going to want to meet you."

"You want to take me home to your sister?" Talia teased. "I didn't know I meant so much to you."

Davin gave her a confused look, the heat rising in his face when he understood.

"Well, I didn't mean ..." Davin started and stopped. "It's just that ..."

"Relax, Davin," Talia replied with a broad smile, enjoying his brief moment of discomfort, "I was just playing with you."

"I knew that," Davin replied, trying to cover for himself.

"Of course you did," Talia nodded, although clearly she said it for his benefit. Davin was about to respond, but she was quick to cut him off. "We need to get out of here."

Nodding, he ran up the stairs to the balcony, Talia close on his heels.

He had wanted to curl around the balcony and make for the corridor that would take them back to the crevice through which they had first entered the Rock.

He growled in frustration, realizing that they needed a new plan.

He had caught a glimpse of several large shadows racing down that passageway. More Stalkers to join the fun.

Having no other options, Davin sprinted down the corridor through which the Stalker Roosarian had just created had exited.

"Davin, do you have any idea where you're going?" Talia was right behind him. She was spending just as much time looking over her shoulder as she was making sure that she didn't trip into Davin since she was following him so closely.

Three Stalkers emerged from the passageway that Davin had wanted to take initially, joining the hunt. Worse, the noises coming from farther down that same tunnel suggested that even more of the beasts were in pursuit.

"Some idea," Davin called over his shoulder.

"You're not filling me with confidence."

"That doesn't surprise me in the least," Davin replied with a bark of laughter.

Talia answered with a laugh of her own. Davin seemed to be enjoying himself way too much. Talia couldn't quite believe it …

Actually, she could. And she didn't even want to consider what that meant.

They ran twenty more yards down the corridor before they came to a junction. They could continue forward through the gloom, or they could turn toward the right or the left, the passageway that met the one they were in curling down in those directions.

Davin didn't hesitate, heading toward the left.

Talia didn't know why he selected that direction. But that didn't matter. With the Stalkers gaining on them, she had no choice but to follow.

Just seconds after they started on their new route, they both heard a scrabbling behind them accompanied by several angry shrieks. The sound made them both smile.

The Stalkers chasing them had trouble negotiating the turn without slowing down. Several had slipped and tumbled past the junction, the others getting mixed into the tangle of legs and arms.

Talia would have found it all quite amusing if not for the fact that she was certain that the Stalkers would be after them again in just a matter of seconds.

They only made it fifty yards farther down the corridor when Talia sensed the first of the Stalkers to regain their feet coming after them again.

"Davin, they'll be on us in seconds."

"I know," he replied, not lessening his pace, actually increasing it and forcing Talia to stay with him.

"We're going in a circle, Davin."

"I'm aware of that," he replied over his shoulder.

"How does that help us? We have no chance of getting away from the Stalkers. They're too fast."

"I'm not trying to get away from them," Davin explained.

"What are you talking about?" Talia demanded, not understanding what he had in mind. Hoping that he had something in mind.

"I'm trying to stall them. Not escape them."

Seconds later, Davin skidded to a stop. They were back where the tunnel they had taken to enter the Rock shifted from rough-hewn rock to carved stone.

As he worked his way deeper beneath the citadel, Davin's overriding concern was whether a Stalker was waiting in the gloom to attack them. But he also had made note of the passageway.

To the left torches affixed to the wall led back toward the circular chamber. To the right, there was only darkness.

Davin gave Talia a satisfied nod.

She heard the sound of the surf breaking against the shore and smelled the sea. A hundred yards away. No more than that. She was certain.

Could they actually make it? she wondered. They were so close.

"Clever," Talia said, impressed by Davin's strategy, disappointed that she hadn't thought of it herself.

"I do what I can."

"That you do," Talia agreed, her response heartfelt and lacking the sarcasm of her last.

Not seeing the tell-tale blood-red orbs ahead of her, she ran for a few dozen yards into the darkness that led toward the beach, then stopped abruptly when she realized that she was alone.

Davin hadn't gone with her. Instead, he was staring up at the ceiling for some reason that she didn't understand.

"Davin, come on!" Talia ordered. "We need to go. This is our chance."

She could hear the clack of the Stalkers' claws as they sprinted down the curling corridor toward Davin.

"You're right. *We* barely stand a chance. But *you* have a good chance."

"What are you talking ..."

Davin turned his back toward her, then drove his spear into the ceiling. He did it again. And again. And again. With the same force and rapidity as if he were trying to kill a Stalker.

"Run!" Davin shouted over his shoulder.

"Davin, what are you doing?" Talia demanded. At the same time, she scurried back twenty feet when she heard the sound of cracking stone coming from the ceiling above her.

Talia hadn't noticed it on the way through the corridor. Davin had.

Large wooden blocks crisscrossed the ceiling. Supporting it. The stonemasons had gotten only so far in their work, leaving the rest of the passageway for some other time, though still wary of its stability.

Davin wouldn't have even realized it if he hadn't tripped on the small rocks scattered across the floor that he paid little attention to when he and Talia first made their way toward the chamber at the far end.

Now, however, he was glad for his clumsiness. He glanced up at the ceiling for just a brief second. With each strike of his spear, the cloud of dust billowed and expanded, more dirt and shards of rock sprinkling down from above.

Believing that he had loosened the stone above him just enough, doing his best to ignore the Stalkers rushing hungrily toward him, and only partially succeeding as his heart began to race out of fear rather than exertion, Davin stayed on task by shifting his attention to the support beams.

Davin grinned. With one good strike where the joints met across the ceiling, he heard the first creaking protest he so desperately wanted. His second well-placed strike gave him another, much louder crack.

He was definitely on the right track. Just one more good blow should do it.

When the blade of his spear punched into the joint just above his head a third time, the last of the structure's resistance disappeared.

Davin shouted in triumph at the same time that he stumbled back, barely avoiding the several tons of stone and dirt, mixed in with a good number of fractured support beams, that crashed down to the floor.

Before the dust even settled, Davin turned to face the onrushing Stalkers.

The monsters were only twenty feet away from him.

Six in all.

Not good odds, but he hadn't expected them to be any better.

Understanding what fate awaited him, his initial instinct was to rush at the beasts. If he got lucky, he might be able to kill one, maybe two, before they killed him.

He held back, however, deciding not to accelerate the timing of his own demise.

Then, much to his surprise, the Stalkers stopped.

Maybe it was because of disappointment. One of their prey had escaped.

Davin didn't know, and he didn't care.

He did know that he had succeeded.

The corridor was blocked. There was no way that the Stalkers could get at Talia now.

As he had told her, she was more important than he was. Even more so now since she carried the vial of roiling black liquid.

"Davin, what did you do?" Talia shouted from the other side of the pile of debris, her anger knowing almost no bounds.

"I gave you a chance," he cried, his voice muffled by the stone and dirt. "Now make the most of it. Go! Get out of here!"

"I won't!" Talia refused. "I'm not leaving you, Davin."

Davin never took his eyes away from the Stalkers. The beasts were fixed in place. Staring at him. Not yet attacking. Strangely passive. For now.

He certainly appreciated the delay.

"Run!" ordered Davin. "Get the vial to Bryen or Rafia. They need to know how the Stalkers are made. They need to destroy the source. They'll know what to do."

"Davin, I'm not leaving you!"

Talia's refusal tugged at Davin's heart. He valued her loyalty and even more what else he heard in her voice. But that loyalty would do neither of them any good right then.

"Talia, you need to go. Now. Please."

"Davin, I can't ..."

"Talia!" Davin said sharply. "Please. I spoke truly before. You know it as well as I do. You're more important than I am. You can't deny that. Don't waste the time that I've given you."

Talia stared at the pile of rocks, dirt, and broken timbers that prevented her from going to Davin's aid and kept her safe from the Stalkers.

She had never been as angry as she was at that very moment.

How could he do this to her?

How could he do this for her?

He had no right!

In one sense she felt betrayed. In another, she felt …

That was a path, even then, upon which she was not yet ready to tread.

Yet she understood what he had done.

Why Davin was willing to sacrifice himself for her. Why he was willing to leave her.

More aggravating, she couldn't find fault with Davin's reasoning. That's what bothered her the most.

Not what he did. Rather the fact that he had acknowledged the truth before she did.

She was angry not because of what he had done.

She was angry because of what he had said. And what he had not said but still was undeniable.

"You better survive this foolish decision of yours, Davin, because I plan on killing you myself!"

Spitting out a dozen curses that she had learned from the sailors on her ships, she heeded Davin even though she didn't want to.

Turning on her heel, she sprinted down the tunnel toward the sea.

HEARING nothing but silence on the other side of the pile of rubble, Davin closed his eyes for a brief moment in relief. Talia had done as he had asked. Reluctantly. But she was gone.

That's all that mattered.

At least now he wouldn't die in vain.

And he had little doubt that he was going to die.

He was the Crimson Giant. That was correct.

Only the Volkun had demonstrated greater skill in the Pit than he had. That was correct as well.

But he wasn't a fool.

He knew what the result would be when the combat began against six Stalkers.

He should have been raging against his fate. He had every right to do so.

But he didn't.

Instead, he felt lucky.

He should have died many times over while he fought on the white sand. But he hadn't.

Sometimes because of his expertise and his skill. Sometimes because of his luck.

He should have died several times while fighting the Ghoules and the Echidnae. But he hadn't.

He really should have died when he attacked the Bakunawa in the Burnt Ocean. But he hadn't.

So many times he had cheated death, still alive just by the skin of his teeth.

Now, however, he didn't think that he was going to escape the fate that he deserved.

Strangely, that didn't bother him. Perhaps it was because he believed that he was going to die having done something worthwhile. Something useful.

Taking some solace from that fact, he prepared to meet the Stalkers' expected rush.

Weirdly, the Stalkers made no move to come at him even though he had nowhere to go. Even though he would be an easy kill for so many of the monsters.

Instead, they stared at him a while longer and then, when Davin heard the stomp of boots coming down the shadowy hallway, the Stalkers stepped back around the curling corridor and disappeared.

What was going on?

The answer to his question came marching around the

bend. Several dozen soldiers, hands on the hilts of their swords, halted just twenty feet away from him.

Out of the frying pan and into the fire.

Or was it the other way around, Davin wondered. Out of the fire and into the frying pan.

Which was a worse fate?

Dying at the claws of the Stalkers or dying at the hands of these soldiers?

He was still trying to answer that question when the soldiers standing in the center of the corridor stepped to the side, allowing Hakea Roosarian to walk through their ranks.

She stopped when she was only ten feet away from him, clearly not worried that he held a spear in his hands.

The staring began again. This time between the gladiator and the Governor of Fal Carrach.

Talia wanted Hakea Roosarian dead. And for good reason.

He wondered whether he should make a play for her. It might be the only chance that he got.

Just one well-placed lunge and it could all be over. Yet for some reason he got the sense that maybe now wasn't the right time.

"Continuing to fight will only lead to your death," Hakea said, breaking Davin out of his thoughts.

He shrugged. "Dying doesn't bother me."

"No, I don't expect that it does."

She studied him for a few seconds more. She was angry that it had come to this, but in the larger scheme of things, it didn't matter.

Hakea's nemesis would be dead soon enough, and she would regain the solution that she had stolen.

Confident of that, she allowed her curiosity to come to the fore. There was something about this gladiator that had pulled at her the very first time she had met him that was only stronger now.

"Was it worth it?" she wondered. "Sacrificing yourself for her?"

"I thought it was very gallant on my part," Davin replied with a mischievous grin and a wink, placing the butt of his spear on the stone floor and leaning against his weapon in a pose of seeming indifference, as if the reality of so many soldiers standing ready to skewer him didn't bother him in the least.

"Gallant or foolish? Often there is little difference between the two."

"True," Davin admitted with a nod, "I'll give you that. Still, I'll stick with gallant. It makes me feel better about myself."

Hakea laughed at that, not quite believing that he could offer a hint of fun while facing such dreadful circumstances.

What was it about this gladiator that so appealed to her? It had to be more than just his gallows humor. "You can keep fighting and ensure your death, or you can surrender, and we can have a conversation."

"A conversation about what?" asked Davin, never expecting the offer.

"A conversation that would benefit us both."

18

INTO THE FRYING PAN

"Does this remind you of anything?" Bryen asked.

"It makes me think of Battersea, which makes sense considering my uncle grew up there and rules here now. It's just that ..."

Aislinn wasn't quite sure what it was that was bothering her. She had sensed it before they even walked through the western gate.

"It's what?" prodded Bryen.

"It doesn't feel right," Aislinn murmured finally, still having some difficulty putting her thoughts into words.

Bryen nodded, although he doubted that Aislinn could see the movement. They both wore their cloaks, cowls hiding their faces, to guard against more than just the crisp breeze that felt even colder thanks to the perpetual shadow in which the town resided, courtesy of the towering peak rising above it.

Of course, hiding Aislinn's face was more important than hiding his. Her uncle may have given a description of her to the Northern Guard.

He doubted that anyone knew him here. Nevertheless, Bryen had split apart the Spear of the Magii, sheathing the two component pieces across his back. It was too distinctive a weapon and too memorable, so best to keep it out of sight.

"How so?"

Aislinn began to reply several times but didn't. She continued to allow her gaze to wander over all that was occurring around them.

What was it that made the skin on the back of her neck prickle?

Aislinn desperately wanted to believe that her uncle had nothing to do with all that they had learned regarding the more nefarious activities taking place in New Caledonia.

Bryen understood that. He wanted to believe it as well.

It would make their arrival here that much easier.

Yet neither of them was willing to make an assumption based on what they wanted. They needed to make decisions based on what was. Because their lives depended on those decisions.

As Declan had taught him and then hammered into his head time after time, doing all that he could to ensure that Bryen never forgot this particular lesson, trust was earned, never given.

Therefore, better to be cautious. They still intended to introduce themselves to her uncle and his wife. On their terms, however.

Neither had any desire to see the inside of a cell or worse.

"Like a siege mentality?" Bryen offered.

Aislinn turned toward him, catching his eyes. She nodded slowly and then her eyes swept past him as she continued to take in all that was Shadow's Reach while they made their way through the city's crowded streets.

"Exactly that," she agreed.

"It could be the Wraiths," Bryen suggested. "Perhaps the Stalkers as well."

"Yes, I'm sure that has a great deal to do with it."

Aislinn stopped, her frustration mounting. Bryen was right, but then again he wasn't.

She felt as if there was more to her sense of unease than just the obvious.

Not wanting to get run over by the many teams of horses pulling large wagons packed with covered cargo down the cobblestones, she sidestepped off the street and found a safe place under the awning of a spice seller who appeared to be doing a very brisk business.

Bryen stepped up next to her. He could tell that she was more than just perplexed.

"Use the Talent," Bryen urged. He had been doing that to supplement his other senses as soon as they reached the top of the several-mile-long tor. What he had discovered as they approached Shadow's Reach didn't surprise him.

If he had not extended his senses with the Talent, from what he could see and hear, Shadow's Reach, although a bit rough around the edges, appeared to be nothing more than a prosperous town that was rapidly growing into a city.

In fact, the original stone walls already had outgrown their utility. Several neighborhoods sprouting beyond the palisades on the southern side of the city.

The new walls were being built, although that construction wasn't yet complete. And, anticipating future growth, the survey work extended the palisades a good half mile beyond the current perimeter of the city.

Most eye-catching were the half-dozen cranes towering over the main square. All of them were in close proximity to one another. All of them were being used to construct what he had learned from a vendor selling hotcakes was the Shadow Keep.

With that fortress would come administrative offices, a public works department, a training ground, and improved barracks for the Northern Guard. The entire complex was encircled by a rampart that was twice as tall as the town's fifty-foot wall. It seemed that the primary delay in constructing the keep was the circular dome that was to be a testament to the Governor and his rule.

Unnecessary in Bryen's opinion, but his perspective counted for very little. He didn't grow up with the power and privilege granted to a ducal family in Caledonia.

The markets they had walked through as they slowly made their way toward the city center were bustling with activity. All of the vendors were doing a brisk business. And there was no lack of goods. Stalls for food and produce and the other necessities of life were situated in the many squares located throughout Shadow's Reach while along the edge shops selling high-end items that you would expect to see in any Caledonian city attracted those with more to spend.

All that suggested a prosperity to be savored. Yet there was an underlying current that disturbed those very obvious signs of success.

Fear.

In itself that wasn't surprising based on the constant peril presented by the Wraiths. However, Bryen didn't believe that sense of alarm mixed with anxiety resulted just from the monsters that hunted around the city when the fog descended and supposedly had yet to penetrate the walls.

No, that fear resulted because the stories that they had heard obviously were to be believed.

The Wraiths hunted in the streets of Shadow's Reach when the Murk flowed in.

As Aislinn searched around them with the Talent, the spark that flashed in the back of her eyes telling him that she had identified what he knew that she would, Bryen studied one large house that was being built just across the street from where they were standing.

A handful of workers were in the middle of mounting a very sturdy door. The oak was at least several inches thick and double banded in steel. It reminded him of what he would expect to see on a gatehouse.

The windows differed, however. They were smaller than what he had seen in the homes in Tintagel. There was no way that anyone or anything bigger than an average sized man or woman was going to climb through that opening.

With his shoulders, he doubted that he could do it. A Stalker certainly couldn't, nor could a Wraith.

He shifted his gaze to the sharply sloped roof, which with the very steep angle immediately made him think of some of the almost unscalable inclines in the Northern Spine that he and Sirius had struggled up as they sought to escape the Ghoules while making their way to Haven. Another crew of workers was laying what looked to be a very thick fire-hardened tile atop beams that were separated from one another by a space no wider than a foot.

Nothing was going to break into the house through the roof.

And he couldn't be certain, because the workers who were finishing the stone walls on the northern side of the house were blocking his view, but it looked as if they were setting the brick so that there were small gaps running in between the windows at regularly spaced intervals.

Murder slits.

Those living in the home could shoot an arrow or extend a spear or lance through those gaps while enjoying the safety offered by the brick.

So a home, yes, although just as much a small fortress.

And this house was no different from the many others that they had passed as they walked through this section of the city which was inhabited primarily by well-to-do merchants and craftspeople.

Definitely a city under siege, his argument buttressed by the large number of soldiers they had walked past while entering the city gates and the even larger number manning the walls.

The soldiers at the gate hadn't bothered to ask any questions. They didn't seem to really care about who entered Shadow's Reach so long as they were human.

Rather, their focus was on what lay beyond the city.

Their eyes were hard, as if they were accustomed to combat. Yet their eyes also were haunted.

They had experienced things that they didn't want to experience. That they didn't want to remember.

The men and women of the Northern Guard radiated a nervousness as well. Slightly distracted. Perhaps even fearful.

The soldiers atop the parapet, even though they stood near the western gate, positioned themselves so that they could look to the north. That only made sense if their primary threat, the cause of their worry and their fear, came from that direction.

Perhaps not surprising, there were also a great many soldiers in the avenues and alleys. In the markets. On the corners. Standing at the junctions where the larger boulevards met.

Just as obvious as the soldiers were the huge braziers set at regular intervals along all of the larger streets -- fresh wood already in place, the remains of last night's fires swept out before the sun had risen over the peaks to the east -- that matched those running along the parapets.

When all those pyres were lit, night would turn into day.

Unless the Murk came in.

And then there was the final piece that completed the puzzle that was Shadow's Reach.

On every street corner, right next to a brazier, there was a steel post set in place that held a large bell.

A system for warning of what was in the streets ... or soon would be.

"Did you sense it?" asked Bryen.

"I did." Aislinn nodded. "It's very strong here, but I really need to work to find it because it's being concealed."

"That was my thought as well," Bryen agreed.

"I hadn't expected to find it here," Aislinn grumbled, disappointed by her discovery, "or rather I had hoped that we would be free of its presence. Naïve, I know, but there it is."

"Sirius liked to say that the Curse was little different than the Talent. How natural magic was used came down to purpose. Because of that, he liked to argue that the Curse is a perverted form of the Talent. Dark Magii use the Talent, or what used to be the Talent and is now the Curse, for themselves rather than for others. As a result, the Curse and the Talent are inseparable. Where the Talent is ..."

"The Curse will be as well, hidden in the shadows, always there waiting for some fool to make use of it, the fool never realizing the Curse was using them instead," Aislinn finished for him, nodding her head as she remembered having the same exact conversation with her former tutor. "He did like to say that, didn't he?"

"He's proving his point once again, even from the other side," Bryen said with a slight smile.

"That he is."

Just as Bryen did, Aislinn sensed a very faint touch of the Curse permeating the city. It was barely there, just teasing her at the edge of her senses.

Even so, it was widespread. There no matter what direction she searched, consuming all of the city and in fact expanding out over the entire tor upon which it was built. It was quite clear that whoever or whatever in Shadow's Reach had sold themselves to the Curse exercised a great deal more of the tainted power than was revealed by Aislinn and Bryen's survey.

Aislinn didn't know the cause for the Curse proliferating throughout the city and beyond. A person, a monster, perhaps even an artifact. It could be any or all or none, or some other threat entirely that she had never encountered before.

That was in part why she so wanted to locate the source. The other, larger part being her need to know if her uncle was involved in any way.

"Shall we continue to wander?" suggested Bryen. "See what we see?"

Aislinn nodded. "You want to identify the source?"

"A worthwhile objective, but no promises in that regard," Bryen replied. "The Curse is very weak here near the wall. It grows stronger as we move closer to the city center."

"Then perhaps we head in a roundabout way toward the Shadow Keep?" Aislinn's worry continued to grow. Moving closer to the construction meant moving closer to where her uncle resided. "See if we can narrow down where we need to look?"

"That works for me."

Aislinn led the way as she and Bryen started to walk through the streets again, taking their time, using up the last few hours of the morning. During their wandering they confirmed their initial sense of the city, that miasma of trepidation having woven itself into the very fabric of everyday life.

Hidden beneath that was the faint hint of corruption that tickled their senses and slowly intensified as they circled their way toward the unfinished citadel that was built on a broad rather than steep hill that dominated the rest of the aspiring city.

"You ready to say hello to your uncle?" Bryen asked. He didn't believe that there was much more to be revealed about the city without introducing themselves to the Governor and Lady Winborne, because he was beginning to think that their questions regarding the Curse only could be answered at the citadel.

"Soon," Aislinn murmured, having reached much the same

conclusion as Bryen. "I was thinking that we might want to get a bite to eat first."

She motioned toward a tavern on the other side of the square they had just entered that, based on the number of people going in and out, appeared to be quite prosperous. The road that would take them to the top of the plateau and the Shadow Keep began on the northern side of the square next to the tavern, which meant that many of the people working in the citadel probably frequented the establishment.

Bryen smiled and then nodded, striding across the square, Aislinn right next to him. There was no better way to get the gossip of what was going on in a city than to spend some time talking with a tavern owner in the know.

"Do you think it's her?"

"It's hard to say," Nico replied. "I didn't see much of her."

He and Mika began following the pair not long after they had walked beneath the portcullis. Neither had gotten a good look at the young woman, so they couldn't say for sure that it was her. Their doubts were reinforced by the fact that based on when she was supposed to have arrived -- several months before -- by all rights she should be dead.

Nevertheless, there was something about the woman that had caught their attention. An assuredness about her. A sense of purpose.

If not the woman they were looking for, than a woman of importance and likely wealth considering the cut of her clothes. A woman they should be able to roll on their own.

Still, better to let the boss know and let him decide. He took a dim view of freelancing if he didn't get a cut or it got in the way of a regular job.

"Mackey in the tavern?" Nico asked.

"I expect he is," Mika replied. "He only leaves if it's necessary. Besides, he was meeting with some of the boys this morning about a new contract with Arjen. He's probably got an entire crew in there right now."

Nico nodded. "Stay here and wait for the pair. If they come out before I do, follow them and I'll find you."

"You're going to tell Mackey?"

"I will. He'll see them. He can decide. And if he doesn't think she's the one we're looking for, then we can go after the both of them on our own. Put a few more golds in our pockets."

"You sure about that?"

"What are you worried about, Mika?"

"Both of them make me nervous."

"What are you talking about?" Nico demanded. "A rich woman with one bodyguard? They make you nervous?"

Mika shrugged. "Just a feeling, that's all. I get the sense they know how to use their weapons."

"We know how to use our weapons too," Nico countered, placing a hand on the hilt of his short sword to emphasize his point.

Nico was about to tell Mika to grow a pair. He stopped himself before the words came out. He had gotten a similar feeling, although he didn't want to admit it. Besides, Mika usually wasn't wrong about these things.

"If Mackey says we can go after them, I'll get a few more of the boys to go with us. No reason to take any unnecessary risks."

～

"WHY THIS ONE?" Bryen asked once they entered the establishment and selected a quiet table in the back that gave them a view of the tavern's courtyard through the windows that ran along the back wall. No one else sat near them, everyone else preferring to be closer to the bar.

"It's close to the citadel," Aislinn replied. "Busy but not too busy at this time of day."

"There's more to it than that," Bryen hinted, catching the gleam in her eyes even as she kept her hood up.

"And the tavern keeper is doing some not necessarily legitimate business out the back," she replied, nodding toward the stables that were visible through the window.

Several wagons were being loaded and unloaded with a good number of toughs lounging around. Clearly, those men weren't soldiers. And they weren't merchant guards, who usually displayed some modicum of discipline.

"Whoever owns the tavern is doing more than providing food and drink, a place to sleep, and even a little entertainment," Aislinn concluded. "They're doing just as good a business if not better in items that aren't always readily available."

"You mean items that the Governor might want to tax or might not want in his city in the first place."

"Correct," Aislinn confirmed, watching for a few seconds more as one of the wagons, packed and with the cargo tied down, was hitched to a team of horses and then taken out of the courtyard, a fist of toughs accompanying it.

As soon as that wagon was gone, another was pushed into place by the remaining hoodlums. Before the wagon even had been set into place, another team of workers emerged from the storeroom right next to the stables and began to stock it with an assortment of products packed in a variety of different-sized crates, tarps to be hung over the cargo at the ready once those loading the wagon were done.

"How do you know all this?" This was a side of Aislinn that Bryen had yet to see, and it appealed to him.

"It's just one of the things you have to know if you're the

daughter of a Duke," Aislinn replied with a shrug of her shoulders, "and there's something else that I learned as well."

"What's that?"

"Get all the information that you can from a tavern owner likely making more money out of the back of his shop than the front," she replied, nodding out the window, "because they know more about what's going on in the city than anyone else."

As if he knew that Bryen and Aislinn were speaking about him, a man with a very large belly hanging over a white apron waddled over.

"A pleasure to have you in my establishment, my lady. My lord." He hesitated before addressing Bryen, not certain if he was a lord or just a well-dressed guard. Therefore, he erred on the side of giving too much respect rather than too little.

"Your name, good sir?" Aislinn asked, giving the tavern owner a broad smile.

His cheeks were bright red. Likely less from the pleasure of their arrival as from the struggle of having to walk the forty feet from behind the bar to their table.

"Arjen, my lady," he replied, giving her a slight bow.

He didn't know this young woman or young man. That didn't matter, however.

What mattered to him were their clothes. Not too ostentatious, although clearly well made. So they had money.

And that's what he was most interested in. Separating them from their coin.

"Arjen, what do you have for us today?"

"Are you in need of a room, my lady?"

"No, thank you Arjen. Just a good meal and perhaps a brief conversation."

Arjen nodded. "For the meal, I can offer you fresh bread and a lamb stew that's been simmering since this morning."

"That sounds wonderful, Arjen."

"For two then?" he asked.

"Yes, for two."

Arjen motioned to the barkeep, holding up two fingers. "Ale as well?"

"Yes, thank you," Aislinn replied.

Arjen got the barkeep's attention again, holding two fingers in the air and tipping them toward his throat.

"All that will be over in just a few minutes," Arjen said, returning his attention to Aislinn.

"Wonderful," Aislinn replied. "I was wondering if you might have a few minutes to talk."

"I would love to, my lady," Arjen tsked, "but we're quite busy at the moment." He nodded behind him.

Aislinn smiled. Other than the small group of men in a nook on the far side of the bar, it was quiet. The lunch crowd had already come and gone, and the evening's festivities wouldn't begin for another few hours.

She pulled a few silvers from her pouch and placed them on the table. "Perhaps not as busy as you say it is. At least for a few minutes."

Arjen's eyes flicked down, fixing on the gleam of the silver. With a surprising speed for such a large man, Arjen swiped once across the table with the towel in his hand. When he was done, the silvers were gone.

Then, he pulled up a chair and sat down at the end of the table. "I guess I could spare a few minutes."

Bryen nodded toward the brazier and the bell on the far side of the square that were visible through the front window. "How often?"

"Too often, my lord," Arjen replied, shaking his head sadly. "Now five, maybe six times a month."

"The Wraiths?"

"Yes, the blasted Wraiths. A scourge on us." He grumbled a few more words under his breath. "You've heard of them?"

"We have," Aislinn confirmed. "From all reports, lethal adversaries."

"Indeed, my lady. Incredibly lethal."

"What do they look like?"

Arjen shrugged. "We don't really know, my lord. With their coloring, both flesh and armor, they blend in too well with the Murk. Most of the soldiers I've asked that very same question say that they're like tall skeletons with their skin pulled tight around their bones."

"That sounds quite unpleasant," Aislinn said. "It must be dreadful when the Wraiths come."

"Indeed, my lady," Arjen confirmed with a nod. "Quite dreadful. Every soldier I've spoken to says that they've never met the like before."

"The Northern Guard has yet to kill any of these Wraiths?" Bryen assumed that if they had they would have paraded the bodies around the city in an effort to build the confidence of the populace during what was becoming a more and more difficult and tense time.

Arjen seemed reluctant to answer the question at first, perhaps out of embarrassment or respect for his friends serving in the Guard. He did when he saw the hard look in Bryen's eyes. A look that was harder than any the many soldiers who visited his establishment had ever given him when things weren't going well for them at the gaming tables in the other room.

"No, my lord. None as yet."

"Though not for lack of trying."

"Definitely not, my lord. The Northern Guard are well trained. Their Captain, Argenta Rensom, is well respected, and she knows her business." Arjen leaned in close as if he was sharing a secret. "It's the Murk, my lord."

"How so, Arjen?"

"These Wraiths live in the Murk, my lady. We don't. They use the Murk to their advantage. We don't know how."

"At least not yet."

"Perhaps, my lord. Although I don't have a lot of faith that we will ever be able to deal with these monsters in the mist effectively. It's hard to kill what you can't see."

"A very astute point, Arjen," Bryen replied with a nod. "Have the Wraiths made it into the city?"

Arjen stared at Bryen for several seconds, distinctly uncomfortable. It could be the scars on his cheek and neck. It could be the sense of competence and power that radiated from him. Maybe the eyes.

"If you talk to the Governor, the answer would be no," Arjen replied carefully.

"And if you talked to anyone else?" Aislinn prodded.

"The answer would be yes. You saw some of the houses being built when you came into the city?"

Aislinn and Bryen both nodded.

"I guess it's hard to miss," Arjen continued. "Those buildings are supposed to offer better protection than an establishment like mine can provide. But they're expensive. That being the case, people would only go to the trouble of building them if there was a necessity for doing so."

"What do you do when the Murk covers the city?" asked Bryen.

Arjen flicked his eyes toward the ceiling. Aislinn and Bryen looked up, seeing the heavy slabs of wood locked in place.

"Heavy shutters is the best that I can do, my lord. Four inches thick. Wrapped in steel bands. We swing those down, lock them, grab our swords, and hope for the best. So far, the Wraiths have left us alone."

"That sounds like a very uncomfortable position to be in," Bryen prompted. "Waiting to see if the Wraiths are going to come after you."

"It is, indeed, my lord. But that's our lot right now until the Governor figures out how to deal with these Wraiths."

"Do you believe that he will, Arjen?" Aislinn was curious as to how the tavern keeper viewed her uncle.

"The good Governor Kendric Winborne and the Northern Guard have done what they can," Arjen began cautiously. "As I said, Captain Rensom is quite competent. It's the difficult circumstances, is all. I have no doubt that he and that wife of his will find a solution."

"His wife?"

"Yes, the Lady Ursina. Wherever Lord Winborne is, she is. They're like two peas in a pod."

Aislinn nodded at that. What Arjen was telling them matched what Benin and his soldiers had told her, as well as what Talia Carlomin and Jakob Kestrel had shared. Although Arjen had phrased it in a more positive light.

From what the others had said, they made it seem like the partnership between Kendric and Ursina was weighted in a particular direction. Hers.

"How many Wraiths come at one time?"

"No one really knows for sure, my lord."

"But I'm sure you've heard rumors," Aislinn pushed gently. She smiled and placed a few more silvers on the table. With another fast swipe of Arjen's towel, the coins disappeared.

Arjen leaned in toward them, placing his elbows on the table. His expression became sly.

"I do hear a few things."

"I get the feeling that you hear more than just a few things, Arjen. I get the feeling that you hear quite a lot."

Arjen beamed at Aislinn, interpreting her comments as a compliment. "Quite so, my lady. I have it on good authority from one of the soldiers on the wall that it's only been scouting parties so far. No more than fifteen or twenty Wraiths at one time."

"You're certain, Arjen?"

So few attackers and yet so much done to defend the city? If what the tavern keeper was telling them was accurate, and he had no cause to think that it wasn't, then that turned what Bryen had viewed as a challenging situation into something much worse.

"Quite certain, my lord. No more than that. Every soldier who comes down from the Shadow Keep for a drink, a meal, a little gaming, or maybe a little fun with the fairer sex all say the same."

"Yet even with so few attacking the Wraiths have gotten over the wall and into the city proper?"

"Unfortunately so, my lord. Several homes have been attacked. The newer homes."

Bryen nodded at that. "They got in despite all that's being done to keep them out."

"That's what the soldiers say, my lord. They don't want to admit it, but they can't hide the truth."

"Which is why you haven't put much effort into doing more than fortifying the shutters and strengthening the door," mused Aislinn.

"That's correct, my lady. No point in wasting money." Arjen shrugged then, as if it was just simple business sense.

Bryen thought about that. So few Wraiths attacking the city at one time. Some of those Wraiths entering the city. There was only one good reason for doing that.

"The Wraiths are a bit of a mystery." Aislinn believed that there was little more that she could extract from Arjen on that topic. Although he had proven quite helpful in confirming what they already knew as well as providing some useful nuggets relevant to her uncle and aunt. "What of the Stalkers?"

"They're not as much of a threat, my lady. At least to those living in the city. In that respect, you have nothing to fear. But beyond the wall ..." Arjen leaned back then, crossing his arms over his bulging belly, giving Bryen and Aislinn a broad smile and a lift of his eyebrows.

"What's going on beyond the wall, Arjen?" Aislinn wondered. She placed a hand on Bryen's forearm, seeing how her Protector's brow had furrowed and knowing what that meant.

Arjen missed Bryen's reaction, keeping his eyes focused on Aislinn. He nodded almost imperceptibly toward the table, a reminder of what he required if he was to continue the conversation.

"Information first, Arjen," Aislinn said with a smile that didn't match her flinty expression.

Arjen studied the young woman, wondering who was in charge between the two. When his eyes drifted over toward Bryen, seeing his frigid expression, he decided that it didn't matter.

Better not to make the young lord angry.

"My brother has a farm about a league beyond the walls. Toward the west. Not too far from the edge of the tor upon which Shadow's Reach has been built. In fact, it's from him that I get all of my vegetables. The best in the Territory as you'll soon discover."

"We're looking forward to them," Aislinn confirmed with a bright smile.

Arjen gave her a nod of appreciation. He chose to not look at Bryen, who without saying or doing anything was making him sweat even more profusely than he usually did.

"Anyway, my brother won't go out at night. Not unless he has all of his crew with him."

"Stalkers?"

"That's what he told me, my lady. There have been stories of people being attacked, a few killed, at farms not too far from his. He'd like to avoid that. As soon as the sun sets, his family and all of his workers stay inside." He motioned toward the shutters latched above them. "He's made the same provisions as I have."

"It's worked for him?"

"So far. He said that there was one night that he was certain one of the Stalkers was working its way around the outside of his home, looking for some way to get in. My brother heard a noise not long after he and his family had gone to bed, a scrape that sounded like a claw cutting its way through wood. Since the shutters were in place and a few men are always on guard they didn't investigate until the morning, although none of them got any more sleep that night."

"It was a Stalker?"

"My brother believes it was, my lady. Several large splinters had been gouged out of a shutter, but that was it. Thankfully. These shutters likely offer little protection against the Wraiths, no more than a minor deterrent, but they seem to work well against the Stalkers."

"Are all those farms near the border of the tor?" Bryen asked.

Arjen thought about his question for a minute. "Yes, they are, now that you mention it."

"And no other attacks near the tor in any other direction?"

"None that I've heard, my lord. Just on the western side where my brother and his family live."

Aislinn and Bryen shared a look. They had seen the crevices and caves that pockmarked the base of the tor when they were approaching Shadow's Reach from that direction. As a result, they were both wondering the same thing.

How far within the tor did those caves reach?

Aislinn placed a few more silvers on the table, which quickly disappeared beneath Arjen's towel.

"My thanks, Arjen. We do appreciate your help."

"A pleasure to be of service, my lady," the tavern keeper replied. He pushed himself up from his chair and glanced toward the bar. "It looks like Charlotte is bringing your ale and food over now. If you ever need anything in the future, you know where to find me. I can provide information and a great deal more than that based on your needs."

"We'll keep that in mind, Arjen, thank you," Aislinn replied. She lifted a finger as if she just remembered something. "Actually, there is one more thing."

"What would that be, my lady?" Arjen helped Charlotte set the bowls of steaming stew onto the table.

"We've heard good things about the work a blacksmith has been doing in Shadow's Reach."

"Which blacksmith would that be, my lady? There are many, but I know them all."

"Juliette."

"What do you make of them?"

"Nothing good," Benin replied.

The former Sergeant in the Royal Guard leaned against the bar, staring intently at his mug of ale most of the time. When he wasn't, he was glancing surreptitiously to the side, taking the measure of the men sitting in a large nook in the back of the tavern.

"Agreed," Tomas replied.

Tomas, a former scout, never once looked in the direction of the men. He kept his back to them at all times and the cowl of his cloak over his head despite the fact that they were inside. Both practices weren't really all that uncommon.

Half the people in the tavern kept their hoods up, either preferring the privacy or not wanting to be identified. And there was a good reason for the latter.

The swinging doors just behind the bar where a bruiser stood on each side took you through to the more profitable side of the tavern keeper's legitimate business. It had a strange name.

The Market.

Although the premise was much the same as any market you might find in Ballinasloe, this one specialized in a particular commodity. You could purchase almost anything once you walked through those doors when it came to the pleasures of the flesh.

"What's your take on them, Tomas?"

The soldier shrugged. He had not yet looked at them directly. He had picked up enough by watching the reflection in the mirror, the principal reason that he and Benin had forced the two patrons who had been sitting there before them to move on sooner than they would have liked.

"I think they're the crew we're looking for," he said softly. "Mugs of ale never far from their hands, yet they barely touch them. And, instead of allowing their eyes to wander over the many pretty serving ladies in this establishment, they didn't take their eyes from the Lady Winborne while she was speaking with the proprietor."

Benin nodded. He had seen much the same and reached the same conclusion. "You do realize that those pretty serving ladies are a great deal more than just pretty serving ladies."

"That did not go unnoticed," Tomas replied, giving his former Sergeant a look that could not be misinterpreted. "Once a scout, always a scout."

Benin snorted at Tomas' humor. "They're leaving."

"Not surprising," Tomas said. "Their target is leaving as well."

"That she is," Benin replied, glimpsing in the mirror Lady Winborne walking out of the establishment with her everpresent Protector at her back. "Shall we?"

"Give it a moment," Tomas replied. "I'm sure the Protector is well aware of what's going on around him. If any of them go after the Lady Winborne, he'll take care of them if she doesn't do it herself. Besides, we'll have no trouble keeping track of this crew."

Benin grunted his agreement, using the brief time that he had to finish his ale.

Once all the men who had been sitting in the back had left, and both Tomas and Benin had looked around the tavern to make sure that none of the other patrons were waiting to see if anyone followed them, they pushed off from the bar and headed toward the door.

Benin welcomed the cool touch of the fresh air coming off the mountain that rose above them when he stepped outside. He and Tomas stood in the busy square. Lord Keldragan and Lady Winborne were nowhere in sight. Nor were the men they had been watching in the tavern.

"You'll be able to find them?"

"With little trouble at all," Tomas replied.

"Good," Benin nodded. "Stay close. Just not too close. I'll get the boys."

"And when you catch up to me?" Tomas asked as Benin headed toward the corner that would give him access to the alley.

"Then we have a little fun."

"Are you Juliette?"

Aislinn stood at the counter that fronted the blacksmith's shop. She could hear the pounding and clanging in the back room, catching glimpses of the work being done through the open doorway. Every so often blasts of flame shot up into the air as the apprentices worked the bellows.

"I am," she replied warily, her eyes tightening. With barely a look, she could tell that these two were not quite what they appeared to be. Particularly the young man. Those dead eyes of his made her shiver despite the heat coming from the smithy at her back. "Is there a particular piece that I can help you with? We do every kind of work here."

"Not a piece," Aislinn clarified, "rather a person."

"I'm sorry, my lady. I don't quite understand."

"There's nothing to apologize for, Juliette," Aislinn replied, trying to put her at ease. "A friend told us that another of our friends was working here. We were hoping to speak with him."

"And who would this friend be, my lady?" A sick feeling settled in Juliette's stomach, already knowing how the young woman was going to answer.

"Jurgen Klines. We were told he was working here. May we speak with him?"

Juliette stared at the woman for quite some time, not saying anything, not sure how she wanted to handle this situation.

She didn't know these two. Although she knew that they were dangerous, she didn't think that they were a threat to Jurgen.

Still, she couldn't help but feel the need to be protective of her favorite blacksmith.

"I'm sorry, my lady. But he's not in the shop. He's making a delivery to a customer right now."

"Juliette, I appreciate what you're doing for Jurgen," Aislinn replied, giving the smith a knowing look. "Loyalty such as yours is hard to find." She kept to herself that she knew that Juliette's response wasn't based solely on loyalty. There was something else there as well, although it wasn't her place to raise it. "Even so, I would appreciate it if you'd allow Jurgen the chance to decide on his own whether to meet with us. I would simply ask that you talk with him now. Time is of some importance in this matter."

"He knows you?" Juliette finally asked, still not willing to commit to what she was going to do next.

"He does."

"Who should I say is calling?" If these two were here to cause trouble, she had no doubt that Jurgen could handle himself. As could the seven other smiths working in the back with him and the twice as many apprentices. Her business had doubled soon after Jurgen began shaping steel again.

"The Lady and her Protector."

"The Lady and her Protector?" Juliette's right eyebrow rose. "Really?"

Aislinn nodded, not bothering to explain.

Juliette, caught off guard, nodded as well, though with less confidence, then stepped into the back.

Just a few seconds later the Blademaster appeared wearing a leather apron and using a cloth to wipe ash and grime from his hands.

"You're late," he said, giving Aislinn and Bryen a big smile.

"It was unavoidable," Aislinn replied. She reached over the counter and pulled Jurgen in for a hug.

19

PAIN AND FLAME

The pitch black gradually shifted to a nighttime darkness as Talia sprinted through the rock-ribbed tunnel, keeping one hand out to the side so that her fingers brushed lightly along the wall.

With every step she took, Talia cursed Davin's name.

What was he thinking?

Was he even thinking?

Knowing him, probably not.

He was just doing what he did normally. Giving in to whatever impulse teased him at that specific moment.

She shook her head. Davin deserved more from her.

He did what he did because he believed that it was the right thing to do.

But how could he do that?

How could he sacrifice himself for her?

He had no right to do that! Absolutely no right whatsoever!

Growling, using her anger to drive herself forward, she thought about the gladiator who had in an instant become her Protector.

But that wasn't quite right, was it?

He had always been her Protector.

The moment she had met him he had taken on that role, whether she wanted to admit it to herself or not.

She swept her free hand across her face to wipe away the drops of sweat that were close to becoming a trickle, using the motion to clear her mind.

She needed to focus.

She needed to do as she had promised Davin that she would.

The vial first.

Nothing else mattered in that moment other than getting the vial to someone who could do something with it.

To do that, she had to get out from beneath the Rock and then back to her enclave.

If Sirena and her Guard still held the compound, then she had a chance. From there, she could do what was required of her.

After that, she would come back for Davin. Then she would worry about Roosarian.

All she could do was hope that Davin was still alive when she returned. For Roosarian's sake he better be.

Still, she couldn't escape the worm of doubt wiggling its way through her. Not after seeing what was coming for him before he decided to play the hero and give her this opportunity to escape what was most assuredly a gruesome death.

As she approached the end of the tunnel, an intermittent grey softened the darkness thanks to the light of the moon peeking out from behind the clouds. Those all too brief hints of illumination gave her welcome pulses of hope.

She growled in frustration again, knowing the danger of giving in to that feeling. Like a wheel rolling downhill, Davin's words played repetitively through her head.

"Hoping doesn't make it real."

He had said that quite a lot. More than he probably should have, in her opinion.

Still, she couldn't dispute the accuracy of one of his favored sayings.

Talia snorted out a sharp, almost silent laugh. Even now, when she faced mortal peril, Davin was still pestering her with one of his many maxims.

And he was full of them. He seemed to pick up aphorisms just as easily as a child picked up marbles.

She snorted softly again. Clearly, if his words popped into her head at a time like this, then she was spending way too much time with him. And if she was doing that, then she was …

Talia pushed that distracting possibility from her mind, not wanting to take that path to its inevitable conclusion. The path that had been confusing her the last few weeks.

Davin had bought her some time. How much, she didn't know.

She needed to make the most of it. She needed to make his sacrifice worthwhile.

Stalkers could still come after her. They likely would. They likely already were.

Davin's quick thinking had eliminated one route that connected the Rock to the beach. She assumed that there were others that remained open beneath the citadel.

Talia stopped abruptly, as quietly as she could, almost tripping on the loose rock beneath her feet.

The sound of the waves rolling gently in a regular rhythm against the shore was more prominent. The smell of the salt in the seawater was getting stronger.

She was still in darkness, but the flashes of moonlight, visible just thirty yards farther down the tunnel, were gaining strength. She could just make out at the far end the cut to the right that would take her out to the beach.

She was almost there. Not very far to go at all, and then she would be free of the Rock.

Although not its denizens.

Because it wasn't the sound of the surf or the smell of the sea that had stopped her in her tracks.

No, it was what she hadn't wanted to hear. That she had been hoping, against Davin's annoying though timely advice, that she wouldn't hear.

For just a heartbeat, she thought that she had imagined it. That she could just continue out onto the beach.

She probably should. Because she was losing precious time. She had no doubt that the Stalkers were already after her.

She ignored that urge.

Instead, she listened to her good sense, which was telling her to heed the warning that prickled along the skin at the back of her neck.

Closing her eyes, her vision useless in the gloom, she allowed her other senses to tell her what might be lurking around her.

She didn't hear anything except for the crash of the waves. She didn't smell anything other than the sea.

Even so, she knew that she had done the right thing. Because she sensed that she wasn't alone anymore.

There was something else here in the darkness with her.

A heavy presence.

A deadly presence.

She just didn't know where yet.

Waiting a few seconds more, a light rumble and a soft hiss at the far end of the tunnel that she could barely hear above the waves confirmed her fears.

A Stalker.

Waiting for her to simplify its task. To give it an easy kill.

She opened her eyes then, willing herself to see in the mix of darkness and shadow.

It was a wasted effort. She couldn't see a thing. Except for her goal.

The entrance to the natural corridor that led out toward the beach.

The moonlight had turned the black to a deep grey there.

It was just enough of a change for her to make out a large shadow coloring the wall that shouldn't be there.

As soon as the moon disappeared behind the clouds, the shadow was gone, fading back into the darkness.

Scarcely a memory. Perhaps never there.

Another low rumble followed by a soft hiss.

Then there was nothing but silence, other than the steady rumble of the surf calling to her.

It was almost as if the monster knew that she was there and knew as well that she knew. That the monster wanted to give her a hint that she couldn't escape so that she would make a mistake.

The Stalker's cunning frightened her, but she refused to allow her terror to get in the way of what she needed to do.

She remained still, barely breathing.

She had to decide quickly on her next step. Because she was running out of time.

Regardless of what she tried, she needed to be smart and careful.

Stalkers hunted in the darkness with a remarkable skill, latching on instantly to any sound or movement.

Yet despite all that, despite being aware of where her enemy was positioned, no certain strategy came to mind.

Just an instant later, another of Davin's many sayings passed through her mind.

"Even if you don't know what to do, seize the initiative. Don't cede it to your opponent."

She cursed Davin again. Silently.

He should have been here with her! They both could have escaped. Not just her.

A scrape at the far end of the tunnel focused her thoughts.

She couldn't see the Stalker in the darkness.

But she could sense the monster.

She could feel how the beast invaded the narrow space of the tunnel with his terrifying presence.

The Stalker was coming toward her. Working its way slowly down the corridor.

Not in a rush. Not making a sound.

Already in control of the engagement.

Talia almost gasped in fear. She contained the noise just in time.

The Stalker knew that she was there. But the monster didn't know where exactly.

At least she still had a chance. She could still seize the initiative if she was clever and quick.

With the darkness, there was no way that she would be able to see her attacker. Not unless the moon broke through the clouds at the exact right moment.

Davin's words quashed that false desire just as soon as it came to mind.

"Hoping doesn't make it real."

Davin was right.

She hated him for it. And she needed him to get out of her head.

A flash of red drew her gaze. Only twenty yards in front of her. Just to her right.

There was no way that she could identify the Stalker based on where she stood in the tunnel and the suffocating darkness.

Except for the eyes.

Those blood-red eyes.

That's what she searched for now as she sought to pierce the gloom.

Finally, after several excruciating minutes had passed, she thought that she caught another glimpse about ten yards to her left.

Blood red.

The flash was gone just as swiftly as it had been there.

The monster still didn't know where she was. The Stalker only knew that she was somewhere in the tunnel.

Talia waited a few minutes more.

She understood that no matter how much she disliked it, she had to allow this combat – because that's what it was, a strange form of combat – to play out to the very end.

To play out to the point where she could seize the initiative.

She didn't see the Stalker.

She didn't hear the Stalker.

But she could feel the monster's unnerving presence drawing closer.

There!

Again.

The flash of blood red. The color disappeared just as quickly as she glimpsed it.

No more than five yards away.

Approaching from her left now.

Just as she anticipated.

The Stalker knew she was there. Somewhere.

But because the monster didn't know exactly where she was, her hunter had to zigzag toward her.

Clever.

By doing so the Stalker eliminated any chance of her slipping by him.

If she moved or made a sound, he would take her. While his movement would bring him right up to her eventually.

It was only a matter of time before the monster gained its kill.

She needed to do something to throw the monster off its rhythm.

That thought driving her, slowly, so slowly that it didn't even feel like she was moving, she bent down and picked up a small rock.

Talia took a deep breath to calm herself.

Either this worked or she died.

Simple as that.

There was no other option.

Davin would have accepted those odds without hesitation. It was harder for her.

The Stalker continued to draw closer.

The monster's very presence threatened to steal her breath away.

Five yards away. No more. Maybe even closer.

Where were the eyes? She needed to see the eyes if she was to have any chance of success.

There!

The flash of blood red.

She had been wrong.

Dangerously so.

Not five yards away.

Only two yards away.

Still coming toward her, moving on an angle from the left to the right.

If the Stalker continued on its current path, the monster would pass right by her before coming back toward her from the right to the left.

When her hunter did that, it would walk right into her if she didn't move. And she couldn't move. That's what the Stalker wanted.

Understanding that it was do or die, Talia placed her free hand on the hilt of the dagger in the sheath strapped to her thigh.

The Stalker was no more than a yard to her front now. The monster would walk right past her, missing her by no more than a few feet.

Then when it reached the far wall it would have her.

She couldn't allow that to happen.

If she was going to have any chance at all of surviving this combat, she needed to seize the initiative.

Now!

With the flick of her wrist, she threw the small stone to her right side. The direction in which the Stalker already was moving.

When the pebble hit the wall, she felt the large presence streak by her, tuned into the unexpected noise.

The Stalker was fast.

Although not so fast that Talia couldn't punch up and out with her dagger that was free of its sheath in an instant.

Whether it was a lucky strike or skill, Talia didn't know, and she really didn't care. All that mattered to her was that she felt that brief moment of resistance as she stabbed. That was followed by the wet trickle of blood that ran down her grip and onto her hand when she pulled the blade back just as quickly.

Right on target.

The Stalker hissed in anger, never expecting to have been tricked in such a way.

Talia scooted a few feet to the side, not seeing, just sensing the monster's claw swipe through the space in which she had been crouching.

Still not able to identify her adversary in the gloom, she fought based on instinct. She punched up with her dagger again, smiling viciously when her steel met the momentary resistance of the Stalker's hardened almost armored flesh before the strength of her blow drove it deep into the muscle beneath.

The Stalker growled.

This time she believed the monster's response was based more on pain than anger.

She had no good way of knowing because of the near total darkness, but she guessed that she had stabbed the beast in the gut or the groin.

Staying low, Talia pivoted and stabbed again.

She earned another hiss for her efforts.

She had taken control of the fight. She was sure of it.

Because this time the Stalker's shriek of pain was tinged with fear. The anger was gone.

The kidney. Talia was sure of it.

Sensing the claw swiping toward her again, on a lower arc this time -- the Stalker having a better sense of where she was now – Talia rolled forward, in the same motion stabbing with a backhanded blow.

Another grunt of pain accompanied by a burgeoning fear.

Talia ignored it. She punched her steel again through the back of the Stalker's knee.

Caught by surprise, and already slowing because of the severity of the wounds inflicted upon it, the Stalker dropped to its one good knee, its damaged joint crumpling beneath it, unable to bear the creature's weight.

Before the monster could even think about pushing itself back to its clawed feet and coming after her, Talia stabbed one more time with her dagger. She then sprinted toward the cut in the tunnel and the grey gloom that beckoned to her.

She didn't know if she had killed the Stalker.

But that wasn't as important as ensuring that the Stalker couldn't pursue her.

Talia believed that with her final blow she had stabbed through the Stalker's muscled back and right into its heart.

She hoped that she had.

The poor, unfortunate man the Stalker once had been didn't deserve the existence that had been forced upon him.

Banishing that thought, she pumped her legs faster when she saw the gleaming moonlight that revealed the very end of the tunnel.

She was desperate to get out from beneath the Rock.

When she emerged from the passageway, she didn't stop, sprinting down the beach. Not toward the longboat that she and Davin had pulled onto the rocky shore not so long ago.

Instead, she turned toward the northern tip of the island and the pier connected to the main gate of the citadel.

Talia only had one oar in her longboat. To get back to her docks, she needed to row against the current.

She couldn't do that with just one oar. The current would win.

Staying close to the side of the fortress as she raced along the beach, she welcomed the darkness that hid her.

She stopped every few seconds. Listening. Looking for any movement. Wanting to make sure that she was alone.

And she was.

For now.

For how much longer she had no idea.

She slowed when she reached the rocks that formed the small breakwater. Climbing carefully, she peeked over the outcropping.

The pier was just on the other side, no more than fifty yards away. A straight shot down the beach once she cleared the breakwater.

Despite the late hour, it was well lit. The braziers running all the way down both sides of the pier blazed fiercely.

That was accompanied by a bustle of activity. Soldiers at the end of the dock were checking their armor and their weapons, getting ready to travel across the harbor once the sailors finished preparing Roosarian's launch, which was tied close to the shore.

Blast it!

All Talia needed was an oar.

Just one stinking oar!

If she could steal the one oar, then she could get back to her enclave and come back with as many squads as weren't needed to hold the gate and save Davin from the terrible fate that awaited him.

Yet how was she supposed to save Davin if she couldn't steal one stinking oar?

Then the truth struck her. Hard. Like a slap across the face.

She probably couldn't save Davin.

No matter how hard she tried.

No matter how fast she got off the cay and returned with Sirena and the Carlomin Guard.

"Hoping doesn't make it real." She heard Davin's voice playing through her head with that snarky tone of his. Again.

She hated when he did that!

Why couldn't he just stay quiet?

Davin was one of the best fighters that she had ever had the privilege of watching. One on one, whether Stalker or human or some other beast or monster, she didn't believe that any of them could defeat him.

Even he, though, the Crimson Giant, one of the most famed gladiators to ever battle in the Pit, stood little chance against six Stalkers at one time.

No one could survive a duel against that many Stalkers.

It was impossible.

Her entire body went cold when she finally admitted the truth to herself.

Tears began to form at the corner of her eyes. She wiped them away before they could flow down her cheeks.

She didn't have time for this. She couldn't allow herself to be distracted.

Talia tried to convince herself that Davin was just a gladiator. Just a fighter. Just someone working with her at the request of another.

However, at the same time a small part of herself that was gaining a stronger voice was telling her that she was lying to herself.

That Davin was so much more to her than just a fighter.

He was a friend, a comrade, a ...

Talia locked away that train of thought and used the cold within her to harden her resolve. She would get off this island, and she would come back for him.

If he was alive, she would save him.

If he wasn't ...

She couldn't think about that possibility now.

It would only get in the way of what she needed to do.

She had to figure out how to get down to the dock.

Glimpsing several longboats tied up to the far end of the dock that she believed that she could manage on her own, she gave up on her idea of stealing an oar.

Better and faster to just pilfer a longboat.

Yet there was no easy way to get down there from where she was without being seen by the soldiers gathered at the end of the pier. Maybe she could slip into the surf and swim along the shore then around the breakwater and to the dock.

For a few seconds she mused about what might be her only option.

Before she could make her decision, the decision was made for her.

Talia rolled off the top of the rock just as a Stalker's claw slashed down where her back had been. The monster succeeded in gouging out several long slivers of stone, missing her spine by no more than a knuckle.

She had been so focused on what she needed to do next that she had allowed the beast to sneak up on her.

She'd been a fool, and her ineptitude had almost cost her life.

Knowing that she couldn't restrain her motion, Talia allowed the momentum to take her. She fell ten feet, landing hard on her back on the beach, the blow knocking the air from her lungs.

Struggling to breathe, she looked up.

The Stalker stood atop the rock, backlit by the moon that picked that very moment to peek through the clouds.

The monster stared down at her with a terrible hunger in its blood-red eyes.

And not just one Stalker. Two more joined the first monster, all of them desperate for her blood.

Even as she acknowledged the seriousness of her situation, her brain continued to work on unimportant matters, such as the fact that she knew for certain now that there were other passages beneath the Rock that led out onto the beach.

Useful information if she actually got off the island and then made it back to attack the citadel. She'd just need to find the entrances.

Completely useless if one of these monsters slaughtered her before she got to a longboat.

Seeing the first Stalker tense, all her thoughts shifted toward one objective and one objective only.

Escape.

Talia pushed herself up, then sprinted and stumbled through the sand, gasping for the breath that was slow to return.

She evaded the Stalker by no more than a second.

Her hunter jumped off the rock, his clawed feet slamming down into the sand right where she had been lying just a moment before.

Two more heavy thumps followed.

All three of the monsters were on the beach and taking up the chase.

Finally getting some air back into her lungs, Talia ran as fast as she could through the sand and toward the false safety of the dock and the light.

If the Stalkers didn't kill her, the soldiers probably would.

In her opinion, better steel than claw. She stood a better chance against the soldiers than the monsters eating up the ground behind her.

Racing out of the darkness and into the light, jumping onto the pier and running toward the very end, she ignored the soldiers and sailors who stared at her, dumbfounded, not knowing who she could be or where she had come from.

She was only concerned about the Stalkers who were right on her heels.

The monsters' shrieks of anticipation sent a shiver down her spine and gave her a much-needed burst of speed.

She didn't bother to look back. She didn't have to.

She could hear the Stalkers' clawed feet ripping into the wooden dock.

The monsters were gaining on her.

Her fear driving her forward, she kept her gaze focused on her goal at the very far end of the pier.

She didn't even see the stunned stares of the soldiers and sailors working on the dock, now realizing that they faced a much greater threat than just a lone woman who shouldn't have been there.

Even so, none of them had yet to move. None of them quite believed what they were witnessing.

That didn't last for more than a heartbeat more.

Feeling the lead Stalker closing the distance between them, the shadow of the beast falling on her, Talia understood that she only had seconds before the monster drove its claws into her back.

Dreading the thought of that, she skidded to a stop and turned to face her attacker.

If she was going to die, then she was going to die on her terms.

If Davin could face half a dozen Stalkers beneath the Rock, then she could take on these three.

Or rather just one, she realized, taking in with a brief glance everything that was happening on the dock.

It was chaos.

There were four Stalkers on the pier now. Not three.

The one racing toward her was only a few steps away. Caught up in their bloodlust, the three others had given up the chase for a time, the soldiers and sailors drawing their notice.

Forgetting about her and having plenty of prey right in their midst, the other Stalkers rampaged through the unprepared men.

Bodies littered the pier in the direction from which she had come, none of them Stalkers.

Even so, the soldiers and a few of the sailors were finding their backbone. They were forming into small squads and trying to corner the Stalkers. Or at least make it more difficult for the monsters to gain their kills.

Smart.

Whether it worked or not remained to be seen with the Stalkers' blood up.

But that wasn't her concern.

She didn't care about what happened to the men working for Roosarian. She only cared about the Stalker who was reaching for her.

Right before the Stalker stabbed its claws into her flesh, she pulled free the small dagger sheathed on her wrist that was hidden beneath her shirtsleeve.

With a quick flick, the steel shot through the air.

The Stalker's blood-red eyes widened in shock as the

monster skidded past her and slammed headfirst into one of the pier's wooden posts. Its claws went to its throat, reaching for the dagger that stuck out from beneath its chin.

The monster succeeded in removing the small blade, but that proved to be a bad decision.

As soon as the steel came free, a gush of blood followed.

The Stalker scrabbled uselessly at the wound as it gasped for air and slowly choked to death.

Talia took full advantage of her good throw and the Stalker's poor choice. Racing past the monster, she kicked out with her leg.

Not at the Stalker. The monster was dead. It was just a matter of time.

Rather, she aimed for the brazier that burned right next to the post.

It didn't take much with the momentum that she had built up.

The heavy brazier toppled onto the dock, sending flaming wood, embers, and ash spreading in all directions.

Pleased with her success, Talia sped down the dock, her goal in sight. Along the way she kicked over every brazier she came across, adding to the flames that already were consuming the middle section of the pier.

She heard what was going on behind her. The screams and shrieks, most human, a few not.

She felt the rush of heat as the flames spread rapidly.

She didn't turn around.

She didn't know if any of the other Stalkers were coming for her. Or the soldiers.

She ignored it all because she didn't care.

All she cared about was the longboat that she had selected that was just twenty feet in front of her.

Slicing the rope that held the craft in place against the now burning pier, she jumped down.

She grabbed an oar and pushed the longboat away from the dock.

Then she fit both oars into the locks and began rowing out into the harbor, toward the south, fighting the current although still making good progress.

Only when she was a hundred yards away did she finally look up to take in the destruction that she had wrought.

She was more than pleased by the result of her work, however that proved to be only a fleeting thought.

She had escaped. For now.

But she still had a great deal more to do.

Half the pier was burning. The other half would be soon, the fire spreading swiftly in both directions, aided by the gusty wind coming off the water that was working into a blazing inferno the flames that shot twenty feet or more into the sky.

Roosarian's launch already was in flames as were all the other craft tied up to the dock except for a few of the longboats at the very end. They would be caught in the conflagration soon as well, the flames licking hungrily down the pier toward them.

Talia couldn't tell for sure because of the smoke and billowing blaze, but if she had to guess it looked like there might be one Stalker still alive. Half as many soldiers as she had seen when she raced up onto the dock with the Stalkers on her heels remained on the one section of the pier that was not yet alight, fighting for their lives against the last of the monsters.

Nodding to herself in grim satisfaction, Talia bent to her task.

Leaning forward, dipping the oars into the water, then pulling back in smooth, long strokes. That was her task now and would remain so until she reached her dock.

She couldn't quite believe that she had managed to escape. But there was no time to congratulate herself.

She escaped because of Davin. She owed him a debt that she doubted she'd ever have the chance to repay.

Even so, she needed to try. Her honor demanded it.

Another emotion swept through her, but that emotion was pointless in her present circumstances.

It would only get in the way of what she needed to do.

She had to get back to the compound. If her docks remained in Carlomin hands – and she believed that they did, because Sirena would never surrender and she was too astute a military commander to be defeated by someone as vain and self-serving as Vanion Oselnik – then once her soldiers had finished with the Fal Carrachian Guard, she would go after the Governor.

Prepared or not, she had to do it.

She had no choice but to make that play now.

She needed to kill Roosarian before Roosarian killed her.

She could only hope that Davin was still alive when she returned to the Rock. And if not ...

If not, she would seek vengeance on the woman responsible for the death of her father and the man who had somehow found a way into her heart.

20

RISING TENSION

"Do you really think it's smart?"

"You'll have to be more specific, Duff."

Jakob and the Highlander were working at the foundry. Or rather where the foundry would be once they completed the roof, which was the task they had taken on that morning. Just a few more struts to be set in place and then the tile would follow.

Jakob was enjoying the work. He hadn't done anything like this since he and his father built the barn on their property in the northernmost section of Roo's Nest.

That seemed like ages ago to Jakob, although it was only a few years' past. Then again, after all that had happened since then, it was.

Helping to build the forge gave him a sense of accomplishment. His progress was obvious and certain.

He needed that now. Because at times his work as the Lord of the Highlands felt anything but certain.

Sometimes his progress in the Highlands was clear. Other times less so.

Most of the time less so, Jakob reluctantly admitted to himself.

Here in the mountains there never seemed to be a straight line to follow to achieve the success that he wanted. Literally at times.

At least when he was building a roof he knew what he was doing.

When it came to freeing the Highlands from the Governor and the monsters stalking its woods, trails, and peaks, more often than not he felt like he didn't have a clue.

That the work was taking too long.

That he needed to move faster.

Right then, he was building a structure of immediate use to the people seeking to make the Highlands their home.

His people, he corrected.

An acknowledgment that still made him uncomfortable.

He had accepted the burden of leadership.

Reluctantly, true.

Still, he had done it.

He didn't really have a choice.

He was responsible for the Highlanders.

For better or worse.

So far for the better, and he would do all that he possibly could to ensure that it was never for the worse.

He smiled as he fitted a joist in position then hammered several forearm-length nails into place.

There was an added benefit to his current efforts. Building this roof didn't require him to kill anything.

He had been doing a good bit of that since he had come to New Caledonia.

Not by choice, of course. Rather out of necessity.

Even so, it was wearing on him.

Believing that the men and women with him were feeling

much the same, Jakob had decided to take a few days at the village so his Highlanders could rest and recuperate after all the clashes they had fought their way through during the last few weeks.

Since Duff had engineered his being named the Lord of the Highlands, Jakob and his supporters had functioned at a brutal pace. Here, they could slow down for a time and plan their next moves rather than running from one wildfire to the next.

With respect to the broch, they were well on their way to finishing the last few items that needed to be completed. In particular, the trapdoor atop the roof, the lack of which had put Duff and his squads at risk when the Stalkers attacked.

While Bertie and Martin managed that task, several teams already had started to build the homes that would circle around the green and then back toward the wood.

The forge, where Jakob and Duff were focusing their efforts, was at the far end of the green, well away from where the first cottages were being raised near the fields that would soon be cleared for plowing and planting.

From where Jakob stood on the roof, it was quite a sight. He felt good about what he was doing.

Only for a moment, however. Because there was always more to do.

By the time he left here, the broch would be complete as would the foundry. Twenty homes would be built with more under construction and the last of the stumps and rocks marring the cleared space removed.

And, of course, they would finish the fences and pens for the animals that would be herded here – horses, goats, sheep, pigs.

He nodded to himself in satisfaction. He hoped that after he and his Marchers dispatched all the threats they were facing, they could turn their full attention to doing this.

Creating.

Not destroying.

With that thought, Jakob shifted his gaze to the far side of the green very near the edge of the forest.

"You know what I'm talking about." Duff pushed himself back to his feet after hammering a long nail into a joist.

They had been at it since before the sun rose above the peaks to the east. Duff needed to take a break and stretch his back. No matter what he told himself, he wasn't as young as he used to be.

"Saraa and Lycia," Jakob murmured.

"Saraa and Lycia," Duff confirmed.

Jakob shook his head, displaying a mixture of aggravation and disappointment. Since being named the Lord of the Highlands against his wishes, although he kept that last part to himself because it would have just made him come across as petulant and Duff would give him a look that he didn't want to deal with, he had solved a great many problems.

He had yet to solve this one.

He had hoped that if the two women spent more time together, they would get to know one another and perhaps stop rubbing each other raw.

A foolish desire, he had discovered. He just hadn't admitted it to himself yet.

Throwing Saraa and Lycia together was like throwing two feral cats in a bag. What came out was never a pretty sight.

Of course, Jakob had a difficult time faulting Lycia. From what he had observed, she had done her best to temper her natural impulse to push back every time Saraa offered an insult or a rude comment. Which was often.

No, the issue wasn't so much what to do about Lycia, but rather what he was supposed to do about Saraa.

She was incredibly loyal. She was one of the first Highlanders he had met upon escaping the slavers and Wraiths.

They had grown close since then.

He and Saraa were friends.

She wanted to be more than friends.

Jakob had balked at her many invitations. Every time.

Not because he didn't enjoy spending time with her.

There was a hard truth getting in the way.

He was still in love with a ghost.

He knew that.

He didn't know what to do about it.

Until he moved on, he couldn't in good conscience respond to Saraa's interest the way that she wanted him to. The way his own body wanted him to on occasion. Because his heart and his mind weren't there as well.

Despite more than a year having passed since Senna's murder, he wasn't yet ready to let her go.

"Any suggestions?" Jakob asked. "Have you had to deal with something like this before?"

"A few times, yes, although the circumstances were different."

"How do you mean?"

"In those cases it was just a matter of soldiers who disliked one another," Duff explained. "There was a simple solution."

"Keep them separated."

"Exactly, and I did. It worked wonders."

"But now?"

"Now there's an added challenge."

Jakob nodded. "Me."

He knew how Saraa felt about him. She knew as well what was holding him back.

Yet despite all that, there was no way that she would leave him for more than a few days, and even then, only if he could convince her that the mission he gave her required her particular skills and couldn't be led by anyone else.

Lycia wouldn't leave him either. She felt a responsibility toward him. She had accepted the assignment given to her, admittedly somewhat reluctantly, but she still meant to see it through.

She had been sent there by Lord Keldragan to provide Jakob with direct assistance and to offer a connection between the two of them. That was a commitment that she would keep, despite all the spite and aggravation that Saraa heaped on her.

"You."

"Then what would you advise?"

"I don't really have much to offer you."

"Really?" Jakob scoffed, giving his friend a curious look, "because much like my father, usually you have advice for me even when I don't want it."

"True," Duff replied with a grin. "But now I really only have a question."

"What would that be?"

"Why did you put them together to work on the fencing at the edge of the wood?"

"I was hoping that by spending time together the intensity of the conflict between them might lessen."

"I'm not really sure that was a good idea," Duff said, shaking his head slowly.

"Why do you say that?"

"Did you ever consider that putting the two together might increase the intensity of the conflict between them?"

"He's doing it again," grumbled Saraa. "I hate it when he thinks he's doing something smart but he's just making a problem worse."

"I'm well aware that he's doing it again. You don't need to keep repeating yourself."

"I just don't like it."

"Neither do I," Lycia replied, "but maybe instead of

complaining about it we can just do the work we're here to do and be done with it. The sooner we're done, the sooner we're away from one another. Fair enough?"

"Fair enough," Saraa agreed.

The Highlander swung a pickaxe into the rocky ground, again and again, allowing her simmering anger to drive her efforts as she dug a hole big enough for the next pilaster.

Saraa and Lycia were almost done with the fence that marked the far edge of the green. They didn't like each other. However, that didn't stop them from putting in an honest shift of work.

They both knew why Jakob had assigned them this task. He was hoping that after their last encounter, in which they had fought together against the Stalker -- Lycia actually saving Saraa's life during that combat -- that experience might serve as an opportunity for the two to make their peace with one another.

It hadn't worked out as he wanted.

Saraa's animosity for Lycia hadn't lessened, and she didn't bother to hide it. In turn, Lycia ignored it, at least as well as she could. So it was no different than any other time they had been forced to work together.

The next few minutes they stayed quiet, focusing on their work. They only had a few more posts to set. After that, it would be a simple matter of fixing the cut timber piled behind them into place.

Job done.

Then they could go their separate ways.

And before Jakob could try to force them together again, they both resolved privately that they would speak to him and convince him of the error of his ways.

Lycia didn't care for her partner. Nevertheless, she was enjoying the work. It gave her a sense of accomplishment that she relished.

Even more, she was enjoying the silence. She was hoping that she could finish this project without having to say another word to her angry partner.

But it wasn't to be.

"You're doing quite a good job," Saraa began.

"Really?" The Highlander's comment confused Lycia. "You mean with respect to the fence?"

"No," Saraa replied, swinging her pickaxe a few more times until she was satisfied that the dirt was loose and the hole was as wide as it needed to be before she went to work with her shovel. "In terms of getting in good with Jakob."

This again. Lycia sighed as she set a pilaster into the hole that she had dug out, now shoveling the dirt back in to ensure its positioning.

She knew this topic was going to raise its ugly head. It was just a matter of when.

Saraa was like a dog with a bone, never willing to let go without a fight.

Lycia really was getting tired of this ridiculousness. Yet she had learned that her not rising to the bait only irritated Saraa all the more, which a small part of her didn't mind in the least but the larger part of her wanted to avoid.

Since there was no point to this discussion, and there was no good resolution, Lycia resolved to stay calm and let the Highlander burn herself out, just as she had done in the past.

"I'm not doing anything more or less than any other Highlander," Lycia replied with a forced calm. "I'm working toward the same objective that you are."

"You're not a Highlander," Saraa hissed, her anger already boiling over and threatening to get the better of her.

"I never said I was," Lycia countered. She kept her voice soft, almost comforting, although it was quite an effort for her to make it so. "I just said I was doing nothing more and nothing less than any other Highlander."

Saraa was about to offer another sharp reply, then stopped herself. She needed to think for a moment, the nuance finally breaking through her anger.

She growled in disgust. None of her barbs ever worked with this gladiator.

It was almost as if the woman was impervious to her insults.

Saraa considered that. She admitted reluctantly that was likely one of the reasons why the woman had survived for so long on the white sand.

And maybe that was the solution she was looking for. If she could maneuver the gladiator in the right direction.

"You really shouldn't be here," Saraa finally said, trying again to worm her way beneath the gladiator's skin. Although this time not for the simple satisfaction of achieving that petty purpose. Rather, she had a larger goal in mind.

"You've told me that before," Lycia replied tiredly.

This was a constant refrain from Saraa. It was less aggravating and more exhausting for Lycia, but she could put up with it as she had done so many times in the past.

"We don't need you here," Saraa continued.

"Yes, I'm aware." Lycia chose not to remind the Highlander that she would have died at the claws of the Stalkers if not for her intervention and assistance. Doing so would have only given the woman something else to argue about.

"Jakob doesn't need you."

"You've told me that before as well." Lycia closed her eyes for a moment, trying to push past her desire to tell the woman to grow up. This was beyond childish. "If Jakob wants me to leave, he can tell me to leave."

As she struggled to set the fencepost in place, Saraa's grimace became a smile.

The night before last she had been speaking with Bertie and Martin. Unknowingly, they had provided her with some information that she believed might allow her to attain her objective.

"When two gladiators had an argument in the Colosseum, and they couldn't come to terms, how did they solve it?"

Lycia was only listening to Saraa's question with half an ear, having grown tired of the conversation and not wanting the annoyance that was tickling at the edge of her consciousness to get the better of her. Instead, she focused on selecting the first few pieces of cut timber that they would nail to the pilasters.

"They challenged one another to a combat in the Pit. They settled any grievance on the white sand."

"To the death?"

"No, Declan never permitted anything like that, although he did understand the necessity of allowing tempers to flow freely at times when there were resentments, whether real or imagined," Lycia replied. "It was only to the blood. The first to draw blood won. The loser had to apologize, make amends in some way, or do whatever they had agreed upon prior to the combat. Since we were imprisoned, that usually just meant that the gladiator who lost the combat needed to stop doing whatever he or she was doing that annoyed the winner."

"Did that happen often?" Saraa was beginning to think that she was on the right path. The path that had eluded her for so long.

"More often than you would think," Lycia replied, carrying over the first few rails to be fixed in place. "Close quarters and all that."

"Then I challenge you," Saraa said, her eyes flashing with pleasure and hate.

Lycia frowned at the Highlander, finding the woman's reaction to be a disturbing combination, bringing to mind some of her previous and now dead opponents from the Colosseum. With this Highlander, however, it didn't surprise her. "Challenge me to what?"

"A combat."

Lycia studied Saraa, her eyes narrowing, understanding now that she had walked right into a trap. "Are you sure you want to do that? You understand the consequences if I accept your request?"

"Are you suggesting that you're a better fighter than I am?"

Lycia gave Saraa a long look. She didn't smile. Rather in an instant the hard, unyielding expression that she adopted right before she walked out onto the white sand fell into place.

"I'm not suggesting anything. I am a better fighter than you are."

Lycia only spoke honestly, something that the still rational part of Saraa's brain understood. Unfortunately, the rational part had been subsumed by the louder, more insistent part that demanded revenge for all the slights the Highlander imagined. The greatest of those being that this woman had pushed herself between Saraa and Jakob.

"Choose the weapon that you'd prefer," Saraa hissed in a frighteningly quiet voice.

After taking a few seconds to analyze the snare that had snagged her, Lycia realized that she had little chance of getting out of this without going through with it.

Better just to engage in the combat and be done with it. Then maybe this Highlander finally would leave her alone.

"You can pick the weapon," Lycia replied calmly. "We need to decide what the victor earns."

"When I win, you get away from Jakob," Lycia replied. "You go back to your Lord Keldragan and tell him to send somebody else if he feels the need to have someone close to the Lord of the Highlands."

"Fair enough." Lycia nodded. She had expected as much. She didn't want to disappoint Bryen, but she doubted that she would. Saraa was more than competent with a blade, but not as skilled as she was. She had spoken truly in that respect. "If I win, then you leave me be. No more dirty looks. No more insults. You treat me like any other Highlander. You don't have to like me, but you need to respect me."

Lycia could tell that her requirement stuck in Saraa's craw by the brief shift in the Highlander's expression, a hint of doubt flashing through her mask of determination. Lycia nodded in satisfaction.

As the combat drew closer, reality was beginning to infringe upon the Highlander's imperfect perspective. She was beginning to remember how Lycia helped her against the Stalkers. She was beginning to remember that Lycia was, in fact, a better fighter than she was.

Nevertheless, Lycia was certain that the Highlander wouldn't back down now. Saraa was desperate for the duel. She wasn't going to give up this opportunity since she had worked so hard for it.

"Agreed," Saraa replied. "Swords." She quickly corrected herself. "One sword." It was hard to miss the twin blades normally strapped across Lycia's back that she had leaned against the section of the fence that they had completed first thing that morning.

Lycia nodded, accepting the terms. She stepped between the fenceposts and into the field.

Digging her heel into the dirt, she walked ten steps farther out before circling around as best as she could, dragging her boot behind her.

The practice ring was rough. It wasn't a perfect circle. But it would do for what the two of them had in mind.

Gliding over to the fence, Lycia pulled a sword free from a scabbard. Nodding to the Highlander to tell her that she was ready, Lycia stepped into the circle.

Saraa hesitated for just a moment before doing the same, her sword, which had been lying in the grass just a few feet away, already in her hand.

There was no pomp or circumstance as there would have been if this were a real combat in the Colosseum. Lycia kept it simple, just as Declan had done, when it was a matter of two gladiators needing to clear the air between them.

"To the blood."

"To the blood," Saraa repeated, her eyes blazing fiercely, finally getting her antagonist where she wanted her, allowing her hate and anger to drown out the faint voices of concern rumbling around in the back of her head.

The Highlander didn't wait, feinting a lunge, pulling back halfway through the motion, waiting to see what Lycia would do in response.

The answer was one that Saraa had never suspected.

The gladiator didn't do anything at all.

She simply stood there. Not impressed. Not moving a muscle. Hilt of her sword gripped lightly in her left hand. One foot slightly in front of the other. Well balanced. Her weight perfectly distributed. Her breathing smooth and even.

That was more than just unsettling, the gladiator's almost preternatural calm. Yet what almost unnerved Saraa were her adversary's eyes.

There was no emotion in them. Not a single drop.

They were cold. Unyielding. Intimidating.

Fearing that she might lose her resolve under that gaze, Saraa lunged again with her blade, this time not a feint.

Lycia pivoted out of the way with barely a thought, the steel passing by her side with more than a foot to spare.

The gladiator made no move to bring her sword up to defend herself. She also made no move to attack Saraa, despite the opening revealed to her.

The Highlander tried again. This time lunging and then slashing with a backhanded slice as she pulled back.

Lycia sidestepped the attack. Once again, she didn't make a

play for Saraa, and she had no need to defend herself, the Highlander's steel never getting close to her.

Saraa growled in anger as she reset herself in the dirt, staring across the ten feet that separated her from her antagonist with a fury that was quickly giving way to embarrassment.

"You need to fight me," Saraa hissed.

"Why?" asked Lycia. "You're doing an excellent job of fighting yourself. You don't need my help."

Saraa's eyes widened at the gentle insult, all of the anger and frustration that had been building up within her exploding outward.

In a blur of motion, Saraa slashed and then slashed again. And again. And again.

Each time, Lycia drifted away from Saraa with an eye-catching fluidity.

The Highlander was fast, but not as fast as she thought she was. Lycia could name at least a dozen fighters she had faced who could move with greater speed and agility than her current opponent.

Yet none had demonstrated the ferocity that Saraa displayed now, the woman driven by her almost uncontrollable rage.

Those other opponents had fought with an economy of motion that was both pleasing to behold and slightly frightening.

Saraa was allowing her emotion to reign, feeding off it, actually, to sustain her attack.

Slicing and cutting.

Slashing and lunging.

Lycia stepped to the side, pivoted, stepped back, circled around, a dance of sorts, allowing the Highlander to tire herself out rather than engage in the way that the woman wanted.

Even as she kept her focus on Saraa, out of the corner of her eye she saw that many of the Highlanders who had been working close to where they were had wandered over. They studied the combat with a discerning gaze, respecting the boundary of the rough circle she had carved into the dirt.

None of them tried to intervene. None of them were foolish enough to do that. And none of them appeared to be worried about how the combat would end.

Most weren't surprised by what was happening. They knew about Saraa's animosity toward Lycia. Seen it. Felt it.

Yet they knew as well just how good a fighter Lycia was. They had observed her in too many clashes to not conclude that there were few who could hope to defeat her.

And certainly not a Highlander who, because of her rising fury at her lack of success, had given in to the need to taunt the gladiator with the desire of throwing her off.

"You don't belong here," Saraa spat as she swung again and again with her sword, this time much as she did with the pickaxe she had been using just minutes before. Her steel dug into the dirt and missed Lycia, the gladiator gliding around the ring with a precision that the Highlander would have found jaw-dropping if she wasn't the one being made to look the fool. "We don't need you."

Lycia chose not to reply, having heard the same from Saraa many times before. Instead, she continued to dance around the Highlander, letting her energy drain away.

Since the Highlander had challenged her, she had counted at least seventeen opportunities to end this combat. To draw the Highlander's blood without causing any undue injury.

She had chosen to hold back. If she ended the combat too quickly, Saraa would not be satisfied. She would not hold to the agreement.

Lycia needed to continue with the duel for a little while longer. She needed the Highlander to reach the obvious conclusion on her own. She needed Saraa to understand that to ever do this again, to even think about lifting her steel against her, was the epitome of folly.

"You're a coward," raged Saraa, spittle flying from her lips, barely able to control her anger now.

Lycia slid out of the way when the Highlander followed her latest insult with a ragged swing through the air, almost slipping in the dirt because she overextended herself.

Lycia didn't bother to counterattack even though that had been another good chance for her.

The Highlander was still angry. There would be no resolution to this combat until Saraa allowed her anger to fade away and she saw this engagement for what it truly was.

A lesson.

One that she would not enjoy, but still she needed to learn.

"You're a fool!" Saraa shouted. She tried again with a lunge that flowed right into a slash and then a backhanded cut.

It was all wasted effort, Lycia easily evading all three strikes.

Saraa swung again, this time a slice aimed for Lycia's throat. "You're just trying to find some way to get into Jakob's bed!"

For the first time since the combat began, the sound of steel striking steel echoed through the small valley.

The gladiator hadn't moved out of the way that time, even though she had been prepared to do so. She had held her ground instead.

Saraa's eyes widened as she stared into Lycia's. The gladiator had stopped her blade with no more than a flick of her wrist and now held Saraa's sword in place with her own with barely any effort at all.

From one breath to the next, Saraa realized that she had overstepped.

That she had made a mistake.

That she was no longer fighting Lycia.

That now she was fighting the Crimson Devil.

〜

"I AGREE with Lycia about our larger strategy," Duff said.

He and Jakob had finished with the beams. Now, they were laying on the roof. If they didn't run into any problems, they'd be done by the end of the day.

"You've spoken with her about it?"

"I have," Duff answered as he shifted a few tiles into place and used a saw to cut another at a right angle. He actually liked this part of the job. It was like putting together a puzzle. "After you mentioned your conversation with her. What you two have in mind, it's the smart thing to do."

"Narrow our focus," Jakob nodded, nailing tiles into place once Duff put them in position.

"Correct. Narrow our focus. Hit hard and fast where it will hurt the most."

"Slavers first, because that means we weaken the Governor at the same time."

"Yes, the correct starting point," murmured Duff, reaching for a few more tiles.

"Eliminate the slavers and next we turn our attention toward the Stalkers because the Highlanders already know how to fight those monsters. Those creatures are tied to the Governor as well, so two birds with one stone."

"There you go," agreed Duff.

"Remove the Stalkers and we remove the fear the Governor has been using against us. Or rather the fear that he has been trying to use against us. It's not really working anymore."

"No, it's not," Duff confirmed with a nod. He reached behind him for a few more tiles. Once he set these in place, they could move to the other side of the roof. "When we remove the slavers and Stalkers from the game board, then it's just us against the Highland Guard, and those bastards are tied to the Stone."

"He's afraid."

"Sharperson is," Duff agreed. "We use that against him, because his fear will limit his options. He'll be playing one game. We'll be playing another. Besides, we have a few tricks up our sleeves."

"That we do."

"And I'm looking forward to making use of them."

"No concerns about the Wraiths?"

"I'm always concerned about the Wraiths," grumbled the Highlander. "However, with the number of brochs that we've built and the number that currently are under construction, we've created enough strongholds to protect against those devils. We can go after them when we're ready because they can't come after us with any hope of success."

"Assuming the Murk doesn't smother us for good," Jakob nodded.

"Always throwing a wet blanket on our plans," grumbled Duff, although he grinned with amusement as he said it. He liked how Jakob always examined a situation or a decision from every possible angle. It would serve him well in the future, just as it was doing now.

"I'm just trying to be realistic," Jakob replied with a shrug of his shoulders. "That will happen. You know it will. It's just a matter of when. Then we'll have no choice but to take the fight to the Wraiths."

"I know," Duff muttered. "I agree with you. And I'm actually looking forward to it now that we can fight the monsters in the mist."

"Which is why..." prodded Jakob.

"Which is why we need to move fast. Remove the slavers. Remove the Stalkers. Remove the Governor and the Highland Guard. Consolidate our control over the Highlands. Then we can deal with the Wraiths without having to divide our focus."

"And no worries about the other Governors?"

"Talia Carlomin should have a good grip on Fal Carrach by then, and if not she'll be giving Roosarian fits."

"What about the Northern Territory?"

"That is a bit of a wildcard."

"The Governor?"

"Kendric Winborne?" Duff leaned back on his heels, considering the question. "No, not him. From what I understand, he's the straightforward type."

"His wife?"

"That would be my guess," replied Duff, bending back to his task. "Although they seem to have quite a lot to handle at the moment, and with the Lord Keldragan and the Lady Winborne deciding to visit, I expect that Kendric and his wife won't be able to look in our direction for quite some time."

"So when all is said and done, really quite a simple strategy." Jakob offered the Highlander a grin and a lift of his eyebrows.

"Anything but," Duff grumbled. "Nevertheless, when you consider how far we've come, and the advantage that you give us, both in leadership and the Talent, why not believe that we can make this happen?"

"I never said I didn't," countered Jakob. "I just said that I was trying to be realistic."

"I hear you, and I agree with you. We do need to be realistic. And I think this approach that you worked out with Lycia is realistic. We just need to be ready to adjust." Duff pushed himself up from where he had been kneeling, needing to stretch his back again.

Swinging a hammer didn't bother him. Working on a roof the entire morning, standing and kneeling again and again, crouching, his bad knees aching before he had even begun the work, was making the muscles along his spine tighten up.

The pain in his knees was a constant, but he could deal

with it. He just didn't need another part of his battered body bothering him at the same time.

"Best laid plans and all that," continued Duff.

Jakob nodded. "You're willing to wait a little longer before challenging the monsters in the mist?"

Duff grimaced, not so much from the stiffness and the pain that radiated down from his neck into his lower back that now mimicked that in his knees in intensity, but rather from the need to wait before going after the threat that angered him the most.

The brochs were absolutely essential. They had proven their utility time after time. Without them, the Highlanders had no good defense against the creatures haunting the Highlands.

Even so, he hated being cooped up in the towers.

"Although it hurts me to say so, yes. I view the Wraiths as the greatest peril out of all the ones that we face. You're right."

Duff offered a conclusion that he knew to be the truth after so many instances of hiding from and now fighting in the grasping grey, the last only possible thanks to Jakob. "Eventually the Murk will settle here, and we'll have no choice but to fight them. But, at this moment in time, I believe that we can't address the Wraiths as we need to until we've unseated Sharperson and eliminated the Highland Guard. You need to be firmly ensconced on whatever throne that bastard is using in the Stone before we go after the Wraiths and impress upon them the cost of entering the Highlands. All of our resources need to be directed toward that goal. We can't allow ourselves to be distracted."

"I have no desire to sit on a throne," Jakob protested.

"I know you don't," Duff replied. "That's one of the reasons I like you." He clapped Jakob on the shoulder, although not hard enough to knock him off the roof. "You knew that this would happen going into all this. You have no choice now. In for a penny, in for a pound as they say. As the Lord of the Highlands, you need to ..."

"I know, I know," Jakob replied as he shook his head in irritation. "I know what I must do." That phrase jolted a memory loose, his father's words streaking through his brain. *You must do what you must do*. His father was right again, even from the other side. "But that doesn't mean that I have to like it."

"I never thought that you would," Duff replied.

"Then we're of the same mind on what we need to do."

"Glad to hear it," the Highlander replied, preparing to carry several stacks of tiles to the other side of the roof. "When do we start?"

"In just a few days' time," Jakob replied. "Once we're finished here."

"You already have a target in mind?"

"I do."

Duff waited for Jakob to say more, but then he realized that something else had captured his friend's attention. Jakob's expression had changed to one that the Highlander knew quite well.

He was using the Talent to search around them. Jakob had identified something of interest.

Whether it was something about which they needed to be concerned, Duff didn't know yet.

"Duff! Jakob!" Tommie approached the foundry at a trot, bow in hand, arrow on the string.

Probably a concern, Duff concluded.

"What did you find?" the Highlander asked Jakob, ignoring Tommie for the time being.

"I'm not sure," Jakob replied, releasing his hold on the Talent and coming back to himself.

"What do you mean you're not sure?" Duff hated not knowing what he didn't know. "You're always sure."

"This time I'm not sure," Jakob replied, clearly as frustrated as Duff was. "It's faint, very faint, although growing in strength. I've come across this feeling, but I can't place it. I can't get a sense ..." Jakob's brow furrowed. "It couldn't be, could it?" Clearly the last was meant for himself and not Duff.

"Is it a good feeling or a bad feeling?"

"That cemetery was about a league to the north, wasn't it?" Jakob's mind was working over the problem, not really listening to Duff.

"What does a cemetery have to do with this feeling that's bothering you?" Duff demanded in confusion.

"Jakob!"

Duff never got an answer to his question. Tommie stood in front of the foundry, her call knocking Jakob out from beneath his thoughts.

"What's the matter, Tommie?" Jakob asked, his mind still examining the frigid, musty feeling that plagued him. There was a darkness linked to it, but not like the darkness he associated with the Stalkers or the Wraiths.

This darkness was older. Ancient.

For some reason that he didn't yet understand, it made him think of an open crypt.

Jakob's eyes sharpened. He did understand. He just didn't want to. Not now.

"The Murk coming in with the Wraiths?" Duff asked, although from where he stood he saw nothing but clear skies. The tell-tale fists of grey mist that would be punching through the mountains to the north if those monsters were advancing with the smothering mist were nowhere to be seen.

"No, not Wraiths," called Tommie. "Not Stalkers either. So no worries in that respect. The problem is a little closer to home."

Tommie pointed toward the other side of the village where they had finished clearing the trees just yesterday. The Highlanders working over there were standing in a circle, a few even cheering.

Jakob closed his eyes and shook his head in aggravation when he heard the sharp clash of steel on steel. It seemed that Duff was right. Having Lycia and Saraa work together was a bad idea.

Especially at a time like this.

"It was only a matter of time," muttered Duff. "You know Saraa. When she has a burr under her saddle …"

"I know, I know," Jakob muttered.

Jakob walked over to the ladder that he and Duff had used to climb to the roof. Placing his legs on the outside, he slid down to the ground.

"Come on," he called to Duff over his shoulder. "We need to put a stop to this before anyone gets hurt. There are bigger issues that we need to address."

Jakob was already running toward the far side of the green. Duff followed him at a slower pace. With his knees and back bothering him, he took his time as he climbed down the ladder.

Tommie stood below him, holding the ladder in place. There to help, but not entirely. She was telling him to be careful while at the same time saying how much she was enjoying the view of his rear.

Blasted woman! grumbled Duff, although he didn't increase his pace.

However, Tommie's comment did make Jakob run faster. He had no desire to hear that conversation.

And he had no desire for any of his Highlanders to get hurt without good cause. Not with that sense of frigid rot teasing him.

He could only hope that Lycia didn't kill Saraa.

The Highlander was a good fighter. An excellent fighter compared to most of the men and women who had joined him in the battle against the Governor and the monsters plaguing these peaks.

But Lycia was better.

Everyone knew it.

Except perhaps for Saraa.

21

A WELCOME RECEPTION

"Aislinn! I can't believe you made it. We were so concerned about you."

Kendric Winborne strode into the main audience chamber with a huge smile, arms open wide. "We thought we lost you." He gave his niece a long hug and then stepped back, hands on her shoulders, taking a good look at her. "I just couldn't bear the thought."

The young girl he had last seen almost a decade ago was now a young woman. Confident. Sure of herself. More a veteran of what the world had to offer her, both good and bad. He wasn't surprised.

However, he wasn't certain what to make of the scarred warrior with the very cold eyes who stood right next to her. With barely a look, that young man made him feel distinctly uncomfortable.

"We almost didn't, Uncle Kendric." She remembered her uncle's warmth and his ready smile, which offered a stark contrast to the seriousness regularly projected by her father. A trait that she valued while he lived in Battersea. Needing the balance.

"You'll need to tell us all about it at dinner," he replied, still staring at the young man.

His growing discomfort was transforming slowly into a shadow of fear, which translated to a shiver that ran down his spine. With that hard gaze of his, it was almost as if the young man was measuring him with a single glance. Based on the expression he offered Kendric, or the lack thereof, clearly he wasn't all that impressed by what he discovered.

"Us?" asked Aislinn.

"Yes, us," Kendric replied, his smile somehow growing even wider. "You haven't met my lovely wife. Your aunt. Ursina."

"I'm looking forward to it," Aislinn replied, although the smile she gave him was somewhat forced, what she had heard of her uncle's wife playing through her mind and coloring her perspective.

"She should be along any minute now. She was taking care of some business below the keep."

"Below the keep?"

"Yes, as you probably saw, construction on the Shadow Keep continues. She's been working with the stonemasons these last few days as we prepare to set the dome in place atop the main building and install the stained glass. It needs to be done correctly, and Ursina is making sure that there aren't any last-minute issues."

Kendric shifted his focus back to the intimidating young man. His discomfiture had very little to do with the double-bladed spear that the young man held so comfortably in his hands.

Aislinn's companion had yet to move or say anything. Kendric found that to be particularly disconcerting because he wasn't used to such stillness. It seemed unnatural to him since he was constantly talking and always in motion.

"You're the one they talk about, aren't you?"

"You'll have to be more specific," Bryen replied after his

eyes narrowed, not feeling the need to ease the conversation along.

"Aislinn's Protector."

"Former Protector," Aislinn corrected.

"Yes, Aislinn is quite capable of protecting herself," Bryen offered, although he didn't provide any more details beyond that.

"Of that I have no doubt, having crossed swords with her in the practice ring." Kendric gave his niece another smile at the memory. "Former Protector. My apologies. The Volkun. The gladiator responsible for the downfall of the Beleron dynasty."

"Only in part," Bryen clarified. "I had a great deal of help. Particularly from Aislinn."

"Uncle Kendric, this is Bryen Keldragan."

"Truly a pleasure young man." Kendric stepped forward, offering his hand. Bryen shook it. "Perhaps at dinner you can tell me more of your adventures. I've also heard a great deal about this Blood Company of yours. I have so many questions. I was hoping you might be able to help with some of the challenges I face in building the Northern Guard into a respected fighting unit."

Before Bryen could reply, a melodic voice cut in from behind them. "As do I. Although my first question is quite basic, I'm afraid. I'm truly curious as to why these two young people made such a perilous journey to visit us here. Not that it isn't a delight to have them here with us, but such a risk taken by the heir to the Southern Marches. I was so worried because of your unusually long delay."

Aislinn and Bryen turned, watching as a petite woman – beautiful, strong featured, sharp eyes that obviously didn't miss anything -- strode into the audience chamber. She stepped up to Kendric, rubbing his forearm as she leaned up on her toes to give him a warm kiss on his cheek.

"My apologies for not being here when you arrived. I was

delayed by another matter. One that required my full attention."

"Ursina, my niece Aislinn and her Protector ..." Kendric quickly corrected himself. "I'm sorry, force of habit. Her companion Bryen Keldragan."

"A former Protector," Ursina mused with a raised eyebrow. "I never knew that such a thing was possible."

"Neither did we," Aislinn replied.

"And yet he still wears the collar." Ursina nodded toward the silver torque circling Bryen's neck. She cocked her eyebrow, as if she had learned something exceedingly important, or was about to. "Why is that?"

"Why not?" Bryen asked in response.

"It's a fair question." Ursina lifted her chin at his answer, not sure whether she should take it as a challenge.

"I've given a fair answer," Bryen replied calmly. "Every question doesn't deserve a response. We can't always get what we want."

"Is he always so difficult?" Ursina turned her attention toward Aislinn. It was quite obvious that her amused tone was forced.

During the brief conversation between Ursina and Bryen, Aislinn had studied the woman standing before her. She should have assumed as much. She sensed the power within her. "This isn't Bryen being difficult. This is Bryen being Bryen."

Ursina chuckled softly at that. "I see your uncle in you. A sharpness ... although not necessarily of wit. At least not all the time."

"And you're the woman who caught my uncle's eye," Aislinn said in a much too sweet tone.

She tried not to make snap judgments upon meeting someone. Her father had taught her that. However, with Ursina she already had reached some conclusions. Not many of them positive.

"I am, and he mine. Right from the start we knew that we were meant to be together."

"That we did," confirmed Kendric. He hugged his wife to his side, earning a soft giggle from Ursina. "I could never have succeeded here in the Northern Territory without her."

"Such a welcome thing to hear, and so rare these days."

"How so?" asked Kendric.

"Well, when I met Bryen for the first time, I hated him," Aislinn explained with a mild shrug. "I had no interest in him whatsoever."

"As I said, sharp in many ways," Ursina murmured.

"Really?" Kendric looked at Bryen, curious as to how he was going to react.

"The feeling was mutual."

"Yet here you are," Ursina said in a supercilious tone. "Such a welcome sight."

"Here we are," Aislinn confirmed with a sickeningly sweet smile, understanding that in the current conversation what wasn't being said was more important than what was.

"And why are you here, my dear?" Ursina returned to her original question. "I'm still quite curious as to why your father would allow his only daughter and heir to risk the voyage across the Burnt Ocean. Ships go missing every week." Her tone suggested that she wouldn't have been bothered in the least if that same fate had befallen Aislinn's vessel.

"Ursina, we can discuss all that at dinner." Kendric was worried that his wife's intensity, a trait of hers that he valued most of the time, might get in the way of his niece gaining a good initial impression of his wife.

"It's all right, Uncle Kendric." Aislinn turned her keen gaze onto the woman who had stolen her uncle's heart. Examining her again, this time with a sharper eye, Aislinn was sure of it.

She'd talk with Bryen to confirm her suspicions once they were alone. "It's not a secret and likely the same reason you came here, Ursina."

"What would that be, my dear?"

"New beginnings, Ursina. Just like most everyone else here in the Territories."

Ursina stared hard at the Lady of the Southern Marches. She wasn't sure how to take what Aislinn had said, concerned that Kendric's niece might know more than she should.

Giving in to her nature, she chose to interpret Aislinn's response as a threat, and that only confirmed her initial read of the young woman. She wanted something. Likely at her expense.

"Sometimes new beginnings aren't what you hope them to be. Sometimes it's better to be satisfied with what you already have."

"Very true." Aislinn didn't miss at what Ursina was hinting. "Although there's really no way to find out other than to try, now is there?"

"Well said, Aislinn," Kendric interrupted. "A topic to continue later tonight."

Before Ursina could override her husband and continue with her line of questioning, Aislinn took advantage of the momentary break in the conversation.

"Yes, there is so much I'm looking forward to talking with you about tonight, Uncle Kendric. You as well, Ursina. I have so much to learn about you."

"Likewise, my dear." Ursina's smile didn't match the coldness in her eyes as she engaged in a staring match with her husband's niece.

"And there is so much that we've already learned on our way here."

"Really?" asked Kendric. "Like what?"

"We can talk tonight, Uncle," Aislinn said, not missing how

her last comment caught him off guard. She loved her uncle. But she remembered who he had been. She didn't know who he was now. She needed to be careful until she could figure that out and determine whether she should be concerned about Kendric, Ursina, or both. "Perhaps you could show us to our rooms. I'm quite tired from our journey and would like to rest for a few hours before we get together over a meal."

"Of course, Aislinn," Kendric replied with a broad smile. "Follow me and I'll take you to the chamberlain. He'll get you situated."

Offering his arm, Kendric led Aislinn from the chamber. Bryen followed right behind. Although not before giving Ursina a nod and a knowing look that he was certain was going to annoy her.

And it did.

Even so, Ursina refused to reveal her irritation as she stood there beneath the dais, watching them go.

Her husband didn't want to believe it, but after speaking with the young woman for only a few minutes, gauging her, she knew Aislinn Winborne for what she truly was.

A threat.

Probably the greatest threat to her and her husband's rule that they'd faced so far. More dangerous even than the Wraiths.

She had expected as much, which was why she had gone to such great lengths to ensure this encounter never occurred.

Yet all that scheming had been for nought.

She was disappointed by that. Not at her conclusion. Rather that her carefully made plans hadn't worked out as she wanted.

She hated it when one of her strategies never bore the fruit that she anticipated.

Not only had Aislinn and her Protector survived the journey across the Burnt Ocean, but they had evaded the dangers lurking in New Caledonia. Including those dangers that she had a hand in placing on the board.

A pity.

She had put a great deal of effort into what should have been a simple task all with no positive result.

But no matter.

It would be easier for her here in Shadow's Reach.

She could oversee personally what needed to be done.

She could make sure that Aislinn Winborne and her Protector didn't put at risk all of her hard work of the last few years.

She was so close. So close that she refused to allow anything or anyone to get in her way.

No matter the cost required.

22

THE WALKING DEAD

Martin and Bertie stood in the front rank of observers. They had a feeling that it would come to this. They knew as well how it was going to end.

Although they made no move to intervene.

Doing that would have been stupid. It might even earn them a touch of steel.

They understood that for better or worse, this needed to play out.

Hopefully, it would end without a body lying in the mud. They had their doubts about that, however.

They knew Saraa. What she was like. How she thought. What happened when she wasn't thinking.

And she wasn't thinking as she faced off against Lycia.

She was emotional.

She was letting her rage drive her.

Saraa fought like a demon, her steel singing through the air. A whirlwind of movement and hate.

She was consumed by a manic energy, and she sought to make the most of it. Clearly, she wasn't interested in the restriction that she and Lycia had put in place.

To the blood.

Not to the death.

Neither Martin nor Bertie were too worried about that. None of Saraa's rabid attacks were having any effect on the gladiator.

They could tell that even though Lycia was engaging more now, spending just as much time gliding out of the way as she was using her sword to defend herself, she was still holding back.

How she was doing it ...

They didn't know, and it was quite impressive. Because they doubted that either of them could ignore Saraa's last insult.

They would have given in to their outrage.

Then again, they weren't the Crimson Devil.

The flinty mask that descended over Lycia's face at the start of the combat had only grown colder. As if she was done humoring a petulant child.

She was beginning to test Saraa on occasion now, throwing her off the rhythm that she had fallen into, just to let her know that her repetitive assaults would be coming to an end soon. A warning of sorts that failed to register with Saraa.

Martin and Bertie both were certain that Lycia had identified the Highlander's tendencies right at the start of the combat if not before steel had been drawn. She wouldn't have been worth her salt in the Pit if she hadn't.

They were astounded by the gladiator's composure. Despite the venom that Saraa spit at her, Lycia didn't give in to the taunts and barbs, even though none of the Highlanders who stood around the ragged circle would fault her if she did.

"You're a whore!" Saraa shouted angrily. She stepped back, breathing heavily, tired, vexed, indignant, shocked, after missing with another slash, her steel cutting through air instead of her hated competitor's flesh.

Martin and Bertie both closed their eyes and sighed at the

same time. That had been the last straw. They had seen how the skin around Lycia's eyes crinkled at the insult.

The gladiator was done with the combat. She was done with Saraa. She'd had more than enough of this farce.

Just as they anticipated, the tenor of the duel changed in a heartbeat.

Lycia cut with her blade from right to left, starting at the shoulder and finishing at the hip. It was a fast attack. Also obvious.

Just as she wanted.

Saraa got her sword up just in time. Even so, because of the power behind Lycia's strike, Saraa almost dropped her blade, not ready for such a forceful stroke.

She scrambled back, swinging with her sword down to her left, thinking that she was going to block the slice that Lycia already had directed toward her hip.

She was caught out, and she didn't even know it.

Lycia's move was just a feint.

With a blinding speed, Lycia slashed from left to right, hip to chest.

Taken by surprise at how quickly the gladiator shifted her attack, Saraa didn't bother to get her sword up to block the blow. She couldn't.

She was too busy falling on her backside into the mud that she and Lycia had churned up as they moved around the roughly drawn ring.

To break her fall, putting out her hands, she lost her sword. She was reaching for it, about to roll out of the way as soon as she grasped the hilt again, when Saraa froze.

"I am many things," Lycia said in a chilling voice that promised a swift and certain end. "I have had to be many things in order to survive. But I am not a whore, and I never will be a whore."

The gladiator stood right next to Saraa, her sharp steel

pressed against the Highlander's throat, although not yet drawing blood.

Martin and Bertie, as well as all the other Highlanders, watched with bated breath. They had reached the climax of the scene.

One gentle touch from Lycia's blade and the Highlander would bleed out. Just a nick, no more, and her life would be over.

Yet Lycia did nothing more than stand there calmly. Steel unwavering. Blade held in an iron grip.

"You remember the agreement," Lycia reminded her reluctant and embarrassed captive.

"I do," grumbled Saraa, almost choking on her words. She was less concerned about how close she was to death than she was about what was required since the gladiator had bested her.

"Will you adhere to the agreement?"

Saraa hesitated, actually thinking about her response. Actually wondering if she could extricate herself from this impossible situation.

Those thoughts fled when she felt Lycia press the steel a bit harder into her neck, though still not drawing blood.

"I will," Saraa replied in a deflated tone, hating herself for her perceived cowardice.

Lycia waited for several heartbeats, keeping her blade in position. She didn't really trust Saraa. Nevertheless, despite the insults and the taunts and the aggravations, she had no desire to kill her. She nodded.

"Then we are done."

Removing her steel from the Highlander's throat, Lycia sliced across Saraa's forearm with her blade, a thin streak of red welling up and dripping down into the dirt.

Lycia stepped back then. When she did, a collective sigh of

relief ran through those who had gathered to watch the combat.

That sigh quickly changed to a gasp of shock when Saraa pushed herself up and out of the mud faster than a squirrel scrambling for a nut, sword back in her hand.

She swung wildly for Lycia's neck, her face a mask of rage, her reason having fled her.

Lycia held her ground, eyes narrowing, sweeping her sword in front of her to knock away the blade.

She had expected that this would happen. She didn't think the Highlander could adhere to the rules. That Saraa would let go of their conflict.

Much to her adversary's chagrin, Lycia had been ready for the dishonorable attack.

Saraa swung again with her sword, just as wildly. She wasn't thinking now. There was only her rage. Her embarrassment. Her hate.

Lycia parried the slash with no more than a flick of her wrist.

And then again. And again. And one more time.

It continued for more than a minute.

Saraa attacking, always attacking, knowing only her fury.

Lycia standing strong, barely moving, defending herself with a remarkable skill.

Until she grew tired of this new exercise.

When Saraa next attacked, Lycia knocked the blade away and stepped forward, driving her shoulder into the Highlander's chest.

The hard blow sent the Highlander sprawling into the mud on her back, sword flying free from her hand.

For several seconds, Saraa lay there, unable to breathe. When she was finally able to draw air into her lungs again, she began to roll over, wheezing, searching in the mud for the hilt of her weapon.

"Yield." Lycia stood over Saraa, pressing her steel against her opponent's jugular. Her eyes were cold. Flinty. Uncaring. She wasn't breathing hard. Completely in control of herself.

She had no compunction whatsoever about slicing the Highlander's throat. It would take no more than the flick of her wrist. And it would be justified. None of the Highlanders standing around the ring would dispute that.

Saraa was still gasping for breath, not quite understanding how she had ended up back on the ground. Her hair matted to her forehead with sweat. Most of her body covered in mud.

She didn't respond, her eyes darting from side to side.

Lycia saw it in the Highlander's wild expression, just as she had seen it so many times before.

Saraa didn't want to yield. She was desperate not to give up the fight.

Despite the steel right up against her flesh, she was still looking for a way out. For a way to flip the odds.

Perhaps a little more of an incentive would bring the woman back to reality.

Lycia pressed the blade against Saraa's throat, cutting into her skin, drawing a thin trickle of blood. She needed to make sure that Saraa understood the seriousness of the situation that she had created.

Lycia's desire not to kill her opponent disappeared as soon as the Highlander broke faith with her. Yet now, she faced something of a dilemma herself.

Even if Saraa obeyed her, even if she capitulated, Lycia would need to worry about a knife in the back.

"Sometimes steel is the best answer."

Another of Declan's many sayings passed through her mind as she considered what she should do next. He was probably right. Killing Saraa would be the easiest and safest conclusion. Justified as well.

Good advice, but it wasn't what she wanted to hear.

Lycia was tired of killing. So she gave the Highlander one more chance.

"Yield," Lycia repeated calmly, her voice as hard as iron.

Saraa's eyes widened. The sharp command shattered the madness that had seized her.

Yet still she hesitated. She refused to allow the combat to end in this way.

"Yield," ordered a commanding voice from outside the circle.

Jakob stood there. Both Lycia and Saraa glanced his way.

He wasn't happy, his face a thundercloud.

Duff, Martin, and Bertie stood with him. Their expressions just as grim.

Saraa locked eyes with Jakob, trying to communicate all that she was feeling. Desperate to explain why she had challenged Lycia. How she was trying to protect him.

From the gladiator.

From himself.

The look in his eyes told her that it was too late. That she had made a terrible mistake. That she had allowed her anger and her desire to cloud her judgment.

An unforgivable error.

Because Jakob's flinty gaze never changed. And she realized then as he stared at her that he was not the young man who had caught her eye when she first met him. The young man who had given her a smile even though he had a nasty wound across his brow that would have put most others on a stretcher.

He wasn't the young man who had unknowingly captured her heart.

He was the Lord of the Highlands.

He was lost to her.

Closing her eyes, tears beginning to form, Saraa nodded, then dropped her head. She had been beaten. By the gladiator. By her own weakness.

Lycia stepped back then, giving Jakob a nod that was both an apology and thanks that he had stopped the fight before she had to kill the Highlander.

Jakob stepped up to Saraa then, offering his hand to help her back to her feet.

"We're going to talk about this later," he said quietly so that no one else could hear.

Saraa grimaced, her expression revealing her misery.

Jakob turned to Lycia next. "I'm sorry."

Lycia nodded, not knowing what to say. She had expected an upbraiding. Not an apology.

"And thank you," Jakob continued.

He knew just as everyone else who had watched the combat that Lycia could have killed Saraa. And none of them would have blamed her if she did.

Yet still she held back even though that would have been the easiest solution to the conflict between them.

Jakob was going to say more when he turned away abruptly. He looked out across the partially cleared field that was still marred by several large rocks and a few tree stumps.

The wood on the far side was quiet. Too quiet.

No sound. No movement.

But that burgeoning scent of menace was unmistakable.

That feeling that had bothered him when he stood atop the foundry was stronger now, and it was moving toward him at a rapid pace.

That frigid cold of the crypt.

That ancient mustiness mixed with an evil that made his blood turn to ice.

That teased at his memories.

That offered him the promise of a never-ending death.

Then he had it.

Then he knew.

He should have figured it out right from the start, but he had been distracted by the duel between Saraa and Lycia.

He had been blinded by his own desires as well. He had hoped that this would never happen again.

But hope was a fickle mistress. He should have simply assumed that another meeting was inevitable, because Aloysius had told him that it would be.

Reaching for the Talent, he extended his senses into the wood all the way to the cemetery.

He cursed himself for taking so long to figure this out. For not taking the time to prepare.

Just as he feared.

He recognized the darkness that was approaching. He had fought it before.

He had almost died in that kitchen. The woman he had loved had died there.

"Jakob!"

Duff stood next to Jakob when he came back to himself. The monsters were only two hundred yards away and closing fast.

They might, just might, have enough time.

"Jakob, what is it?" Lycia came up on his other side.

He didn't have time to explain. Not yet.

"Marchers, form shield wall!" Jakob ordered, his voice sharp, measured, in control. "Shields facing the wood!"

His command put the Highlanders into immediate motion, the men and women scrambling into place, not needing to look for their weapons because even when they were in what they considered a safe place, they always kept their scuta and their steel close at hand.

Even Saraa. Beaten and distraught just a second before, still she found a place right behind the shields, her sword back in her hand.

Although they were unable to get a good look at them

because of the play of the shadows in among the trees, the Highlanders began to pick out figures moving through the wood.

Then a few breaths later, the fiends raced out from between the heart trees.

The eyes of many a Marcher widened when they took in what charged toward them. A few even took a step back.

Stalkers and Wraiths were bad enough.

But this?

These monsters sent a chill down the spine of every Highlander.

Before they could take another step back, Jakob was there, preferred double-bladed daggers in hand.

"We will stand fast, Marchers!" the Lord of the Highlands roared. "We will stand strong! We will stand free!"

"JUST BECAUSE THEY'RE dead doesn't mean they can't die!" Duff shouted.

He was trying to instill some confidence in his Highlanders. He feared that it wasn't working, as even he struggled to make sense of what he spouted.

He chalked it up to nerves. He had fought a great many opponents ever since he first picked up a blade. And in all that time, never a creature that had risen from the grave.

"Really? That's what you decided to say?" Tommie stood right next to him, half as many arrows in her quiver as she had at the beginning of the fight. As usual, spectacles safely nestled in the leather pouch around her neck.

"It's the only thing that came to mind," grumbled Duff, disappointed in himself.

He knew that what he said sounded foolish. He was a bit out of sorts. He would be the first to admit that even he, who entered every fight with a barely repressed excitement, had been knocked off balance by what he was battling now.

Maybe that's why he felt the need to say something. The Highlanders had removed a handful of the undead from the fight. But no more than that. And their circumstances were only becoming more precarious as the revenant horde pressed forward.

The undead never stopped. They fought and fought and then fought some more.

Growling.

Hissing.

Biting.

Clawing.

Stabbing.

Swinging.

Slashing.

Staying true to their only goal.

Killing the living.

Duff swung his overlarge blacksmith's hammer over Martin's shoulder. The Highlander held his shield in place, the crush to his front, preventing three of the undead from penetrating the shield wall.

When the head of Duff's hammer hit the top of the woman's head, the skull shattered, and the rising from the grave collapsed, now no more than a pile of bones.

Duff assumed that it was a woman. It was hard to tell because of the state of her decomposition. He spotted a few loose, long strands of dried out, brittle hair extending from her skull before he crushed it as well as several fragments of cloth that suggested the corpse had been buried wearing a dress that extended down below her knees. Beyond that, the creature he had destroyed had been nothing more than a skeleton.

Some of the other undead were more easily identified. The

primary factors for determining that were how long they had been dead and where they had been lain to rest.

Some were old and moldy. They had been in the ground for years. Nothing more than bones covered in whatever ragged clothing they had been buried in that had not yet disintegrated completely. Just like the woman.

Some were desiccated and withered. Whole, their dried flesh constricting their skeletal frames. Those probably had emerged from cairns where it was dry and cool.

Others were fresher, flesh and muscle hanging from the bone. Dead less than a year. Maybe just months. In fact, Duff recognized a few of the undead as former friends and acquaintances.

An even more unsettling proposition for Duff and the Highlanders when they recognized their attackers. They did their best to ignore their horror, knowing that their lives depended on staying focused on their task.

It was fairly easy to tell which of the undead had died of natural causes and which had not. Several of the skeletons displayed broken, cracked, or chipped bones. Obviously the work of a blade. And those with meat, tendons, and ligaments still hanging from those bones revealed the wounds that had put them in the ground.

"Maybe less talking and more fighting," grumbled Tommie. She pulled back on her string, releasing the arrow nocked there.

The shaft struck true. Just as it always did.

Right through the gaping eye socket of one of the skeletal-like undead seeking to breach the shield wall.

This revenant carried an old, rusted sword. A few of them did. Most of them just used their jagged digits to scratch against the steel or bite at it with their teeth.

The power of Tommie's strike was enough to snap the undead's head back, breaking its neck. Even so, the undead didn't collapse to the ground. It was held in place by the horde of revenants around him.

Not unexpectedly, the undead Tommie had targeted, arrow sticking out from where an eye had once been, rejoined the attack immediately despite the horrific angle of his neck, head lolling to the right side.

Jakob had warned them that there was only one way to destroy the undead with steel. An arrow through the eye wasn't it.

The Highlanders had succeeded in keeping the undead in place once the crush smashed into the shield wall, the creatures demonstrating little in the way of tactics, simply trying to overwhelm them through sheer ferocity and the weight of numbers.

Duff doubted that would last for much longer. More of the undead were sprinting, scrambling, or hobbling, depending on their physical condition, out from the wood. A stream of revenants that only now was beginning to trickle off, and that at a very slow pace.

Duff had faith in the fighters with him. But he understood the reality of their situation.

Eventually, the undead would achieve the break they desired, and then those monsters would swarm over his Highlanders ... if Jakob waited too long.

"Watch the flank!" Bertie shouted.

He held the very end of the line, shield in hand. The undead coming at him from straight ahead couldn't get past him. However, he couldn't manage the undead to his front and also defend against the monsters who were about to curl around the line and come at him and the Highlanders behind him from the side.

Duff took a few steps in that direction, thinking that he could help his friend. A false hope as he returned just a few breaths later to the center of the line.

He couldn't go to Bertie's aid. The center of the shield wall was bulging back toward him, the hundreds of undead and the pressure they were applying threatening to split the line in two.

He had no choice. He had to stay here. He had to ensure that they held in the middle.

Just then, the first crack in the center of the steel wall appeared. One of the fresher undead, the flesh still gracing his bones, what looked to be a former soldier because of the blade in his hand, was pushing his way between the shields.

Duff swung his hammer with all the strength that he could muster, the steel head cracking with a lethal finality against the undead's jaw and separating the head from the neck.

The undead dropped where he stood, the evil force that had resurrected the corpse vanishing as soon as the skull was ripped from the spine.

Duff grinned with grim satisfaction. Just like Jakob said would happen.

When fighting undead with steel you had to remove the head or crush it. That was the only effective method for stopping one of these monsters.

Cutting off limbs. Stabbing the undead in the chest. Shooting an arrow where an eye had been. None of that had any effect.

It might slow the creatures down, but they still kept coming.

And there was only one other way to destroy them.

Fire.

Jakob put that method into play as soon as the last of the undead straggled out of the wood. A lone skeleton wearing a ragged shirt and breeches followed the pack, pulling itself across the ground because its legs ended at the knees.

He understood the seriousness of the situation. That the threat of the undead overrunning the Highlanders was all too real.

He needed to delay, however. He needed to ensure that

there were no more of the monsters still lurking in the shadows of the forest.

He started with the undead that were pushing their way around the flank that Bertie anchored.

Reaching for the Talent, he connected the energy surging through him with the power contained within the Blood Ruby, allowing the artifact to magnify his already formidable strength. As he did so, the jewel hanging around his neck, usually cool, offered him a comfortable warmth as the energy within the stone joined with the natural magic that Jakob called upon.

He employed the skill that Aloysius taught him right before that terrible night that had set him on his current course, taking him across the Burnt Ocean and into the Highlands, fighting the same monsters now that he had sought to escape then.

A ball of energy no larger than his fist shot from his palm. The white-hot power streaked with red sizzled through the air and slammed into the chest of a revenant who was reaching for Bertie's shoulder.

With a bright flash and whoosh of air that sounded like a small explosion, the undead disintegrated into a cloud of black ash. The sphere of energy kept going, blasting through five more of the undead before slamming into a tree on the far side of the green.

Pleased by his initial success, and seeking to take advantage of the fact that the Draugr were pressed together so tightly, Jakob didn't bother to select his targets. Instead, he concentrated on where the Highlanders were facing the greatest pressure, shooting sphere after sphere of energy from both palms, the power tearing through the revenants, the monsters from the grave having no defense against the Talent amplified by the power of the Blood Ruby.

In less than a minute, it was done. Jakob only having to

send a handful of spheres ripping through the last of the undead who continued to fight, including the skeleton at the back of the pack who really never got into the battle.

The dead were at peace once more. This time for good.

Once they were ash, they could not rise again.

The Highlanders lowered their shields, staring in shock at the thick layer of charred flakes that covered the ground to their front. They tried to make sense of what they had just fought.

This was nothing like the Stalkers or the Wraiths or the slavers. They could kill those adversaries.

But the dead rising from the grave?

That was a difficult concept to wrap their minds around.

"What were they?" Duff walked up to Jakob, gripping his hammer in one hand, the haft still covered in pieces of bone and dried flesh. "I get the feeling you've faced these monsters before."

"I have," Jakob replied. Closing his eyes, he tried to calm himself. His nerves threatening to get the better of him. He should have known better. He should have expected this. "They're Draugr."

"Draugr?" mused Duff, shaking his head as if it was unfortunately beginning to make sense. Although it really didn't. Or rather he didn't want it to. The Highlanders faced enough challenges as it was. They didn't need to add another to the list. "Draugr are a myth. A story from the far north designed to frighten unruly children."

Jakob stepped a few feet to the side, staring down at the black ash, sliding a foot through the cinders. "Not any longer. As we've learned, there's little difference between myth and reality. It's just a matter of belief."

"How did you know how to fight them?" Lycia stepped up right next to him. She had anchored the other side of the line, using her twin swords to ensure the Draugr couldn't flank them from that direction.

"I came up against them once before," Jakob replied quietly, seemingly lost in thought.

Or rather lost in his memories, Lycia guessed. "When?"

It was like pulling teeth to get information out of Jakob sometimes, but she sensed that on this topic she couldn't push him as she might another matter. He would tell her what he wanted her to know when he was ready.

"Right before I left Caledonia," he replied after a few heartbeats, eyes still focused on the ash.

Lycia hoped that Jakob would say more. He didn't.

Instead, he stood there, stuck in his memories, tears forming in the corners of his flashing green eyes.

"I was right about Lycia and Saraa."

Duff and Jakob sat on the roof of the broch. The full moon shone down brightly upon them. They would close the trapdoor when they went back inside.

All of the Highlanders would be spending the night in the tower. Just in case.

There were no Stalkers about. The Murk was well to the north, far above the Northern Peaks.

Even so, Jakob was concerned about the Draugr. He had destroyed all of the undead who had attacked them. But he wouldn't believe that they were free of those monsters until they went to that cemetery in the morning to confirm that there weren't any more bodies in the ground that needed to be dug up and burned.

He didn't think that they would find any. Still, he didn't want to take any chances.

"You were," Jakob replied. He had no trouble admitting that

he had been wrong. He never had. Another trait that he had picked up from his father.

"You need to keep those two away from one another," Duff advised. "I don't trust Saraa. Her feelings for you are getting in the way of her thinking clearly."

"I know," Jakob murmured as he scanned the forest and the mountains surrounding the small valley. Quiet. Peaceful. A nice change compared to what they had faced earlier in the day. "That will be my primary objective from this night forward."

"I'm glad to hear it." Duff leaned his forearms against the parapet, staring out at the Highlands. The moon. The stars. A beautiful sight. And one of the reasons why he knew his coming here and then staying in the mountains rather than meeting his brother on the Western Isle was the right thing to do. "I never expected such a reaction from Saraa."

"Neither did I," Jakob replied. "She didn't seem herself."

"Maybe she wasn't," Duff agreed. "Love can do strange things to a person."

"True." Jakob didn't really want to follow the path that Duff had put in front of him. Because his mind had begun working its way down another trail. He had begun to wonder whether there was more to Saraa's emotions than just love.

"Draugr," Duff murmured. "I never thought it possible. Ever since I got here, it's just one story after another coming to life." Duff smiled at his own bad joke. "In a manner of speaking, of course."

"I didn't want to believe it myself the first time."

"You mentioned you have some experience with these monsters," Duff prodded gently.

"I do," Jakob replied. "I never told you about Senna, did I?"

"No, you didn't."

Jakob nodded, keeping his eyes on the mountains to the north. Willing to share, but only to a point. "I loved her. She loved me. I was going to marry her."

"The Draugr?"

"Yes. I found her. Dead. In her family's kitchen. All of her family as well. The Draugr killed her and them. They were waiting for me."

Sensing that Jakob didn't want to talk more about an experience he had yet to get past completely, Duff redirected the conversation to what he believed was the most important topic. "Why are the Draugr here? Why were they set against us?"

"They serve the Ancient One," Jakob replied calmly.

"The Ancient One?" Duff allowed that to simmer in his brain, working hard to control the buzz of concern. "Another story that I thought was just a story."

"Unfortunately, it's more than a story. The Ancient One is real."

"The Ancient One is here as well? In New Caledonia?"

"No, not yet. But he wants to be. The Draugr do his bidding. From what I learned from a friend, the Ancient One is seeking to break out of the Spirit World. If he can do that, then he can bring the Natural World and the Spirit World together. He can rule both because we have few defenses against him."

"If the Ancient One is still locked away in the Spirit World, then how did these Draugr come to life? He can touch the Natural World from the Spirit World?"

"That's a good question," Jakob replied. "I never got the chance to ask Aloysius if the Ancient One can touch the Natural World himself from where he is imprisoned or he requires proxies."

"Assuming that he can't, hoping that he can't, then how?"

"A Skath."

The color drained from Duff's face as he began to understand. A Skath was another monster of mythology. Or so he had been taught.

He realized that his mother had been teaching him not

stories but rather history. Just a history that no one wanted to remember.

The Skath were the Disciples of the Ancient One. The stories said -- histories he corrected in his own mind – these handpicked men and women sold their souls for the power gifted to them by the greatest evil ever faced by the Realms. These greedy, power-hungry, deluded fools didn't realize or didn't care about the true cost of swearing allegiance to a creature of such malevolence.

The Skath were stronger than the strongest of the Magii. A single touch by one of those monsters was said to be enough for the creature to drain the victim of his soul, leaving nothing more than a shadow behind that died a slow, excruciating death.

"Where did the dead come from? There were quite a lot of them."

"You don't think it was that cemetery?" Jakob asked.

"It was, but there were too many Draugr to come from just that cemetery. We haven't used it for very long."

Jakob thought about that. Duff made an excellent point. Curious, he reached for the Talent and extended his senses.

It didn't take him long to find what he was searching for, blaming himself for not checking more thoroughly the first time.

"There used to be a mine not too far from here?"

Duff nodded. "There was. Not any longer, however. It closed down before I got to the Highlands."

That made sense. Because Jakob's brief examination confirmed that the mine had been abandoned several years before. "From what I could see, hundreds of people died while being forced to work there. There's a large burial pit at the end of one of the shafts."

"There's the answer," Duff agreed. "That mine was shuttered when the veins dried up." The Highlander stretched his back. It had been a long day and working on the foundry's roof for most of the morning hadn't helped during the battle against the Draugr. "Now we know where the Draugr came from. Although we don't know why they came here."

"I think I know," Jakob replied, turning away from the mountains and focusing his attention on Duff.

"You know?"

"Do you want the good news first or the bad news?"

"Good news," Duff replied, his level of worry increasing.

"They weren't here for you. Or I should say they weren't here for the Highlanders."

Duff had a sense of where this was going. "The bad news?"

"The Skath sent the Draugr after me."

"Why?"

Jakob sighed, then reached beneath his shirt and pulled out the necklace. He held out the jewel, which Duff could see quite easily thanks to the strength of the moonlight. "Because I'm the bearer of the Blood Ruby. From what Aloysius told me before I left for New Caledonia, I'm the only one who can stop the Ancient One."

"You?" Duff tried to keep the disbelief from his voice, but he failed. It had been a very long day.

"That's what he said," Jakob replied with a shrug, his voice a mix of resignation and disappointment.

"With that? A ruby?"

"With this and another artifact I have yet to acquire."

"Seriously? A Magus told you this?"

Jakob offered an apology with his next shrug. "He did, and after what just happened, I have no cause to disbelieve him."

Duff thought about what Jakob said, a bemused smile breaking out on his craggy face. "So in addition to Wraiths and Stalkers and slavers we need to deal with Draugr as well. You certainly do have a knack for picking up enemies."

"It certainly feels that way," muttered Jakob, "although I

might be able to do something to ensure the Draugr and the other servants of the Ancient One leave us be, at least for the time being."

"What would that be?"

"Declan put me in touch with Magus Rafia. I spoke with her about this."

"Really?"

"Yes. She told me how I might be able to use the Talent to shield the Blood Ruby so that it's invisible to those searching for it."

"You haven't tried to do that yet?"

"Not yet," Jakob admitted, realizing with regret that he shouldn't have delayed. If he had been quicker, he wouldn't have put the lives of his Highlanders unnecessarily at risk. "I've been a little busy the last few weeks."

"I'll grant you that. But you'll try what the Magus suggested? I don't want to add Draugr, Skath, and the Ancient One to the list of monsters that we're battling. At least not yet. We've got enough on our plate as it is."

"As soon as we're done talking I'll do as Rafia taught me."

"Then consider this conversation over. I'd prefer to deal with the living for a little while longer before taking on the dead."

23

AN UNTENABLE OFFER

"You know, it's not like I'm going to go anywhere." Davin was tired and in pain. Blood trickled from a handful of slashes across his chest and forearms, one of the Stalker's claws ripping through his leather armor. He felt as if he had spent the entire night fighting on the white sand. And he really wanted to sit down. "All of this seems a bit much just for me."

Once the soldiers seized him in the tunnel beneath the Rock, Hakea Roosarian had them take Davin up to her private office. Since then, he had been waiting for more than an hour.

Two soldiers, weapons drawn, stood in every entrance. Two stood right behind him, spearpoints pricking his back. All this even though his hands were shackled and fixed to a chain running around his waist while another chain connected his manacles to the collar they had locked around his neck.

After thinking about it, he decided that right at that moment, he would have preferred to be back on the white sand. He had never lost in the Colosseum. And after a combat in the Pit he could see the physick and then relax in his cell, spend time with his sister, his friends. Try to forget that the following morning he would need to begin training for his next fight.

He couldn't do that now.

Even more galling, for the first time he had lost a combat.

Well, that wasn't exactly right, now was it.

Davin wasn't yet willing to concede that point.

He had achieved his objective. Talia had gotten away.

At least he hoped that she had gotten away.

No, he was certain that she had gotten away. If she hadn't, Roosarian would have made a big deal about that, parading Talia in front of him so that she could taunt him.

Talia was safely away. Hopefully with the vial.

If she didn't have that piece of evidence, then all their effort and sacrifice would have been for nought.

And he hadn't lost the combat against the Stalkers or the soldiers. He reached that conclusion as he used the next few minutes to review all that had happened since he and Talia escaped the Stalkers swarming the pier.

He had simply chosen not to fight. Exercising a modicum of restraint. A first for him.

Lycia would have been proud of him, he was certain.

And it seemed like the right decision at the time.

Why throw away his life if he had a chance to learn something that he might be able to put to use later?

Assuming that he could escape or Roosarian didn't just kill him outright.

Yet there was no point in thinking on that now. He had made his decision. What's done was done.

Davin grinned then, remembering one of Declan's favorite sayings.

"Death doesn't choose us. We choose our death."

Being realistic, he didn't hold out much hope that he would escape. Nevertheless, he promised himself that he would try to live up to one of Declan's favorite maxims. He would try to make his friends proud even if he never saw them again.

Because he knew that he had made the right choice. He did

the right thing, sacrificing himself so that Talia had the opportunity to get away.

"I like to be certain," Hakea Roosarian said as she strode into her office, "and I like seeing you in chains. There's some aspect to it all that appeals to me."

Davin had a snarky reply on the tip of his tongue, then decided to keep it to himself. It could be taken several ways. The most obvious of which was turning his mind down a road better left untraveled.

"From what I've seen of you, you're just one surprise after another," Hakea continued after she rounded her desk.

"I do my best," Davin replied, giving her a wink and a grin, taking her words as a compliment.

"And even in circumstances such as this that irrepressible personality of yours still can't contain itself."

"Guilty," Davin replied, smiling even more broadly. He was pleased by her comment. Even though he sensed the sarcasm that was laced within it, he chose to ignore it.

Hakea was losing the fight to hold back the smile that threatened to break free, so she dropped down into her chair, using the motion to hide her grin. When she lifted her head, her expression was hard. She was all business again.

For quite a long time, she studied him. Not saying a word.

She thought that her examination of the Crimson Giant would make him uncomfortable. Clearly it didn't.

Despite the gladiator being bruised and battered, bleeding from how many wounds she didn't know, more scratches than she could count in his armor, as well as several rips in the leather, he appeared to be completely at his ease. As if his capture was no more than another obstacle that needed to be overcome.

The Stalkers hadn't fazed him. Nor did the soldiers positioned around him.

He just stared right back at her.

Giving her a cocky smile.

He didn't seem angry.

In fact, she thought that she saw a spark of amusement in the back of his eyes. As if he was simply curious as to why he was still alive. Although it was also quite clear that he knew that she wanted something from him.

She realized at the conclusion of her examination that in different circumstances this gladiator could have been more than just a glorified fighter. So much more.

There was a spark in him that she rarely saw in anyone else.

Davin tried not to chuckle as Roosarian examined him, working hard to keep a straight face. To not allow his irrepressible personality as she had called it to shine through.

Her scrutiny didn't bother Davin. He was used to it after his time in the Colosseum, every flaw examined by fifty thousand bloodthirsty spectators.

He couldn't tell what she was thinking. He wished that he could.

Because there was something about her look that suggested that his own death might not be the worst conclusion that he needed to worry about. That she might have some other fate in mind for him. Although what that could be he had not a clue.

"So we meet again," Hakea began.

"That we do," Davin replied, not feeling the need to be disagreeable yet.

"Hakea."

"Excuse me?"

"Hakea. You may call me by my first name. A rare honor for most."

"That's very kind of you, Governor Roosarian."

"Always difficult, are you?" Hakea actually enjoyed his spark of harmless defiance.

She didn't mind a little insolence. It showed spirit. So long as it was infrequent and didn't get in the way of what she would require of him.

"So I've been told," Davin replied.

"You should have sought me out for work when I suggested it. You wouldn't be here now if you did. You'd be down on the dock with me at this very moment enjoying the spoils of my victory."

"Spilt milk," Davin replied with a shrug. "I made my decision. Now I need to deal with the consequences. That's just the way of it in this world. Decision and consequence. Over and over. Until you go to the other side."

"That is how you view the world? I can have you killed any time I like, but you seem completely unconcerned." She bit her lip, then nodded her head slowly, slightly revising her opinion of him. Yes, a little spirit could prove useful and be used in so many different ways. Some of them quite fun, in fact. "I must say, that's quite a fatalistic perspective that you have."

Davin shrugged again, one of his favorite mannerisms for communicating. "Just another day on the white sand."

"You were never afraid of dying in the Pit?"

"No, there are worse things than death."

"Such as?"

"Such as not meeting your own expectations. Those of your friends. The people who care about you and you care about."

"I never took you for having a soft heart. Your feats on the white sand preceded you here."

"I was forced to fight in the Pit. I didn't have a choice."

"There are many people in this world who are forced to do what they don't want to do. Who don't have a choice."

"And the world is poorer for it." Davin's eyes narrowed, beginning to really understand the woman who was seeking to manipulate him. "A person is best measured not by what they accomplish when they are forced to a task, but rather what they accomplish when they choose to take on a task."

"Apparently I have a philosopher standing before me," Hakea nodded sagely.

"No, just a gladiator who has seen more of the world than he has wanted to."

Hakea considered Davin for a few heartbeats more. There was some aspect to this fighter that wouldn't allow her to take her eyes away from him.

Not a confidence or a swagger. Rather, a cool resolve. A viewpoint on the world that allowed him to see past the deceptions of life and glimpse the simpler truths.

"Really? That's what you believe?" Hakea placed her elbows on her desk and leaned forward, her eyes flashing when they locked onto those of the gladiator. "The Crimson Giant standing before me. Black and blue. Bloody and battered. One of the most famed gladiators to ever fight in the Pit. Beaten. Chained. At my mercy. There seems to be little choice involved in your current predicament."

"That's one way to look at it."

"There's another way?" she asked with a raised eyebrow. "If there is, please, share it with me. I can't wait to hear what you have to say."

"I could say that I have you exactly where I want you."

Hakea chuckled at that, a deep-throated laugh that made Davin grin. "And where would that be, Davin. That is your name, isn't it? Davin Noname?"

"It is."

"And you're still going with Noname?"

"I am."

"Why is that? I would have thought that you would have come up with something better by now."

"It's grown on me. I like the sound of it. Besides, I couldn't think of anything better."

"Why not?"

"I've been busy."

"Really. Doing what?"

"Sinking pirate ships. Killing Stalkers."

"You're proud of that?" A hint of heat seeped into Hakea's voice.

She didn't want to admit it, but the man standing before her had played a large role in stifling her efforts to gain control of the shipping along the east coast of New Caledonia. She could kill him now and be done with him, earning some measure of revenge. But where was the fun in that?

Studying Roosarian, Davin could tell by her tone that he had struck a nerve. That only made his usual smile brighter. "Not proud. It was necessary. No more than that."

"And you do that?"

"Do what?"

"What's necessary," prodded Hakea.

"When I have the capacity to do something and it's necessary ... yes. I do. Just as you do what you need to do for yourself."

"That's a harsh assessment." Hakea leaned back into her chair, strangely enjoying this conversation with the gladiator. "You don't know me. You think you do. But you don't."

"I know enough about you to know that I'm speaking the truth."

"So sure of yourself, aren't you?"

"In this ... yes."

"Then I won't bother to deny it."

"Why make such a big deal out of it then?"

"Because I enjoy talking with you. You challenge me."

Davin nodded. "I've heard that before as well."

"I don't doubt it," Hakea replied with a soft chuckle. "I don't see how you could think that you have me where you want me. Most men rarely do."

Davin ignored her last comment, not wanting to be led down a rabbit hole. "You're here, talking with me. I'm learning more about you. You're not out in the harbor, trying again to gain control of the Carlomin docks since your Captain Oselnik and the Fal Carrachian Guard failed so miserably at that task the first time."

"Why do you believe my Guard won't make it onto the Carlomin docks?"

"Because I trained them," Davin replied. Not gloating in any way. Simply stating what he took to be a fact. "With Captain Makarin leading them, you won't get past the gate. But you already know that. Which is why I'm still alive and you feel the need to talk."

Hakea forced out a laugh, trying to make this gladiator believe that his words were nothing more than words to her. That there was no truth behind him. Because she refused to admit that he was right.

She had spoken to Ronild when he returned from the harbor. The lack of success in breaking through the Carlomin gate and the fact that Talia Carlomin had escaped the Rock had made her decision for her before she came in to deal with the gladiator.

Those two failures ate at her in a way that she refused to reveal. She would maintain her calm even though she desired nothing more than to rush down to the harbor and take charge of the attack herself. Then, once she broke onto the Carlomin docks, she would kill the mother and the daughter.

Her greatest problem solved.

With a swift slice of her sword.

Although she feared that might be more dream than reality after what Ronild reported.

The gladiator was correct. She did need him ... at least for a little while longer. Assuming that he acquiesced to what she was going to require of him.

"You're so sure of yourself."

"I am," Davin agreed. "Even more so, I'm sure of the Carlomin Guard."

That stopped Hakea for a moment. "So confident, gladiator."

Davin couldn't miss her belittling tone. He ignored it. "Only when it's deserved."

"You should know, Davin Noname, that I am here because I choose to be. All is well on the Carlomin docks."

"For you or for the Carlomins?" Davin asked. He saw the rise that he got out of her with that comment, her face coloring, so he decided to press her. "Because it seems that you could deal with me whenever you want. And if you were successful against the Carlomins, you'd be down there right now like a conquering hero." He shrugged, or at least tried to, finding the effort difficult because of the chains and his manacles. "You're here. Dealing with me. That tells me all that I need to know."

"That can all wait, Davin Noname. You don't know of what you ..."

He cut her off, continuing with his thought. "That your attack on the Carlomins didn't play out as you anticipated. Once again, Lady Carlomin has made your life more difficult than you wanted it to be."

For the first time she noted amusement in his expression, irritated by it. "I can claim my victory whenever I want, Davin Noname. I choose to be here now. Because we have much to discuss."

"And what is it that we have to discuss?"

"You and me."

"I didn't know that there was a you and me." There was a hint of surprise in his voice.

Hakea pushed herself up from her chair and walked around her desk. She hesitated for just a breath.

She didn't remember just how big and tall he was until she was standing right next to him. But she couldn't stop now.

Doing that would make her appear weak. And no matter the situation, she refused to appear weak. She would die first.

Besides, his hands and feet were manacled with a chain linking them together and he was easily controlled because of the collar around his neck.

She knew he was fast. Skilled. Deadly.

But there would be little that he could do to her if he tried now. Although she didn't think that he would.

He was too curious, and she really wanted to make use of that interest.

"There could be a you and me."

"You and me?" Davin turned the words over in his mouth as if he were tasting a drink that had soured. "Sad to say, I'm intrigued. How so?"

"You don't have to die here in the Rock."

"Really? That's news to me. Because I thought that was a given once you threw me in chains."

"Nothing in life is ever set in stone, Davin Noname. You should know that. You began life on the streets of Tintagel. Continued it on the white sand of the Pit. Then became a key leader among the Blood Company. You helped to save Caledonia from the Ghoule Overlord and his Legions. Now you've come here. There's no reason for your journey to end in this room. Perhaps we could begin a new journey together."

"Really?" Davin was enjoying the conversation, even as he wondered and worried about how she had learned so much about him.

"Really." Hakea began to walk around him then, trailing a finger along his back and then his chest as she circled him. She didn't appear to be put off by the sweat and blood. In fact, it brought a flush to her cheeks. "As you said, sometimes we don't have a choice. We all do what is necessary to survive."

"You must do what you must do," Davin murmured.

"What was that?" Hakea asked.

"Something a good friend of mine likes to say. You must do what you must do."

"Perhaps you should take your friend's advice. Perhaps you should do what you must do in order to survive. Because that's really what it's come down to."

"And what would that be?"

"Do what you must do," Hakea urged. "Swear loyalty to me. Serve me."

Davin chuckled at that, not believing his ears and struggling not to give free reign to his good humor. "And if I did, you would trust me? After I worked against you with such great effect?"

"I would," Hakea replied with a strange confidence.

"Why?"

"Because from what I've learned about you, you're an honorable man."

"If I'm an honorable man then why would you think that I would break the promise I made to Talia Carlomin?"

"Because honorable men will often change their perspective when their lives depend on it." Hakea's finger continued to trail along Davin's chest. "And when a better offer is made."

Davin stared hard at Hakea. There was something specific that she wanted from him. He just wasn't sure what.

"I fought in the Pit for five years. As I said, I'm not afraid to die. I doubt there's an offer that you could make that would be sweet enough for me to break faith with Talia Carlomin."

Hakea stepped back then, although not very far. Just far enough so that she could look into the gladiator's eyes without having to bend her neck backward since he was so much taller than she was.

"I believe you."

"Then why are you making this offer? As a friend of mine likes to say, death doesn't choose us. We choose our death."

"You certainly do have a lot of friends with sayings."

"That I do," he replied with pride.

She stepped up close to him then, her hand resting on his chest, pressing hard against his armor. With her other hand, she tugged on the chain that connected his manacles to the steel collar around his neck, pulling his head down so that she could look directly into his eyes.

She was so close that if she wanted to, she could stick out her tongue and lick his lips. An urge that she chose not to give in to. Although it was remarkably tempting.

"That's a good saying. I like it. But it's wrong. Because I can be the one who chooses how you die. I can be the one who chooses whether you die. I can be the one who makes you beg me to die. Because I'm the one who can make you do whatever I want you to do."

"How is it that you're going to get me to do whatever it is that you want me to do?"

Hakea smiled then, licking her lips as she ran her free hand down his leg.

Rather than continue with the motion, she pulled her hand away at the last possible second and slipped it into her pocket.

With an even bigger smile she pulled out a vial of black fluid that looked exactly the same as the one he and Talia had stolen from the secret chamber beneath the Rock.

That got his attention, Davin's eyebrows shooting up as he realized that maybe his decision to sacrifice himself might not have been the best one. Perhaps it would have been better for him to die with his spear in his hand.

"Think about what I said. You have no leverage. You will help me. One way or the other. Either as you are now or as a Stalker. You choose."

THE END OF BOOK 6

I HOPE you enjoyed Book 6 of *The Tales of the Territories*. Keep reading for a sneak peek at Book 7, *Shadow's Reach*.

BONUS MATERIAL

If you really enjoyed this story, I need you to do me a HUGE favor – please follow me on Amazon and BookBub. And if you have a few minutes, consider writing a review.

Keep reading for two chapters from *Shadow's Reach,* Book 7 in my series *The Tales of the Territories.* Order Book 7 from my author website PeterWachtBooks.com. Also available on Amazon.

PETER WACHT

SHADOW'S REACH

7

Shadow's Reach
By Peter Wacht

Book 7 of The Tales of the Territories

Published in the United States by Kestrel Media Group LLC.

ISBN: 978-1-950236-50-3

eBook ISBN: 978-1-950236-51-0

Library of Congress Control Number: 2024913372

❋ Created with Vellum

1. STRANGE KIND OF PLEASURE

"One more time, Alister," Hakea Roosarian purred. Her voice was soft. Seductive. "Just so he understands."

The whip whistled through the air, slicing across Davin's back and leaving a hiss of static in the air, a few seconds of expectant silence following behind it.

Davin held his breath, gritting his teeth, his entire body tensing against the pain. He refused to call out. He refused to give the Governor of Fal Carrach the satisfaction that she craved.

He began to breathe again when the sizzle across his back slowly, excruciatingly transitioned into the slow burn that he welcomed. Relished, in fact. Harnessing it just as Declan had taught him. Using the stinging throb to strengthen his resolve.

The pain a palliative of sorts.

A reminder that he was still alive.

What he was experiencing now was no worse than any of his combats on the white sand.

It was all the same.

The pain.

The exhaustion.

The struggle for clarity.

But no fear.

Never fear.

Declan and his incessant training made sure of that.

This was just another contest.

A contest of wills.

He had never lost in the Pit.

He refused to lose now.

"Again, Alister. One more time. We want the Crimson Giant to remember this experience for however much longer he continues to draw breath."

Davin's expression didn't change when the whip bit into his back again. To maintain his concentration and his control, he needed to find a focal point.

With that in mind, he stared at Hakea Roosarian. His eyes cold. Dispassionate. Never revealing what he was truly feeling.

The Governor stood before him offering an imperious gaze and an arrogant smirk. She tried to avoid his eyes, but she couldn't. His frigid orbs catching her. And once he had her, Davin didn't let go.

He wanted to send her a clear message.

He wanted her to see only two truths.

The first, purpose.

The second, a promise.

Once he was certain there was no confusion between them, he gave her a small smile filled with a menace that made her take a step back.

Out of surprise, not fear. That's what Hakea told herself. Because the gladiator wasn't going anywhere. And he certainly wasn't in a position to make his promise real.

Davin stood in the same circular chamber from which he and Talia had stolen the vial of black liquid only a few hours before.

Behind him were the two cells draped in a deep pall. Yet

now they only contained the Stalkers that Roosarian had created. Just a drop of the Curse in fluid form all that was required for each horrid transformation.

The shadows hid the monsters' features, although Davin had no trouble seeing them in his mind's eye. During the last few months, he had become much too familiar with their razor-sharp claws, long fangs, and mottled black flesh that resembled melted wax. The only feature visible in the shadowy gloom that nestled around the Stalkers, just as always was the case, were their brightly burning blood-red eyes.

Davin ignored the monstrosities. They were a threat, but they were not the immediate threat.

He forced himself to keep his gaze fixed on the source of his torment. The petite woman with a sword on each hip who took a sadistic pleasure from the punishment that she was inflicting upon him.

He hadn't noticed the rungs set in the floor the first time he entered the chamber, his focus solely on stealing the vile liquid that turned men and women into monsters. But he noticed them now. Those steel rungs allowed Roosarian to chain him and have her way with him as she was doing now.

The soldier tasked with whipping him gave Davin just enough chain so that he could stand to his full height. No more than that, however. Because of that limitation, he couldn't raise his arms or shift his feet more than a few inches in any direction.

He wore only his breeches and boots. As expected, the torturer had removed Davin's leather armor before he began his less than tender ministrations. Davin's shirt now no more than a bloody rag, most of it shredded, just a few strips of cloth still keeping it across his shoulders.

Davin could no longer recall how many strikes of the whip he had suffered through to reach this point. He had lost count, finding the exercise of keeping track too tiring.

He had tried to retreat into his mind. To separate the physical punishment that his body was enduring from his spirit.

It was easier to do that at the beginning of this torture session. It had gotten more difficult for him as his pain and suffering intensified with every slash of the whip, the knotted leather leaving one bloody streak after another across his broad back.

"There is no point in fighting the inevitable, Davin Noname," smirked Hakea as she sought to re-exert her authority. She was impressed by his persistence. Nevertheless, she believed that it would only take him so far. "You will give me what I want in the end. You know it just as well as I do. So there's really no point in continuing to resist."

Davin did his best to ignore her taunt, somewhat discomfited because it held the unnerving ring of truth to it. Gritting his teeth to the point where he thought they might crack, he hardened his expression until his face resembled a stone.

He would not allow her to take from him who he truly was.

He would not allow her to make him into who she wanted him to be.

To that end, Davin stared right into Hakea Roosarian's eyes. Refusing to blink.

He would make this hard on her. He would make her understand that a gladiator of the Pit could not be broken.

He had fought men and women on the white sand. He had fought Ghoules and Echidna and Slayers. He had fought Stalkers. He had even fought a Bakunawa, which, thinking back, was not one of his better decisions.

Even so, he had survived each combat. Often when he didn't deserve to. Always ready to go to the other side.

His honor, his integrity, intact.

Because when it was time for him to journey to the other side that would be all that he would have.

She might kill him.

She probably would.

But he would not give her what she wanted.

That thought driving him, he refused to give her the satisfaction of knowing that she was hurting him. He would not allow her to shatter his strength of will.

Because that's the only way she could win. That was the only way that she could get what she wanted.

She needed to break him. And despite the agony that his back had become, that wasn't going to happen.

He would live with the pain.

He would savor the pain.

The more he hurt, the more he knew that he was winning.

The more he knew that he was still alive.

Hakea stared right back at Davin, trying to match his expression with her own. She would not be the one to give in during this battle of wills.

She would win in the end. She was sure of that, her eyes sparking with pleasure as she took in the gladiator, because she always did.

Her lips curled into a small smile while she studied him. Then she bit her lip.

He was tough. There was no question about that. Tougher than any person she had ever met before.

That only made what she was doing to him now all the more fun. All the more exciting. Almost intoxicating, in fact.

No one had done it before.

But she would.

She was the one who was going to break the Crimson Giant.

One way or the other, one of the most famous gladiators to ever fight in the Pit was going to do her bidding. Become her servant. Whether he wanted to or not.

"Davin Noname," she purred quietly. She knew that he still heard her even over the sharp crack of the leather whip striking his back with a frightening consistency. She shook her head then as if she were disappointed in him. Although she really wasn't. She was impressed. Even slightly aroused. "We didn't have to be here doing this. We could have been doing something else. Something much more exciting. Much more fun. Back in my chambers. Just you and me."

The gladiator didn't respond. His expression didn't change.

Davin simply stared at her.

She couldn't see a speck of emotion in his eyes.

She knew it was there, however. Just locked away for the time being.

She would worry it free soon enough.

Once she found the key to unlock him.

And she would find that key.

Because she was very skilled at getting what she wanted.

She mulled the gladiator's name as Alister slashed into his back in that steady, comfortable rhythm that the soldier had perfected, a bloody spray erupting every time the leather struck Davin's flesh.

She had been right the first time that she met the gladiator. The first time that she felt that spark between them.

It had been instantaneous. The moment their eyes met on the Carlomin dock.

There had been a promise there of what could be. Why the gladiator couldn't see that as she did, Hakea didn't know.

She would make him see it nonetheless. She would make him understand why he should have left Talia Carlomin's service and joined her.

Why he didn't, she still couldn't understand. She couldn't quite come to grips with the strange sense of loyalty he demonstrated toward that blasted woman.

Most any other man would have acknowledged the precarity of his position and acceded to her demands without a second thought.

The gladiator hadn't, however.

Why?

Why so obstinate?

As she thought about that, she shook her head in disappointment once again. He had been such a fool. If he had been smarter, they truly could have had so much fun together.

But now ...

Now it was too late.

He was too stubborn. Too unwilling to see and understand the larger picture that she had placed before him.

That lack of vision was going to cost him. More than he anticipated, in fact.

Although she did have to admit that she was quite enjoying this spectacle. This show that he was putting on for her.

Her eyes gleamed as they wandered over him. Every scar that crisscrossed his body told a story, and she wanted to hear each one. She wanted him even more than she had wanted him before.

But sadly, it wasn't to be.

Because the red-haired fighter who had been quick with a grin and a wink wasn't there.

She wasn't staring at Davin Noname any longer.

No, the Crimson Giant stood before her now.

Bloody and beaten, true, yet still defiant.

That's what she wanted. His recalcitrance gave her a thrill that she hadn't experienced in quite some time.

"Your loyalty is misplaced, gladiator," Hakea finally said very softly, as if she were sharing a secret with him. "You know that. Yet still you force this punishment upon yourself."

She didn't expect him to answer, although she was pleased when he did.

"You know that my decision is made. I will not do as you want. No matter what you do to me, I will not kill Talia Carlomin for you."

"So you'd rather die for her?" Hakea tsked, shaking her

head with regret. "That seems such a waste. She's going to die anyway. You know that. And there's nothing that you can do to prevent her death. Why not hasten it for her? Ensure that it's painless. Ensure that it's done quickly and correctly so that she doesn't suffer."

"Gladiators of the Pit are unique, Hakea," Davin replied quietly. He took advantage of the short break given to him as his torturer halted his labor at his mistress' nod. The soldier stepped back and flung the whip over his shoulder, fully expecting to put it to use again soon, working out the tired muscles in his arm and shoulder while he waited. "Death doesn't choose us. We choose our death. I will not kill someone who doesn't deserve it."

"Even if your death means you never leave this chamber as you are?" Hakea asked, enjoying ever so much the brief spark of fear that flashed across his face when he realized what she meant.

"Even so." Davin's voice wasn't as strong as it had been before. The whipping affecting him. The veiled threat more.

"I don't understand this loyalty of yours." Hakea stepped right up to Davin, making sure that his eyes were locked onto hers, before she began to walk around him. She trailed a finger along his chest as she did so before moving to his back.

"Obviously you have some useful skills. Perhaps you'd still be willing to use those skills for me without having to continue this game between us. Without having to reach the pointless end toward which you're forcing us."

She stopped for just a moment, taking her time as she traced with one finger a long scar along his side that slid below his trousers, before she started walking around him again. "We could achieve a great deal together. We could be unstoppable."

She halted right in front of him then, giving him a suggestive look. When he didn't respond as she wanted him to, Hakea grabbed the chain attached to the collar around his neck and pulled his head down so that their noses were no more than an inch apart.

"All this could stop, Davin Noname. All you need to do to make that happen is agree to do what I want you to do. All you need to do is kill Talia Carlomin. Why is that so hard for you?"

She leaned up then, kissing him roughly. Hungrily. She allowed her lips to linger on his, relishing the blood and the sweat that she tasted.

When she pulled back, she smiled brightly and then laughed softly. She was beginning to understand the source of his rebelliousness.

"There's more than just loyalty between you and Talia Carlomin, isn't there?"

Davin kept his expression the same as it had been – strong, flinty, cold -- even as his emotions roiled within him.

"There's nothing between me and Talia Carlomin," Davin replied softly. "It's a matter of honor. Nothing more than that."

"Honor? Really?" She chuckled softly. "You killed how many? Hundreds? No, that's probably too low. It must be thousands. And despite that you're still not willing to kill one woman to save your own life and ensure a prosperous future for yourself? I find that hard to believe. No one can be so selfless."

"I've been forced to kill, that's true. I don't view myself as a killer."

Hakea laughed at that. "Then you're just kidding yourself. We're all killers, Davin Noname. When the circumstances require it."

Hakea pulled on the chain again, pressing her lips against his even more roughly this time. Her ardor intensifying.

Davin had no choice but to comply, unable to pull away because of the irons and the collar.

Hakea released his lips and stepped back, although not

before she gave him a painful bite on his lower lip that drew blood.

"You would rather suffer here for that fool Carlomin? I thought you were smarter than that, gladiator?"

"You're right. I am smarter than that. I already bet on the winning horse. And you're not it. My dying doesn't matter. She'll still beat you even after I go to the other side."

Hakea's eyes widened at his comment. Infuriated, she drew the dagger from her hip. With a lightning fast slice, she cut across his chest, a thin stream of blood sheeting down his abdomen.

"You think you can stand up to me?" Hakea hissed. She wanted to cut him again. To make him flinch since he hadn't the first time. Her natural reaction to crush anyone who resisted her. Yet for some reason she didn't quite understand she held back.

"I already am, Hakea. You know it just as well as I do. Do what you will. You won't get what you want from me. I will never serve you."

"You're not afraid of much, are you?" she asked.

"Why would you say that?" Davin needed the distraction. The longer he could draw this out the more time he would gain to steel himself for when the whipping started again. Likely as soon as Hakea tired of this conversation. "I'm frightened by many things actually."

"Really. I would think that right now you were frightened only of me."

"Although I'm sure you'd like to hear that, no. I'm not frightened of you."

"Why not?" Hakea asked, more curious now than angry.

"Because you're not scary enough. You're predictable."

"I'm not scary enough?" Now she was getting angry. She held the bloody dagger in front of his face. "I could cut you again. And again. And again. I could cut you until you resembled nothing more than a slab of meat."

"You could, that's true. But again, where's the imagination in that? It's all very predictable. Just like I said." Before Hakea could interrupt him, he offered more of an explanation.

"Now spiders ... spiders are scary. For example, the widowmaker spider. You wouldn't even know that little nasty, which could fit easily in the palm of your closed fist, was there until you felt its bite. And then you'd only have hours left to live. In fact, one of the gladiators I knew in the Pit was bitten by one of those tiny monsters. He started bleeding from his nose, his eyes, his ears, and no one knew why until the physick arrived after he died and showed us that the widowmaker had nested in his armpit, eating its way into his flesh. That spider was going to use that gladiator to plant its eggs. Now that's scary. And then there's this centipede ..."

"Enough, Davin Noname," growled Hakea. "I am not interested in insects."

"What's the matter? You wanted to know what I was afraid of and why I wasn't afraid of you. That widowmaker spider ..."

"Stop!" shouted Hakea, having lost patience.

Now it was Davin's turn to give her a smile and a lift of his eyebrows, gaining the reaction that he wanted.

"I should have assumed that you would be difficult."

"You should have, yes," agreed Davin.

"Clearly you're familiar with pain. Clearly you're not afraid of Stalkers, because they are little different than some of the monsters you've fought in the Pit."

"That's true," Davin agreed.

"And you're not afraid of death."

"Right again," Davin said, trying to nod and not able to because of the chain and the collar. "Since we've worked all that out, there's really no reason to continue with all this. It doesn't help either of us."

"Maybe," Hakea replied, appreciating his attempt to extricate himself from his difficult circumstances. "Then again, doing what you don't want me to do doesn't have to be about you. It could be about me."

"I'm afraid to ask," Davin grumbled.

That comment brought Hakea's smile back. "You see, Davin Noname, if you haven't figured it out by now, I enjoy inflicting pain. And you have a very high tolerance. That just means that I have to try a bit harder, and that only will make it that much more fun for me."

"I doubt that you could do any worse than you've already done," Davin replied, although he wondered right after he said those words whether he was going to regret uttering them.

"I'll have my fun with you, Davin Noname, and when I'm done with you, I'll do what I need to do. What was that saying your friend had? You must do what you must do?"

Davin nodded, even though he tried to stop himself, becoming even more concerned when he saw how Hakea's expression shifted from menacing to almost barbaric.

"A very appropriate saying for our current intractable situation," Hakea continued. "Because you will do what you must do. But after I'm done with you, you will do it for me. Believe that. Think about that for the next little while. If your perspective doesn't change, then I will do what I must do."

It was then that she reached into her pocket and pulled out the small glass vial, holding it up so that he could see the roiling black fluid contained within it.

Davin steeled himself as best as he could. He feared it might come to this.

He had the tolerance for a great deal of pain. A great deal of suffering.

He knew that.

He knew that he could stand almost anything she might do to him.

He certainly didn't fear death.

But he did fear what one drop of that black liquid could do if it was forced down his throat.

"So this is how the Crimson Giant meets his end?" Hakea mused, her smile fiendish as she rubbed the glass vial against his cheek. A promise of a type. "The terror of the white sand. What a waste."

"Like I said ..."

"Yes, yes, yes, I know. Death doesn't choose you. You choose your death. Very trite. And it will mean nothing in the end." She stepped back then, slipping the vial back into her pocket. "One way or the other, you will kill Talia Carlomin for me. Because if you continue to resist, I'm not going to kill you. I'm going to turn you into a monster instead. You'll die. Or this part of you will die while the monster that's inside you will live. And you'll know it the entire time. Think about that for a few days and then tell me you're still willing to disobey me. Tell me you still refuse to kill Talia Carlomin. Because one way or the other you will obey me. You will kill her."

2. THE NEXT STEP

"Anything to worry about? I don't care much for surprises."

"You know, I never noticed that about you."

"You don't need to offer your dry wit all the time," Lycia murmured, the tone of her voice suggesting that she was both testy and slightly amused. "Discretion is permitted on occasion."

"I'll remember that for the future," Jakob replied softly, only listening to what the gladiator had to say with half an ear.

More intent on the perspective provided by the four kestrels soaring above the three mountains that resembled a trident and rose right in front of him. It was slightly disorienting for him when the kestrels dove and curled tightly through the sky, allowing the air currents to guide them where they would.

It was a small price to pay. His ability to connect to the raptors with the Talent and see what they saw gave him a viewpoint he couldn't have gained otherwise.

Their sharp gazes revealed the narrow, rough trail that led down through the forest to the hollow that fronted the central peak and focused on features of the environment that might have slipped right by him.

"Well?" Lycia prompted.

"Well what?" Jakob asked.

He was studying the approach to the only mine that was still functioning in the northwest section of the Highlands, looking for any hides or good spots for ambushes. There were many. All unoccupied.

If he moved forward with his plan, he would be exposing the hundred Highlanders with him to the risk of attack from behind. He wanted to avoid that. Because just like Lycia, he didn't like surprises.

"Is there anything to worry about?" Lycia asked again, her tone more demanding.

As they got to know each other better, Jakob revealed more of his personality. She learned that sometimes he liked to be difficult just to be difficult. And sometimes he was just distracted. At the moment, she didn't know which one it was.

"Nothing that I can see. Just give me a few more minutes. I want to make sure. If we're going to take this risk, I want it to be a calculated one."

He had confirmed already that there were no Stalkers in the surrounding area. He extended his senses for more than fifty leagues, all the way to the east and the coast, hunting for any monsters still lurking about.

Jakob was pleased to confirm what he already knew.

It validated his decision to work with Declan and the Blood Company and give them the responsibility for clearing the Highlands of the Stalkers since those monsters concentrated so much of their attention near the crossing to the Isle of Mist.

From what he could determine, there were large swathes of the Highlands free of those monsters now. And, in a few months, if all went to plan, the Stalkers would be an afterthought within the peaks.

Nevertheless, Jakob understood that achieving their objective wouldn't be as easy as he hoped it would be. Nothing ever went to plan. His father had taught him that. And he had experienced it too many times himself to ignore that lesson.

Thus his desire to ensure that what he had in mind for the Highlanders' attack on the mine was based on the reality of their current situation and not on what he wanted it to be.

Because there were still monsters that needed to be eliminated. It just so happened that here the bulk of those monsters took human form.

"It just seems a little too easy," Lycia said softly as she lay among the rocks next to Jakob, watching from the ridge that allowed them to look down upon the entire hollow.

From all appearances, taking the mine should be a fairly simple task. Based on the number of guards they identified, the Highlanders would face little resistance when they freed the slaves.

Yet, if that was so, then why was she so unsettled?

Maybe it was because the gladiator didn't trust what she saw.

As they journeyed between the peaks now at their back and approached the mine through the wood, they hadn't run into any patrols or guard posts. Perhaps the slavers were unconcerned because the mine was situated within the wilder terrain of the Highlands. Perhaps they were just lazy after several years of being left alone. Or perhaps there was another more dangerous variable in play.

Maybe Lycia's unease resulted from the fact that there was only one way to reach their objective, the heart trees so dense that they had to take the trail that led down from the mountains and through the small forest. It wouldn't take many soldiers coming at them from behind to block the path and trap them in the small valley, the soaring mountains around them offering few options for escape.

Shaking her head in annoyance, Lycia returned her focus to

their target. The main entrance to the mine was located in the central mountain.

There were two smaller tunnels visible in the base, each one a hundred yards away from the opening that was wide enough for twenty soldiers to march through standing abreast of one another. There were no tunnels visible in the mountains on either side.

A small village had grown up around the entrance to the mine, a large dirt field separating the mine from the first of the ramshackle buildings. A stockade curved around the hamlet. The crescent-shaped wall was anchored against the sides of the central mountain.

The wall was only fifteen feet in height. Easily scaled if the defenders atop the parapet didn't realize that they were under attack. And, based on the space between the soldiers standing atop the barrier, the Highlanders should be able to make it to the top and gain a foothold even if the alarm was given.

This mine really was no different than the others that they had scouted previously. In fact, the defenses here appeared to be weaker than they were at the other mines.

Maybe that was why things didn't feel right.

The guards standing atop the wall appeared bored and disinterested. They were in a static position, not moving along the parapet, staring out at the wood and looking for any sign of intruders, though just as much observing what was happening in the compound. And there was a good reason for that.

Most people's eyes were drawn to movement.

There was no activity in the valley other than the slaves forced to work in the mines moving back and forth between the small village and the entrance.

This mine was in a remote location in the Highlands. There were no brochs within twenty leagues and those few settlers who attempted to make their way in the surrounding mountains already had been scooped up by the slavers.

"What's the matter?"

He was looking at Lycia now, his sharp green eyes capturing her gaze, her breath catching for just a few heartbeats. She shrugged, unable to give him a good reason for her apprehension. "It just seems too easy to me. There's something about all this that doesn't smell quite right."

"What are you so worried about?" Saraa lay hidden among the rocks on Jakob's other side. "We've been eliminating the Stalkers and pressing the slavers. Sharperson is afraid. He's terrified of challenging Jakob. He knows what will happen if he does. That's why the bulk of his troops are protecting the Stone. That's why we've got an easy task here if we're quick about it."

Since the combat between them, Saraa had adhered to her promise to treat Lycia with less animosity, although it was obvious that doing so pained her. She could barely contain her contempt for how Jakob permitted Lycia to play such a large role in what they were trying to accomplish in the Highlands.

Saraa believed that she was right. The gladiator didn't belong there with them. Lycia was a threat to what they were trying to achieve. Unfortunately, Jakob didn't see it that way. Only she did.

She couldn't do anything about that fact now. Not yet anyway. But she would when the time was right.

And who knows? Maybe her problem would work itself out all on its own in the clash to come.

"Don't you get the sense that they're waiting for something to happen?" urged Lycia. "As if what we're seeing now is just an act? It's almost like they want us to attack."

"That would mean that they know we're here," scoffed Saraa.

"Exactly right," Lycia affirmed.

Jakob nodded slowly as he continued to study the layout of the stockade. "Lycia makes a good point. This mine is just as large and productive as all the others that are still functioning in the Highlands. Yet there are fewer guards on the walls. Fewer slavers walking about. Fewer workers in the village and going to and from the mine."

"The slavers and miners are probably in the mine," Saraa advised. "My guess would be that they don't need as many guards here since this location is so difficult to reach. Sharperson likely believes that we'll keep our focus on the coast. There's more work for us there. More to gain."

"And what of those tracks we saw when we were making our way here?" countered Lycia. "What we found on the trail hinted at a large party coming here during the last few days. Who are they? Where are they?"

Jakob nodded. They had picked out the signs as they worked their way down the trail and into the hollow. A hundred people. Maybe more. It was hard to be exact because last night's steady, drenching rain had washed out a good part of the path.

It could have been more miners making their way here just as Saraa proposed. Or it could have been something else entirely. Something more worrisome.

"Don't look a gift horse in the mouth," argued Saraa. "That was probably just another gang of miners. Several, in fact. With what we're seeing in front of us, it certainly points to that. They've been letting the product pile up here rather than taking it back through the mountains. They waited too long. They need to get it out. Simple as that." She turned her gaze toward Jakob, her eyes almost pleading. "This is too good an opportunity to pass up, Jakob. We need to take advantage of what the slavers are giving us."

"That's the problem," Lycia challenged. "If I was looking to set a trap for us, this is how I would do it. Give us a target we can't resist and defenses that appear to be lacking."

"Is the great Crimson Devil frightened?" Saraa snorted.

Lycia, who had kept her attention on the mine below the

ridge, turned her harsh gaze toward the Highlander. She didn't take insults well. She never had.

Before she gave free reign to her temper, she took a breath to calm herself. Saraa was simply trying to get a rise out of her. Rather than give her the satisfaction, Lycia smiled sweetly instead of snapping at her.

"Frightened, no. I'm not," Lycia replied. "But I'm not stupid." Before Saraa could poke at her again, Lycia pleased by the Highlander's offended expression, she continued, making her argument one more time. "By all rights, yes, this should be an easy raid for us. Not as many guards as you would expect. Not as many people in the village as you would expect. A load of ore and other metals, maybe even some jewels, waiting for us. But I don't like it. I say we wait until we get a better sense of what we're facing here. Waiting doesn't hurt us. It will just give us a broader view."

"Wait?" hissed Saraa. "If we wait, we could lose this chance."

"What's wrong with waiting?" countered Lycia. "We know there are no threats around us. There are no companies of Sharperson's Guard coming to bottle us up in this valley. What's the rush? Why not spend a little more time scouting before we make our move?"

Jakob ignored the bickering that circulated quietly around him. Saraa and Lycia didn't have any more arguments to make for their differing perspectives, so it swiftly devolved into repeating what they had said already.

Frustrating, yes. Even more so because both had good points.

Saraa was correct. This really was an excellent opportunity.

They were isolated here, and as Lycia had noted, they didn't have to fear the Governor's soldiers coming up behind them. There were only five working mines remaining in the Highlands. If they eliminated this one, they'd be turning the screws even tighter on the good Governor Sharperson.

It would take them one more step – one very large step – closer to freeing the Highlands from his grasp.

Sharperson would become more desperate. Perhaps even make a mistake. Maybe even weaken his forces around the Stone and give the Highlanders the chance to make a play for his citadel.

Take his fortress and Sharperson would be on the run if they didn't catch him there. He would have to leave the Highlands. And if he wasn't in the Highlands, he could do very little to stop the Highlanders from claiming what belonged to them.

Unfortunately, Lycia was correct as well.

Much of what he saw before him didn't feel right. He agreed with her on that. Maybe those tracks were workers coming to take back to the Stone the ore and jewels that had been dug out of the mine.

More than a hundred pallets on sleds were lined up off to the side of the main entrance. Many of them full.

The trails through this part of the Highlands were too narrow for horses and wagons. It made sense to assume that the workers who might have been brought here would be tasked with delivering those sleds to the Governor.

Which meant that the Highlanders could seize the mine, free even more miners than they anticipated, and prevent Sharperson from making use of the riches waiting to be transported back to the Stone.

That thought appealed to Jakob. Even so, Lycia's concern stayed with him.

It could be an opportunity.

It could be a trap.

Then again, it could be both.

It probably was.

Because he could hear his father's voice in his head telling him that this was all just a little too easy. Just as Lycia warned.

Wanting to get rid of his father's voice, Jakob released the stream of the Talent that connected him to the kestrels flying above them. He redirected his focus toward the mine and the mountains themselves.

He took his time, thorough with his evaluation. There were more men and women working in the mines than he thought there would be. Although that could be explained by the several dozen empty sleds waiting to be filled that were lined up next to those piled high with the natural resources that Sharperson relied upon.

However, if those people in the mines were the cause of the tracks that survived during last night's downpours, then why was he filled with such an acute sense of foreboding?

His concern now had nothing to do with Lycia's hesitation. There was something not quite right about the scene set out before him.

It didn't take him long to figure it out.

A large number of the people working in the mines weren't actually working. Rather, they were gathered together in caverns just off the main path that led deeper into the mine.

They weren't doing anything at all. Resting. Sleeping. Just waiting.

There was no maybe about it when he concentrated on the group closest to the main entrance.

Definitely soldiers, not miners. A lot of them.

Close to three hundred and more than enough to make the tracks they had seen on the trail.

Lycia was right to be concerned.

So what else could be waiting for them in the mines?

He got the feeling that it wasn't just the soldiers loyal to the Governor.

Jakob extended his search with the Talent, reaching deeper

into the mountain. Exploring the shafts that led a mile or more beneath the ground and that were free of both slavers and miners both.

Jakob nodded to himself. He should have assumed as much.

It was definitely a trap.

Although it was an opportunity as well.

But why here?

Why would Sharperson believe that he would come here?

Why order so many soldiers here?

There was no way around it. The Governor would have had to have known that Jakob was coming here and when. It was the only way to get the soldiers here before him. Otherwise, he was wasting resources that he could use elsewhere. And Jakob knew that Sharperson loathed doing that.

That question faded away for a time when Duff walked up the slope, waiting for Jakob, Lycia, and Saraa to slide back down through the dirt and shale before they stood up.

The Highlander had been coordinating the scouting that was taking place along the edge of the wood. He wanted to find any weaknesses in the wall that they might be able to exploit.

Duff trusted Jakob and his use of the Talent. Even so, he liked to see things for himself. It was a habit that had been ingrained within him by the Blademaster, and he was reluctant to let it go.

"Are those two going to bicker all day?" grumbled Duff.

"Seems like it," Jakob replied when he stepped up next to the Highlander, whose ever present hammer rested on his shoulder.

The Highlander smiled at that, then crawled up to the top of the ridge so that he could survey the target before sliding back down.

"What did you decide?" he asked.

"We've got a surprise waiting for us."

"The tracks?" asked Lycia.

Jakob nodded.

Lycia gave Saraa a triumphant grin that only served to escalate the argument between the two.

"Even so, we're going to make a play for the mine," Jakob said, ignoring the tension between the two, "but we're going to go about it a bit differently than we discussed originally." His decision cut off the quiet wrangling between Saraa and Lycia.

"What did you have in mind?" Duff shifted his hammer from one shoulder to the other. "I take it that we have some unwanted visitors waiting for us in the mine?"

"We do," Jakob confirmed. "If we're fast, we could turn what they have planned for us against them."

"Sounds good to me. The lads and lasses want to make a try of it. They know how important this is to our larger effort."

Jakob nodded, understanding. He also relayed with a glance that after this conversation he and Duff needed to have another one. Just the two of them.

"A squad will advance first into the compound to get eyes on the mine entrance and eliminate any guards wandering the village at night. They will serve as an initial skirmish line before the bulk of our forces come over the wall and then move through the village."

"I want that responsibility," Saraa said.

Jakob nodded. "So long as you're careful."

"I'm always careful."

Jakob grunted at that, not entirely convinced. "While Saraa is scouting the compound and the entrance to the mine, the rest of us will take the wall. We'll keep a reserve here in the wood. Just a few squads. Just in case."

"It's a trap?" asked Lycia, already knowing the answer but wanting to hear it.

Jakob nodded. "But also an opportunity." That last mollified Saraa, who was about to offer a few choice words to rebut any argument Lycia might offer. "If we can turn the trap to our advantage. That's going to be the primary challenge."

"How do you propose to do that?" asked Duff.

Jakob took the next few minutes to explain. "Saraa, why don't you get your squad ready. It should be dark within the hour."

"With pleasure," she replied, scrambling down the slope and disappearing into the wood.

Jakob turned his gaze to his second in command.

"What do you need?" asked Duff.

Jakob explained.

"I'll do what I can," nodded Duff.

"Thank you."

"And the other matter?"

"It will have to wait. There's nothing to be done about it now."

"Fair enough," Duff nodded, although based on Jakob's expression, he really wanted to know what was bothering him. "I take it that you're going for the wall?"

"I am."

"Lycia will be going with you?"

"I will," Lycia replied before Jakob could respond, "whether he likes it or not."

"Good," Duff grumbled. "Hopefully she can keep you out of trouble. Because if this doesn't work the way we want it to, we're all dead."

"Thanks for the vote of confidence," Jakob deadpanned.

"I do my best," Duff replied, his ready grin breaking free. "Now let's get to it. One way or the other, this is going to be quite a fight."

The end of the chapter.

To keep reading *Shadow's Reach*, visit my author website at PeterWachtBooks.com or Amazon.